PERRIN'S THROAT DRIED;
SHE WET HER LIPS.

She ordered herself to step away from him. But she couldn't. Oh God, she could not move, could hardly breathe. A hot tingle of anticipation shot through her body as electric as the stars flashing in the steamy night. "I see you every morning and every evening," she whispered in a husky voice.

"You don't speak a word that isn't necessary, then you run away." His eyes plundered her face, ravished her lips.

The night closed in to suffocate h Years of wanting—something—tightened h t and vibrated through her limbs. We him thinned her voice. His face, as t esire as her own, his face that she had d ed of waking and sleeping. A groan closed her throat. "Cody, please. No . . . "

One powerful hand caught her waist and pulled her roughly against him. The instant his arms closed around her, her head spun and she knew she was lost . . .

Books by Maggie Osborne

THE WIVES OF BOWIE STONE
THE SEDUCTION OF SAMANTHA KINCADE
BRIDES OF PRAIRIE GOLD

Published by
WARNER BOOKS

MAGGIE OSBORNE

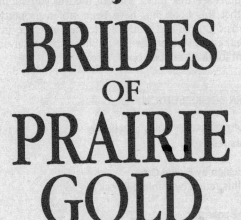

BRIDES
OF
PRAIRIE
GOLD

WARNER BOOKS

A Time Warner Company

WARNER BOOKS EDITION

Cover design by Elaine Groh
Cover illustration by Danielo Ducak

Warner Books, Inc.
1271 Avenue of the Americas
New York, NY 10020

Visit our web site at
http://pathfinder.com/twep

 A Time Warner Company

Printed in the United States of America

First Printing: August, 1996

10 9 8 7 6 5 4 3 2 1

Dedication

This book is affectionately dedicated to the people who made my life miserable while I was writing it:

To: Todd, Jeff, Chris, and Nathan. Dave and Jimmy. John, Jay, and John. Dave, Dirk, K.C., and Charlie. Frankie and his crew. Bill. Tom and Tony. Wayne, Ed, Pete, Jason. John K., Rick R., Dave S. Leland. Michael, and my hero, Tim. Victoria. Larry and Doug. And to Henry, with thanks for the grapefruit and peaches.

Most of all this book is for Stew and Louise Janz.

Thanks to all of you for making our dream come true!

BRIDES
OF
PRAIRIE
GOLD

My Journal, March, 1852. Finally the waiting has ended! At the end of the month, the bride train will embark on a journey that will take us half way across a continent. We'll be on the trail for two and a half thousand miles, and for nearly six months. We shall encounter dangerous weather and wildlife, and many perils. Some in our party will take seriously ill, some may even die though I shudder to speak of such things. If anyone were wagonmaster other than my dearest Cody, I would shake with apprehension.

I thought he would take me in his arms the instant I entered the interview room and met with him for the first time since we promised ourselves to each other. Oh how my heart beat with anticipation. But he spoke to me as if we were meeting for the first time, as if I were merely responding to the advertisement for Oregon brides like all the other applicants.

Dear journal, I was so bewildered and shocked. Then he smiled and said I reminded him of someone, and my heart sang. I understood at once that this was a secret message. Until he offered this assurance, I wasn't sure if joining the bride train was what he wanted me to do. I even worried that I might have imagined everything, that I might be as queer in the head as she said I was.

I would have thrown myself into his arms during the interview, but then he smiled and said he had reached the age when everyone reminded him of someone. This comment was not meant to wound, but to warn. Otherwise, his scout would have discovered us locked in each other's arms.

I don't understand why we must conceal our love for one another, but it is clear that we must. I trust Cody has good reason and will explain when he judges the moment ripe.

Meanwhile, I rejoice that we are finally together again with no obstacles and the future bright before us.

It relieves the pressure behind my heart to write these words. I have never before kept a journal, but now I understand why nearly all the brides have vowed to record their thoughts throughout the journey. There is comfort in seeing these words on the page: I love him, I love him.

CHAPTER
* 1 *

My Journal, April, 1852. My heart is filled with sorrow at the thought of leaving Chastity, and family and friends. But oh joy, how the spirit soars at the promise of Oregon. And a husband! Hilda Clum

"Here comes trouble," Smokey Joe announced cheerfully. He lowered a hundred-pound canvas sack of flour to the ground beside the cook wagon, then straightened and thumbed back his hat before he slid Cody a sidelong grin.

Cody glanced up from the list he was checking against the provisions waiting to be loaded and frowned at Smokey's grin. Nothing entertained Cody's trail cook more than trouble that arrived with someone else's name on it.

"Right now I'm glad I ain't you, Capt'n," Smokey Joe added, his grin widening. He tilted the wide brim of his hat, directing Cody's attention toward the row of wagons they had ferried across the Missouri yesterday. "Think I'll just make myself scarce."

Cody tucked the provisions list inside his vest and glanced down the row of wagons, noting the alignment and bright canvas tops. Later today he and his teamsters would bring the cattle and oxen across the river; tomorrow the long journey would begin.

He hadn't expected trouble until they were well under way, but Smokey Joe had called it right. Two of the brides he was commissioned to transport from Chastity, Missouri, to Clampet Falls, Oregon, were marching down the row of wagons, grim-faced and tight-lipped, skirts billowing and flapping in the cold wind like the dark wings of mythical Furies.

Suppressing a sigh, Cody leaned against the back wheel of the cook wagon, folded his arms across his chest, and observed their furious advance.

The willowy blonde draped in deep mourning was Miss Augusta Boyd. During her interview, she had made certain that Cody understood she reigned as the society belle of Chastity, the implication being that her name and position merited deference and esteem.

Perhaps the obligations of society in Chastity, Missouri, demanded the profusion of ribbon, braid, and fringe trimming her dark pelisse and skirts. On the other hand, for all Cody knew of women's fashion, it was possible that lavishly adorned mourning had become the mode everywhere.

The small brunette with flaming cheeks, he recalled, was Mrs. Perrin Waverly, a widow of several years' standing. Her plain brown dress was not richly trimmed nor as well cut as that of the imperious Miss Boyd, and she didn't wear a warm wool pelisse but clutched a yarn shawl over slender shoulders.

Cody remembered their names and a little of their history because Miss Boyd and Mrs. Waverly were far and away the best-looking women among his eleven charges. He found it curious that women as beautiful as these two had agreed to undertake an arduous, two-thousand-mile journey to marry a stranger.

At the moment they both looked angry enough to chew rocks. Fists pressing down their crinolines, they advanced at a rapid pace as if each feared the other would reach him first.

Augusta Boyd won the race. She halted in front of him in a swirl of black crepe, her china-blue eyes frigid with outrage.

"Mr. Snow!" A cold breeze tossed the ribbons trimming her bonnet and pelisse, imparting the impression that even her clothing quivered with anger. "I demand a word with you!"

Cody glanced at Perrin Waverly as she arrived a step behind Augusta Boyd. He couldn't tell if her cheeks were fiery with anger or from the chill in the air. He guessed a bit of both. For an instant her deep-lashed cinnamon eyes met Cody's gaze, then she abruptly turned toward the river and faced the town of Chastity on the opposite bank. She gripped the shawl close to her throat and lowered her head.

Cody lifted his hat and stepped away from the wagon wheel. "Good morning, ladies."

"I will not share a wagon with this . . . this *creature*!" Augusta Boyd announced furiously. Twin circles of scarlet flamed on her pale cheeks. "I demand that you order your men to stop loading *her* goods into *my* wagon!"

Cody's jaw tightened. He didn't take kindly to demands, didn't warm to orders issued by his passengers. It required an effort to hold his tongue, required a reminder that dealing with women was not, and could not, be the same as dealing with men.

In the expectant silence that followed Augusta Boyd's outburst, Cody slid a curious look toward the "creature." Wind buffeted Perrin Waverly's small, stiff form, molding her skirts around shapely hips and thighs. Her cheeks burned and she kept her gaze fixed on the skeletal trees outlining the dirt streets of Chastity. At this moment she looked as if she were held upright solely by anger and embarrassment.

"I could place Mrs. Waverly with Miss Hilda Clum," Cody decided after a minute, looking back and forth between the two women. When Mrs. Waverly didn't speak, he returned his attention to Miss Boyd. "Are you willing to ride alone, Miss Boyd? Drive your oxen with no relief?"

"Certainly not!" she snapped, giving him a look of irritation and incredulity. A slight shudder convulsed her shoulders. She shot a venomous glance toward Mrs. Waverly. "I expect you to remove her goods from my wagon at once!"

Before Cody could reply, Augusta Boyd whirled in a billow of black crepe flounces and departed the way she had come, carrying her head high.

Narrowing his gaze, Cody watched her cut a wide path around the piles of goods stacked behind and to the sides of each wagon awaiting loading. He noticed that she nodded regally in response to greetings from the other brides, but didn't pause to speak.

She had departed too soon. Cody decided he had a few things to say to Miss Augusta Boyd. But first there was the problem of Mrs. Waverly.

"I take it that you and Miss Boyd are acquainted," he commented dryly, studying Perrin Waverly's profile. The curve of her bonnet hid her eyes, but he glimpsed a slender nose and a well-shaped chin that trembled with anger.

"Indirectly," she replied after a minute. Her voice was low and throaty as if the cold wind had settled there. She pulled the shawl tighter around her shoulders, clutching the edges near the high collar of her dress. "I'm sorry for this inconvenience."

As tact didn't rank high among his qualities, Cody couldn't think of a soft way to ask the next question. "Is there any reason why Miss Clum might object to sharing a wagon with you?"

Perrin Waverly flinched, then squared her shoulders with an obvious effort. "Possibly," she admitted after another pause. Waves of angry humiliation rolled off of her and crashed against Cody's chest. He cursed beneath his breath. Curiosity was exactly the type of involvement he didn't welcome, didn't need.

He didn't want to know the brides personally, wasn't concerned about them as individuals; he rejected any speculation about their choices. He chose to consider them as cargo, freight he was paid to haul. Unfortunately, though it grated against his better judgment, he couldn't help wondering what in the hell little Mrs. Waverly had done to incur the wrath of the regal Miss Boyd.

"Miss Clum is the schoolteacher, isn't she?" Her throaty voice made him suddenly think of French corsets and lace garters, an image distinctly at odds with her plain, high-necked gown.

"I'll speak to Miss Clum on your behalf."

Suspicion flashed in Mrs. Waverly's brown eyes, eyes too large for her small face and delicate features. "I will speak to Miss Clum myself, Mr. Snow."

He shrugged. She was glaring at him as if he'd given offense by offering to intervene. Before his irritation mounted, her expression dissolved into uncertainty. "If Miss Clum won't agree to let me share her wagon . . ."

"Then we have a serious problem." Even angry and embarrassed by the scene with Augusta Boyd, she was truly a beautiful woman, not the sort of woman he had expected to find on this journey. "If Miss Clum refuses, then I can't accommodate you on this journey. Unless you resolve your dispute with Miss Boyd."

"That isn't possible," she said sharply, turning away from him to face the river.

From this angle, glimpses of gabled rooftops and brick chimneys could be seen through the winter-bare branches of thick elms and cottonwoods. The largest house, Cody had been informed, was the Boyd mansion, which Augusta Boyd had recently sold. Mrs. Waverly gazed at Miss Boyd's house with an unreadable expression.

After a moment she straightened her spine and smoothed down her skirts. "Well. There's no sense putting it off."

In silence, Cody accompanied her as far as the third wagon. The women working around the first two wagons did not greet Mrs. Waverly or acknowledge her in any way. He was thinking about that when they reached Hilda Clum's wagon. Hilda was moving her trunks and sacks of provisions herself, placing them in the order she wanted everything loaded into the wagon.

Aside from bright, intelligent brown eyes, Hilda Clum was about as plain a woman as any Cody had encountered. Broad Slavic features topped well-fleshed bones; she was put together as sturdily as the wagon behind her. On the plus side, she seemed practical, efficient, and cheerful. Cody had yet to discover her without a smile. He had liked her at once.

He tipped his hat. "Miss Clum. Are you acquainted with Mrs. Waverly?"

Hilda Clum's eyes widened and she hesitated before answering. "I have not actually met Mrs. Waverly, but Chastity is small enough that of course I've . . . heard of her." Hilda dusted bare hands together and kicked her skirts forward between the boxes littering the ground. "The only bride that I do not recognize by sight is Miss Munger. Jane Munger is from St. Joseph, isn't she?"

Mrs. Waverly cast Cody a steady, narrow-eyed look that told him to go on about his business and leave her to hers. It occurred to him that this was one bride who did not particularly like men.

That, thank God, was not his problem. But he felt a flash of sympathy for the poor bridegroom awaiting her arrival in Oregon. The man would get a beauty, but he'd also get a spit-in-your-eye attitude. After watching the women study each other for a moment, he left them to reach an accommodation if they could.

Striding down the line of wagons, he nodded to women busily checking lists against their provisions, and automatically skimmed a critical eye over canvas and axles and the iron tires rimming the wheels.

At the last wagon, Heck Kelsey, Miles Dawson, and John Voss stood off to one side of an astounding number of boxes and trunks. They smoked, wasting time, and watched Miss Augusta Boyd with unhappy expressions. She glared back at them with eyes flashing anger and contempt.

"Thank goodness you've finally come," she said, hurrying forward. "These—men!—refuse to do as I order. They won't remove Mrs. Waverly's boxes from my wagon!"

Cody narrowed his eyes on her smooth oval face, noting a perfect complexion, thick-lashed blue eyes, and a rosy mouth. "My men don't take orders from anyone but me."

Irritation quirked her mouth and her gloves fluttered in an impatient gesture. "Then *you* tell them!"

He nodded at Heck Kelsey before he touched Augusta Boyd's elbow and led her several yards from the wagon. She was tall enough that the lip of her black bonnet nearly reached Cody's eyes, taller than Ellen had been. As always, Ellen's memory blindsided him. He stared down at the blond fringe curling on Augusta Boyd's brow, the color so like Ellen's, and felt a flash of white-hot anger.

"First, you do not issue orders to my men," he said bluntly. "You don't demand; you don't insist. Second, the men in Oregon are paying for these wagons and paying the fare for your passage, but they are not paying for drivers. Either you drive your wagon or you don't go. And third, just so you understand, no one gets preferential treatment on this journey."

Instantly her smile snapped into shock and outrage. "My father was a respected banker and the mayor of Chastity for three terms!" When Cody's expression didn't alter, she added, "That's our home over there." She nodded toward an impressive mansion showing through the trees. "My father was the most esteemed—"

"I don't care if your father ruled the Western world, Miss Boyd." Shock silenced her. "On my train, all passengers are equal. You drive your wagon, you cook your meals, you set up your tent, just like everyone else. You pull your share of the load or there's no place for you here."

Anger frosted her blue eyes. Her chin rose imperiously. "I am a lady, Mr. Snow. It is outrageous that Mr. Clampet, my intended husband, did not provide a driver for my use and I shall speak sharply on this subject when I meet him." She glared at the men removing Mrs. Waverly's goods from her wagon. "It's clear that I'll need an additional wagon to accommodate my furnishings and linens. I'm sure you'll agree to that requirement at least."

Cody ground his teeth and swallowed a swear word. "One wagon was ordered and paid for; one wagon is what you get. What won't fit into one wagon stays behind," he said, striving for patience.

"But my furnishings!"

At the conclusion of ten minutes of pleading on her part and implacability on his part, moisture and resentment appeared in Miss Boyd's eyes, but she finally, sullenly, accepted that her furnishings would not accompany her to Oregon.

"If I had known of these restrictions in advance . . ." she whispered, pressing gloved fingers to trembling eyelids.

"Miss Boyd, have you ever driven oxen?" Looking at her, he couldn't imagine she had attempted anything more strenuous than wielding an embroidery needle.

"My maid, Cora, will drive the wagon," she said, her gaze mourning the heavy furniture that would remain behind.

"Your maid?" Incredulity blanked his expression.

"Cora Thorp. She grew up on a farm. I suppose she knows about things like driving a wagon." After throwing Cody a glance that labeled him an unfeeling brute, she turned her face away. "Will that be all, Mr. Snow?"

Cody stared, his mind leaping to accommodate the addition of a passenger of whom he had no previous knowledge. A maid. After an inner struggle, he conceded there was space for Cora Thorp now that Mrs. Waverly had gone to Miss Clum. At least he hoped Mrs. Waverly had worked it out with Miss Hilda Clum.

"This is a long journey, Miss Boyd, and I don't want any unnecessary problems. If there's . . ." he paused, "anyone on this train that you can't get along with, then you need to reconsider this expedition. We're going to run into enough problems with forces we can't control."

"If you're referring to that creature," she said, speaking between perfect teeth, "she's the person who should be put off this train! She is a woman of the lowest possible character. Her presence dishonors all decent women!"

"If you're accusing Mrs. Waverly of something, you'll have to be specific."

Her chin rose another notch and crimson flared on her throat and cheeks. "Ladies do not speak of such matters!"

He stared down at her and felt his eyes narrow in irritation and impatience. "As far as I'm concerned, Mrs. Waverly has as much right to be here as anyone. If you decide to stay with the train, then I expect you and Mrs. Waverly to ignore your differences, at least until we arrive in Clampet Falls. Is that understood?"

Fresh shock dropped a film of moisture across her eyes. "I have *never* been spoken to in that tone of voice!"

When he noticed the tears, Cody felt like shouting and kicking something. Her tears and injured expression were intended to be weapons as potent as her dimples and tiny waist. What she didn't grasp was that he recognized the display of waterworks as female manipulation. The only effect of her tears was to further exasperate and irritate him.

"Remember what I said." Deliberately neglecting to tip his hat, he strode away from her, so annoyed that he didn't notice Mrs. Perrin Waverly until he nearly walked on her hems.

After a swift glance toward Augusta Boyd, Perrin Waverly informed him that Hilda Clum had agreed that she could share Miss Clum's wagon. Her face was pinched and pale with relief.

"Excellent," he said sharply. He left instructions with Heck and the boys, then strode away before he said something about women that he would undoubtedly regret.

When he reached Smokey Joe's cook wagon, he poured a tin mug of thick coffee from the ancient blackened pot that Smokey kept boiling whenever the wagons weren't in motion. From the corner of his eye, he watched Webb Coate, his scout, ride up and tie his horse to the back of the wagon.

"Smokey says you had a little problem." Grinning, Webb shook back a mane of shoulder-length black hair, then removed a cup from one of the boxes on the ground. He reached for the coffeepot.

"I'm asking myself what possessed me to agree to take a bunch of temperamental women to Oregon," Cody remarked sourly.

Webb laughed, black eyes sparkling. "If I remember the wager, you bet the first problem would be swimming the oxen and cattle. Or maybe something to do with the molasses. Smokey and I figure you owe us a bottle of rye whiskey."

Cody knelt beside the cook fire and cupped his hands around the coffee mug. He managed a smile. "Haven't you heard? It's illegal to give whiskey to Indians."

"Half Indian," Webb corrected. His voice blended an exotic mix of English, French, Sioux, and the American west. Cradling his cup, he leaned against the wheel of the wagon and inspected the sky. "It's going to freeze tonight. We'll have hard ground when we roll out."

"Did Murchason depart on schedule this morning?"

Webb nodded, thin sunlight sliding in his blue-black hair. "Murchason's train is a day ahead of us. Rochack will be a couple of days behind."

"The word is cholera and measles are all along the trail."

"Fresh graves every day. We'll avoid the usual campsites." Webb tossed back the last drops of his coffee and glanced down the line of wagons. "The tall blond woman, wearing mourning . . . a widow?"

Cody studied Coate's bronze face. "She's mourning her father, the sainted Mr. Boyd."

"She's a beautiful woman."

"She's a pain in the ass. Forget it, old friend. Each of these women has a bridegroom waiting in Oregon. If you're in the market for a wife, you'd do better to make the choice after you return home to England."

Webb didn't comment. He continued to gaze down the row toward Augusta Boyd's wagon. Then he slapped Cody on the back. "Come on, Captain. If we don't get those oxen across the river, this train isn't going anywhere."

Cody rose to his feet and finished his coffee, catching a glimpse of Perrin Waverly and Hilda Clum dragging boxes around their wagon. Mrs. Waverly had the largest, loveliest brown eyes he had ever seen. And a chip on her shoulder as big as a buffalo.

The predeparture meeting was scheduled for seven o'clock in the small hall at the back of Brady's Mercantile. Most of the brides arrived with their wagon partners, chatting excitedly, debating the order in which they had loaded their goods into the wagons, deepening their acquaintance.

Cody waited near the lanterns at the front of the room, trying to place names with faces as the women chose seats. Two weeks ago he'd conducted a private interview with each of them, inviting each to select a letter introducing a prospective bridegroom.

During the interviews he had ascertained that the brides were in good health and able to work. He made certain they understood they didn't have to marry the men in Oregon if they could reimburse the cost of their journey. That made them lucky. As he understood it, the usual procedure required a marriage at the end of the journey, like it or not.

He recognized Augusta Boyd, of course, as she selected a seat in the front row. She was probably the only bride who could actually repay her bridegroom's expenses if she chose to forgo marriage. Cody doubted the others had the money to buy their way out if the bridegrooms weren't what they hoped for or expected.

For tonight's meeting, Augusta had changed into a black velvet gown that enhanced her blond beauty. Cody considered the fringe on her forehead, then shifted his glance to the small sullen girl at her side. This, he assumed, was Cora Thorp, the maid. Cora Thorp was small but wiry, with a demeanor that suggested low expectations and a lengthy acquaintance with hard labor.

Perrin Waverly caught his eye next. She chose a seat in the back row and took a long time arranging her skirts. None of the others sat next to her. Cody studied her downcast eyes and the neat center part that showed at the front of her bonnet, then he let his glance move forward.

The sisters, Mem Grant and Bootie Glover, were a mismatched pair, he decided with some amusement. Mem, the older and a spinster, was auburn-haired and topped five feet nine inches, extraordinarily tall for a woman. The widow, Bootie, was six inches shorter, with reddish gold hair, and clung to her sister's arm like an ornament. The widowed sister concerned him. He hoped she was less dependent on the older one than it appeared.

As he watched the other brides enter the room, he was able to recall the names of only two of the remaining seven. One was Sarah Jennings, another widow and the oldest of the women at twenty-nine; her wagon partner was Lucy Hastings, the youngest. Seventeen and sweetly pretty, Lucy was the only one who had actually met her intended husband, a friend of her father's.

When the eleven brides were assembled Cody cleared his throat, offered a few opening remarks, then introduced his men. "Webb Coate is our scout, and the most important man on this expedition."

Augusta Boyd and Bootie Glover, the widowed sister, frowned at Webb when he stepped forward and inclined his head with a white-toothed smile. Tonight he wore tailored broadcloth and a snowy stock instead of his usual buckskins.

"Webb will select our noon stopovers and evening campsites. Grass and water are the essential requirements for a successful journey; it's Webb's job to make sure we find them. Webb's made this trip before; he's one of the best scouts in the west. We won't cross an inch of ground that Webb doesn't recognize. Next, I want you to meet the men's cook, Smokey Joe Riley."

Smokey Joe flipped back a long graying ponytail, then stepped forward with a wave and a grin.

"Smokey knows all the tricks of cooking over an open fire. If you have any culinary questions, he'll be glad to offer suggestions and advice. Course you'll have to put up with his temper. . . ." Cody smiled, then motioned Heck Kelsey forward. "Heck is our blacksmith and all-around handyman. He'll keep the horses and oxen shod and make any repairs we need. When Heck isn't whittling or mimicking accents, he can work miracles with a broken wheel or a busted set of harness."

Heck smiled, turned red at the attention of so many females, then stepped back against the wall.

"These last four gentlemen are our teamsters, Miles Dawson, John Voss, Bill Macy, and Jeb Holden. Miles and John will tend the oxen and cattle. John will also drive a freight wagon, and Bill and Jeb will drive the molasses wagons. Most of you have met these young fellows, since they're the ones who helped load your goods."

Cody waited until the teamsters stepped back before he continued.

"Today was the first and last time anyone will help you load or unload your wagons. The boys are going to be too busy from here on with their own duties. There will be times when it will be necessary for you to unload your wagons to dry out your goods, or to lighten a ferry crossing. That's why you were instructed to pack light in units that you can move yourselves."

He gazed at a small sea of bonnets, examining sober eyes.

"Tomorrow morning we embark on a journey that will take us halfway across a continent. We'll be on the trail for two and a half thousand miles, and over five months. We're going to encounter all kinds of weather and problems we can't anticipate now. Several of you will fall seriously ill along the trail; one or two in our party will die. These are facts based on experience."

A gasp hissed across the room and several gloved hands flew to soft bosoms. The women slid anxious looks toward one another, then fastened their eyes back on Cody.

"There's cholera and measles on the trail; dysentery is a common ailment. We're going to ford rivers and cross mountains. It's going to rain, hail, and snow on you, and for most of the trip, the sun is going to broil you alive. We'll encounter every type of wildlife you can name, some of it dangerous."

"Will we encounter hostile Indians?" Augusta Boyd inquired, looking at Webb Coate with an expression of distaste.

Cody frowned. "To date, there have been numerous incidents of Indians stealing cattle, but few reports of hostilities.

From Fort Laramie on, we'll encounter many Indians seeking to trade items of clothing for food or vice versa. By that point you'll be glad to see them, glad for the variety of fresh fish or venison."

He waited until the women stopped murmuring, then responded to a raised hand. "Yes?"

Sarah Jennings, whose late husband had been an army major, stood before her chair. "A few of us are wondering about the freight wagons, Mr. Snow. What are you hauling?"

"I'm glad you asked. We're taking molasses and a load of carbines and ammunition all the way to Clampet Falls. Both loads are part of your future. I own one of the molasses wagons; your prospective bridegrooms own the second wagon. Your bridegrooms and I own the carbines and ammunition jointly. Eventual profits should be high enough for your bridegrooms to build each of you a house. We all have a stake in getting the freight to its destination."

Sarah Jennings sat down, one eyebrow cocked, a puzzled expression on her face. Cody could almost hear her computing the price of molasses and wondering how the profits could be as lucrative as he claimed.

"Ladies, a well-organized wagon train performs as a unit. If one of us has trouble, we all have trouble. It's imperative that you set aside personal dislikes or prejudices and function as a team. I cannot stress this too strongly." He looked at Augusta Boyd, who returned his gaze with a cool stare. Perrin Waverly's beautiful face remained expressionless.

"My responsibility is to deliver you safe and sound to your bridegrooms in Clampet Falls, Oregon. I won't have time to deal with petty disputes or small problems. Therefore, before we leave here, I want you to select a representative for the group. If one of your oxen throws a shoe, I don't want to hear about it. You tell your representative and she arranges with Heck Kelsey to take care of it. If someone falls ill, you inform the representative. If it's serious, she'll inform me. That's how it will work."

After he finished the rest of his speech, which was frankly

designed to scare hell out of them and weed out those who might be having second thoughts, the women pulled their chairs into a circle and began the process of selecting a leader. Cody dismissed his men, but remained behind to discover which of the brides he would have to deal with on a daily basis.

Since voting wasn't an act that sprang to a woman's mind, the women decided to select their representative by drawing lots. Cody had sworn not to interfere and he didn't, but this method impressed him as inefficient and the least likely to produce a qualified leader. He folded his arms across his chest, leaned against the wall, and watched in silence, attempting to judge the women's characters by what they said and who said it.

"Whoever draws the X will be our representative," Hilda Clum suggested. As a teacher Miss Clum was accustomed to addressing a group. In Cody's opinion, Hilda Clum would have been an excellent choice as the women's representative.

"But what if young Lucy draws the X?" Sarah Jennings smiled at Lucy Hastings and pressed her hand. "I like Lucy as much as any young woman I've met, but I think even Lucy will agree that she's too young to accept this responsibility."

Sarah Jennings would also be a good choice. When Major Jennings was alive, Sarah had traveled with him from one army post to another. She impressed Cody as practical and sensible.

Mem Grant, the spinster sister, nodded agreement. "Several of us may shrink from serving as representative. Perhaps only those who are willing to assume that duty should draw."

"Does everyone concur? Good." Hilda Clum beamed. "Mem, would you borrow Mr. Snow's hat, place the slips of paper inside, and begin the draw?"

Cody offered his hat to Mem Grant, admiring the gleam of auburn curling from her bonnet, and watched as she moved around the circle offering slips of paper to those who wished to draw. Mem Grant was a tall, handsome woman, the type of woman whom some men would see as plain and others would see as striking.

The vague unfocused bride—Cody thought her name was Winnie something-or-other—didn't seem to grasp what was happening and passed on the drawing. So did Thea Reeves, a pretty, dreamy-eyed fairy of a woman. She smiled and shook her head when Mem paused in front of her. Lucy Hastings, the seventeen-year-old, declined to draw. And so did Jane Munger, the only bride who didn't live in or around Chastity, Missouri.

"I'm the stranger in the group," Miss Munger explained. "It would be better if the representative is someone the rest of you know and trust."

The rest of the brides drew a slip of paper from Cody's hat, exchanging sidelong glances when little Mrs. Waverly hesitated, then also drew one of the papers.

"Well?" Sarah Jennings inquired. "Who drew the X?" Cody spotted the false tone covering her disappointment. Mrs. Jennings had wanted the position. He regretted that she hadn't gotten it.

"I did," Perrin Waverly whispered. She stared at her slip of paper in disbelief.

Cody sighed. Observing her consternation, he sensed pride had motivated her to draw rather than an actual desire to be the women's representative. She continued to examine the marked slip of paper with a shocked expression.

Augusta Boyd stiffened. "I will not take orders or accept decisions from that creature! We will have to draw again."

During the ensuing abrupt silence, Cody wrestled with his decision not to interfere. Judging by the reactions of the other brides, Perrin Waverly was something of an outcast. She was probably a poor choice as their representative. But it struck in his craw that Augusta Boyd appeared to believe the world should spin to her tune. He kept his mouth shut, but only with great effort.

The silence continued until Ona Norris, one of the

younger brides, appealed to Cody. "Perhaps Mr. Snow should—"

He raised his hands. "Work it out among yourselves."

Uneasily, they turned back to each other while Cody continued to gaze at Miss Ona Norris. Ona Norris was barely into her twenties, pretty in the way that young women always seemed pretty, youth placing a bloom on otherwise conventional features.

Jane Munger, sharp-eyed and sharp-featured, finally spoke. "Everyone here knows everyone else, so maybe you see things differently than I do. Maybe you think it makes sense to keep drawing from Mr. Snow's hat until Miss Boyd approves of whoever pulls the X." She looked at Augusta and raised an eyebrow. "But I think we should honor our agreement. We agreed to accept as our representative whoever drew the X."

Perrin Waverly lifted grateful eyes to Jane Munger. Her cheeks had turned fiery after Augusta's comment.

Hilda Clum and Sarah Jennings glanced at each other, then Sarah cleared her throat.

"Miss Munger is correct." She cast a troubled glance toward Perrin Waverly, speaking with obvious reluctance. "If we begin reneging on our agreements at this point, it doesn't augur well for the journey." Clearly, her statement made her uncomfortable, but she turned to Perrin, drew a breath, and said, "Therefore, I agree that the choice is made."

"I concur," Hilda Clum added after a brief hesitation.

Mem Grant nodded and elbowed her sister, but Bootie Glover sat twisting her hands together and gazing at Augusta with an uncertain expression as if she sided with Augusta but lacked the courage to stand against the majority.

Mem muttered a sound of exasperation. "My sister and I support Mrs. Waverly in accordance with our prior agreement."

Eventually, reluctantly, all the women grudgingly nodded assent except Augusta and Winnie something-or-other. Uninterested in the discussion, Winnie dreamily contemplated the flame dancing within a lantern glass.

Perrin rose in front of her chair and pressed her gloves together. "I've never done anything like this, but I pledge that I'll do my best to represent our interests to Mr. Snow." Briefly her cinnamon-colored eyes flicked toward his. Then she glanced at Augusta Boyd's rigid expression of loathing and bit her lower lip. "If I have to make decisions, I'll do so fairly."

Augusta stood and snapped her fingers at her maid. Cora Thorp pushed to her feet and handed Augusta a small beaded purse.

"You'll regret that you refused to take my advice to choose someone else," Augusta announced curtly. "I doubt it will take long for Mrs. Waverly's low character to reveal itself. I predict we shall all suffer for tonight's lapse of judgment."

Sweeping her velvet skirts to one side, she tossed her blond curls and glided from the meeting room, Cora Thorp a step behind her. The other brides smoothed their skirts or gloves, looking everywhere except at Perrin.

Perrin Waverly stood as straight and stiff as a ramrod, her hands in small, shaking balls by her sides. Although her lips trembled and humiliation pulsed on her cheeks, she spoke in a steady voice.

"Mr. Brady was kind to allow us the use of his hall. I'm sure he would appreciate it if we restore his chairs to their original places," she said quietly.

Grateful for a task to relieve the awkwardness, the women jumped to their feet and scraped their chairs back into line.

"Be at your wagons by five-thirty," Cody called as they hurried toward the door. "We depart at six o'clock sharp." He touched Perrin Waverly's arm, holding her back.

When the others had departed, he detailed her duties as the women's representative and suggested they meet for a few minutes every evening. While he talked, she straightened the rows of chairs, turned down the wicks in the lanterns.

"May I escort you home, Mrs. Waverly?" he inquired politely as they emerged from Brady's Mercantile and stepped into the darkness draping Main street. The lanterns on a gig bounced past them then receded. Otherwise the street was deserted.

"No!" she said sharply. She glanced toward a low light shining in the apothecary's bay window, then she sighed and spoke in a milder tone. "Thank you, but I'm just around the corner."

Silk roses adorned the brim of her bonnet; the color had faded to a dusky pink that matched the color of her lips. "Tell me something. You don't seem to lack spirit, so why do you allow Miss Boyd to insult you?"

He could have kicked himself. But despite his intention not to get involved with these women, he had always cheered for the runt of the litter. And that was Mrs. Waverly. Although she'd been affirmed as the women's representative, none of the brides truly accepted her except Jane Munger, a stranger to the group.

Instantly she stiffened and lowered her head. "I doubt my problems would interest you, Mr. Snow."

In other words, mind your own business, Cody thought. And she was right. "Sorry I asked," he muttered, angry with himself. He had no idea why he felt so drawn to this small prickly woman or why she had scratched his interest. Runts were always more trouble than the rest of the litter.

She clutched her shawl tightly against her throat, seeking protection from the chill night breeze. "Good night, sir."

"Good night." And good riddance, he silently added, vowing to put her out of his mind. The brides were just freight, he reminded himself as he watched her walk away from him.

When she reached the corner, she turned abruptly and stared back, her features lit by the dim light in the window of the apothecary. "Sometimes people don't have choices." She delivered the statement in a defensive tone that dared him to disagree. He could have sworn thorns sprouted from the faded roses trimming her bonnet.

"I believe people always have choices, but I'll concede that sometimes it doesn't appear that way."

"You're wrong," she stated flatly. "Sometimes there are no alternatives, none at all. Regardless, everyone deserves a fresh beginning. That isn't asking too much."

He didn't understand her defiant tone. The conversation seemed too mild to warrant the angry tremble in her voice. "I'm definitely in favor of second chances," he agreed, frowning.

She nodded curtly, then spun on her toes, leaving him to watch the seductive sway of her skirts as she marched beyond the apothecary's window. Cody imagined he spotted a giant shadow cast by the chip on her shoulder.

"Damn it." He waited until she rounded the corner like a soldier on parade. And he caught himself wondering how she would look with a smile curving those beautiful lips. He hated it, truly hated it, that such a thought would enter his mind.

Three-quarters of the town rose early on a chill spring morning to see the brides off. Church ladies passed out hot coffee and tarts baked in honor of the occasion. A sprightly fiddler moved through the crowd playing a wedding polka and encouraging hand clapping and a spontaneous jig here and there. During the night a well-meaning prankster had painted OREGON OR BUST on several of the wagons and a cheer went up at the sight.

Other than Perrin Waverly, Jane Munger, and the sisters, Mem Grant and Bootie Glover, all the brides had a collection of family or friends to wish them bon voyage and good luck. Hurried embraces were exchanged, tears shed, and last-minute gifts pressed into trembling hands. Then Smokey Joe Riley banged his dinner gong, signaling it was time to climb aboard the wagons.

Webb Coate cantered to a stop beside Cody at the head of the line and they watched with thin smiles as the women decided who would drive first before they took up the reins trailing across the broad backs of the oxen. One of the cattle tied behind Thea Reeves and Ona Norris's wagon broke loose. Midway down the line, a bonnet tumbled under the wheels.

"It will be a damned miracle if we get these women to Oregon," Cody observed, watching a young boy rush to toss the crushed bonnet back toward a wagon seat. The throng of spectators cheered as Miles Dawson jumped from his horse to retie the cow to the back of Miss Reeves's and Miss Norris's wagon.

Webb turned sparkling black eyes toward the low hills they would cross before nightfall. His hair lifted off his shoulders and the fringe on his buckskins fluttered in the cold wind.

"We'll make twelve miles even with a late start."

Cody looked at him. "You love this, don't you?"

"I'd give half of my father's fortune to do nothing but scout trains for the rest of my life."

Cody's smile broadened. "That sound you hear is not the wind. It's your father rolling in his grave."

Webb laughed. "Actually, I think he would have understood. What's hard for me to understand is why you've decided this is your last trip."

"You know the reasons."

Someday soon the plains would explode into violence. Each time Cody led a train through Indian territory, he observed fresh confirmation of growing anger and unrest. He had friends in both the Indian and white cultures and he wanted no part of the coming conflagration. That it would come, he could no longer doubt.

"Well, Captain." Webb leaned on the carbine resting across his thighs. "Are we ready or are we going to sit here all day?"

Cody looked down the line of wagons toward the townsfolk bunched together near the ferry. He thought about the eleven greenhorn women in his charge, twelve if he counted the maid. God help them all and keep them safe.

He removed his hat and swept it in a broad wave above his head.

"Wagoooons hooooo! Move 'em out!"

The journey began.

CHAPTER

* 2 *

They rolled past the first graves shortly after the noon rest on the third day.

"Mr. Coate says it's cholera." Drawing her shawl tighter around her shoulders, Perrin peered at the mounded earth through a thin fall of spring snow. She tried not to think about how cold her feet were. "They didn't get very far."

The wagon she shared with Hilda Clum tilted over a large stone, then rocked past the pair of wooden crosses. Falling snow obscured any names that might have been carved in remembrance.

"My mother says it isn't the destination that's important, it's the journey." Hilda accepted the reins from Perrin; it was her turn to drive the oxen. She peered through the snowflakes at the wooden markers. "I hope their journey was a happy one."

Now that Perrin didn't have to worry about the oxen, she relaxed her spine against the short wooden seat with a sigh and considered her own life's journey. So far, life's road had been rocky, strewn with obstacles and problems. Most of her problems could be laid squarely at the feet of some man.

Men took. That's how it was and had always been. Garin Waverly had taken her confidence and self-esteem and crushed them beneath his bootheels; Joseph had taken her reputation and cast her good name to the winds.

There was no reason to assume that the unknown bridegroom awaiting her arrival in Oregon would be any less of a thief. He would take her body, her labor, and her future. And she would have no say in the matter, no choice.

She touched the fingertips of her gloves to her forehead. "Odd, isn't it? How small decisions can lead to such enormous consequences," she murmured, not realizing she spoke aloud. "One day you take stock, and you don't really know how you got to where you are. But chances are, the first step began with a small decision."

Seeing the graves called to mind all the people she had lost. Her parents, the aunt and uncle who had raised her, her husband. A friend here, an acquaintance there.

Joseph was her most recent loss, though she couldn't properly mourn him. To be absolutely honest, Perrin wasn't sure how deeply she grieved Joseph's death. Her feelings were so mixed about him. There was affection, yes, and gratitude, certainly, but also a deep reservoir of resentment and anger.

It was Joseph who had prompted her thought about small decisions leading to large consequences. An insignificant decision to accept a ride in Joseph's carriage to escape a sudden downpour had eventually led to her flight from Chastity, Missouri.

Actually, the beginnings were even more trivial. Perrin would marry an Oregon stranger because it had rained on a certain morning a year ago when she had decided to walk to Brady's Mercantile to beg for an extension of credit.

Or maybe she was sitting on this wagon because Garin Waverly had died needlessly, leaving her destitute, which had led to an accumulation of debt at Mr. Brady's store, which had caused her to walk out on a rainy morning, and that in turn had led to accepting a ride in Joseph's carriage.

Or perhaps she would wed a stranger because Garin Waverly and his brother had purchased her uncle's riverside warehouse and thus she and Garin had met and decided to marry, which had led to Garin's jealousy, which had led to that terrible moment in the street and the sound of gunfire, which resulted in Garin dying needlessly, which had . . . Perrin rubbed at the headache forming behind her forehead.

Hilda coughed into her hand and shook her head to dislodge the snowflakes accumulating on the brim of her bonnet. "Everyone makes mistakes," she said after a minute. She gave Perrin a quick look of curiosity mixed with sympathy. "*Ja*. Sometimes we all do things that we later regret."

Perrin nodded gratefully. After three days together, she could guess this was Hilda's way of saying that she didn't judge or condemn. The problem was, Perrin doubted the other brides would be as generous. By now Augusta would have made sure that all of them knew. If they hadn't heard rumors beforehand.

Ducking her head, she picked at her gloves and realized there wouldn't really be a fresh beginning for her. With Augusta on this train, Perrin was taking her reputation with her.

"I don't know why I'm here," she said in a low puzzled voice, gazing at the slanting curtain of falling snow. "I keep wondering if I'd changed one small decision, maybe a decision I made years ago, maybe I would be somewhere else now."

"I know exactly why I am going to Oregon," Hilda offered with a chuckle. "I am twenty-eight years old, plain as a boot, and I have never had a single marriage offer. This is my chance to marry and have children of my own. I will not likely have another." Cold silvery vapor plumed before her lips. "With more and more families going to Oregon, I expect there will be opportunities for teachers. In every way, this is the best thing that has ever happened to me," she added brightly.

Perrin examined Hilda's expression and wondered how she could sound so cheerful when they were both feeling wretched, suffering the effects of coach fever.

All the women except Sarah Jennings were ill with coach fever, which Sarah said the army referred to as motion sickness. Despite Smokey Joe's advice that they suck on pebbles, the only genuine relief arrived when the wagons halted and the rocking, shaking, jarring, jostling mercifully stopped.

"I'm concerned about Winnie Larson," Perrin remarked. Despite the snow and frigid temperature, she blotted feverish perspiration from her brow and stifled a groan as the wagon tilted and rocked over another large stone. "Winnie is still our worst case. Jane Munger made her a bed in the back of their wagon. Jane's driving the team with no relief."

Conversation diverted her thoughts from a queasy stomach and the headache banging at her temples. She tried not to think about the unrelenting rocking motion, the hard wooden seat bruising her tailbone, or the icy fingers of cold creeping into her gloves and down her collar. Cody Snow had grinned and promised the coach fever would pass, but so far it hadn't.

Cody Snow was another subject Perrin didn't want to consider right now. She hadn't made up her mind how she felt about him or how to take him. It irritated her that she wasted so much time thinking about him and planning their evening meetings.

"Winnie's mother and mine knew each other in Germany," Hilda offered. Her face was red with cold above the scarf wrapped around her throat.

"Then you and Winnie are friends?" Perrin hoped the question didn't betray her surprise. Hilda's sunny intelligence seemed at wide variance with Winnie's drifting lack of focus. Whenever Perrin encountered Winnie Larson, as recently as during the noon rest, Winnie appeared drowsy and withdrawn. She was agreeable in a distracted sort of way, but her attention wandered in realms an observer couldn't follow.

"I do not really know her." Hilda glanced at Perrin. "The Larsons live in Chastity; we live three miles out." She explained that the Clum family owned a prosperous dairy farm, whereas the Larsons were town people.

Perrin sucked on her pebble and watched the snowflakes swirling over farmland and low hills. The landscape hadn't yet changed much.

"How much longer do you suppose Mr. Snow and Mr. Coate will continue before we stop for the night?" Hilda shivered, then wiped her nose and eyed the snow collecting on the oxen's backs.

"Not long, I hope."

The coach fever would ease when the wagons halted. But their problems wouldn't end. The last two nights had re-

vealed that only Sarah Jennings had the slightest inkling how
to cook in the open. A few of the brides had gone to bed hungry. Others, like Perrin and Hilda, had choked down charred
biscuits; hard, half-cooked beans; and coffee that tasted like
flavored creek water. At least the weather had been dry and
Hilda had managed to get their fire going. Ona Norris and
Thea Reeves had given up and ended by accepting Sarah
Jennings's invitation to join her and Lucy Hastings for
warmth and a bite of the stew that made Sarah the envy of
everyone who walked within sniffing distance.

Following supper came the problem of erecting their
sleeping tents. The first night the teamsters had helped those
baffled by poles and tie-downs, but last night they had all
had to manage on their own. Since Winnie was too ill to help
Jane, Perrin had lent Jane a hand while Hilda assisted Cora
Thorp with the tent Cora shared with Augusta Boyd. As far
as Perrin knew, Augusta had not done two minutes worth of
driving, cooking, or physical labor.

Thinking about Augusta Boyd and how much Augusta
hated her made Perrin's stomach cramp. Changing direction,
she let her thoughts wander to Cody Snow. His handsome,
rugged face sprang into her mind, one eyebrow lifted in a
roguish expression.

She couldn't decide what Cody was all about. During their
two brief meetings since they'd been on the trail he had
treated Perrin with unfailing politeness, but he'd erected a
barrier between them. At first she told herself that his mind
was focused on the numerous details that had to be addressed
to ensure a successful journey. Then, she couldn't help it, she
started worrying and wondering if he had heard the gossip
about her.

Well, she didn't care. She straightened on the hard wagon
seat and glared at the falling snow. Cody Snow and his blue,
blue eyes meant nothing to her. She and Cody Snow would
begin and end this miserable journey as strangers. That's
how it had to be. And that's exactly what Perrin wanted. Ob-
viously, it was what Cody wanted too.

She had no idea why she suddenly felt sad.

Bootie Glover leaned to the fire and extended her gloves over the flames that Mem had finally managed to coax into life.

"My head is still reeling, my bottom hurts, and I'm freezing! I swan, Mem, I've never been so miserable in my life!"

Mem paused to watch snowflakes tumbling into the biscuit dough she stirred on the wagon sideboard. Wearing gloves made her actions clumsy, but she'd pulled the gloves back on after her fingers started to tingle and turn blue with cold. A sudden smile curved her lips. The unusually cold weather and cooking with her gloves on would make an entertaining story for her trip journal.

"Don't stand too close to the flames," she called absently, glancing at Bootie. "Mind your hem."

"Can't we have a larger fire? Some of the others have bigger fires than ours."

Mem pressed her lips together and strove for patience. "If you want to go search for more wood, we can have a larger fire," she said finally.

Bootie peered uncertainly into the snowy darkness. "It's black out there, and everything's covered by drifts. There might be wild animals roaming around."

"Then stop complaining."

"Well, you don't need to snap." Bootie turned toward Mem with a liquid-eyed look of injury. "And I wasn't complaining. I was just stating facts. It *is* freezing. And there probably *are* wild animals out there." After a minute she sighed and added, "And our fire *is* smaller than everyone else's."

Mem pulled off balls of dough and arranged them in the skillet. At least Bootie had found something to complain about besides coach fever, her favorite topic along the trail. The only relief from an ongoing monologue of symptoms had come when they rolled past the graves.

Seeing the graves had prompted Bootie to recite a tearful

remembrance of their mother's death, then recount her two miscarriages and agonize over the infant who had died in childbirth. The next set of snowy graves had brought on sobs mourning the deaths of their father and Bootie's husband, Robert.

Mem wrapped a scarf more securely around her throat, shoved a lock of auburn hair into her bonnet, then cut slices of ham into a second skillet and continued the dialogue going on inside her head. She supposed all spinsters talked to themselves.

She told herself that she didn't feel any less deeply about their shared losses, but she thought it depressing to dwell on painful subjects. She didn't refuse to discuss the death of their loved ones because she was cold inside, as Bootie so wrongly hinted, but because the pain was too great, and she preferred to look forward rather than back. When she did look backward, she chose to remember happy, pleasant moments, rather than drown herself in sadness and loss. She was not a cold woman, far from it. Glancing up from the skillet, she watched Bootie leaning over the flames and thought how shocked her sister would be to know just how brightly burned Mem's inner fires.

Bootie moved one of the camp chairs that Mem had dragged from the back of the wagon, and sat as close as she dared to the small fire. She pressed a hand to her stomach and groaned.

"I still feel like I'm rocking. And I'm so cold. We haven't had a decent meal and so far this whole journey has been so purely awful that I'm wondering why we agreed to go west."

Mem placed the skillets on the fire, then studied her sister's face in the light leaping from the flames. Bootie had always been the pretty sister, the amiable sister, the sister with the beaus and later a husband. Robert Glover had been charmed by Bootie's fluttery helplessness and by her reliance on his judgment and guidance. To Mem's knowledge, Robert had never noticed that Bootie depended not only on him, but on whoever happened to be nearby. And, of course, there was always someone nearby to smooth over Bootie's mistakes or her tactless remarks, to step in when responsibilities became overwhelming, or to flatten the bumps that appeared on Bootie's road.

"Why *did* you decide to come?" Mem asked.

"Why, to be with you, of course." Bootie's eyebrows lifted and she looked puzzled that Mem had posed the question.

The answer bowed Mem's head with guilt. She ground her teeth together.

Bootie and Robert had given her a home. They had genuinely welcomed her and had treated her as a valued sister and not as a servant, as happened to so many spinsters dependent upon a relative's largesse. She had no right to wish that Bootie had not accompanied her on this adventure. Her resentment was a shameful example of gross ingratitude.

To make amends, she offered Bootie the best, uncharred biscuits and the pinkest slices of ham. As further penance, she listened with as much patience as she could muster to a comparison of Augusta Boyd's mourning garb to their own plainer attire. And she assured Bootie that the lack of a few ribbons and furbelows did not mean they mourned the loss of their father less than Augusta mourned the loss of hers.

"And Robert," Bootie added with a catch in her throat. "I begged him not to accompany Father downriver. I pleaded."

"I know you did," Mem said soothingly. She felt trapped and wild inside. There was so much life out there, teeming all around them, but all they could talk about was death or illness.

Later, when they lay in their frigid tent, bundled in thick quilts, Mem silently chastised herself for wishing Bootie had remained in Chastity, and she waged a battle against the resentment she couldn't seem to vanquish.

But this trip should have been hers and hers alone. When she first spotted the advertisement for Oregon wives that Cody Snow had placed in the *Chastity Gazetteer*, every dream she had ever wistfully dismissed again sprang to vibrant life.

At once she envisioned herself traveling to Oregon, and she eavesdropped on future generations as they related her story in tones of awe and admiration. Her descendants would marvel at the courage required to cross half a continent, to conquer dangers only hinted at in Mem's journal. They would shake their heads and exchange wide-eyed glances when they read about fording wild rivers or preparing a meal while wearing gloves. In her lovely fantasy, her descendants would memorialize her as a brave pioneer spirit. Instead of being an invisible branch on the family tree, Mem would blossom forth as an inspiration to future generations.

But Bootie had spoiled the dream. Now Mem had to share her story. And if a fluttery little thing like Bootie Grant Glover could cross half a continent, then doing so could only be a tame adventure. The tale became ordinary.

Mem sighed and gazed at the roof of the tent.

She should have been born a man. If she had been a man she would have traveled the seven seas, founded a nation, invented an object to change the world. She would have opened continents, forged constitutions, battled unknown dangers. Oh, she would have had such experiences, such grand escapades.

But destiny had decreed otherwise. Fate had made her a woman, a spinster with a life as dull as a weed. This journey to Oregon was her one and only opportunity for a taste of adventure and a sense of true accomplishment.

She thought it unfortunate that her grand adventure came at the cost of taking a husband, but the price was one she was willing to pay. Even if Peter Sails, the man whose letter she had chosen, turned out to be a bore or a brute, she would always have this journey to remember. And she would have a home of her own and eventually perhaps she would have children. All in all, she couldn't regret her decision to journey to Oregon.

Except Bootie had insisted on tagging along. Her sister

would rather accept a new husband than be left behind. And now, instead of missing Bootie as Mem had expected, she was getting one of her headaches from listening to Bootie's soft snores. She had to resist an urge to dig an elbow into her sister's side.

A whooshing noise sounded overhead and the tent roof collapsed on top of them. Bootie thrashed awake with a scream as Mem struggled to sit up and shove the heavy, snow-laden canvas away from her face.

"Stop screaming, we aren't being attacked. We didn't set the poles well enough, that's all. The roof has come down." Laboring to kick off the quilts, she punched the canvas to knock off the snow, then fought to hold it up so Bootie could crawl outside.

When Mem followed on her hands and knees, a brown hand appeared and she clasped it gratefully, pulling up to her feet.

"Thank you," she said to Webb Coate, pushing back her hair and peering at him through the snowy darkness. Mem was tall enough that there weren't many men she had to look up to see. Tilting her head back, she unexpectedly experienced a delicious sense of what it might feel like to be small and feminine. The strange sensation made her feel positively giddy.

"I heard a scream," Webb said. "Are you all right?" He spoke with a slight but intriguing accent that Mem couldn't place.

"Is anyone injured?" Cody Snow demanded, striding forward with a torch. When he approached near enough to spot the collapsed tent, he nodded with relief that the problem wasn't worse.

"I swan," Bootie gasped, patting her hair, her bosom, her cheeks. "I was sound asleep then something heavy fell on me and I thought sure I was smothering and—" She looked as if she might swoon. Had they been sleeping in nightgowns instead of their day clothes, Mem suspected Bootie would indeed have fainted, considering it the proper thing to do.

Also, she noticed that Bootie's remarks were addressed solely to Cody Snow. Bootie ignored Webb Coate. Mem tossed back the thick braid that fell over her shoulder and smoothed down her skirts. Sometimes she wondered how she and Bootie could possibly share the same blood.

"Thank you for arriving so swiftly," she said to Mr. Coate. Aside from being an extraordinarily handsome man, which Mem didn't care about, Webb Coate's history intrigued her. Had his parents been married? How had they met? Which parent had raised him, Indian or white? The answers were none of her affair, of course. But curiosity had always been her most troublesome trait.

"We'll have your tent restored in a few minutes," Coate said, smiling at the long rope of auburn hair that swung over her breast.

"Will you hold this?" Cody Snow gave Mem his torch, then the two men fixed the tent in less time than it had taken Mem to merely unfold it. After Bootie crawled back inside, diving into her quilts, Mem thanked them again and watched as they walked away, moving toward the fire that burned beside the cook wagon.

She heard Cody murmur something that made Webb laugh and she decided the collapsed tent was one incident that she would not record in her journal. Mem Grant, founder of nations, the great adventuress, could not erect a tent sturdily enough to withstand a few inches of snow.

Disgusted and sighing at her foolishness, she crawled inside the tent and rolled into her blankets.

"It was nice of Mr. Snow to arrive so quickly to help us," Bootie murmured drowsily.

"It was Mr. Coate who dragged you outside," Mem said tartly. The little smacking sounds that Bootie made immediately prior to falling asleep irritated her no end.

"Him! He's just an Indian. A half-breed."

"He's a man like any other."

Not quite like any other. Most men weren't as tall as Webb Coate, and didn't have a thick mane of black hair, or teeth as white as eggshell. Not many men had piqued Mem's interest as did Mr. Coate. There were a thousand questions she wished to ask him about the legacy of two cultures.

But she didn't fall asleep thinking about Webb Coate. She drifted away borne on plans of how best to plant her tent poles.

"At least it's warmer today," Augusta commented. Leaning to one side, she peered past the wagons ahead of them, watching the teamsters ride back and forth across a small flat stream, shouting the cattle and oxen forward through the water.

They'd been on the trail only five days and already Augusta had learned to hate creeks. Yesterday, one of the heavy molasses wagons had become mired in the mud of a streambed and the men had spent three hours getting it unstuck while everyone else waited.

So far Augusta had not discovered a single pleasantry to relieve the inconvenience and tedium of the journey. The next few months promised little more than a continuing series of discomforts and indignities.

Now that she didn't suffer coach fever as badly, she noticed the chill more. Especially at night, when she and Cora had to sleep on the ground in a tent. And with her appetite returning, it had become abundantly apparent that Cora Thorp was no cook.

Last night Augusta had stared down at a gray congealing bowl of gravy and had actually considered finagling an invitation to Sarah Jennings's fire. Because of Sarah's connection to her Jennings in-laws, Sarah was the most socially acceptable of the brides. Unfortunately, Sarah's years as an army wife had exerted a coarsening effect. She was far too frank and plainspoken for true gentility. Still, Sarah Jennings was the only bride who could produce a decent meal over an open fire.

But the worst part of the journey, Augusta had discovered, was the utter lack of privacy. When one felt compelled to answer a call of nature, one had to hop down from the wagon, dash for a bush or gully, relieve oneself in the open air, then run to catch up to one's wagon while those in the following wagons watched. It was embarrassing and degrading.

Equally as dismaying was the growing problem of cleanliness, something Augusta had not anticipated at all. She hadn't yet figured out how to manage her weekly bath. First, Cody Snow had forced her to leave her tub behind. Second, she had no pot large enough to heat enough water for a full bath. And finally, the Indian didn't always select a campsite within easy walking distance of a stream.

Frowning, she tried to see what was happening ahead.

"Jane Munger's and Winnie Larson's wagon is hung up in the middle of the stream," she said to Cora, sighing deeply. Those lucky enough to have already crossed had climbed out of their wagons and congregated in small groups. Lucy Hastings had wandered off to inspect a prairie dog village, Thea Reeves was sketching the wagon stuck in the middle of the stream. Mem Grant was down beside the stream bank, getting her hems wet and shouting like a hoyden at Jane's and Winnie's oxen.

Augusta released another sigh. There wasn't a single woman on the train whom Augusta recognized as her equal, none with whom she could socialize. She was accustomed to this state of affairs—took pride in it, actually—but occasionally when she observed women chatting and laughing together her chest tightened wistfully and she wished for someone of parallel stature with whom she might develop a friendship. It occurred to her suddenly that she had never really had a close friend.

Cora Thorp leveled a frown on the broad backs of the oxen. "I think you could help out a little." She glared at the reins. "There. I've said it and I'm glad."

"I beg your pardon?"

"I'm doing all the work for both of us. That ain't fair."

Augusta's brows rose and she shifted on the wagon seat, careful to hold her hem away from Cora's muddy boots.

"You're paying for your trip to Oregon through your labors." They had settled this point before departure. If Cora had not agreed to do the work involved, Augusta would never have saddled herself with such sullen and disagreeable company. "I believe you understood the nature of your duties from the outset."

"I didn't know how much work there would be, or that you wouldn't do your share."

"I beg your pardon! My share?"

"Mr. Snow said we each had to pull our own weight." Cora's sharp dark features pinched together. "The others take turns driving or walking. I never get a chance to walk and stretch my legs, I'm always at the reins. Just look at these calluses! And there's no time to visit with anyone at night, not with the cooking and cleaning, then setting up the tent and all."

Augusta closed her eyes against one more slap from destiny's hand. She didn't need a show of rebellion from Cora Thorp; she just didn't need it. Already she was dealing with more than a body should have to bear.

"It isn't too late for you to change your mind about going," she snapped, staring at Cora. "There's a farmhouse up ahead. You could wait there for someone to carry you back to Chastity. I thought you wanted to go to Oregon. I thought you wanted a chance to better yourself."

Cora bit down on her back teeth. "I ain't a slave," she said stubbornly. "Least you could do is say thank you once in a while."

"Oh, for heaven's sakes. Say thank you to a maid?" The suggestion was so ridiculous that Augusta laughed.

"There's another thing," Cora continued, her little dark eyes disappearing into a squint. "I ain't been paid in five weeks!"

Instantly Augusta's amusement died and she went cold inside. "I told you," she said when she was certain her voice would emerge without a quiver. "Mr. Clampet, my intended bridegroom, will pay you when we reach Clampet Falls."

"Well, what if he don't? You haven't met him; you don't know him or what he's willing to pay for. What if this Mr. Clampet says he didn't order no maid?"

"The town was named after Mr. Clampet's family. He's a wealthy man." She hoped and prayed that this was true.

"No, sir, I ain't going to wait. I want what's owed me. I want my back wages now."

"I'll think about it," Augusta said sharply.

The congestion ahead cleared as Jane Munger's and Winnie Larson's wagon lurched out of the mud and splashed onto the opposite low bank. The women atop the rise cheered.

Cora flicked the reins and their wagon moved forward a space as Webb Coate rode toward them. His black eyes skimmed Cora and settled on Augusta.

"When it's your turn to cross, don't hesitate. Keep the animals moving at a steady pace." The darkness of his intense gaze released a cloud of butterflies in Augusta's stomach, and she swallowed a sudden dryness in her mouth. "If you'll water your oxen now, out of a bucket, they'll be less inclined to stop midstream." He studied Augusta a minute, then tipped his hat and rode toward the wagon behind them to repeat the message.

Augusta pressed a hand to her bosom and caught a breath. "Insolent creature! How dare he look at me like that!"

Webb Coate was dark and handsome and exotic. A hideously shameful image flashed in her mind: a strong brown hand, the fingers opened against pale milky skin.

A gasp broke from her throat and she gave her head a violent shake. The brute was an Indian, for heaven's sake. Uneducated, lazy, a savage. He hadn't looked drunk, but he probably was. Indians were notorious liquor-hounds. The women on this train would be lucky if Coate didn't rape and murder them all.

Sighing heavily, Cora set the wagon brake, then gathered her skirts to climb down and fetch the bucket tied to the side. She glared up at Augusta.

"I ain't going to dress your hair or lace your corset anymore, so don't even ask. I just don't have time. Besides, everyone else stopped wearing corsets on the second day."

"Well!" Augusta stared. "Someone is forgetting her place!"

Things had come to a pretty pass when her own maid threatened her. The idea! Demanding payment, refusing her duties . . . truly it was an insult of the highest water. Tears of frustration moistened Augusta's blue eyes. As her corset laced up the back, she couldn't possibly maintain her standards without Cora's assistance. If Cora meant what she threatened, then another humiliating indignity loomed on the horizon.

And all of this misfortune was her father's fault.

If her father hadn't squandered his fortune, and part of the bank's, if he hadn't committed suicide, Augusta would not have had to sell her home to pay debts, would not have had to travel to some barbaric territory to marry a stranger. It was her father's fault that she was sitting in a covered wagon being threatened by her own maid. His fault that she was shockingly, unbelievably destitute.

The lesson was clear. Without money, a person had no choices at all. Her father had killed himself rather than live without money. Now his daughter was vulnerable to white trash like Cora Thorp, the daughter of a gravedigger, for heaven's sake. And Mrs. Thorp took in other people's laundry.

If she hadn't been wearing gloves, Augusta's fingernails would have cut deeply into her smooth palms.

Red-hot resentment burned through her body, shocking her to the toes of her fashionable boots. It didn't seem possible that she could resent or blame her adored father, but when she thought about his liaison with that creature Perrin Waverly, which had led to him leaving his daughter penniless amid the scandal of his suicide, anger swelled into a scalding flash.

All of her life she had been taught that Boyds were special, several cuts above ordinary common folk. Boyds had sailed on the Mayflower; Boyds had distinguished themselves in the Revolutionary War. Boyds enjoyed wealth and privilege. The Boyd men were giants in business and politics; Boyd women graced society at its pinnacle and married men like their fathers.

Except Augusta. There had been no man in Chastity good enough to marry Augusta Boyd. That had been her father's judgment, and an opinion Augusta shared. It was far better to remain a Boyd spinster and devote her life to her father than to marry beneath herself.

That future was no longer possible, because her father had forgotten who he was. He had forgotten that Boyds didn't lose their fortunes, didn't alter the books of their own bank. Boyds did not place a noose around their necks and step off of a chair.

Now, because of her father's mistakes, Augusta was penniless and driven to marry a common stranger to survive. It still did not seem possible or real.

The scandal of his suicide was even worse than the scandal he'd caused with Perrin Waverly. Augusta would have killed herself if she had believed for a minute that anyone knew the humiliating truth about her father's financial devastation. It would be unendurable if people knew she was penniless, reduced to the same common level as . . . as Cora Thorp. Good Lord.

Miles Dawson waved and shouted. "Move your wagon up, miss."

With a start, Augusta emerged from her misery and dashed at the tears hanging on her lashes. She gripped the wooden seat and called for Cora.

"I'm here." Sullenly, Cora climbed up on the seat and released the brake. She slapped the reins across the oxen's back and they crossed the stream without trouble.

Eventually all the wagons reformed in a line and returned to the ruts winding across the prairie. Here and there green shoots sprouted out of winter-brown. But Augusta didn't notice the greening earth. Nor did she hear the rattle of harness or the sound of women's voices calling to one another.

Each revolution of the wheels whispered: No money; no choices. No money; no choices.

Whenever she thought of the future and the stranger waiting for her in Oregon, when she thought of Cora demanding her pay, or wondered if her provisions would last until she reached Clampet Falls, desperation glazed her eyes and she felt physically ill.

Cody lifted a stick out of Smokey Joe's fire, lit a cigar, then leaned against the back wheel of the cook wagon, studying the camp. At night the wagons formed a square, four wagons to a side, with the animals corraled in the center. Unless there was reason to expect danger, the women cooked and slept outside the square. It wasn't ideal, as he couldn't see all of the women at once, but it was the safest arrangement for the animals.

Before he let his mind release the day's small problems, he listened to his men exchanging tall tales around Smokey's fire. Heck Kelsey amused them by spinning yarns in different accents. Heck was solid and dependable, as honest as a collection plate. He'd already proven his worth by repairing an axle that broke on the second day.

The four teamsters laughed and joked, filled with high spirits and young enough to believe there was no obstacle they couldn't conquer. Overconfidence could be a problem, and it concerned Cody. But as long as their showing off didn't get out of hand, he didn't mind the competition among them or that they flirted with the younger brides.

A sound caught his attention and he stiffened and peered into the darkness, not relaxing until he recognized Webb's owl call. Minutes later Webb loomed out of the night near one of the molasses wagons. Cody waited while Webb unsaddled his mustang, watered and fed it, then turned it in to the enclosed square.

After washing at the water barrel, Webb accepted a platter

of venison from Smokey Joe, then glanced at Cody. Cody nodded, and they walked into the darkness away from the others.

Webb speared a chunk of venison on the tip of his knife, chewed, and they both scanned the dark ridge of a low hill.

"We'll camp near Addison's farm the night after tomorrow," Webb said after a minute. "There's good water."

Cody smoked his cigar and waited.

"Jake Quinton is there."

Cody flipped his cigar into the darkness. "Is there another campsite other than Addison's place?"

"I'm avoiding the usual sites. We're seeing too many graves; there's too much risk of cholera, typhoid, or measles."

"Jake Quinton." Cody swore and ground his teeth.

"I spoke to Ed Addison. He says Quinton's been hanging around his farm for several days. Quinton's heard about the brides. He's curious what other freight we're carrying."

Cody jammed his hands in his back pockets and tilted his head to look at the inky sky. Clouds blotted the stars. A cold wind blew steadily from the north. Turning, he gazed toward the ring of cook fires circling the wagons. Here and there a woman's form passed in front of wind-tossed flames.

His history with Quinton tracked back five years. Jake Quinton had deserted during a summer campaign in the Dakota Territory. When the patrol returned him to the post, it had fallen to Captain Cody Snow to decide if Quinton would hang or be confined to the stockade at hard labor for six months.

"He's sworn to kill you. You know that."

Cody watched as the women began to extinguish their fires and drift toward the sleeping tents.

He should have hanged Jake Quinton.

CHAPTER
* 3 *

A fast stream, swollen by spring melt, tumbled across Ed Addison's farmland. The water was clean and sweet, the ground level, and Addison earned a tidy profit by allowing trains to camp on his acreage. Addison sold grain for weary animals, his wife and daughters peddled eggs and handicrafts, and one of his sons hawked cider out of a wooden stand near a weathered silo.

"We'll rest here for a day," Cody informed Perrin. Shading his eyes against the morning glare, he looked toward Addison's farmhouse about three-quarters of a mile in the distance. "Tell the women they can bathe in the stream and do laundry, get some baking done ahead. I don't know when our next rest day will be."

Immediately Perrin's spirits soared. Although plates of ice rushed along the surface of the stream, the weather had improved in the last few days and the air had warmed. The luxury of a bath and a hair wash would cheer everyone. Smiling, she raised her face to the sun, glorying in the bright morning.

"Are we permitted to walk up to the house?"

Cody's silence became so lengthy that she opened her eyes and studied him as he continued to contemplate the farm buildings on the distant rise. He had an interesting face, Perrin decided, weathered and strongly angled. Vertical lines split his cheeks, the creases deepening when he smiled or frowned. A stubborn jaw framed an uncompromising mouth and lips that were full and wide.

The lines fanning from the corners of his eyes confirmed a life lived out of doors, but more interestingly, they suggested strength of character. Although Perrin hadn't actually seen Cody laugh, she had heard the sound. Like his voice, his laughter was deep, genuine, and resonated with feeling.

"If you go up to the house," he said finally, "go in a group. Not alone."

She nodded, trying to decide if his eyes were blue like the trim on her skirt or like the delphiniums that had bloomed in the garden behind her rented house in Chastity.

A startled blush heated her cheeks as Perrin realized that she hadn't speculated about a man's eyes in years. Suddenly she was very aware of how close they stood, aware of the flannel and leather scent of his shirt and vest.

"I'll inform the others," she said abruptly. Lifting her skirts, she started back toward the wagons.

"Mrs. Waverly?"

After hesitating a moment, Perrin uneasily returned to where he stood, not far from the smithy's wagon. The ring of Heck Kelsey's hammer sang in the clear air. An aroma of sizzling bacon curled from the cook fires, and the smell of strong coffee. It was better to appreciate the perfect spring morning than to marvel at the color of Cody Snow's eyes or to notice that standing near him tightened her nerves.

"We're having a problem. You and me."

Abruptly, Perrin's heart plummeted to her toes. When she stared into Cody's steady gaze, she was certain she read condemnation there. Lowering her head, she blinked rapidly, shocked to discover how much she had hoped that Cody Snow wouldn't hear the gossip about her.

"In the past week," he said, watching her as he lifted a hand and started to tick down his fingers, "Sarah Jennings has come to me with a suggestion that the brides share provisions and a communal cooking fire. Ona Norris has come to me to inquire how many miles we've traveled. Augusta Boyd has come to me to demand bathing facilities. And Thea Reeves has come to me to inquire if I'll pose for one of her sketches." He shook his head and made a sound reminiscent of stones grinding together. "Do you see the problem, Mrs. Waverly?"

A rush of pink tinted her face. She scuffed a boot over the

sun-soft ground and frowned. "I don't know how to make them come to me instead of you."

Cody removed his hat, raked his fingers through a tumble of dark, sweat-damp hair, then he resettled the hat on his head. "You need to figure it out, Mrs. Waverly . . . or we'll have to make other arrangements."

Which meant choosing a new women's representative. The sudden cramp in her stomach told Perrin that she didn't want that to happen. Being the women's representative had become important to her.

Because of the title, the others couldn't shun her outright. When she stopped by their fires in the evening to inquire if there were any problems, they didn't offer her coffee as they did with each other, and they didn't invite her to stay for a chat. But at least they were politely cordial. They didn't snub her or look through her, as they had done before she drew the slip of paper with the X on it.

Moreover, the title and position restored a tiny kernel of something that almost felt like pride, something she hadn't experienced in longer than she could remember.

A sudden choking sensation closed her throat as she tried to imagine the five- or six-month journey with no one to talk to, with no social interchange. No illusion of friendship.

She could not allow that to happen; she couldn't survive it. Being the representative required contact with the others, and it was her fervent secret hope that frequent contact could prove to them that she wasn't a bad person. She had made mistakes, yes, but her mistakes were not the sum total of her character.

Finally, she realized with a jolt of fresh shock, if she weren't the representative, she would have no reason to see or speak to Cody every day.

Right now, she told herself, losing contact with Cody did not loom as a great loss. Right now, Cody Snow was the enemy. Like all men, he threatened to take something away from her, something she valued, something she needed. Her chin rose and her dark eyes snapped and flashed.

"How did you respond to the interruptions that annoy you so much?" she asked in an unsteady voice. If she hadn't been so frightened of losing the representative position, she doubted she would have found the courage to confront him. He was an intimidating man, and confidence was not her strong suit. "Did you answer their inquiries?"

An impatient movement of one large square hand dismissed her question. "Of course."

"Then you didn't help much, did you?" The words emerged with a sharp edge, propelled by a burst of self-preservation.

It amazed her to discover she possessed the backbone to speak so plainly. But if she had learned nothing else in the last dismal years, she had learned that a man would trample her if she gave him the chance. After Joseph, she had decided it wouldn't happen again. Plus, she needed this position. Her shattered self-esteem desperately required something to build on.

Or maybe she lashed out at Cody because she disliked how flustered it made her feel to be alone with him. She didn't want to feel drawn toward him or any man. She didn't want male scents stirring that hollow space inside her, filling it with strange restless yearnings. Cody made her feel tense and aware of herself as a woman and aware of him as a man, and she didn't like it, didn't want those feelings ever again.

Cody contemplated her squared shoulders and the angry glances that flashed from the sides of her lowered bonnet. He threw back his head and laughed. The sound was as deep and full-bodied as it was surprising. Astonished and offended, Perrin stepped backward from his amusement.

"I'm not laughing at you," he said finally, sensing her offense. "I'm laughing because I made a stupid mistake. You're right. I've undermined you, and I apologize."

Perrin couldn't believe what she heard. Flustered and suspicious, she threw out her hands. "You shouldn't answer their questions. You should direct them to me."

"You're absolutely correct. In the future, if someone approaches me directly, I'll send them right back to you. I'm sorry. I didn't realize I was contributing to the problem."

Perrin stared. Never in a lifetime had she expected to hear a man acknowledge a fault or apologize so readily. Biting her lip, she frowned and examined him with frank distrust.

"If you'll do that," she said slowly, "it would help me enormously."

"I should have spotted the problem myself." He smiled down at her, sunlight slanting across his eyes, making them shine like deep blue crystal. Lightly touching her elbow, he started to lead her toward Smokey Joe's wagon and away from the noise Heck Kelsey made pounding out a length of metal.

But his step faltered and almost instantly he pulled his hand away as if the touch of her scalded him. "Will you accept a cup of cider as a peace offering?"

A warm tingle shot to her wrist and traveled up her shoulder, continuing to radiate from the spot he had touched. Perrin bit her lip and dropped her head. So he was aware of her too. The realization sent a dizzying sensation through her body and she touched her fingertips to her forehead. The last thing she needed was for anyone to observe his sudden awkwardness coupled with the bright bloom on her cheeks, and speculate what it might mean. Fresh rumors would fly, and she could abandon all hope for acceptance.

"Mornin', Miz Waverly." Smokey Joe tipped his hat, then returned to slapping lumps of floured bread dough across the wagon's sideboard. Sunlight cascaded down his long braid in a shine of silver. His drying hair suggested that Smokey Joe had already sampled the stream.

Cody opened the bung on a cider barrel and filled two tin cups. Perrin was careful not to touch his fingers when he extended one to her. "If we can maintain this pace, we should reach Fort Kearney early next week." They moved away from Smokey Joe's fire, and Cody faced toward Addison's farmhouse, his gaze narrowing.

Not wanting to mimic his every move, Perrin shifted in the

other direction to inspect the ruts tracking across the land. Far in the distance, she could see the swaying canvas tops of the train ahead of them. Suddenly she experienced a glorious, blinding impression of curving blue sky, green-brown earth, and the small slow-moving white dots of canvas. The beauty and vibrancy of sky and earth, of blue and green and white raised a lump to her throat. With all her heart she wished she possessed Thea Reeves's talent for art and sketching.

When she turned away, the scene too achingly beautiful to bear, she discovered Cody watching her. "It's just . . ."

"I know," he said softly.

For one strange moment they held each other's eyes and Perrin's chest tightened at the unexpected intimacy of sharing an instant of perfect unspoken accord. He knew exactly what she was thinking and feeling; she knew that he shared the same sensations. She didn't recall such a stunning certainty ever happening to her before.

After a minute Cody cleared his throat, then raised the cider to his lips. "How ill is Winnie Larson?"

"We all assumed it was coach fever," Perrin answered slowly, grateful to move beyond the disturbing moment of mutual understanding. "But she should have recovered by now." When she saw a spark of alarm flare in Cody's eyes, she added hastily, "It's not cholera. Sarah Jennings has seen cholera and this isn't it. Winnie isn't feverish or nauseous. She's just . . ." Puzzled, she shook her head. "I don't know."

Winnie Larson's condition had become a continuing and worrisome enigma. She didn't exhibit real symptoms of illness, yet neither was she capable of functioning adequately. When she attempted to help Jane Munger, her wagon partner, her mind drifted in the midst of a task and she seemed to forget what she was doing. Last night, when Perrin had stopped by Jane's and Winnie's wagon, she had discovered Winnie standing beside their cook fire, swaying and smiling into the flames, a pan of bread forgotten in her hand.

Jane had pressed her lips together and shrugged helplessly.

Dark circles rimmed her eyes, and her vivid coloring had dimmed with fatigue.

Perrin frowned. "I've tried speaking to Winnie, but it's like talking to a cloud."

"Are there other problems I should know about?"

She couldn't give up this job, she could not. It felt so good to have a purpose, to believe that she might make a difference, however small. She simply could not let the other brides cast her back into loneliness before she had a chance to redeem herself. Somehow, some way, she vowed to prove to Cody and the others that she was more than her reputation suggested.

"Ona Norris wrenched a finger. Bootie Glover set the grass on fire around her firepit, but Mem put it out." She paused and drew a deep breath as she always did before she could make herself speak Augusta's name. "One of Augusta Boyd's cows is limping."

"Tell Miles Dawson to take a look at it."

When she spoke again, the words came in a fierce rush. "I'm going to succeed as the women's representative, I know I can do this, and I will! But if . . ." She swallowed and made herself go on. "If you find it necessary to replace me . . . I think Sarah Jennings really wants the position. Hilda Clum or Mem Grant would also be good choices."

Two weeks on the trail had revealed which of the brides could be depended on to approach a task straightforwardly and without hesitation or complaint. Sarah, Hilda, and Mem were as different as three women could be, but they were alike in competence, attitude, and strength of character.

"Are you suggesting that I replace you with Mrs. Jennings?"

When Perrin realized how readily the other brides would follow Sarah, or Hilda, or Mem, her heart sank.

But trying had to count for something. Didn't it?

"No. I want you to give me another chance."

He hesitated, then walked out on the short grass budding on the land. Finally he turned and looked at her. "I don't know why, but I'm pulling for you, Mrs. Waverly. I'd like to see you succeed." He tossed the rest of his cider on the ground. "Don't misunderstand. This gets corrected or we make a change. I don't have time for constant interruptions. If you can't handle being the women's representative, I expect Sarah Jennings can."

"I can do it!"

"Show me."

Turning so abruptly that her skirts billowed behind her, Perrin walked away before he could see the tears of frustration that sprang into her eyes. All right. Now all she had to do was figure out how to make the women come to her instead of bothering Cody. And she had to fight her attraction to him. She would. She had to.

Miles Dawson and John Voss strung a rope down to the stream so none of the women would slip and fall, and they hacked a crude path through the thicket of willows crowding the banks. A second, separate bathing spot was designated for the men.

Though the brides agreed the males in their train appeared to be honorable, they also knew the young teamsters could be prankish, so Perrin Waverly volunteered to stand guard at the top of the rope and chase away any male who wandered too near. With their privacy ensured, the other women could enjoy their first bath since the journey had begun. Everyone hurried through irksome chores in anticipation of the treat.

Hastily, Mem Grant lined up tins of rising bread dough, crowding the pans along the wagon's sideboard. That done, she filled a large pot with water from the barrel she would replenish later today, and put the supper beans to soak. Next, she sorted the laundry into piles and located a cake of mild soap that would serve for laundry and for a bath. Lye soap would have been better for the laundry, but she couldn't find her wash supplies.

"Where are our towels?" she muttered in exasperation. Mem couldn't stand fully erect inside the wagon, couldn't

reach the trunks in the back of the wagon bed. She had believed she had planned the load carefully with everyday
needs within easy reach, then the food barrels, and finally the
items they would not require until they reached Oregon and
set up housekeeping. Frowning, she tried to recall who had
packed the linens. Surely Bootie hadn't packed their towels
in the Oregon trunks.

"It's warm today, but the wind is chilly," Bootie called,
raising her voice so Mem could hear her inside the wagon.
She wrapped dust-caked skirts around the bundles of soiled
linen so their petticoats couldn't be seen. "Augusta said there
was ice in the water."

"A brisk dip will be invigorating. Where on earth are the
towels?"

"I've never bathed outside, or in front of other people,"
Bootie added. Mem glanced out the back of the wagon and
saw her sister wringing her hands and glaring as if the air
and sunshine were enemies. "But if Augusta can bathe in a
stream, so can I."

"You certainly can if you want to be clean. Heaven knows
when we'll have another chance." To fend off the headache
building at the top of her spine, Mem planned how she
would describe stream bathing in her journal. She would
make it sound exciting and extraordinary to her descendants,
perhaps amusing. But the words wouldn't form in her mind.
Right now all she could think about was the anticipated pleasure of washing the travel grime off her skin and trail dust
out of her hair.

Bootie offered a hand when she climbed down from the
wagon, but Mem waved it away. If she relied on Bootie,
chances were they'd both fall to the ground. "We'll use these
old shawls as towels until I can find ours." She lifted a bundle of laundry, waited for Bootie to gather a pile, then they
walked toward the ropes the teamsters had strung.

"Oh! I meant to ask. Do you recall the names carved on
the crosses we passed last night?"

Mem looked at her sister. "What is the point of filling your trip journal with the names of people who have died?"

She didn't understand Bootie's obsession with the graves they passed every day or so. Here they were, having the grand adventure of their lives. There were a thousand new and exciting experiences to record. The first river crossing, the first antelope sighted, the first meal that wasn't raw or overcooked, the first warm day, the first bath in a cold rushing stream.

A fringe of reddish gold hair and Bootie's frowning gray eyes were all that showed above her bundle of laundry. "Augusta says it's important to make sure those poor unfortunates are not forgotten."

"Then let Augusta record their names."

"Augusta says it is our Christian duty to assume this obligation. Besides, I can't think of anything else to write in my journal."

"Augusta says!" Mem rolled her eyes. "I am growing thoroughly weary of hearing that Augusta says this and Augusta says that. Perhaps you've forgotten that less than a month ago, Her Majesty wouldn't deign to give you a nod when she passed you in the street. And frankly, I doubt you'll be deluged with invitations from her once we arrive in Clampet Falls. Why you follow after that woman like a lapdog mystifies me."

Bootie's eyebrows soared above the pile of laundry. "Augusta and I are becoming friends! She's a true lady!"

"So are you. So what? If you ask me, Cora Thorp has more character in her little toe than Augusta Boyd has in her entire snooty body. That poor young Miss Thorp is working herself into a state of exhaustion because your esteemed 'friend' considers herself too refined to lift a finger."

The mere suggestion of Augusta Boyd assisting with the tasks of ordinary mortals appeared to shock Bootie. Mem sighed. She wondered if Bootie had really joined this venture to be with her, or if the appeal of the journey had been that Bootie had finally spied a way to insinuate herself into Augusta Boyd's charmed circle. If Mem had an apple seed for every time Bootie had taken to her bed in grief over being excluded from one of Augusta Boyd's teas or soirees, she could have planted an orchard.

They washed their laundry first, clumsily and not very thoroughly. Smiling, they exchanged excuses with Hilda Clum and Cora Thorp as to why they were not taking time to heat boiling water and do the job properly. Mem was not the only bride to rush through her chores; apparently everyone was impatient for a bath and eager to visit Addison's farmhouse and see what there was to see. Bootie helped her drape their wet petticoats and gowns on willows to dry in the thin spring sunshine, then finally they were free to rush down to the bathing area.

Halting on the path, Mem observed the others for a minute, then laughed out loud with pleasure. Ona Norris and Thea Reeves frolicked in the cold water like young otters, splashing and shrieking and laughing as their skin turned red with cold. Sarah Jennings stood in water fluming around her knees, wearing a white shimmy and pantaloons, washing Lucy Hastings's hair. Cora Thorp, Hilda, and Jane Munger pressed head to wet head, examining a family of sand turtles they had found along the bank.

Bootie and Augusta huddled on the stream bank in dismayed silence, the sun shining on loosened tresses of reddish gold and blond, contemplating the cold tumbling water with dread. They could stand there all day if they liked, Mem decided, but not her. She threw off her gown and petticoats, then ran forward in her chemise and pantaloons and plunged into the stream, yelping when the icy flow struck her skin.

Lord, Lord, it was marvelous. An experience that was simply incomparable. How many women ever had the opportunity to bathe in the open air like a child of nature? After splashing water up her arms and over the goose bumps rising on her shoulders, Mem tugged her hair loose, then bent at the waist and let the heavy spill of auburn drop into the water. She laughed with joy as frigid water stung her scalp like icy needles. If she hadn't been a dignified twenty-eight year old, she would have joined the younger women splashing and chasing each other through the shallows. She was sorely tempted. But she had promised to relieve Perrin at the top of the rope, and it wouldn't be fair to waste time in play.

When she stood upright to wring the water from her hair, she noticed that Bootie and Augusta still shivered on the bank, as dry as two Methodists, cringing from flying droplets and shuddering. As might have been predicted, Augusta's pantaloons were trimmed with expensive imported lace and her chemise had been tailored to her trim body instead of fitting loose like everyone else's did. Augusta observed Ona's and Thea's frolics with an expression of superiority and distaste.

Mem truly did not comprehend Bootie's infatuation with Augusta Boyd. In Chastity, Augusta had been a distant queenly figure, too elevated by society and her own imagination to take notice of the likes of Bootie Glover or Mem Grant.

A closer acquaintance forced by the trail had not improved Mem's impression. In her opinion, Augusta Boyd was self-absorbed, selfish, standoffish, and a generally useless woman. She was curt to the teamsters, imperious with Mr. Snow, and painfully rude to Webb Coate. She was barely civil to poor Cora Thorp and seldom mingled with the other brides. If Augusta Boyd was the product of money and position, then Mem was glad she had neither.

Quickly she finished washing, glorying in the tingle of the cold water and in feeling clean again, then she dashed out of the stream, toweled her skin and hair, and hastily dressed.

"I'm sorry I didn't come sooner," she apologized to Perrin. Extending her hands, she laughed at the fiery glow on her pale, redhead's skin. "The water was wonderful! I hated to get out."

When Perrin Waverly smiled, she was truly beautiful. Studying her, Mem decided that Perrin was, quite simply, one of the loveliest-looking women she had ever met. On the surface, Mrs. Waverly was small and delicate, but Mem sensed strength beneath those fine bones. It required strength and courage to face down the rumors Mem suspected Perrin must surely know were circulating among the women.

Mem had no idea whether the gossip was true; she didn't know if Perrin Waverly actually was a fallen woman. But she had considered the matter and had concluded that she personally didn't care.

In Mem's opinion, all women were but one catastrophic disaster away from sinking into shame. If Bootie and Robert had not offered Mem a home, she didn't know what might have become of her. Maybe she too . . . but that didn't bear thinking about. In fact, it impressed her as rather hilarious that she, a virgin spinster, could even think about taking a lover on a paying basis. It was a good thing that Bootie couldn't read her mind.

Nevertheless, it wouldn't do to rush to judgment as regards the choices Mrs. Waverly had made.

"Are you and Hilda planning to visit the Addison farm this afternoon?" Mem asked.

Perrin touched the dusty bun coiled at the nape of her neck and gazed toward the sounds of splashing and shouts of laughter. Eagerness sparkled in her large dark eyes. "I'm going, but Hilda hasn't decided yet."

"If you like . . ." Mem paused, then finished her thought before she could change her mind "I'll wait while you do your laundry and bathe. We could walk up to the farmhouse together." A decision which was certain to scandalize Bootie.

Perrin's head jerked up, and a leap of gratitude moistened her eyes. "I'd like that," she said in a low voice. "Very much. I promise I won't be long."

"Don't hurry on my account. I need to finish some baking before we go, and I promised myself I'd reorganize our wagon."

Perrin touched Mem's sleeve, then started down the path to the stream, pausing once to look at Mem over her shoulder.

After peering around to make sure none of the teamsters were lurking about, Mem sat on a large stone and fluffed a sheet of wet hair across her shoulders to dry.

In her mind she continued to see Perrin's large eyes and moist gratitude. A sigh lifted Mem's bosom. It was time someone besides Hilda Clum offered Perrin Waverly a little support. "There but for the grace of God . . ."

There was precious little to see at the farmhouse, Augusta decided. She had walked this distance for nothing. The Addison boy's cider looked weak and it cost three pennies a cup. Still, she was thirsty after the trek so she poked about her purse with a stricken expression and pretended to Bootie that she had forgotten to bring any money. Permitting Bootie to buy her a cup of weak cider meant she had to put up with Bootie for the rest of the afternoon, and that would be a trial, but she deserved a cup of cider.

The cider was as watery as she had predicted, but cool. After refreshing themselves, she and Bootie paid a duty call on Mrs. Addison at the house. The rooms were large and airy, but the furnishings proved as dismal as Mrs. Addison's outdated gown.

"No sense of fashion at all," Augusta commented as they stepped off the porch and opened their parasols.

"None," Bootie echoed.

They strolled about the yard before stopping at a safe distance from the well housing, where three Indians sat on the bare ground, two men and a woman, expressionlessly extending their palms in silent appeal for coins. It was disgusting. Some of the brides gathered around them, and as Augusta watched, Lucy Hastings actually gave one of the creatures a nickel.

"She is a preacher's daughter, but still . . ."

Bootie was about to agree, but before she could speak, Cora Thorp broke away from the group circled around the Indians and joined them, a determined look pinching her small sour features.

"The least you could do is buy me a cup of cider too," Cora snapped, her expression daring Augusta to disagree.

"Excuse us, will you?" she said to Bootie, then clutched Cora's elbow and drew her away from eavesdroppers. "How dare you address me in that tone!"

Cora's chin came up. "I could buy my own cool drink if you'd pay me what I'm owed! And a trinket too if I wanted one. But I suppose that ain't going to happen, leastways not right now. So you can just give me enough for a cup of cider!"

Icy fingers gripped Augusta's stomach. She didn't know what she was going to do. Cora was becoming more belligerent by the day, relentlessly demanding her wages. And Augusta couldn't pay them. Pride, and fear of exposure, was turning her into a nervous Nellie. She stared at Cora's cheap bonnet and jutting chin, and wondered how much time she had left before Cora started complaining about her wages in front of the other brides.

The possibility made Augusta feel faint. She couldn't bear it that the pride of the Boyds rested on the crumbling discretion of a gravedigger's daughter. She would die, absolutely die of shame if the others discovered that she had only forty dollars to see her through to Oregon. Forty dollars was her entire fortune, all that remained after she had paid her father's debts and repaid the money he had embezzled from his own bank.

And Cora wanted one-eighth of it. If Augusta paid Cora five dollars to clear her back wages, she would have only thirty-five dollars to last five months and two thousand miles.

For a moment she stared into Cora's challenging eyes and she hated Cora Thorp with a passion she hadn't known she was capable of feeling. Then, tight-lipped and trembling, she opened the drawstring on the little purse dangling from her wrist and repeated the charade she had performed earlier for Bootie Glover.

"I've spent the money I brought," she informed Cora in her most imperious tones.

"You had money for *your* cider," Cora said, not believing her. "I want some too." She stamped her boot on the ground. "Damn it, I want my wages!"

"Hush!" Panicked perspiration sprouted under Augusta's arms. "You don't need to shout. I . . . I'll pay you a dollar when we get back to the wagon."

"Good. But I want some cider *now*!"

Horrified by Cora's rising voice, Augusta swiftly looked around to see if anyone had heard. She had to do something quickly. "Wait here, you sniveling little chippy!"

Instead of boxing Cora's ears as she yearned to do, she made herself stroll back to Bootie's side. "My dear Bootie, I do hate to impose on your good nature, but poor Cora forgot to bring any coins with her, and you know I did too—so silly of us both—so I wonder if you might lend me another three pennies. It's hot in the sun, and the poor thing would enjoy a sip of something cool."

Bootie leaned around her to peer at Cora, then spoke in a whisper. "She sounded so demanding. Do you permit her to speak to you in that tone very often?"

Augusta unclenched her jaw and lifted a gloved hand in an airy gesture of forgiveness. "She's hot and tired, poor thing. One must be charitable and take circumstances into account."

Bootie opened the drawstring on her little purse. "I swan, Augusta. You're truly a marvel of generosity."

"How kind of you to notice," Augusta murmured, lowering her lashes modestly.

Once she had Bootie's three pennies in her hand, she returned to Cora and slapped the coins against the palm of Cora's mended glove. "There! Are you satisfied?"

"No," Cora said sullenly, counting the pennies. "And I won't be until I get *all* my back wages!"

"Hush!" Panicked, Augusta prayed that no one had overheard. Bootie was watching, but Augusta didn't think she was close enough to hear. She fervently hoped not. A rivulet of nervous perspiration zigzagged between her breasts. Her lips trembled.

Hands clenched at her sides, eyes narrowed, she watched Cora walk toward the Addison boy's cider stand, imagining a swagger. Anger and despair twitched her lips. Cora was going to humiliate and destroy her; Cora was going to trample everything the Boyds had represented since the Mayflower.

With the help of the Boyd attorney, Augusta had managed to salvage the debacle of her father's disgrace and keep the worst of it from becoming public knowledge. But she didn't know how to stop Cora. For that, she needed money.

For a moment her shoulders sagged and helpless tears swam in her eyes. She couldn't manufacture money out of wishes and desperation.

It was the only thing she thought about, day and night. She desperately needed money to pay Cora's wages and shut her up, but there was no possibility of getting any. Every night while Cora slept, Augusta counted her forty dollars, again and again, praying that she had erred and her purse would yield hundreds.

"Augusta?" Bootie called.

"In a moment," she answered, hoping her voice didn't sound moist or teary. You are a Boyd, she reminded herself angrily, taking courage from the proud old name. Boyds do not make a public spectacle of themselves.

Now she noticed the group of hard-eyed men loitering beneath a budding cottonwood, watching her. Addison's farm appeared to be a gathering spot for all manner of unsavory characters. Dirty, bearded, and half drunk, the men looked like cutthroats all. She slashed them a glance of disdain before she rejoined Bootie.

"Any one of them would knock a woman over the head to steal the earrings from her ears. It's disgraceful that Mr. Snow and that Indian would expose us to such a low element!"

"I couldn't agree more," Bootie said with a sniff.

Bootie would have agreed if Augusta had claimed the sky was made of blue pudding. Actually, Augusta expected those she allowed into her circle to agree with her, but occasionally unthinking acquiescence could be annoying.

One of the men under the trees detached himself from his cronies, wiped a sleeve across his mouth, and ambled toward them, his strange yellowish eyes fixed on Augusta's breasts.

" 'Scuse me, ladies. Are you two of them brides off Captain Cody Snow's train?"

Augusta cast him a freezing glance and turned her back, but not before she noticed that his beard was ragged and untrimmed and he reeked of cheap whiskey. She was utterly offended that he imagined a lady such as herself would recognize his existence or speak to him.

Bootie's hands fluttered to her bonnet strings. She cast an uncertain look toward Augusta's stony profile. "Ah . . . well, yes, we are."

Augusta sighed. Bootie Glover was such a silly, irritating little creature. If she could have caught Bootie's eye without facing the reprobate, she would have brought the brainless twit to her knees with one of her famous icy glares.

"Me and the boys was wondering . . . what's ole Cody carrying in them freight wagons?"

"Are you a friend of Mr. Snow's?"

Augusta longed to give Bootie a slap. She could hear Bootie's voice oozing trust. The woman was hopeless. Was there no one to whom she wouldn't speak? Had she no standards at all?

"I've known the Captain for years, ma'am. Served under his command in the army, I did."

"Oh. Well, then, I suppose it's all right to tell. We're transporting arms to Oregon, and molasses to Fort Laramie."

"Do tell. Molasses and arms. Did I hear you right, ma'am? You did say molasses?"

"Two wagons full," Bootie offered brightly. "We're going to sell the—"

Augusta could not endure it another minute. Turning, she

gripped Bootie's arm, squeezing hard enough to cut off the flow of words.

"If you wish to discuss our business," she said in a frigid voice, addressing both Bootie and the drunk, "I suggest you do so with Mr. Snow." Turning, she dragged Bootie away from the man.

"In case I don't see *Mister* Snow, you tell him that you met Jake Quinton. You tell the son of a bitch that old Jake ain't forgot nothing."

The menace in his tone made Augusta look back despite herself. She stared into the meanest, coldest, most frightening smile she had ever seen. A prickle of fear shuddered down her spine. At once she knew she would see that terrible smile and those yellowish snake eyes in her nightmares. Panicked, she frantically looked for Miles Dawson and Bill Macy, the teamsters who had accompanied the women to the farmhouse. She didn't see either of them.

"You seem . . . What's wrong?" Bootie asked anxiously, trotting along beside her. "He said he was Mr. Snow's friend."

"Hush," Augusta hissed. "That man is no friend of Mr. Snow's." When she darted another quick glance over her shoulder, she saw Jake Quinton licking his lips, his hard slitted eyes studying the sway of their skirts.

"Dear God," Augusta muttered. Her lips were dry as toast.

A rush of relief nearly overwhelmed her when she spotted Webb Coate and Cody Snow striding toward the farmhouse. But when she dared another frightened glance toward the men beneath the cottonwoods, Jake Quinton had vanished.

"Thank heavens!"

Lifting her skirts, she hurried forward to relay Jake Quinton's message and to berate Webb Coate for choosing this terrible place as a campsite.

Her heart beat a little faster as she noticed Coate watching her approach, a condition she stubbornly attributed to her upset regarding Jake Quinton's threatening manner.

Augusta Boyd would *never* disgrace herself by feeling any attraction toward an Indian. She had standards.

CHAPTER
* 4 *

My Journal, April 18, 1852: Every day we rotate the wagons. The lead wagon goes to the back and everyone moves up a space. All of us hate being last because the dust is so bad. It gets in our mouths and eyes, on our clothes, and it scums the water buckets.

The lead spot is best because I can see him. He rides out ahead most of the day, but occasionally he drops back alongside the first wagon. I've noticed that he usually comes to my side whether I'm driving the oxen or taking my rest, but not always and I understand that. He doesn't want the others to notice that he favors me.

He doesn't say anything of a personal nature, nothing that would cause anyone to gossip about us. But sometimes his guard drops and I see his feelings in his eyes. Then he says things that are meant for my ears alone, but disguised so an eavesdropper would hear nothing to suspect. Still, it seems he could find a way for us to be alone. And he has yet to come right out and declare his feelings.

It thrills me that we share the secret of our love, but I struggle to understand why we must pretend to be strangers. My day is broken into the moments I see him, and the hours when I must suffer his absence. I need to be alone with him, need to hear him explain this game we're playing. I need to know the reason, need to hear it stated from his own beloved lips.

We have waited so long, lost to each other and believing we could have no future together, I tell myself I can wait longer if we must, but I wish so greatly that it could be otherwise. It shames me to confess that I don't always understand his secret messages, although I understand the glances he sends me, and I comfort my heart with the love I read in his gaze. I have loved him for so long.

We can see Fort Kearney in the distance and will camp there for a day of rest. The Fort does not look like much.

It rained again yesterday. We see graves beside the trail every day. One of the teamsters got stepped on by an ox. Most of us have set aside any pretense at finery and wear old wash dresses of plain wool or serge. No one except Augusta still wears crinolines.

I long for him so much that I fear I will reveal our secret. I plunged my hand in the coals of our campfire; burning flesh cooled the heat of my yearning.

CHAPTER
* 5 *

The chilly, overcast morning seemed more a reminder of winter than an affirmation of spring, Perrin thought, watching the men work. Heck Kelsey and the teamsters inched along the line of wagons, caulking bottom boards with tar and pitch to prevent the waters of the Platte from soaking into wagon beds. Ordinarily the broad but shallow river reached only knee high on a man, but swollen by the spring melt, the water had risen to four and a half feet. The crossing would be difficult.

Perrin joined Hilda on a muddy bank overlooking the turgid flow. From here, they had a clear view of wagons from other trains struggling to cross the river, and they could see the entire length of their own train. They watched Cody Snow shouting orders and moving along the line to inspect the teamsters' work.

"For the rest of my life I'll associate the smell of tar with being wet and cold," Perrin murmured, speaking against the wind. She drew her shawl tighter around her shoulders and dodged a breeze-blown tumbleweed. She had lost count of the number of river crossings, all of them difficult.

"*Ja.*" Hilda sighed and tucked a strand of blond hair beneath the braided coronet that crossed the top of her head like a tiara. "Mr. Kelsey says the crossing will take all afternoon and into the evening." They both glanced at the leaden sky. "I hope it doesn't snow or rain again."

Perrin dreaded the fording. Despite its comparatively shallow depth, the Platte was noted for unpredictable currents, quicksand, and shifting banks. It wasn't one river, but a series of streams that wound together like an intricate water braid, the strands interspersed with sandbars. They would have to cross six of the streams, each presenting its own peculiar set of problems.

"I overheard Smokey Joe telling Mr. Snow that the Platte is too thick to drink and too thin to plow," Perrin said, trying to smile. Automatically her gaze followed Cody along the length of the wagons. Usually the sight of him grounded her anxieties about any particular difficulty, but raised anxieties of a different sort. She didn't permit herself to analyze those anxieties.

Her shoulders tensed when she noticed he'd stopped to talk to Jane Munger. She fervently hoped Jane hadn't interrupted him with something trivial. Cody would be concerned about the upcoming crossing, and he was waiting for Webb Coate to return from a scouting trip to Fort Kearney on the north side of the river.

As Perrin watched, her hopes sank. Cody swung in her direction and pointed, saying something to Jane, then Jane stiffened and strode forward, heading toward the muddy point where Perrin and Hilda stood braced against the wind. Cody continued to stare toward Perrin's flapping skirts until he was certain she had noticed his frown.

Perrin swallowed a sigh. Last week, she had handled a myriad of small problems, all of them referred back to her by Cody, who had let her know the interruptions had not ceased. None of the brides were accustomed to taking problems to a woman; their instinct was to approach the man in charge. They resented being turned back to Perrin.

Regardless, Perrin had helped a distraught Lucy Hastings locate the family Bible she had feared left behind at their last camp; she had found Hilda's wandering cow; she had traded a bottle of castor oil for a bottle of peppermint oil to treat Ona Norris's earache; she had asked Smokey Joe for answers to Thea Reeves's questions about the bison they would be seeing soon.

These problems or questions had loomed large for the women involved, but none had been overwhelming for Perrin. She was discovering that helping others satisfied a deep-seated need. But none of the problems so far had been as serious as the problem she suspected Jane Munger was bringing her.

Jane marched across the muddy ground with no thought for her hem or boots, her face clamped in an angry scowl. When Perrin first met Jane at Cody's predeparture meeting in Brady's hall, she had admired Jane's high coloring and glossy dark hair, had thought her pretty, though sharp-featured. Now Jane's cheeks were pale and drawn with weariness. Dark circles ringed her eyes. The luster had faded from her skin and hair, and her lips trembled.

Jane started talking before she reached them. "I've spent all my life in towns. Before this, I'd never ridden in a covered wagon, had never driven oxen, never cooked outside or slept outside. I've known hardship, but nothing like this!"

Hilda slid a quick look at Perrin, then backed away. "I'll finish packing for the crossing." She hurried toward the wagons.

"I would never have agreed to join this train had I known that I'd be doing *all* the work! I was told I would have a wagon partner who would share in the duties!"

"Jane—"

"I can't continue. I'm exhausted! And look at my hands." Jerking off her gloves, she extended shaking palms smeared with the bloody fluid of broken blisters. "And look at this!" She held out her skirt to show Perrin burned spots along the hem where sparks from open fires had charred the wool. "Everyone else gets a rest from driving the oxen, gets to walk a bit behind the wagons and visit awhile. But not me. Winnie can't drive, couldn't be trusted to drive if she would try. And everyone else takes turns doing the cooking or the laundry or setting up the tent or milking in the mornings or baking or searching for firewood. But I have to do it *all* because Winnie Larson can't do *anything*!" Her hands flew up to cover her face, and her shoulders shook. Her voice cracked and sank to a whisper. "This isn't fair!"

"No, it isn't," Perrin gently agreed. Stepping forward, she hesitated, then placed an arm around Jane's trembling shoulders and led her toward an abandoned water barrel. When Jane was seated, Perrin knelt at her side.

"It's only been three weeks, but I'm so exhausted that I'm afraid I'll fall asleep at the reins. I'm too tired even to eat. Last night rain washed inside our tent and soaked our bedrolls, and I slept through it." Jane covered her eyes with a shaking hand. "Then this morning, I had to spread out our blankets and sheets to dry. But it's going to snow or rain again and they'll never get dry. Tonight we'll sleep in cold wet blankets, and it's just the last . . . the last . . . I just can't *do* this!"

Dropping her hand from her face, she gripped Perrin's fingers so hard that Perrin couldn't suppress a wince. "Please. I can't go back, I just can't! Oh, God, I don't know what to do! I can't go back, but I can't make it all the way to Oregon doing the work of two people!"

Withdrawing her hands from Jane's grip, Perrin patted her shoulder. "I'll speak to Winnie again," she said, frowning toward the line of wagons. Winnie Larson sat on the tailgate of the wagon she shared with Jane. The distance was too great for Perrin to see what object Winnie held in her hand, but it seemed to absorb her attention to the exclusion of all else. She appeared oblivious to the frenzied preparations occurring around her. She wore no shawl or hat, apparently unaware of the wind and cold.

"Talking does no good," Jane cried, anguish lifting her voice. "You must know that by now! The only thing that's going to help is for someone to take the laudanum away from her!"

Perrin's head jerked up. "What are you talking about?"

"Winnie is a laudanum addict!" Jane wiped her eyes and returned Perrin's incredulous stare. "You didn't know?" Sudden confusion drew her eyebrows together. "But I thought . . . you all know each other, so I assumed . . ."

"Oh, Jane. You thought we burdened you with Winnie because none of us wanted the extra work of taking care of her?"

When Jane nodded, carefully watching her expression, Perrin shook her head and took the other woman's hands in hers.

"I swear to you, this is the first I've heard about Winnie and laudanum. I know Winnie's father is the chemist in Chastity, and I've run into Winnie and her mother in Brady's Mercantile, but until this journey, I'd never actually met her or exchanged a word with her." She considered a moment. "It's my guess that few of the others know her well either."

Jane's shoulders collapsed and she pulled one trembling hand free and pressed it against her eyelids. "If that's true, then I've done all of you an injustice. I've been so angry because I thought . . ." She waved a hand and shook her head, then gazed into Perrin's wide eyes. "I don't know what to do."

Perrin's first anxious instinct was to run pell-mell toward the wagons and throw this problem at Cody. She checked the urge with difficulty. "Did you tell Mr. Snow about Winnie?"

"I didn't get that far before he sent me to you."

Think it through, Perrin urged herself, wringing her hands. If Cody knew about Winnie, what would he expect her to do?

Rocking back on her heels, she studied the dark clouds scudding low to the earth. The sky was gray, the river gleamed like bands of gray ribbon, her thoughts were gray. She didn't have the faintest idea how to approach this problem. But she knew she needed to solve it herself, without asking Cody's advice.

"Can you manage a little longer?" she inquired finally, lowering her gaze to Jane's face. "I need to think about this."

Jane turned weary eyes toward the low banks beyond the two-mile expanse of water. Every inch of the crossing was fraught with dangerous possibilities, promised to be a battle. The other brides would have help from their partner or at least encouragement. But she would endure the ordeal alone, with Winnie daydreaming in a makeshift bed in the back of the wagon.

Finally she nodded. Lowering her head, she examined the raw blisters on her palms. "I'm so tired," she whispered. "So bone-deep tired. But I can go a little farther if I know an end is coming." Lifting her head, she stared hard into Perrin's eyes. "I can't go back to Missouri. That's impossible. But it will break my health to continue like this. Please help me."

"I will," Perrin promised. She pressed Jane's hands, then released them and helped her to stand.

Alone on the riverbank, she watched Jane return to the wagons, her hem and steps dragging. With all her worried heart, Perrin wished she knew what to do. But there was a hole in her mind where a solution should have been. This problem was too large to grasp.

Then she spotted Cody, watching her. He stood beside one of the teamsters, a bucket of tar in his hand. For a long moment they gazed at each other across the broad expanse of muddy earth.

Still watching her, Cody removed his hat and waved it in the air to alert Smokey Joe. Smokey Joe pounded his dinner gong, signaling it was time for the women to return to the wagons. As Perrin hurried toward her wagon, she noticed that Cody still watched her. His hard scrutiny should have worried her, and it did, but it also gave her a tiny secret thrill of pleasure.

Her heart sank. There was something about dangerous roguish men that had always appealed to her. Perhaps it was their stubborn refusal to be manipulated or their relentless confidence or their disregard for rules other than their own. Perhaps it was the open speculation that smoldered in their eyes when they gazed at a woman who intrigued their interest.

Face flaming, Perrin hastily pulled herself onto the wagon seat, where she could no longer see him.

Several trains camped near Fort Kearney, resting from the arduous river crossing, drying goods soaked by rain or river water, and crowding the post stores to replenish provisions.

After three weeks on the trail, most immigrants discovered they had overestimated the need for some items and had seriously underestimated the need for others. Consequently, the post stores conducted a brisk business, callously charging outrageously high prices, secure in the knowledge that travelers were at least five weeks away from the next opportunity to purchase supplies.

Augusta's frustration was like a vise tightening around her chest, anxious tears clogging her throat. Simply everything was going wrong.

First, the tar had not held on the bottom of her wagon and river water had seeped into the bed, soaking her good linens. Worse, twenty pounds of sugar, her entire supply, had rolled out of the gutta-percha bag that was supposed to protect it. The sugar had dissolved and flowed away. The twenty-pound sack should have lasted the entire journey; now it was gone.

Next, Cora had gotten frightened and drew up on the reins, causing them to stall on a sand bank in the middle of the Platte. The teamsters rode into the river to assist them, but they couldn't help the ox, who, stupid thing, was sinking in a bog of quicksand. All they could do was cut the ox from the yoke and watch helplessly as the heavy animal sank beneath the water.

Then, as if there hadn't been enough misfortune, icy rain poured from the skies in buckets, drenching them before they completed the crossing. Later, Cora tried to cook their supper in streaming rain—an impossible task—so they had gone to bed hungry, trying to sleep with half-frozen raindrops soaking through their tent and dripping on their faces all night.

And the final disappointment—after days of anticipation, Fort Kearney had turned out to be nothing more than a dismal collection of log shacks set alongside a square that was a sea of churned-up mud, horse droppings, and tobacco juice.

Augusta stepped up on the boardwalk erected before the stores and stared down at the disgusting mess clinging to her boots. The tassels were ruined and so was her sodden hem.

She swallowed hard and blinked against the tears stinging her eyelids. She would not cry, she absolutely would *not*.

"Well? Are we going inside the store, or ain't we?" Cora asked crossly. Rain had all but melted the pasteboard lining of her sunbonnet, and the brim now sagged and flopped in her eyes.

In other circumstances, Augusta might have laughed. Still, by choosing to wear a bonnet that was already ruined, Cora didn't have to worry about spoiling a good one. But then, Cora didn't concern herself with maintaining the standards of gentility. A gravedigger's daughter had no family name to live up to.

"I haven't decided if I'll purchase anything," Augusta said, turning her eyes away from the tempting items arrayed in the store window. Soldiers and travelers clogged the square, further churning the mud. Wagons piled high with provisions moved out the open end and empty wagons rolled in to take their place.

Cora leaned to examine the goods in the window, then threw out her hands. "We can't go all the way to Oregon without sugar," she said in a voice sulky with impatience. "You might believe you can sweeten your coffee merely by sticking your finger in it, but believe me, it ain't going to happen that way. Plus, you need to replace the ox we lost."

"And whose fault was that?" Augusta snapped, stepping aside to allow a man and a woman to enter the store. Before the door closed, she caught a tantalizing glimpse of cloth bolts and medicals and intriguing barrels and leather goods.

Cora stared at her. "Maybe if you'd take the reins once in a while, you'd find out it ain't so easy to drive several yokes of oxen! Especially when the wagon is mostly floating and there's water rushing all around you!"

Augusta lifted her chin. "Some people make do with only six oxen, so we can get along nicely with seven."

Discreet inquiries had elicited the shocking information that the price of an ox could run as high as eleven dollars. It wasn't fair. The silly animals were prone to foot disease, could go lame in a heartbeat, and were dumber than an earthworm.

"Well, we do need sugar." Cora entered the store and let the door bang behind her.

Grinding her teeth, Augusta squeezed the little purse dangling from her wrist and fervently wished it would magically grow fat beneath her anxious fingers. Sugar, she had learned, was selling for the dismaying price of twenty cents a pound. To replace what the river had stolen would cost four dollars. And to buy fresh eggs, which made her salivate and nearly swoon to think about, would cost fifteen cents a dozen.

Biting her lip to hold back tears of anger and self-pity, she paced along the mud-caked boardwalk, performing the arithmetic again and again in her mind.

Shock glazed her blue eyes. She had thirty-five dollars to see her through five months and two thousand miles. "Oops." Mem Grant caught Augusta's arm as they collided near the store's entry. When Augusta didn't apologize, Mem did, speaking in a cool voice. "I beg your pardon. I fear I wasn't paying attention."

Augusta acknowledged the apology with a distracted nod, then turned toward a voice speaking above her hat.

"Good afternoon, ladies."

Both women looked up at Webb Coate as he tipped his hat and smiled. Augusta caught a breath and felt Mem do the same. She had an impression of flowing dark hair, lustrous black eyes, and white, white teeth in a darkly bronzed face. A warm shiver skittered toward her toes.

Webb's gaze skimmed her ornate bonnet and the gauze tied beneath her chin. "I'd suggest that you ladies buy the widest-brimmed hats you can find. We'll be into hot weather soon."

"Dry warm weather can't come soon enough for me." Mem lifted her damp skirts and laughed at the mud pasting the folds together. "A little sunshine sounds like a boon from heaven."

Webb smiled, seeming to notice Mem for the first time.

"If you aren't carrying lip salve, it would be wise to buy some while you can. Wind and that sunshine you're so eager to see can wreak havoc on a pale complexion."

Augusta gasped. She could not believe her ears. Quivering with indignation, she drew to her full height. "Your advice is neither wanted nor welcome," she snapped, letting her eyes go frosty with offense. "Should you make intimate remarks in the future, we will complain to Mr. Snow!"

Webb stared at her and something dark and challenging gleamed in his black eyes. Then he touched his fingertips to his hat brim, nodded, and stepped off the boardwalk. He crossed the square toward the saddle shop where Cody waited.

The instant he turned his back, Mem's fingers dug into Augusta's arm. "You are the rudest, most self-inflated woman I have ever had the misfortune to encounter!"

"I beg your pardon! That half-breed mentioned our lips and our complexions! Such personal remarks are not to be tolerated from a white man, let alone an Indian!"

Mem leaned down until her eyes reached a level with Augusta's. "Don't ever—not ever again!—include me in anything you say. Don't presume to say 'we.' You speak solely for yourself, Miss Boyd. You do not speak for Mem Grant!"

"Well!"

Thoroughly angry and offended, Augusta watched Mem stride down the boardwalk with a face so stormy that even hardened soldiers hastened to scurry out of her path.

"Well!" she said again, lifting her chin. It was certainly evident which sister had the breeding in *that* family.

As if her thoughts had conjured reality, Bootie came rushing out of the store, halted in a swirl of skirts, and inspected a cameo watch pinned to an imitation cashmere shawl.

"Oh, dear. I'm going to be late for Perrin's meeting. Mem will be furious." She looked up and saw Augusta watching with a cool expression. "Have you seen my sister?"

Silently, Augusta nodded toward Mem's retreating figure. Bootie took a few steps in pursuit, then halted. "Aren't you coming? The meeting is scheduled to begin in a few minutes."

Augusta tossed her head, feeling her blond curls give a satisfying bounce against the top of her shoulders. "That creature has nothing to say that I choose to hear. I can't imagine you would respond to her summons either. Perhaps you would prefer to return inside with me?"

An agony of indecision pinched Bootie's expression. She gazed toward Mem, who had reached the end of the boardwalk, and high color flooded her cheeks.

"Id like to, I really would, but . . . well, Mem made me promise that I'd attend Mrs. Waverly's meeting, and . . ." she shrugged helplessly. "Any other time . . . but I . . ."

Augusta released her with an impatient flick of her fingertips. "Run along, then," she said coldly. She watched Bootie hurry along the muddy boardwalk, taking Augusta's hopes with her. She had counted on persuading Bootie to buy her a dozen eggs.

Involuntarily, she glanced at the little gold watch pinned to her own genuine cashmere shawl. The creature's meeting was due to begin in fifteen minutes. Well, she would not be present.

Inside the store, she inhaled a blend of tantalizing aromas, her mouth watering at the scent of pickles and onions, coffee beans and smoked sausage. After inspecting the tumble of goods tossed willy-nilly on the shelves, she paused before a piled stack of sugar bags, wishing she could purchase something smaller than a ten-pound sack.

"Ain't you going to Mrs. Waverly's meeting?" Cora asked innocently, appearing from another aisle.

"Hardly!" A pungent scent wafted from the black licorice whip Cora was chewing. "And neither are you!" She stared at the bag of licorice Cora clutched in her hand. The rich dark aroma filled her nostrils.

Cora's eyes narrowed. "I am too going! I guess I can go wherever I want when I ain't working!" Turning abruptly, she hurried down a narrow aisle and left the store.

Heartsick, Augusta stared at the bags of sugar without seeing them. Licorice. Cora had spent part of her dollar on licorice. Augusta had surrendered one whole precious dollar so that stupid, wasteful Cora could buy licorice.

A flood tide of rage, frustration, and helplessness almost knocked her to her knees. Despairing, she pressed her purse against her side. Oh, God. What was she going to do?

Cody watched Webb's dark face as he wound through the traffic clogging the post square. He moved forward as Webb stepped onto the boardwalk. "We'll stop in at Rogue Street on the way back to camp. Looks like you could use a drink."

Rogue Street was situated outside the post, a collection of saloons, washhouses, and whores' cribs. They entered the last saloon in the row and took a table near a cracked window that gave them a view of the post's entrance gate. Miles Dawson, the head teamster, would remain at the post until the last of the brides, Augusta Boyd, returned to camp. Cody wouldn't relax until all his passengers had returned to the train.

Tilting his chair against the rough log wall of the saloon, he scanned the faces of the men crowding a faro bank. "I knew the commander of this fort when I was in the army. Willis says Jake Quinton passed through about four days ago."

Webb tossed back a whiskey. "I would have thought Quinton had had his fill of army posts."

"Willis thinks Quinton and his men robbed Jed Lexy's train."

Webb nodded. "I'll tell the watch to keep their eyes open."

They never left the guns and molasses wagons unguarded. Someone was always posted on look out, day and night. Both men were fully aware the freight they carried made the train a target for marauders like Quinton and his gang.

Cody poured a second round of whiskey. "This is none of my business, but I keep telling you she's poison, old friend."

"You're right. It's none of your business. And it's not my

place to mention that you regard all women as lethal since Ellen died." Webb turned his gaze toward the window and the view of the post entrance.

Cody didn't answer, but Webb's observation stung as it was intended to. When Ellen and her newborn son had died a day after the birthing, he had gone crazy. The craziness eventually cost him his career in the army, but that no longer mattered. What mattered was he never wanted to endure that kind of pain again.

Webb turned his shot glass between long elegant fingers. "You worry me, my friend."

"You worry about you; I'll worry about me," Cody muttered.

"You're letting what happened poison your thoughts against all women." He tossed back the whiskey. "That's why you're planning to settle in Oregon at the end of this trip."

Cody almost laughed. "Because there aren't many women in Oregon? Is that what you think?"

Webb smiled. "If the cargo we're carrying is any indication, there don't seem to be many temptations in Oregon."

Cody let his chair bump down on the sawdust floor, then stood and resettled his hat. "Heck and Miles will be looking for us to relieve them back at camp."

The two men strode down Rogue Street, accustomed to seeing other men step out of their path.

"You know, Coate," Cody commented as they left the boardwalk and slogged through the mud toward the train. "I hate it when you go analytical on me. That's part of the Indian culture that I really don't warm to."

Webb laughed and returned Cody's grin. "You don't like hearing the truth, white eyes."

"What do you red devils know about truth?" They both laughed.

As they approached the campsite, Cody noticed the Chastity brides had gathered a short distance from the squared wagons. The women's camp chairs were arranged in a half circle to face Perrin Waverly.

"What's that all about?" Webb inquired.

"Damned if I know." A twitch of curiosity furrowed his brow. "I wasn't invited."

Perrin Waverly occupied his thoughts more frequently than he cared to admit. She was beautiful and she was an outcast, two conditions guaranteed to pique a man's interest. What surprised him and aroused his grudging admiration was her quiet fortitude. She was doggedly determined to succeed as the women's representative regardless of how little the other brides cooperated with her efforts or how coldly they treated her.

As he and Webb entered camp, he watched her step to the front of the assembled brides, and it occurred to him that courage came in many forms.

CHAPTER

* 6 *

Perrin hadn't known how many, if any, of the women would attend her meeting. She suspected they came largely in response to Mem's cajoling, bullying, and veiled threats. She located Mem's erect figure in the midst of the group and cast her a look of heartfelt gratitude. Unfortunately, Mem couldn't help her conduct the meeting. That she had to accomplish on her own.

Although she had rehearsed for two days, she hadn't realized how unnerving it would be to address a group, especially a group who preferred visiting with each other to listening to anything Perrin Waverly might have to say.

Some of the women darned stockings or mended torn hems while they chatted; Sarah Jennings stirred a cake bowl in her lap. Thea Reeves had opened her sketchbook and kept looking up at Perrin, then down at a stick of charcoal that appeared to fly across the page. Cora gave Lucy a licorice whip, and they whispered together. Ona Norris busily pressed the season's first tiny wildflowers between the pages of her trip journal.

"Excuse me?" It wasn't a good beginning. She sounded timid and tentative. And the suspicion that Thea might be sketching her portrait tied her stomach in knots. Swallowing hard, she began again. "May I have your attention, please?"

Gradually, the women quieted and raised inquisitive faces. All those eyes, resistant and judgmental, drove Perrin's speech out of her mind. The saliva dried in her mouth.

"I've never made a speech before," she admitted in a low voice, floundering, wondering if they could see her lips tremble.

"Louder," Hilda prompted gently.

Perrin cleared her throat. To bolster her courage, she had tucked her most prized possession beneath her bodice. She touched her chest and traced the old valentine lying next to her skin. Over the years the lettering had faded, and now only she could make out the inscription: *To my beloved wife, Charlotte.* The valentine was all she had left of her parents.

She clasped her hands tightly and cast a quick glance toward Jane Munger, who sat a little apart from the others. Jane's tired eyes fastened on Perrin with hope and anxiety.

Perrin drew a deep breath. "I've asked you here because we have a problem that I can't solve without your assistance."

"What kind of a problem do we have?" Sarah Jennings asked crisply. She handed the cake bowl to young Lucy Hastings, who set aside her licorice whip to take a turn at stirring.

Whatever Perrin did, Sarah was there looking over her shoulder, subtly implying she could have done it better. Nevertheless, Perrin admired Sarah Jennings. Sarah brought cheerfulness to a no-nonsense personality, and she wasn't shy about speaking her mind. During her years as an army wife, she had learned to approach problems as challenges, could cope with whatever obstacles fate tossed in her path. Perrin had to admit that Sarah would be a good ally in a crisis.

"Can you hear in back?" Perrin looked toward the last row where the younger women sat, Thea Reeves, Lucy Hastings, and Ona Norris. Thea glanced up from her sketch pad and nodded. So did Lucy. Ona Norris set aside her pressed flowers and frowned. It was painfully obvious that Ona disliked Perrin. The girl hadn't spoken a dozen words to her since the journey began.

"I believe we're all aware that Winnie Larson is ill." Perrin twined her fingers together and pressed shaking hands against her skirt. "I have recently learned the nature of Winnie's illness, and I've confirmed the information to my own satisfaction." She gazed back at the sea of eyes.

"It's cholera!" Bootie gasped. Lifting the chemise she'd

been mending, she used it to fan her face and fell back in her chair in a near swoon. "I knew it! We're all going to die!"

"It's not cholera," Perrin hastily assured them. "Winnie Larson is dependent on laudanum, which is an opium product. She's retaining water, she isn't eating, and she's dangerously weak. She's drifting in a world of her own."

The brides stared at Perrin. She imagined she could see them remembering that Winnie's father was Chastity's chemist, could sense them picturing the row of laudanum bottles on the shelves behind the tall counter at the rear of the Larson apothecary.

"I have something to say." Reluctantly, Hilda rose to her feet and faced the group." I should have told this before." She cast Perrin an apologetic look, then wrapped her hands in the folds of her apron. "My mother and Winnie's mother are friends. I recall my mother saying . . ." Her face flushed and she gazed down at the ground. "This is gossip, and I hate to . . ."

Mem's brown eyes sharpened. "If you have information that would help, it's your duty to tell us." Sarah murmured agreement.

"*Ja*. This I know." Hilda bit her lip and lifted her head. "Three years ago the man Winnie believed she would marry, married someone else." One of the younger women on the back row gasped. "That is when Mrs. Larson began to believe that Winnie was, ah, taking medicine from her father's store."

"Stealing laudanum, you mean?" Sarah asked.

Hilda nodded unhappily. "The Larsons thought Winnie would recover from her depression, but she did not. She withdrew from society and her family, mourning her lost beau. The Larsons thought they could wean her from the laudanum, but they could not. Somehow she always managed to get more." She paused. "If my mother is correct, it was Mr. Larson's idea to put Winnie on this train. I doubt she was given a choice. It is possible that Winnie does not understand where she is going. Occasionally she seems to believe that she is going to join the man who left her."

"Oh, dear." Bootie's hands fluttered in the vicinity of her bosom. "You should have informed Mr. Snow about this matter before we departed."

Hilda turned apologetic eyes to Jane. "I am sorry I did not tell him. But I hoped Winnie would not be able to get any laudanum on the journey. I hoped she would recover and perhaps find happiness in Oregon."

Hilda sat down in a pool of silence. Perrin could hear the shouts and noise drifting from the distant saloons along Rogue Street. She could hear Smokey Joe playing his mouth harp on the far side of the wagons' squared formation. She wished Hilda had trusted her enough to share this information earlier.

She stepped forward. "Jane can't continue taking care of Winnie and doing all the work for both of them." The group shifted to examine Jane's gaunt face and the circles of fatigue bruising her eyes. "The question is, what do we do about this situation? I need your suggestions, and your help."

Ona Norris stood on the back row. Her shiny dark hair was neatly parted down the center and swept back from her face into a tidy bun. "This is not our problem. I think we should tell Mr. Snow about it." Blushing, she dropped her gaze and sat down.

"I considered that," Perrin admitted. Looking over their heads, she noticed Cody and Webb returning from the post, walking toward the wagons. She could feel Cody's stormy eyes narrowed down on her. "But I've concluded Mr. Snow's likely solution will be to send Winnie back to Chastity." She hesitated. "If our final consensus is that we wash our hands of the affair and give the problem to Mr. Snow, then of course that's what I will do."

Sarah rose before her chair. "If the captain sends Winnie back to Chastity, that solves the problem for everyone."

"But I sense you have something else in mind. Is that correct?" Mem inquired, raising an eyebrow.

She did. The problem lay in convincing them. "If Winnie is sent home, she'll return to a situation where she has demonstrated she can get as much laudanum as she wants. From what Hilda has told us, it sounds as if Winnie's family has given up on her." She scanned each face. "Sending Winnie back to Chastity won't solve Winnie's problem, or Jane's problem. Jane will be left with no partner, she'll still have to drive the oxen with no relief, will still have no assistance with the work involved."

Mem broke the ensuing silence. "What are you suggesting?"

Perrin's cheeks heated, and she shifted uncomfortably. "I'd like to help Winnie. Her parents have abandoned her; must we abandon her too?"

Sarah's voice broke a sudden and absolute silence. "I believe I see where this is leading."

"If she doesn't stop taking laudanum, Winnie will die. Sooner or later that's what will happen. I propose that we find Winnie's laudanum and destroy the bottles. That we nurse her through the recovery process and back to health."

When it became apparent that no one would comment, Perrin continued. "Winnie has a chance for a fresh start, but only if she's well enough to take it, and only with our help." Caught up in the passion of conviction, Perrin forgot her rehearsed speech, forgot her nervousness. For twenty minutes, she spoke from the heart, appealing to the caregiver in the women before her.

Sarah pursed her lips when Perrin paused. "Mrs. Waverly, have you ever dealt with a medical addiction before?"

"No, I haven't."

"I haven't either. But I've heard that stopping opium, even milder forms like laudanum, is dangerous and can be life-threatening. And there is no guarantee that Winnie would not return to laudanum at the first opportunity."

"But if she stops taking it, and if she survives, then she has a chance to live and possibly be happy," Mem said. "She has no chance at all if Mr. Snow sends her back to Chastity."

"*Ja*, I believe this too," Hilda agreed. "If we send her back, Winnie will never get a husband."

Perrin waited, but no one else spoke. "If we fail, then I agree we must give the problem to Mr. Snow, and he'll undoubtedly send Winnie home." Slowly Perrin scanned the faces frowning back at her. "If we attempt this, one of us will have to stay with Winnie all the time. This will cause hardship for our wagon partners. It will mean missing sleep, missing our rest periods. But first we need to decide if we want to try to give Winnie a chance to rebuild her life."

Lucy Hastings stood and brushed down her skirts with a decisive gesture. Her pink cheeks shone with youthful righteousness. "I'd like to think if I needed help that you would all try to help me," she stated in a voice that shook from the embarrassment of addressing a gathering. "I believe with the Lord's assistance, we can save Miss Larson from the evil that afflicts her." Hastily, she sat down and looked at her hands.

Cora Thorp jumped to her feet. "I ain't a bride, and I don't have no say here, but if it helps any, I can tell you there ain't nothing in Chastity, Missouri. Everybody here knows that or we wouldn't be on this train. But there might be something for all of us in Oregon. If Miss Larson was thinking straight, I say she'd beg you not to send her back. I know I'd sure hate it if you sent *me* back!" She sat down, thrust out her chin, and pulled another licorice whip out of the bag in her lap.

"Jane?" They all followed Perrin's gaze. "Our decision will affect you. Do you have an opinion?"

Jane Munger closed her eyes and swayed on her chair, then she looked at the group. A tired sigh lifted her chest. "I agree with Mrs. Waverly. Don't send Winnie back." She gazed at Perrin. "If you're determined to do this, I'm willing to help."

Mem nodded briskly. "Then it appears we're agreed. We'll take away Winnie's laudanum, and we'll do what we must to nurse her back to health."

"Thank you," Perrin whispered. She cleared her throat and spoke in a louder voice. "Those who wish to be involved, please speak to your wagon partner and make sure she is willing to assume the extra burdens caused by your absence. Hilda? Perhaps you could check with everyone and make a list of those who are willing to sit with Winnie. Mem? Would you organize a schedule?" She clenched her fists and inhaled deeply. "Tomorrow morning before we get under way, Jane and I will search the wagon. We will dispose of Winnie's laudanum." She lifted an eyebrow in Jane's direction, waited for Jane's nod.

"You'll need help," Sarah said after a lengthy pause. "I'll come after I've done the milking."

"God bless you all," Lucy Hastings stated brightly. "I'll pray for our success."

Sarah stood and looked hard at Perrin. Then she nodded to herself, picked up her chair, and called to Lucy. Mem gave Perrin a thumbs-up sign before she headed back to her wagon.

After the women had dispersed, Perrin rescued a licorice whip that had fallen from Cora's bag and retrieved a forgotten sock. She stood alone gazing back at Jane's and Winnie's wagon. She had persuaded the brides to attack Winnie's problem. She hoped to heaven that she had made the right decision.

A weighty mantle descended and settled heavily across her shoulders. If they succeeded in coaxing Winnie back to health, their success would be due to the joint efforts of those who chose to participate. But if they failed, the fault would be hers alone.

Winnie's panicked screams awoke the camp and brought everyone running through the hazy darkness of predawn. They arrived to find Jane inside the wagon and Perrin on the ground struggling with a frantic Winnie.

"I can't hold her," Perrin gasped. Once the first laudanum bottle had appeared, Winnie had smiled and lifted her hand.

Instead of giving it to her, Jane had tossed the bottle to Perrin, who smashed it over the back wheel. When the second laudanum bottle shattered in a shower of glass and liquid, Winnie began to grasp what was happening. In a flash, she transformed into a screaming, spitting, fighting virago. Clawing and kicking, she tried to fight past Perrin and climb into the wagon.

"I am strong," Hilda shouted, running toward the struggling women. "I will hold her." Sarah came right behind her. Together, they pulled Winnie off Perrin and wrestled her away from the wagon. Her shrill despairing screams continued, clawing on nerves like squeaky chalk raked down a slate board.

Leaning against the tailgate and fighting to catch her breath, Perrin touched the scratches on her cheek, then inspected a smear of blood across her fingertips. "Are you all right?" Jane called, peering out of the wagon bed. She tossed two more laudanum bottles to Lucy Hastings, who told the devil to get behind her before she smashed the bottles on the wheel.

"I wouldn't have believed she could be that strong. Keep searching. I'll return in a minute." The sky had brightened enough that she spotted Cody standing behind the women, his narrowed eyes sweeping the scene. When her gaze met his, he scowled and jerked his head, then walked away from the crowd. Perrin stiffened her backbone, sucked in a deep breath, then moved through the silent spectators to follow him.

"You want to know what this is all about," she said when she caught up to him away from the wagons.

"I know what this is about," he snapped. When her eyebrows lifted, he glared down at her. "Ona Norris told me."

"Ona?" It shouldn't have surprised her, but it did. Fumbling in her sleeve, she found her handkerchief and gingerly pressed it against the row of scratches stinging her cheek.

"Miss Norris correctly believes this is a problem that should have been brought to me. And she correctly believes that Miss Larson is a danger to Jane Munger and to everyone on this train. Why the hell didn't you tell me about this?"

He loomed in the milky shadows like a statue depicting angry masculinity. The lines splitting his cheeks had deepened, his jaw had hardened, and his steely, storm-blue gaze didn't waver.

Perrin pulled back her shoulders. "You instructed me to handle whatever problems arose."

Cody threw out his hands in a gesture of exasperation, then fisted them on his hips and glared down at her. "You and I are having difficulty understanding one another. I don't want to be bothered with trivialities, but I sure as hell want to know when I've got one passenger so exhausted she's reeling, and another who's drinking tincture of opium by the bottleful!"

"Mr. Snow—"

He lifted a hand to silence her. "Winnie Larson's problem is a problem for everyone on this train. Therefore, Winnie Larson is going home. I'll arrange for her to stay at Fort Kearney until Commander Willis can put her on a train headed east."

Perrin grabbed his arm, feeling his muscles stiffen at her touch. "Please, Mr. Snow! Cody, please listen!"

"You've got one minute," he said angrily, staring at her.

And she could very well waste that minute thinking about the iron cords of muscle banded beneath her fingertips. Swallowing hard, Perrin removed her hand from his arm and scrubbed her palm against her skirts as if she could rub away the sensation of heat and power.

"If you send Winnie back to Chastity, back to her family and her father's apothecary, she'll never get well. She'll keep drinking laudanum until she dies! She'll never marry or have a family of her own. Please, I'm begging you. Give us this chance to help her! If we fail, *then* send her back. But give Winnie a chance! It's the only chance she'll ever have!"

"Damn it!" Turning away from her, he took a few steps toward the fort. She could see his jaw working, watched him rub his arm where she had gripped it.

"Most of the women agree. We want to do this. Please . . . please allow us to try!"

When he turned toward her, his lips were tight. "What makes you think Winnie Larson wants your help?"

"Right now all Winnie knows is that her heart hurts and the laudanum makes the pain go away." Suddenly Perrin was talking about herself instead of Winnie. Moving forward, she clasped his arm again, ignoring the way her stomach tightened when she touched him. "Winnie deserves a second chance! Don't condemn her out of hand, Cody. Don't do that. She tried to survive in the only way she saw open to her. And she made a mistake. With our help, maybe she can undo that mistake! Don't you see? There's a new life waiting in Oregon. Give her a chance for that life! Please, give me . . ." She wet her lips and shook her head. "Give Winnie a chance to live again!"

He stood so close that her body tensed at the heat coming off of him; she could smell the grease that weatherproofed his jacket, inhaled the scent of leather, rawhide, and man. Dismay curled her hands into fists. Even in the thick of pleading for Winnie, she couldn't set aside her awareness of Cody Snow as a man.

Not taking his eyes from the scratches on her cheek, he removed a thin cigar from his inside pocket and lit it. For a full minute he smoked in silence.

"At least one person doesn't agree with your decision. There may be others."

Perrin inspected the blood on her handkerchief, then refolded it and pressed it against her cheek. She watched the smoke from his cigar curl over his hat brim, finding it easier to look away from dangerous blue eyes that seemed to see inside her. "I'm sorry to learn that Miss Norris disagrees so strongly. But I assure you most of the brides are willing to help."

She had pleaded, had said everything she could. Now all

she could do was wait and watch Cody stare into the distance. He smoked with his back to her, grimly watching the group gathered around Winnie's wagon. Winnie's anguished screams and sobs rent the chill morning; the sound of smashing glass seemed loud and discordant in the clear air.

"All right," Cody finally agreed. "I'll let you attempt this. But I'll be watching, Perrin. If any more of my passengers become dangerously weakened by overwork, or if it looks like this wild plan isn't going to work, I'll intercede, and there won't be any further discussion. At that point, Winnie Larson goes home. Do you understand?"

Weak with relief, Perrin stared at his profile, thinking it looked chiseled in stone. Cody Snow was an astounding man. When she had followed him onto the prairie, she wouldn't have given two pennies for her chances to persuade him. It occurred to her that she couldn't name one other man who might have listened to her appeal with an open mind, or who would have adjusted his own opinion so swiftly, albeit grudgingly.

"Thank you," she whispered. "If Winnie were thinking logically, I believe she would thank you too."

He gazed at her for a long moment, letting her see the doubt narrowing his eyes. "Make no mistake. I'm not agreeing to this fool experiment for Winnie's sake." She folded her arms under her breasts and lifted her chin. "My policy is to encourage passengers to settle problems among themselves and to intercede only if they run into trouble. Plus, if you succeed, your success should take you a long way toward securing your place with the others. And that will make my life a hell of a lot easier."

"And if I fail?" she asked softly, wadding the bloody handkerchief inside her fist.

They studied each other beneath the lightening sky. "We'll talk about that when it happens."

When it happens. So he expected her to fail. Maybe the others did too.

Well, she was going to succeed. She had a lot to prove, to herself and to the other brides. And to Cody Snow.

Mem had never seen anyone suffer the way Winnie Larson suffered during the following week. It was sheer hell for everyone. To spare the others the sound of Winnie's screams and pleas, Jane's and Winnie's wagon assumed the last position in the line for the duration; the dust was choking and unremitting. But during the night, even those on the far side of the squared formation heard Winnie's shouts and threats and pleading screams.

It was as terrible to watch as it was to hear. Winnie shook uncontrollably; she was violently ill. She wet herself, and she couldn't get warm. She sobbed and spit blood as her tortured body jackknifed into convulsions. She tried to strike out at the women who sat by her side day and night, but her thin arms were so weak she could hardly raise them. She threatened, beseeched, promised the earth for a sip, just one sip of laudanum.

It was the most horrifying experience Mem had ever undergone, draining physically, mentally, and emotionally to everyone involved.

"I have come to relieve you," Hilda called softly, climbing into the wagon. A bar of moonlight fell across the wagon floor when she lifted the canvas flap. As weary as everyone was, Hilda had still taken time to pin her braids neatly across the crown of her head and dress in a tidy wool skirt and waist. "She's sleeping?" she asked Mem in relief.

"Just in the last few minutes. And Thea said she asked for something to eat earlier." This was a first, and an event worth celebrating, as they were all desperately worried about Winnie's bony wrists and thin body. They feared she lacked the strength to survive the wracking torments her body was undergoing.

"Her appetite is returning!" The news infused new energy in Hilda's large frame. She squeezed Mem's hand and tears glistened around the sudden brightness in her eyes. "Praise God! If she will eat, she will grow strong again."

Mem returned the pressure of Hilda's fingers, then climbed out of the wagon into the darkness of the wee hours. It was never silent on the trail, even at night. She heard oxen and cattle shifting within the square, heard the distant lonely howl of a wolf. These were sounds she would always associate with the journey west, along with the rattle of harness, the clang of pots and pans banging together like cymbals, and the crunch of iron tires against exposed rock.

Tilting her head, hoping to relieve the tension in her neck, she examined a sweeping dark canopy spangled by the fiery blaze of distant worlds. Imagining worlds on stars was a fanciful thought, one that would have surprised most of the people who believed they knew her. If her headache hadn't pained her so greatly, Mem might have smiled.

Instead, recognizing that her headache was too severe to permit sleep, she considered walking awhile. Sometimes walking helped. Lifting her hems, she took a few steps toward the open darkness before she remembered the night watch, stationed near the arms and molasses wagons. If the men heard someone moving beyond the perimeter, they might mistakenly shoot her. Still, being shot at was almost preferable to crawling into her tent and lying there sleepless, listening to Bootie make little smacking sounds.

After a moment of indecision, Mem sighed, then turned her steps toward the embers glowing in the pit of Smokey Joe's cook fire. It was a less appealing but safer choice. The light from the coals was so low that she didn't realize someone else was sitting beside the cook pit until she had walked up to the pot hanger and extended her palms over the heat. "Oh!"

"Good evening, Miss Grant. Sorry if I startled you." An exotic blend of accents told her who spoke.

"It's so late that I wasn't expecting to find anyone awake except the watch. May I join you?"

"Please do."

Gathering her skirts around her hips, she sank to the same log on which Webb Coate sat. He edged to one side to make room, then watched as she crossed her ankles and stretched her feet so the warmth of the embers reached the soles of her boots.

"The days are warmer, but the nights are still cold," she said, drawing her shawl to her throat. "Why aren't you sleeping?"

"Either Cody or myself has joined the watch since this business with Miss Larson began." An orange flicker revealed his smile. "Most of you aren't aware of it, but you have an escort to and from Miss Larson's wagon."

In this light she noticed his Indian heritage more starkly than in the brightness of day. Shadows emphasized his strong nose and clean hard jaw. The glow from the embers smoothed a forehead Mem surprised herself by wanting to touch.

"The ordeal with Winnie has been hard on everyone. But Sarah Jennings believes we've passed the crisis point. Sarah predicts that Winnie's pain will lessen with every passing day." Mem prayed it was true. Closing her eyes, she touched her fingertips to her forehead and the headache behind it. "Regardless of the outcome, Mr. Coate, I'm truly glad we did this."

"Are you in pain, Miss Grant?"

She felt his black eyes studying her and surprised herself again by enjoying his attention. Suddenly she wanted to lean against him and sleep with her head on his shoulder. The odd yearning gave her a tiny shock and made her blink. This was certainly a night for frivolous speculation.

"It's only a headache," she said with a dismissive wave. "I have them frequently. It's nothing important."

Webb removed a knife from the sheath at his waist and leaned forward, idly whittling slivers from a stick of wood. "My mother's people believe no ache or pain is unimportant. They believe that aches and pains are the voice of the body."

"Really?" Fascinated, Mem strained to see his face in the dim glow. "What is the body saying when it aches?"

He turned dark sober eyes toward her. "It's saying: Make this ache go away."

She stared, then burst into a shout of delighted laughter. Quickly, she clapped a hand over her mouth and hastily looked around, hoping she hadn't awakened anyone.

"Forgive me, Mr. Coate. I don't usually ask stupid questions."

Seeing that she hadn't taken offense, he grinned, his teeth a flash of white in the darkness of face, hair, and night. "Something causes your headaches, Miss Grant. The pain in your head is a request for correction. Your body is telling you that something is amiss."

They sat side by side in front of the fire pit, their faces flickering in the ruddy glow of shifting embers. Mem watched the shavings of pale wood curl away from the stick in his large hand and she imagined Augusta Boyd's outrage had Augusta chanced to see them sitting so close, discussing pains and bodies.

"Unfortunately, I can't correct the cause," she remarked after a minute. Letting her head fall back, she gazed up at the stars.

"Are you certain?"

"Very certain. I can't tell my silly shallow sister whom I love that I wish she had stayed behind in Chastity. I can't tell her that her helplessness and her constant prattle makes me feel like screaming. I can't tell the other brides to stop treating Mrs. Waverly as if she had a disease they could all catch. I can't make them forgive or accept. I can't make Winnie Larson stop craving laudanum, and I can't make Augusta Boyd be less rude or more charitable." She lowered her head and looked into his black eyes. "I can't change an unfair world, Mr. Coate. I can't make every eye see humanity instead of color or a different culture. I can't give women a voice in a man's world. And there's more. I will never do all the things I long to do. I'll never see a storm on the Amazon or sail up the Thames. I'll never stand on an African savanna and watch an elephant raise his trunk against a sunset sky. I will never soar toward heaven in a hot-air balloon, or weep at the beauty of the Louvre."

Webb Coate studied her intently, his hands motionless around the knife and his whittling stick.

"So you see, Mr. Coate," she added softly, mesmerized by his bottomless black eyes, "I cannot treat the cause of my headaches. I can only accept them." Standing, she pushed down her skirts and touched a hand to the auburn tendrils falling from the thick coil wound on her neck. "Good night, sir."

"Sleep well, Miss Grant." As she moved into the darkness, she felt his gaze on the back of her shawl.

There wasn't much left of the night, and Mem doubted it was worth trying to sleep, as Smokey Joe would be banging his gong in an hour or so. As she passed Winnie's wagon, she hard a moan that rose to a heart-wrenching sob, followed by a scream. Pausing, Mem listened for Hilda's soothing murmurs before she moved toward the tent she shared with Bootie.

All of the brides were exhausted and showing the stress of the last terrible week, even Augusta Boyd, who was doing nothing to help with Winnie. Mem made a face and shook her head. Since the incident at Fort Kearney, Her Majesty had not addressed a single word to Mem. That didn't bother her; in fact, she considered Augusta's snub amusing.

But it angered her greatly that Augusta chose to extend her imagined punishment by not speaking to Bootie either. Despite Mem's dislike of Augusta, the woman's supposed friendship was important to Bootie, and Bootie was puzzled and hurt by this recent swerve toward coldness and silence.

A rush of protectiveness and anger tightened Mem's throat and she clenched her fists. For two spits and a spade, she would march over to Augusta's tent, shake the high and mighty creature awake, and give her a scathing piece of her mind.

She had actually turned around before she caught herself. What on earth was she thinking? Appalled, Mem placed one hand on the nearest tent pole and pressed the other to her forehead.

The fatigue and the stress of the last week with Winnie were making all of them as combative as snapping turtles.

CHAPTER
* 7 *

My Journal, May, 1853. Approximately three hundred miles along the trail. We have settled into numbing fatigue and a tedious daily sameness. Tempers flare. We are beginning to know each other.

Sarah Jennings

"I think I see it! Just the top!" Ona Norris exclaimed. "Look. There on the horizon on the south side of the river."

Augusta pushed back the lip of a fashionable straw sunbonnet and peered hard. "I don't see a thing."

"We won't be able to see Courthouse Rock until at least tomorrow evening," Cora insisted, setting two buckets of water beside the back wheel, then stretching her back against her hands. "Mr. Coate said so."

"Him!" Augusta waved a dismissive hand. But the mention of Webb Coate caused her to instinctively scan the site, searching for his tall graceful form even though she knew he and Miles Dawson were away from camp hunting pronghorns. She had watched them ride out minutes after the fog lifted.

Why she wasted so much time watching for Webb Coate and constantly thinking about him mystified her. She supposed her secret fascination had developed because this was the first time she had been exposed to one of his kind at close quarters.

And she had to admit, grudgingly, that Webb Coate wasn't what she had expected. He didn't seem lazy or thieving, and she had yet to catch him reeling about in a drunken state. Nevertheless, she held it uppermost that Coate was a heathen, barely civilized, and like all Indians, not to be trusted. Heaven help her if ever she relaxed her guard. There was no telling what he might do. Something stirred in his eyes when he looked at her, something speculative, dangerous . . . and thrilling.

"Are you cold, Augusta?" Ona inquired. "You shivered."

"Merely a passing chill." She glanced at the afternoon sky. "But now that the sun has reappeared, it should warm up some."

Since entering the Platte Valley, the weather had become troublesome. By midday the air was usually warm, but every afternoon, the temperature plummeted and thunder rumbled down the valley signaling the onset of a chilly afternoon rain.

Yesterday's storm had turned into a steady slashing downpour that continued until morning. Augusta had spent a miserable night trying to sleep beneath a haze of fine drizzle that filtered through the canvas tent roof.

This morning they had awakened, tired and out of sorts, to discover a heavy milky fog clinging to grass and ground, making travel impossible. The women had used the free day to turn out the wagons, bake, catch up on chores that never seemed to end.

Bending over the fire pit, Augusta filled a china pot that had belonged to her mother, waited for the tea to steep, then poured for herself and Ona, trying to bring grace to a ritual never intended to be performed on a barren prairie. As her mother, may she rest in peace, had never surrounded herself with shoddy items, the tea set must have cost a pretty penny. Augusta wondered what the set might fetch today, assuming she could find someone along the trail willing to buy it, and assuming she could bring herself to part with a treasured heirloom.

She also wondered if she had been a tad hasty to invite Ona Norris to address her familiarly. On reflection, she realized that she knew very little about Ona's background.

"I know you came to Chastity from back east . . ." she said pleasantly, hoping to draw out more details. Idly she snapped her fingers at Cora as a reminder to pull another of the folding camp chairs out of the wagon. Couldn't the slow-wit see that they had a guest? One who was standing rather awkwardly, holding her cup and saucer in front of her waist?

"I lived in Washington, D.C., until ten months ago," Ona said evenly. "After my cousin died, I traveled west to Chastity, to live with my mother's brother and his wife."

"I see," Augusta murmured politely, only slightly more enlightened than before her inquiry. No matter. She would learn Ona's story. There was so little to occupy one's interest on this journey that everyone shared their history merely for something to talk about. Undoubtedly Ona's narrative would be short and largely uninteresting. It could hardly be otherwise, as few were blessed with as fascinating a background as a Boyd.

"Well, finally!" Cora dropped the extra chair beside Ona, then walked past the fire and smiled grimly toward the first wagon on their side of the square.

"How many times must I tell you not to interrupt?" Augusta warned sharply. This was one of those days when dealing with Cora unraveled her. The continual whining, complaining, and rude remarks were enough to erode the patience of a saint. "Can't you see that my guest and I are—"

She gasped and stood so abruptly that her cup and saucer clattered from her lap to the muddy ground. No, her eyes did not deceive her. Perrin Waverly was walking directly toward them. Reluctance tagged her steps, but determination firmed her jawline. There was no mistaking the creature's destination.

Augusta whirled to stare hard at Cora's smug expression. "You know something about this, don't you? Why is *she* coming here?"

Cora's dark eyes glittered and her mouth set in a line. "It don't do no good to ask you for my back pay, so I did like Captain Snow said we should. I took my problem to our representative and asked Mrs. Waverly to help me get my money!"

Horror blanched the color from Augusta's face so swiftly that she felt dizzy. Throwing out a hand, she steadied herself against the back of the camp chair. "You told that . . . crea-ture! . . . that I owed you money?" Though it sounded to her as if she screamed the words, her shaking voice emerged in a whisper.

"Maybe now you'll pay me the four dollars you owe me!" Folding her arms across her chest, Cora thrust out her chin, turned her back to Augusta, and waited for Perrin to arrive.

The horror and betrayal staggered Augusta. As if looking through a distorted glass, she noticed that Ona's eyes had narrowed with curiosity. And sudden scalding hatred blurred her vision of Cora. All she saw was a ferretlike sharpness of black hair, black eyes, and black satisfaction. Her fingers twitched with the need to slap the smile off of Cora's face. Every ragged nerve ending screamed at her, ordering her to beat the treacherous snip until she begged forgiveness.

"How *dare* you do this to me!" Gripping the back of the chair with both shaking hands, she prayed that she would re-main upright. Rage and hatred leeched the strength from her muscles.

Perrin approached the fire, then stopped and wet her lips. She nodded with stern politeness to Ona and Cora. "If you would excuse me, please, I'd like a private word with Miss Boyd."

Cora backed away, disappointed that she would not be privy to any unpleasantness on her behalf. Wordlessly, Ona pulled her skirts to one side and walked from the wagon to a position where hearing would be difficult but watching re-mained possible.

Perrin waited, then clasped her hands at her waist. She spoke in a low voice. "Please believe me when I tell you I'd give anything if this wasn't necessary. But I have no choice. Cora came to me in my capacity as representative and . . ."

Augusta didn't hear the rest. Humiliation blinded her, closed her ears. Of all the people in the world who might take it upon themselves to chastise or admonish her, fate had dished up Perrin Waverly. It was beyond endurance. Hideously intolerable. Every terrible thing that had conspired to bring about her ruin could be laid directly at Perrin Waverly's feet.

"Cora understands that she is paying for her journey west through her labor. But she claims that you owe her for—"

"You man-killing whore! If it wasn't for you, my father would still be alive!" The accusation exploded through clenched teeth, like poison lanced from a boil. She had held the hatred inside for so long that the relief of finally saying the words opened a torrent. "You seduced him, then you bled him of every penny he possessed, and now you dare—you *dare*—to come here and demand money from me?" The audacity of it swept her breath away. The magnitude of this outrage made her shake all over with violent emotions impossible to contain a moment longer.

Perrin closed her eyes as if she'd been struck, and oh, how Augusta longed to strike her. She trembled with the need. She wanted to hit and bite and scratch and rend and tear. She wanted to howl at the sky and demand justice from heaven itself.

Perrin spoke in a voice trembling with quiet dignity. "I never asked Joseph for anything. What he gave, he gave freely."

"Liar!" Augusta gripped the top of the chair so fiercely that her fingers turned white. Her eyes burned and her heart slammed in her chest. "My father paid the rent on your house. He paid for the food in your harlot's mouth. He paid your dressmaker and the chemist and he paid your bill at Brady's Mercantile! He rented a gig for your use, and he paid your stables bill. He paid and paid until finally he faced ruin or suicide! That is what *you* did to him. You killed him!"

"No!"

Perrin's face paled and she looked sick. But that was not what Augusta saw. Her fevered state painted a superior sneer on Perrin's lips; she saw a harlot's greed and a harlot's indifference. She saw the whore who had destroyed her father.

"I was as shocked as everyone when Joseph died. Augusta, I promise you it wasn't because of me." Stepping closer, Perrin reached a hand in appeal. "Please. We both cared for him, and he cared for both of us. Can't we—"

"You think my father cared for you? You? You make me laugh! A Boyd would *never* lower himself to give a spit for a low-born harlot! He used you, that's all. Used you as other men undoubtedly have and will in the future!"

Baring her teeth, she slapped Perrin's hand away, putting the full force of her hatred into the blow. And there was so much hatred, so much fear and frustration and helplessness bubbling and boiling inside her like poison.

Of course she had known her father was keeping Perrin. How could she not when everyone in Chastity whispered about the scandal? And oh, the pain of being cast into second place, of discovering that she was not enough for her adored father, that he needed someone besides her, someone he went to in the evenings, leaving her alone to wonder how she had failed him.

And in the end, Perrin hadn't suffered one iota. It hadn't been Perrin Waverly who set aside her grief to frantically deal with hushing up Joseph Boyd's embezzlement. Perrin Waverly hadn't been forced to sell the home where she had grown up, and dispose of treasured belongings to settle debts. Perrin Waverly hadn't fallen from the pinnacle of privilege to the cellar of despair.

Burning rage, and resentment, and a scalding sense of betrayal bit deep into Augusta's mind. The hardship of a journey she loathed and hadn't wanted to undergo. The empty hours, the tedious monotony, the lack of privacy and sleeping on the ground and eating gritty bland food. And at the end of this damnable miserable trek waited a husband whom she didn't know and didn't want. And always—always!—the bone-deep worry, the crippling fear about money.

Perrin snatched back her slapped hand and cradled it against her waist. Shock flamed on her throat and cheeks and she trembled from lips to toes. "Your father was a good man.

Augusta, please. It would pain him deeply to see us at each other's throats."

Only vaguely did Augusta perceive that a crowd had gathered behind Ona and Cora. Only dimly did she realize that her voice had risen to an ugly scream.

"How dare you!" The words, too mild, too inadequate, stuttered from her lips, accompanied by furious droplets of spittle. "How *dare* you suggest that you know what would have pained my father! I was his confidante, not you!"

Fury boiled up before her, red and scorching hot. The stress of her dwindling purse, the strain of the journey, and her hatred for Perrin Waverly exploded inside her like a burst heart. Frothing at the top of the eruption was the humiliation of her father's destitution and his suicide, his betrayal of a daughter who had worshiped the ground he trod. And all of it—all of the darkness in her spirit and the blot on the Boyd name—all of it was this whore's fault.

Her teeth clenched and her fingers curled around the top rung of the folding chair. Blinded by everything Perrin Waverly represented, needing to strike out or blow apart in bloody pieces, she gripped the chair and threw it as hard as she could.

The chair struck Perrin squarely in the torso and knocked her to the ground. In an instant, Augusta flew across the few paces separating them and fell on her, slapping her face, yanking her hair, kicking and scratching and trying to destroy the monster who had seduced her father and ruined his life and hers.

On some level she realized Perrin fought back, but she didn't feel her own hair tearing loose from the scalp, didn't feel the scratches digging down her arms. She had no awareness of the crack in her lip. Lost in the throes of momentary madness, her only reality was the bloodlust roaring inside her head.

Someone had to pay for the terrible things that had happened to Augusta Boyd. Someone had to stand responsible for her devastation; there had to be someone to blame. That someone was Perrin Waverly.

In this moment of madness and fury, she truly believed if Perrin were destroyed, all her problems would vanish. With Perrin gone, her father would stride into camp and rescue his beloved daughter from these commonplace women and the numerous unbearable hardships. Her father would explain that it had all been a mistake. He was alive, and they still owned their large mansion on the riverbank, they still were the wealthy and esteemed Boyds. He would beg her forgiveness and declare his love, he would spend the rest of their lives atoning for the shame and heartache she had suffered in his name.

A rough hand grabbed the collar of her shirtwaist and dragged her up off of Perrin. Iron fingers clamped her arms against her sides and held her tightly against a male body. Still screaming and spitting, fighting to free herself, she watched Cody Snow pick Perrin up by the shoulders and jerk her back against his chest. Panting heavily, Perrin strained against him, kicking and flailing her elbows.

"Let me *go*!" Augusta screamed. When she twisted to see who dared put his hands on a Boyd, she looked into the brilliant black gaze of Webb Coate. Her body went rigid, and revulsion twisted her lips as she felt the heat of him burning along the length of her body, felt his hips molding her buttocks.

"Release me, you savage!"

Perrin shouted, "She started this! She—"

"Shut up, both of you!" Cody roared, his face as dark as Webb's. He gave Perrin a hard shake. "What in the name of God is going on here?"

"She attacked me!" Perrin cried, twisting to look up at him.

"She was my father's whore! It's her fault that—"

"One at a time!"

But they couldn't. Screaming, they shouted accusations and explanations, red-faced and struggling to free themselves until Cody gave Perrin another bone-rattling shake and Webb followed suit. Augusta felt her brains knock against the inside of her skull, felt her bones grind together.

"Quiet! Both of you!" Cody scanned the crowd of appalled onlookers. He glared at Sarah Jennings, who looked utterly thunderstruck. "Did you see what happened here?"

Sarah's head swiveled back and forth between Augusta and Perrin, scanning their muddy hair and clothing, the bloodied lips and scratches. A steady stream of bacon grease flowed into the ground from the pan forgotten in her hand.

Cody barked the same question at Hilda, shaking Perrin into silence when she tried to speak. "You?"

Hilda shook her head. "*Nein.*"

"The whore came to my wagon and she—" But Webb's hand covered her mouth, and Augusta's words were smothered. Frustration choked her.

Ona Norris stepped forward. "Mrs. Waverly provoked Miss Boyd," she stated firmly.

"That isn't what I saw," Jane Munger disagreed. Frowning, she too stepped forward. "Miss Boyd slapped Mrs. Waverly's hand, then threw a chair at her."

Everyone present peered at the broken chair, then examined Augusta's flying muddy hair and torn bodice. Silently, they inspected Perrin's ripped skirt and the new scratches bleeding on her mud-caked cheek. Every face reflected a horrified mixture of shock and disbelief.

Cody exchanged a long glance with Webb. "All right. Each of you return to your wagons." The brides studied his scowl, then hastily dispersed, whispering among themselves. "You too," he growled at Perrin and Augusta. "I'll talk to each of you later."

Gingerly, he released Perrin's shoulders, his body tensed to catch her if she flew at Augusta. But she whirled and ran pell-mell toward her wagon, tripping over her torn hem, breaking into sobs of anger and embarrassment.

The iron fingers opened and Augusta felt Webb step away from her. A button on his fringed jacket caught in her loosened hair and she cried out at the tug against her tender scalp, then she jerked free of him. Knowing they stared at her, she flung an arm over her face and ran toward the back of the wagon, desperate to escape Webb Coate's silent judgment.

Once inside the canvas covering, she stuffed a fist in her mouth until she heard Cody and Webb murmur something to each other, then walk away. Only then did she surrender to the hot tears that flooded her cheeks.

Strangled by humiliation, she fought to make sense of what had happened. The events of the past twenty minutes utterly horrified, mortified, and appalled her. She, Augusta Josepha Boyd, had physically attacked someone. She had rolled in the mud like a fighting sow, like a dockyard harpy. She had done this in full view of Cora Thorp, Ona Norris, Bootie, and the other brides who had come running at the sound of screaming. She had done this in front of the wagonmaster and his Indian.

Shock blinded her. Bitter tears of shame cast her to her knees. She had disgraced a dozen generations of Boyds. And she would rather have died a hundred deaths than face anyone on the train ever again.

Cody waited until the camp settled down for the night, and the women, who had been scurrying from cook fire to cook fire, crawled into their tents. He checked on the animals, shared a smoke with Heck Kelsey and John Voss on the night watch, then he walked along the perimeters of the squared wagons until he reached Perrin's tent. He scratched lightly at the flap.

"Are you asleep?"

"No."

A quiet rustling sounded inside, then she crawled out. He extended a hand and helped her to her feet, noticing that she had changed out of the torn clothing he had last seen her wearing and had done what she could to comb the mud out of her hair. She wore a plain wool gown, buttoned to the throat. A mud-dull, dark braid fell across her shoulder and curved over her breast.

"It'll still be warm by Smokey Joe's fire," Cody said, noticing that her fingers trembled around the edges of her shawl.

She nodded silently and preceded him, seating herself on a buffalo robe thrown over the log beside the fire. She refused to look at him, fixing her gaze on the low flames in the cook pit. Absurdly, she reminded Cody of a painted squaw. One cheek was striped by the healing scratches Winnie Larson had carved. The other cheek had been freshly marked by Augusta Boyd.

Lowering himself to the end of the log, he tried to decide where and how to begin. That he had to think about it surprised him. Ordinarily, he spoke bluntly, without concern as to how his words might be received. But this small woman possessed a puzzling facility for turning his thoughts inside out.

Initially, he had believed that Perrin Waverly was weak, withdrawn, and raw with vulnerability. In retrospect, he saw that she had been unsure of herself and her reception among the others, and with good cause. But she was not weak. After witnessing her tireless efforts with Winnie Larson, after observing how seriously she assumed her position as the women's representative and how she stood up to him, Cody had concluded her backbone was made of iron.

Throughout the last weeks he had overheard bits and pieces of gossipy talk among the brides; still, it had jolted him to hear it confirmed that Perrin had been Joseph Boyd's mistress. What had happened to that iron backbone when Boyd came knocking at her door? Why hadn't she refused him? What on earth had possessed her to throw away her body and her reputation?

As if sensing his speculation, she leaned forward and wrapped her arms around her knees, gazing into the low flames. "You and I have met before, but I don't think you remember."

Cody blinked at her profile and silently swore. She never did what he expected, seldom said what he anticipated. Until this minute, he would have wagered his saddle that she would immediately inundate him with explanations regarding the fight with Augusta Boyd.

"You're mistaken. I'd remember if you and I had met." Drab clothing and faded hats couldn't disguise a beauty as rare as hers. He wouldn't have forgotten her regardless of the circumstances. Her lush compact figure and those lustrous cinnamon eyes would remain in a man's memory long after she had gone.

"It was a brief meeting. We weren't introduced."

"I think you're mistaking me for someone else."

"About three years ago, my husband took me with him on a business trip to St. Louis. Garin and his brother owned a warehouse in Chastity. Down by the river." She fell silent, looking into the flames as if the past flickered in the dying glow. "Garin was a possessive and jealous man. He used to . . ." She shook her head, unconsciously raising both hands as if to ward off a blow. "We were crossing the street. This was our second day in St. Louis. A man bumped into me and I started to fall, but he caught me by the arms. Garin . . ." Closing her eyes, she pressed her fingertips to her bottom lip. "Garin went mad. I guess he thought . . . I don't know. Anyway, he fought with the man. Right there in the middle of the street."

As Cody listened, his memory stirred, bringing forth an event long forgotten. The scene she described formed in his mind and he recalled horses rearing in clouds of dust, drivers and riders struggling not to run down the two brawling men. Now he remembered a woman, dressed in a neat dark cape and gown, frantic and oblivious to the wild-eyed horses and cursing drivers. The sides of her bonnet had concealed her face.

Raising her eyes, Perrin looked into the darkness beyond Smokey Joe's fire, trying to see the prairie wolf who howled near the river. "I didn't see it happen. But the man had a gun; he shot Garin in the stomach. The man kept firing, he must have been crazed, and one of the shots wounded a man on a horse behind me."

She turned her scratched face and gazed into Cody's eyes. "Then you came running out of the smithy. And you shot the man who killed my husband."

Cody remembered. "I found out later that his name was James Amberly. He was a horse trader known for a hair-trigger temper. He'd been in scrapes before."

"I never learned his name. Or yours. I didn't know who you were until you interviewed me for this journey."

The orange shadows cast by the flames made her dark eyes seem too large for her small features and delicate bone structure. To his amazement, he felt an absurd urge to stroke the blue vein that throbbed on the pale skin at her temple.

She turned back toward the fire pit. "Garin's brother sold the warehouse and took his family back east. My portion of the money was enough to care for myself for two years. Then . . ." She lapsed into a long silence. "I had no family to turn to, there was no work to be had. To keep myself alive I would have married any man who asked, but none did. I was desperate. Lucy Hastings's father, the Reverend Mr. Hastings, did what he could to help me. I would have starved if his parishioners hadn't collected food on my behalf. But there were other expenses. A place to live, soap, clothing, shoes. . . ." She touched her forehead.

Bending forward, Cody stirred the coals into a small burst of flame. "Enter the sainted Mr. Joseph Boyd," he said bluntly.

Her head whipped around and she glared at him. "Joseph Boyd was not a saint, but he was kind and generous. He saved my life, Mr. Snow. When I met Joseph, I was at my lowest ebb. I saw no way to survive another winter, and I was considering taking my own life. Of all the people in Chastity, Joseph Boyd was the only one who recognized my desperation and offered meaningful assistance!"

"By making you his mistress?" He didn't know why he felt so angry or why he was prodding her like this. He could not have explained why her story pained him, not if the success of the journey had depended on him doing so. But something about her defense of the man who had ruined her infuriated him.

"No." She came to her feet in an angry swirl of wool and fringe. "Joseph asked nothing but companionship in payment for his kindness. It was me who persuaded him to climb into my bed. Joseph was as lonely as I was, missing his wife as I missed my husband, but with better cause. Yet he never asked me to compromise myself. That was my idea and he resisted it. Make no mistake. Ruining myself was solely my decision. And I threw myself away for the best of reasons. Gratitude and affection."

He stared up at her, astonished by her honesty. And her naïveté. "You only think it was your idea. He manipulated you."

Sudden tears sparkled in her brown eyes. "He said he loved me, and I tried to love him, but . . ." Her hand slashed across her body in a gesture of frustration. "Regardless, I would have married him except neither of us believed Augusta would accept another woman in her home. Then something happened, I don't know what, and Joseph changed. At the end he was anxious, depressed . . . even so it was a terrible shock when I learned that he . . ."

Slowly, Cody stood. "So Augusta hates you because you were her father's mistress."

She cringed from him, pressing both hands to her injured cheeks. She looked sick. "Fighting with Augusta, rolling in the mud . . . it's the most humiliating, most shameful thing that has ever happened to me or that I could possibly imagine."

Her whisper was as husky as her speaking voice. Suddenly Cody pictured her with her rich dark hair spread across a white pillow. A wave of fury rocked him that it had been Boyd who heard her whisper his name in that midnight whisper.

He stood so close that her skirt brushed his legs, and he could smell the cornstarch she had combed through her hair to draw out the mud, sensed the softness of her. His groin tightened and the urge to pull her into his arms nearly overwhelmed him.

He didn't want this. His fists tightened at his sides and he reminded himself that he was finished with women. "I can't have my passengers brawling."

Her body jerked and she squeezed her eyes shut. Thick lashes fringed her cheeks like silky crescents, dark against the paleness of her distress. "I know."

"I don't know how you settle this with Augusta, but either the two of you reach an accommodation or I'll put you both off this train. I've told Augusta the same thing. I won't tolerate fighting among my passengers."

Sudden fear leaped in her eyes. She had no family or she would have appealed to them after the death of her husband. She had no place to go or she wouldn't be here. Her only future waited in Oregon with a man who might be less kind than Joseph Boyd and more abusive than Garin Waverly.

"I'll find a way to appease her," she whispered, stepping back from him. She covered her mouth with a hand and spoke against trembling fingers. "Somehow. I'll try."

"Mem Grant and Hilda Clum approached me on your behalf," he said, annoyed with himself that he was telling her this after he had decided that he wouldn't. "Winnie Larson is recovering, and they credit you for Winnie's returning health. I won't tell you that their support is enthusiastic, but you've made progress."

"Progress? Toward what? Acceptance? These women will never accept me. I represent everything they fear and abhor." She looked away from him. "I haven't had a woman friend in years, Mr. Snow. I no longer even hope for friends."

There was no response he could make.

A rush of color flooded upward from her throat, and sudden tears gathered in her large dark eyes. "But . . . speaking on my behalf was generous of Mem and Hilda. I'm grateful." She bowed her head for a moment, then she surprised him yet again. "I hope someone also spoke for Augusta."

Cody decided he was never going to understand women.

He stared at her, then slowly nodded. "Ona Norris and Bootie Glover."

"Good." She turned into the darkness. "If that's all, then . . . good night." She stumbled over an exposed rock, paused, and stared back at him. "Do you have secrets, Cody Snow? Or are you the only person on this train who doesn't?"

As it didn't seem that she expected a reply, and he wouldn't have answered anyway, he remained silent. He heard her gather her skirts, then stumble through the dark night toward her tent.

Swearing softly, he returned to the log in front of the fire. The flames had died to a bed of glowing orange and black. Patting his pockets, he searched for a smoke, discovering a small bulge in his vest that hadn't been there earlier. Frowning, he fished in the pocket with two fingers and withdrew a yellowish chunk about the size of his belt buckle.

Bending forward, he stirred the coals into a burst of flame, then held the chunk to the light and turned it between his fingers. He couldn't decide what the hell it was. It might have been a piece of hardened sponge, but that seemed so unlikely that he discarded the possibility. It didn't smell like soap. Crumbs rubbed off on his fingertips as he handled the peculiar object, and he touched one to the tip of his tongue.

Cake. It was a hardened piece of bread or cake. And he knew it had not been in his pocket this morning.

"I'll be damned." He couldn't have been more amazed if he'd discovered a gold nugget.

Standing, he peered through the blackness at Perrin's retreating figure, able to discern only a swaying silhouette. Why in the name of reason had she placed a chunk of ancient cake in his pocket? And when had she done it?

Shaking his head, puzzled, he remembered to bank the coals in Smokey Joe's pit before he strode toward the arms and molasses wagons and the sane company of men. A few steps before he reached Heck and John, he tossed the piece of hardened cake in the direction of the prairie wolf still baying at the moon.

CHAPTER
* 8 *

My Journal, May, 1852. Rain, all day yesterday and last night. Our camp flooded, so we went to bed hungry and had to sleep sitting up in the wagons. We've been seeing tornadoes on the plains for the last three days and everyone worries that one will devastate our camp, but so far it hasn't happened.

One of our oxen drank some alkali water, sickened and died. Lost a day of travel so Mr. Kelsey could repair the cracked axle under Sarah and Lucy's wagon. Only made five miles yesterday because the men's cook wagon and one of the heavy molasses wagons got stuck in the mud in one of the gullies we had to cross.

He hasn't said anything about the cake or the ribbon. I thought surely he would say something.

I started thinking that maybe he isn't sure if I remember. If that were true, it would explain why he hasn't spoken openly to me even though he can't hide the love in his eyes. I started wondering if perhaps we are in the midst of a terrible misunderstanding. That maybe he believes I've forgotten everything and truly intend to marry the Oregon man whose letter I picked. So I put the piece of cake in his vest and pinned the yellow ribbon to his saddle blanket to tell him that I've forgotten nothing. But he didn't acknowledge my messages. I thought he would be touched that I've kept these items for so many years, that he would see them as proof of my love and devotion.

I know his duties keep him occupied, and that harlot, Perrin Waverly, won't allow him to speak to us. Everything must go through her. I know he didn't mean that I have to send messages through Perrin, but I don't know how to tell her that the rule does not apply to me without revealing everything. She becomes more puffed up with herself every day.

Augusta says that she throws herself at every man in her path. This is true.

My love and Cody's is like a secret current, strong and pure. I know he is immune to the harlot's charms. But still, it worries me on occasion. If she continues to flaunt herself at him, well . . . Cody is my man.

CHAPTER
* 9 *

"You have the saddest eyes I've ever seen."

Perrin blinked at Winnie in surprise. To the best of her knowledge, this was the first time Winnie had uttered a personal comment to anyone.

"Your eyes are sad too," she said gently, pressing Winnie's hand. "And tired." But now, finally, Winnie's gaze was clear and lucid. The blank, unfocused look had been replaced by quiet sorrow as memory adjusted to returning reality.

"Feeling better?" Perrin inquired, smoothing a drift of dust-dark hair back from Winnie's pale forehead. A year ago Perrin had passed Winnie on the streets of Chastity and she recalled admiring Winnie Larson's tiny waist and delicate features, remembered how pretty Winnie had been. Even then the young woman had been floating inside a laudanum cloud.

"The cramps aren't as bad. Every day is a little easier." Pushing up on an elbow, Winnie peered through the gap between the wagon board and the canvas top. The effort to rise exhausted her and she let her head drop back to the pillow and closed her eyes. "It's blowing too hard to see any trees."

"The emigrants who came before us chopped down most of the trees for firewood. It's hard to find wood for cooking."

The wagon swerved like a boat sliding down a swell and they both braced as iron wheels lurched out of the deep trail ruts and rolled toward a patch of rank grass that would feed the oxen and cattle during the midday rest period.

Winnie gazed up at the canvas, watching it flutter beneath the force of the wind. Dust and sand found the gaps and cracks and settled on her blanket and pillow. Her lips were outlined by a faint muddy tracing. "I know we're going to Oregon. Hilda told me." A moist shine glistened in her eyes. "Billy Morris isn't waiting for me there."

Lowering her head, Perrin stroked the veins evident on the back of the slender hand she cradled in hers. Winnie's wrist was so small, still so dangerously thin. "I'm sorry."

"It's strange . . ." Winnie continued to gaze at the canvas flapping over their heads. A solitary tear hung on her lashes then spilled down her cheek. "I can't remember Billy's face anymore. Or the sound of his voice. I thought I'd never forget the way he held his cigar." Now she lowered her gaze to Perrin. "I've lost three years of my life grieving for a man who wronged me and whose face I can't remember." Her weak laugh was harsh and ended in a fit of coughing. "Can you guess what I do remember?"

In a flash of understanding, Perrin abruptly realized that Winnie's tears were not tears of grief, but tears of anger. Slowly she felt her anxiety subside, and a weight lifted off her shoulders. Winnie was going to make it.

"I remember that he made disgusting noises when he ate. And sometimes flecks of spit bubbled at the corners of his lips while he talked. Once he told me that wives were like children, meant to be seen but not heard. That's what I keep thinking about." She clenched her teeth and her eyes narrowed. "I should have rejoiced when he eloped with Emmy Greene. I should have danced in the streets and celebrated my escape. Instead I turned to opiates . . . How could I have been so stupid?"

"Oh, Winnie," Perrin said softly. She pressed a handkerchief into Winnie's hand and waited while she blew her nose. "The important thing is that you're seeing clearly now."

"I know Lucy will be here soon. But before you go, there's something I want to say." Her fingers tightened around Perrin's hand and her eyes darkened earnestly. "Mem and Hilda told me it was you who saved me from being sent back to Chastity. Thank you from the bottom of my heart for saving my life. I would die if I returned to Chastity, where everything reminds me of Billy. If ever I can do anything to repay you, you have only to ask."

"Winnie . . . do you know that I . . ." Perrin began in a low voice. "I mean, there's gossip that . . ." she couldn't make herself say the words.

A flush of pink stained Winnie's pale throat and cheeks. "I know you're kind. I know you fought to give me a second chance when the others would have washed their hands of me." Her fingers tightened around Perrin's hand and her eyes steadied. "Billy and I . . . we . . ." Her whisper broke on a note of shame. "You and I are not so different."

"Dear Winnie," Perrin whispered, angry tears sparkling in her own eyes. Billy Morris was another man who had taken and used, damn him. She had yet to meet one who didn't. "Billy is behind you and best forgotten. You have a wonderful future waiting in Oregon."

Was that true? Instead of Billy Morris, Winnie would spend the rest of her life with a man whom she hadn't yet met. Maybe he wouldn't make disgusting sounds when he ate, but maybe he'd be quick with his fists. Maybe his tongue would be as sharp as a blade, wielded to carve little pieces out of Winnie's life.

Perrin sighed and struggled to think optimistically. Perhaps Winnie would be lucky enough to marry the one good man in the Oregon Territory. She looked into the girl's tired face and hoped so. For herself . . . well, her expectations were low.

"How can I repay you for all you've done?"

Perrin patted her hand. "The best way to repay all of us is to recover your strength and get well."

"I will," Winnie stated fervently. Her damp bright eyes underscored the promise. "There's a new life waiting for me in Oregon. I don't ever want to return to Chastity."

Lucy Hastings arrived then, bringing fresh bread and a large tin cup of Sarah's nourishing soup. After giving herself the satisfaction of watching Winnie eagerly accept the soup, Perrin climbed down from the wagon. Her boots sank in loose sand and she turned her face out of the scouring wind.

What she wanted most was to bask in the knowledge of

Winnie's gradual recovery, and she wanted to walk the stiffness out of her legs and lower back. But a hard wind and blowing sand argued against a stroll.

Perhaps now was as good a time as any to confront Augusta and get it over with. For two days Perrin had waited for Augusta to come forth with an apology. She should have known it wouldn't happen. Augusta Boyd never apologized.

If they were to reach an accommodation, Perrin would have to be the person who made the approach, and if concessions were to be made, she would have to make them. With great reluctance, she had decided she would do whatever was necessary for one reason: so Cody Snow would not evict her from his train.

Grim-faced and dragging her feet, she turned her steps into the blowing sand and trudged forward in search of Augusta's wagon. With each step, her resentment mounted.

Sand blew into the bacon grease, mixed into the biscuits. It reddened eyes, invaded layers of clothing. There was sand in Augusta's hair, beneath her fingernails, in her tea, and in her blankets. The wretched sand rubbed raw spots on her skin and made her itch all over.

She had believed she could hate nothing more than she hated asking the other women to hold out their skirts and form a shield around her while she answered a call of nature. But she hated the ubiquitous blowing sand even more. And when she spotted Perrin coming toward her with head bowed against the wind, she remembered that she detested Perrin Waverly more than she could possibly hate sand or discomfort or any other thing.

Spinning in furious realization, she yanked down the scarf that protected her nose and mouth from the swirling sand and hissed at Cora. "You talked to her again, didn't you!"

Cora glanced up from the frying pan and the flames that darted and danced in the wind. Defiance hardened her eyes. "You still owe me four dollars! It ain't been paid yet."

Panic gripped Augusta's chest. At once she understood

that if she did not pay Cora immediately, Perrin might deduce that Augusta lacked the funds. The horror of being exposed as a pauper glazed her eyes. Perrin would feel superior to her; Perrin would laugh and tell the others how far the mighty had fallen, Augusta Boyd was no better than anyone else.

She could not bear the scene her imagination sketched. A thousand times no. Never would she ever allow a base creature like Perrin Waverly to feel superior to a Boyd. It was unthinkable, unendurable.

The only way to hold her pride intact was to pay Cora the four dollars. But how could she do it? Then she would have only thirty dollars to see her through the next three-quarters of the journey. What if another ox died? Or her cow? And she would want fresh eggs or vegetables along the way. There was a rip in the tent that could eventually worsen to the extent that she would have to purchase another.

"Oh, God. Oh, God." She couldn't catch her breath.

Wringing her hands, fighting to suppress the hysteria that clogged her throat, Augusta paced against the maddening wind, chewing her lips and trying not to inhale flying sand. What to do? Pay Cora or invent an excuse that no one would believe? Which evil to choose, which? She had to decide right now.

In the end, the decision was instinctive. She watched Perrin walking toward her, then pride reared and vanquished prudence.

Whirling into the blowing sand, she ran to the back of the wagon. In less than two minutes she had climbed inside and opened her beaded purse with shaking hands. "Oh, dear God." Panting with fear and dizzying bitterness, she withdrew four precious dollars. Wrapping her fist around the coins, she clutched them to her breast for a moment and desperately told herself she would not cry. She would *not*.

"Don't think about it," she whispered, blinking rapidly. "Somehow everything will work out. You are a Boyd."

She *would* snag her hem and rip it as she dropped out of

the wagon. And the sandy wind blasted her full in the eyes. Despair bled the color from her lips. But at least the harlot would see with her own eyes that Cora had received her blood money. And it was indeed blood money. Parting with each coin was like tearing off one of her limbs.

"Cora? Here! Take these and get out of my sight!" She flung the gold pieces into the wind as Perrin approached the fire pit. "Don't come back until it's time to get under way!" Right now she didn't trust herself to remain in Cora's presence.

Sputtering with anger, Cora glared, then she crawled around the fire pit, digging the coins out of the sand with her fingers. When she had found them all, she twisted the gold pieces in her handkerchief, then pushed to her feet and stormed away, heading into the wind toward Sarah's and Lucy's wagon. Augusta threw up her hands when she noticed that Cora had abandoned the bacon to burn in the skillet. Rage pounded the base of her skull.

"We need to talk," Perrin said, raising her voice against the blowing sand. Her skirt whipped around her body and she snatched at her shawl before it skittered away.

"You have nothing to say that I want to hear," Augusta said coldly. The stripes healing on Perrin's cheek provided a surge of pleasure. She hoped the scratches stung as painfully as the crack in her lower lip. "Cora received her money," she snapped, starting to turn her back to the creature. "You're dismissed."

"I didn't come about Cora. I came to tell you that what happened between us three days ago cannot, must not happen again!"

God in heaven. Augusta sagged against the back wheel, fighting a scald of vomit that surged in her throat. The money wasn't why the harlot had come.

She stared unseeing at the sandy air. She needn't have paid Cora. She could have kept her four precious dollars.

"I don't know why you decided to travel to Oregon and marry a stranger, but I know why I did," Perrin stated in a level tone. "I have no choice. Therefore, I can't afford to be evicted from this train. You and I will have to tolerate each other, Augusta. We'll have to find a way to coexist for another four months."

A bitter taste flooded Augusta's mouth and coated her tongue. She might have convinced Cora to wait for payment until they reached Oregon. Dear God.

"I'll stay out of your way, and you stay out of mine. When we must converse, surely we can do so in a civilized manner without resorting to physical violence." Perrin stared through the flying grit. "We'll behave like ladies." Her voice sharpened with suppressed anger. "If you think you can do that."

"You insufferable piece of baggage!" Crimson heated her cheeks. It mortified her that a low remark questioning her breeding was even possible. "You provoked what happened. It was your fault! Moreover, you are not a lady and you never will be!"

"Perhaps not. But I can behave like one. I don't slap people or throw chairs at them!" The words were accompanied by a shudder of revulsion.

Oh, how she burned to fly at the creature and claw that contemptuous expression off of her face. The ferocity of her emotions shocked Augusta to the tips of her stockings.

Where in the name of heaven did these sick yearnings for violence spring from, and when had they begun? She stared at the scratches on Perrin's cheek and found they did not satisfy her. She longed to leap forward and draw fresh blood.

Shaking, Augusta willed herself to step backward, opening a space between herself and a nearly overwhelming temptation to attack. She pressed her fingertips to her temples. When had her weapons altered from icy disdain and her own innate superiority to fingernails and teeth? How had such deterioration occurred?

She must be losing her mind. That was the only reasonable explanation. Fear and constant anxiety were destroying her.

"Are we agreed, then?" Perrin demanded, her tone as sharp as a blade. "We will not embarrass ourselves or the others again? We will set aside our dislike for the remainder of the journey and conduct ourselves in a civilized manner?"

"I detest you!"

They glared at each other across the flames leaping in the fire pit. Dark smoke curled from the skillet Cora had abandoned, and the smell of burning bacon invaded their nostrils.

"As you pointed out," Perrin said angrily, "I was not your father's confidante. And I didn't drive him to ruin. He also paid for the mansion *you* lived in and the servants who staffed it. He paid for gowns ordered from Paris and baubles designed in Brussels. He paid for your carriage and the set of matched bays to draw it. He paid for soirees and entertainments. Joseph could have provided for four mistresses for the same money as it cost to maintain one daughter. So if he hanged himself because he faced financial disaster, his difficulties cannot be laid entirely at my door!"

Pride steadied Augusta's cold gaze. Her chin snapped up. "What on earth gave you the impression that my father was suffering financial difficulties?" she demanded furiously.

Perrin stiffened. "You accused me of ruining your father and driving him to suicide."

"I referred to his mental state, not his purse," she said haughtily. "How amusing that you thought yourself powerful enough or clever enough to ruin a man like my father. Ona and Bootie will laugh when I tell them." She forced wooden lips to smile. "You're really quite entertaining. Did you actually imagine that your shabby little rented cottage and your cheap clothing had bankrupted the former mayor of Chastity? You make me laugh."

Perrin stared at her. "You accused me of ruining your father and being the cause of his death. You said that."

Her teeth bared. "He'd be alive today if it wasn't for you! The shame of consorting with a whore, the scandal of it, *that's* what killed him!"

"You're wrong." Perrin clenched her fists at her sides. "Your father wanted to marry me."

"Liar!"

"The only reason I was Joseph's mistress instead of his wife is you and your selfishness. Joseph didn't want you to be uncomfortable in your own home. And he didn't want me to feel unwelcome in what would have been my home too. You never thought that Joseph might be lonely. All you thought about was yourself."

"Get out of my sight! I can't stand to look at you!"

Perrin's dark eyes narrowed, and scarlet patches burned on her cheeks. She opened her mouth, then closed it. Clamping her teeth together, she whirled and walked into Cody Snow, who strode toward them out of the swirling clouds of sand.

"Back in your wagons, ladies. We'll try for another four miles before we stop for the night."

"Get out of my way!" Perrin snapped. His eyebrows lifted as he stepped aside. She tossed her head and twitched her skirts in a furious motion, then stormed past him.

Cody pulled a bandanna up over his nose and mouth to block the sand that blotted the sun and thickened the air. His voice was muffled when he swung toward Augusta.

"Did you two get things settled?"

You're a Boyd, Augusta reminded herself. Boyds didn't discuss personal matters with inferiors. She raised her head and let her eyes look through him.

"Find Cora, if you please, and tell her to return to the wagon."

Cody's eyes narrowed into slits above his bandanna. "If you want your maid, Miss Boyd, then you fetch her." He strode past the burning bacon and in a minute his tall form had been swallowed by the sandstorm.

Cora. The instant Augusta spoke the wretch's name, the full horror of her situation returned in force. She felt as if someone had punched her in the stomach.

What was she going to *do*? Walking around behind the wagon, she bent at the waist and vomited into the flying sand and grit.

"It's a fine day! Finally!" Throwing back her head, and almost losing the man's hat she had borrowed from Heck Kelsey, Mem Grant grinned at two hawks wheeling overhead. Sunlight and a sky that gleamed like an inverted china bowl made her feel better than she'd felt in two weeks. Thank heavens there was no headache today. No headache would dare intrude on this morning's treat.

Webb Coate turned his head and smiled. "Don't celebrate yet. We'll have rain before supper."

"I don't care, it's wonderful now. Just look! Everything is turning green, and—" She stopped and laughed at herself. The "everything" she referred to was tufts of hard buffalo grass fighting to survive on barren sandy hillsides. Here and there a few hardy wildflowers glowed yellow or blue against the earth, but it wasn't difficult to see why emigrants referred to this stretch as the Great American Desert.

She glanced at Webb, admiring the way he sat his horse, as if the two were one body, one mind. His eyes were shaded by his hat brim, but the sunshine fell full upon his lips and lower jaw. Seeing how straight he rode in his saddle, Mem unconsciously straightened her own spine.

Webb spotted the motion, lifted an eyebrow, and waited.

"I may have exaggerated my riding experience just a little," she confessed sheepishly. Daylight showed between the saddle and her behind, which was taking a pounding.

"A little," he repeated, glancing at her gloved hands. She gripped the pommel, hanging on for dear life. "How much riding experience have you actually had?"

She pursed her lips and pretended to consider. "Well, counting today, I've been on a horse four times." She grinned as Webb rolled his black eyes and made a sound deep in his throat. "If I'd told you, you wouldn't have allowed me to come."

"That's right." He shifted the carbine that rested across his thighs and glanced at the train over his shoulder as if thinking about returning her to the wagons.

"This is my first time riding astride, and it's much easier and not nearly as unnerving," Mem said quickly, hoping to

divert his intentions. "I'm glad no one had a lady's saddle."
By now Bootie would have noticed that she was riding like a
man and Mem would hear about it for days. She'd deal with
Bootie later. After all she had undergone to arrange this outing, she wasn't going to spoil it by anticipating trouble.

First she'd had to promise a whole day of driving the oxen
in exchange for Bootie driving them without relief this morning. Then she'd had to convince Miles Dawson to lend her
the use of a horse. Finally, and by far the most difficult obstacle, she'd had to persuade Webb to let her ride with him
out in front of the wagons, just for a few hours.

"I feel as if I've been . . . what's the word?" he asked, still
frowning at her.

"Bamboozled," she supplied with a laugh. "And I'm so
glad. This is absolutely glorious, Mr. Coate. I thank you
from the heart for making it possible!"

The land that looked so drab and flat when viewed from
the seat of a rocking wagon stretched toward the horizon like
an immense rippling blanket woven from threads of green
and gold and brown. When her borrowed horse topped a rise,
Mem gasped and believed that she could see the far edges of
forever. The vast empty spaces exhilarated her, awed her, diminished her to a speck of human insignificance. Measure-
less quantities of air and earth lifted her spirit, glorious and
frightening in the same instant.

"I wouldn't have missed this for the world," she said
softly. "I see why you like riding point. There's no dust and
nothing to block your view. You can pretend you're the only
person on earth."

"Except for the people in the train ahead of us," he said
dryly.

Until he mentioned them, Mem hadn't noticed the white
specks crawling across the landscape far in the distance.
"The eyes of an experienced scout," she murmured, wondering what else he saw that she couldn't.

Long before this morning she had noticed that Webb
Coate was not only the handsomest man she had ever met,

and the most interesting, but his senses were sharper than those of most people. Webb could smell rain when there wasn't a cloud in the sky. He could determine the distance between himself and a coyote solely by listening to the animal's bark. Mem had seen him place his hand on an old campfire and sift the ashes, then state when the ashes had been flame.

Everything about him fascinated her, from the sensual curve of his lips to his blue-black hair to the way he walked, with liquid grace and a soundless step. His voice and the strange blend of accents delighted her ear like a symphony. And she could have listened to his stories about growing up in a Sioux village for the rest of her natural days.

To her utter delight, she and Webb had fallen into a habit of meeting at Smokey Joe's fire pit late at night while the rest of the camp lay sunk in slumber. Like her, he didn't seem to require much sleep, and he appeared to welcome her company as much as she anticipated his.

Sometimes Webb talked about his boyhood with the Teton Sioux, sometimes Mem talked about growing up in Chastity, Missouri. Her contributions to their conversations seemed extraordinarily dull compared to the richness of experience that he had lived. Mostly, what she brought to their nightly meetings was her own viewpoint of the day's happenings, and a mishmash of opinions addressing everything under the sun.

"I love this," she said with a smile and a sigh of pleasure, squinting toward the curving edge where earth met sky. The air was so clear that she swore she could see for thousands of miles.

The trip to Oregon was turning out exactly as she had hoped, a grand adventure even more exciting than she had dared imagine. And she was wresting every pleasure and new experience from the trip that was possible. After much wheedling, Heck Kelsey had let her pound out a horseshoe, Miles Dawson had shown her how to tie a lasso, Smokey Joe had taught her the fine points of dressing out an antelope.

Exhilarated, she had recorded each fresh experience in her journal. She didn't want to forget a single moment of this remarkable journey.

Occasionally, it occurred to her that she was probably the only one of the brides who preferred travel to arrival. She dreaded the day, thankfully still far away, when they would finally drive their wagons into Clampet Falls, Oregon.

"The sky, the air, the river . . ." She inhaled deeply and smiled with joy, wishing the journey would never end. "Are you sorry this is your last trip across the continent?" she asked, enjoying the gleam of sunlight that slid through Webb's black hair. Today he wore it tied at his neck with a strip of rawhide. A dark curl swayed down the back of his buckskin jacket.

"I have promised myself that I'll return someday," he said quietly, his eyes scanning the wide vista, alert to movement. "My father made the same promise," he added after a moment. "But he never returned after the trip to fetch my mother and me."

"Do you miss him?" Mem asked, curiously. She knew Webb's father had died in England earlier in the year. He would return to Devonshire at the conclusion of this journey. Webb was so at one with the land, so natural a part of Mem's vision of the West that she couldn't imagine him living in England.

The strips fringing his jacket and leggings stirred in a meandering breeze. He shifted the carbine to his shoulder.

"My father was a great warrior." When he saw her eyebrows lift, he smiled. "He was an Englishman through and through, but he possessed the qualities of a Sioux warrior. Fearlessness, bravery, intelligence. His fighting ground was Parliament."

Mem urged her horse to keep pace with his, riding close enough that her skirts almost brushed his beaded leggings. "Is your mother still alive? Will she ever return to the American West?" It was rude to ask such personal questions, but she couldn't help herself. She hungered to know everything about him.

Sunlight burnished his face to tones of bronze and copper. "My mother is very much alive, and still beautiful." Then he laughed. "I doubt she has any interest in returning to the West. She's become very attached to English comforts."

Mem pictured a slender graceful woman with large black eyes and Webb's classically sharp profile. Someone beautiful. A sigh twitched her shoulders.

Occasionally she noticed how the teamsters looked after Perrin Waverly and Augusta Boyd when they passed. And she wondered how it might feel to be so beautiful that you turned men's heads. Would it be gloriously satisfying to gaze into a mirror and observe an exquisite creature looking back from the glass? Would it feel exciting and powerful? Saucy and fun? She would never know.

"What is your mother's name?"

Webb glanced at her with an indulgent expression. Her endless curiosity about his native upbringing seemed to amuse him. "Her name is Spring Wind, Miss Grant."

"Spring Wind." She liked the way the name sounded on her tongue, liked how the words fit together and dangled images in her mind. "Do you have an Indian name?"

"Tanka Tunkan. It means Big Stone." He laughed at her puzzled expression, showing a flash of white teeth. "The first time I was allowed to accompany a raiding party against the Crow, as a lowly moccasin carrier for Snow Bird, I had the misfortune to stumble over a large stone and pitch headfirst down the side of a bluff. The noise alerted the Crow hunting camp. Consequently our party returned to the village without having struck a blow. On that day I was named Tanka Tunkan." He smiled at the memory, then explained that a Sioux was given several names during his lifetime: his childhood name, his adolescent name, his adult name, and his true name, which was never shared with anyone. "Had I remained with the village, I would have spent the next years striving to earn a name more worthy of a warrior."

Entranced, Mem studied his strong wide-cheeked face, thinking about the story and trying to picture him as a boy living a life she could only imagine. She wished she knew what his true name was. He was the most exotic man she had ever met.

"While we're speaking of names," she said, taking the opportunity to address something she had been considering, "I think we know each other well enough now that . . . well, I'd like it if you'd call me Mem instead of Miss Grant."

Unexpectedly, he looked away from her and didn't answer. When the silence lengthened and became awkward, she added quickly, "When we're alone together." That comment sounded so much like something Augusta might say that she cringed and hastily amended, "Please call me Mem anytime."

This, she realized at once, would never happen, not in an age when couples married thirty years referred to each other in public as mister and missus. Not at a time when an Indian might be flogged merely for looking too long at a white woman.

Her cheeks heated beneath the brim of her borrowed hat. If she hadn't been astride a horse, knowing she was blushing would have prompted her to throw out her hands in exasperation. She couldn't recall the last time she had blushed.

The longer Webb's silence continued, the hotter her cheeks became and the deeper grew her mortification. Too late she realized she had invited an unseemly and brazen intimacy. He would think less of her for this mishap. Worse, he might decide she was throwing herself at him.

In an agony of embarrassment, she finally made herself break the miserably uncomfortable silence. "Of course if using first names would make you uncomfortable . . ." She spoke in a voice so low that only the sharp ears of a scout could have heard.

Finally he answered, but without looking at her. "I doubt the captain would approve a show of familiarity between his passengers and his men." His expressionless eyes scanned the horizon, lingering on something Mem couldn't see.

Abruptly the pleasure vanished from the day, blotted by the swift descent of excruciating humiliation. The vast open spaces offered a person no place to hide; she had nowhere to turn away from him. Staring straight ahead in a paralysis of embarrassment, she bounced up and down on the silly horse, her cheeks on fire as she realized their hours beside Smokey Joe's embers had meant one thing to her and another to him.

Mem had believed they were developing a rare friendship. Now it seemed obvious that Webb had merely been passing the time by visiting with a foolish woman who couldn't sleep and so had imposed herself on his place by the fire. She had mistaken politeness for pleasure in her company.

With all her heart Mem wished the raw earth would open wide and swallow her whole. One minute there would be a tall plain virgin clinging to a skittish horse, scalded with embarrassment—the next instant, she would disappear and Webb Coate would sigh with relief and ride on blessedly alone.

Suddenly he leaned forward and his mustang shot ahead. The horse sped away so swiftly that Mem almost missed his shout.

"Get Cody!"

Startled out of self-absorption, puzzled, she jerked on the reins of her own horse to stop him from sprinting after the mustang. Her horse wheeled in a circle, fighting her control and giving her a scare before she finally managed to bring him to heel or whatever it was called. When she felt secure enough to look up and ignore her pounding heart, she spotted Webb, already half a mile in front of her, riding hard toward a white dot.

Squinting through the dust kicked up by his horse, she finally recognized the white dot as a lone wagon turned out of the tracks that followed the Platte. Distances were deceptive on the plains, but she guessed the wagon was about five miles ahead.

Even to her inexperienced eye something looked amiss. Wagons seldom traveled alone—had this one been abandoned by the train ahead? Curiosity and an adventurous spirit urged her to follow Webb and discover the situation for herself. But practicality won out as it usually did.

Reluctantly pulling her horse around, she flapped her bootheels against his side and hoped she could stay on his back long enough to carry Webb's message to Cody Snow. Actually, she was grateful for an errand to divert her mind from her humiliation and a disappointment that cut to the quick.

"Mem Grant," she muttered between her teeth, "You are a foolish, fanciful old spinster. Haven't you learned anything in twenty-eight years?" Next year she would look back and laugh at herself for ever thinking that a man like Webb Coate might have considered her interesting or worthy of friendship. She would remember today and she would squirm and chuckle at the brazenness of inviting him to address her familiarly.

But right now, his rejection hurt as badly as the headache that had reappeared to stab the top of her spine.

CHAPTER
* 10 *

Cody cantered back to the wagons and instructed Miles Dawson to bring the train up to within a quarter of a mile of the abandoned wagon. After a quick search, he rode toward a sand hill where Perrin stood waiting.

She faced west toward mounds of purple clouds billowing up along the horizon, watching the lightning that flashed across a dark strip near the earth. Rising wind teased dark tendrils from her bonnet and molded her skirts around a curve of hips and thighs, the sight of which made his stomach suddenly tighten.

She looked so alone with the sky and plains behind her, swaying like a stalk in the wind, that his chest tightened sharply and he surprised himself by wanting to clasp her to his chest and shield her from weather and fate and the loneliness imposed on her by the other brides.

He didn't understand his attraction to this woman, didn't want it. Even if he hadn't decided there would be no more women in his life, he would not have chosen a woman like Perrin Waverly regardless of her beauty. She didn't like men, expected the worst from them. She was stubborn and argumentative.

She had been another's man's mistress.

The push-pull of his relationship with her irritated and mystified him. At the end of each day, she approached their meeting with wary eyes and the ever-present chip on her shoulder, clearly expecting a battle of wills. This despite the fact that he had bent over backward to keep his train running smoothly, which meant he frequently ground his teeth, set aside his gut reaction, and acquiesced to many of her requests.

Then, just about the time that he decided to hell with her and her prickly manner, they shared an instant of perfect accord, a stunning moment when he looked into her face and *knew* that she felt exactly the same emotion he was feeling, or that she assessed a situation precisely as he did. He had never experienced this connection with a woman, this strange unspoken harmony of shared accord.

Such instances threw him off balance by giving him a glimpse of something he couldn't label or identify, but something that made him suddenly ache with a restless loneliness as intense as he felt when riding solo across the prairie. At such times a hollowness opened behind his chest as if he lacked something he hadn't known he was missing.

Riding up alongside her, he frowned down at the oval face tilted up to him. Beneath the lip of her bonnet, her dark hair was parted neatly down the center, drawn toward a heavy knot on her neck. Loose tendrils floated in the breeze and fluttered against her cheeks. Today her eyes seemed enormous, the warm color of his saddle. Her lips reminded him of early strawberries.

He didn't need this. Damn it, he did not want it.

"Tell the women we'll be stopping long enough to bury two people." His voice was harsh, an order, not a request.

She nodded and folded her arms across her breast, facing the lightning that pulsed behind the clouds. "Cholera?"

Watching her face, he suddenly comprehended that lightning frightened her. And he realized that she looked at him with the same apprehensive expression as she regarded the lightning, as if he were hot and dangerous, something wild and beyond understanding, to be feared and avoided.

"It's difficult to tell. They've been dead awhile."

Her thick-lashed eyes swung toward him with a glint of anger. "The previous train passed by without burying them?"

"It won't take long." Several of the brides leaned out of the wagons to watch them talking. It occurred to Cody that at least some secretly hoped Perrin would do something to confirm her reputation as a loose woman, something to condemn her for.

What the hell did they expect her to do? Lean against his

thigh and simper up at him? He tossed a glare toward the avid watchers. Hell, no wonder she stiffened and jerked from an accidental touch. "We should be able to make a few more miles after the burial, before the storm hits."

"Cody?" she called as he was turning his horse. He hauled on the reins and glanced over his shoulder. Today was a day of insights. She never called him Cody except when it was impossible for anyone to overhear and read something into it. "Thank you for being willing to stop and bury those people."

Their eyes held. And God help him, he stared at her wind-molded breasts and thighs and wanted to bed her. He wanted to see those cinnamon eyes gazing up from his pillow, wide and feral with desire. He longed to scatter the pins from her hair and bury his hands in its silken weight. He wanted to make that husky voice whisper his name. Wanted to melt the starch out of her bones. He burned with inner wildness at the thought of her shuddering with pleasure beneath him.

He stared down at her. "Did you pin a short length of faded yellow ribbon to my saddle blanket?"

Her eyebrows soared like silky wings. "No."

Without another word, he rode away from her large brown eyes and visions of naked curves and strawberry lips. Maybe she had pinned the yellow ribbon to his blanket; maybe she hadn't. He didn't know whether to believe her. He couldn't think of anyone else who might have done it.

Damn her. He had more important things to deal with than bits of ancient cake and yellow ribbons, or thinking about rounded hips and small perfect breasts. He didn't want to speculate how her body would feel beneath his, didn't want any of it. There would be no more women in his life. No more betrayals, no more pain written across his heart in a female hand.

Bending over the neck of his buckskin, he galloped back to the abandoned wagon.

Webb had nearly finished digging the first grave. Cody removed a shovel from behind his saddle and lifted his boot to drive the edge into the ground. "Did you discover who they were?" he asked after twenty minutes, taking a break to wipe the sweat from his brow.

Webb nodded toward a man and woman he had covered with a blanket pulled from the back of their wagon. " 'Eaggleston' is carved on the side of the wagon bed. The same name is engraved on a trunk inside."

Mr. Eaggleston had been laid out carefully, his arms folded across his chest, but Webb had found the woman sprawled in a heap at the tail of the wagon, a shovel beside her. "We've been lucky so far," Cody commented before he returned to digging. Because of Webb's judicious campsites and plain good fortune, he hadn't had to dig a grave for one of his passengers. Yet.

An hour later he stood from mounding sand and dirt atop the graves, removed his hat to wipe his temples, then swore between his teeth. Contrary to orders, his train was headed straight for the abandoned wagon instead of staying on the trail as he'd ordered. Miles Dawson rode point, his face flushed and frustrated. Dawson called a halt when the lead wagon came abreast of the graves and he spread his arms in a gesture of exasperation.

"Mr. Snow?" Perrin called.

Cody swung his gaze from Miles Dawson, but not without a narrowed scowl that promised a good cussing later. He watched Perrin and Lucy Hastings striding toward him, the other brides behind them. "What the hell is going on here?" he demanded.

Perrin pressed down her skirts, holding them against the stiffening wind. "Miss Hastings demands, and we all agree, that these poor souls have a service spoken over them."

Irritation reddened his face. A bunch of determined women had overridden his orders and cowed one of his teamsters. He scowled at them, noticing they had gussied up, had washed their faces at the rain barrels, had smoothed their hair. They all wore bonnets and gloves and faces dead set on having their way.

"It's going to rain and we've lost enough time. Get back in your wagons."

None of them moved. "We insist," Sarah Jennings called.

Lucy Hastings lifted her chin in a self-righteous gesture. "It is our Christian duty to give these poor souls a decent burial."

Stepping forward, Perrin fixed him with a stubborn look that Cody was beginning to know all too well. Not a hint of compromise softened her defiant scowl.

"The service needn't be lengthy. You can say a few words, then we'll sing a hymn and end with a prayer. It will only take a few minutes." Twitching her skirts, she walked toward the graves and the others flowed around him, following her. When they reached the mounds, they all turned to look back at him, waiting.

Son of a bitch. Small confrontations like this one, and how they were resolved, could determine the success or failure of a leader and consequently the fate of the train. Cody had seen it happen. Cal Halverson had been ejected from his own train because he hated beans and wouldn't accept a plate of pintos from the wife of an easily offended passenger.

He slapped his hat against his leg and swore. He didn't want a bean or a prayer incident; and it would take longer to argue than to speak a few words. Furious that the brides thought they'd forced him to do something he'd intended to do anyway, only not in front of everyone, he strode toward the graves.

Grinding his teeth, he held his hat against his chest and glared at the freshly washed faces beaming approval at him. "Lord," he began, snapping the word against the wind, "we come before you to commend the Eagglestons into your safe-keeping."

When he glanced up, all heads were bowed except Perrin Waverly's. She was gazing at him with a faint smile on her strawberry lips and the hint of a twinkle in her eyes. But he saw gratitude too, and maybe something more difficult to identify.

He held her gaze so long that two of the brides lifted their heads to look a question at him, and he forgot what he had already said. He drew a breath and began again.

All the time he spoke, he was aware that Perrin Waverly watched him with those large, dark, liquid eyes, aware that he didn't do justice to the Eagglestons because his mind was fixed firmly on the rewards of earth, not on those of heaven.

Augusta had no interest whatsoever in attending a depressing service for two strangers. Instead of following to the grave sites like tailing a herd, she turned her steps in the opposite direction, deciding she'd take a peek at the Eagglestons' wagon.

Lifting on tiptoe, she peered inside the wagon bed. Sand and dust furred several trunks and boxes, but it appeared the Eagglestons had been traveling light, without enough provisions to complete a lengthy journey. Perhaps they hadn't planned on traveling as far as California or Oregon.

It didn't matter to her, and it no longer mattered to the Eagglestons. *They* no longer had to worry themselves sick about provisions or sick oxen. *They* wouldn't spend another sleepless night weeping in despair over a nearly empty purse.

Jerking her skirts away from the snatching branches of a sagebrush clump, she walked away from the wagon, moving on an angle that blocked her sight of the service. Nor could those at the grave sites see her. There was no point calling attention to the fact that she had chosen not to pretend grief for strangers.

However, should anyone inquire, she could truthfully excuse her absence by pleading a headache. Pausing, she pressed her fingertips to her temples and squeezed her eyes against the pain.

Prior to this hideous ordeal, she didn't recall ever having suffered a headache, although it had occasionally seemed expedient to pretend that she did. Now headaches pounded her temples every single day. It felt as if heavy coins flew around inside her skull, slamming the sides of her head and brain.

The cause of her headaches was money, always money. Already it was evident that she would have to buy more bacon and flour when they reached Fort Laramie, and sugar too.

On the days when they stopped early, she upheld her social obligations by inviting Bootie, whom she had forgiven for Mem's transgressions, Ona, Thea, and sometimes Sarah, to take tea by her fire. One couldn't serve a proper tea without small cakes, which consumed more sugar and flour than she would have believed possible. But even as she urged her guests to take more sugar, she counted each grain they stirred into their cups and silently despaired over their lavishness at her expense. Prior to this, she hadn't dreamed how expensive it was to keep up appearances.

Anxiety was killing her in daily doses. She couldn't sleep, could hardly swallow her food. Every minute of every waking day was a continuing nightmare of anxiety about the future, worrying about that inevitable moment when she opened her purse and found nothing inside except the seam at the bottom.

That was the day she would follow her father to the grave, she thought bitterly. Pride would make the decision for her.

After dashing a tear of self-pity, she pressed a hand to her forehead and continued pacing. Lightning flickered on the plains and she wondered if there was some way to attract it on command. A lightning strike would occur so swiftly as to be painless, and then she would never have to suffer again.

Halting, she braced against the endless lunatic wind, surrendering to a moment of hopelessness. The tragedy of her life and situation overwhelmed her. When she stumbled forward, her heel caught in a depression and pitched her to the ground.

For an instant she lay where she had fallen, staring hopelessly at the sky. Even the earth, even her own shoes and feet conspired against her.

Sitting up, she rubbed dusty gloves against her cheeks, then searched the ground with dulled eyes and not much interest to see what had tripped her.

Her shoe had scraped a thin covering of dirt from something that gleamed like brass. She stared at it a minute, then, leaning, she brushed away more loose dirt and discovered a small rectangular box buried in a shallow depression. The box was made of wood with brass corner bracings and a brass plate engraved with the name Edgar Eaggleston.

Instinctively, she cast a quick glance over her shoulder to see if anyone was watching, then tested the lid of the box and discovered it was not locked. A lifetime of proper behavior prevented her from immediately peeking inside. She reminded herself that one didn't invade another's privacy.

Rocking back on her heels, she listened to the hymn being sung not a hundred feet from where she knelt. She couldn't see the others, but she heard Lucy Hastings's sweet voice soaring like a lark, leading them in song.

The thing to do was to inform Mr. Snow at once of her discovery. On the other hand, it didn't seem appropriate to interrupt a funeral service. And, while she waited for the service to conclude, she might as well have a look inside the box. The Eagglestons were, after all, deceased. It wasn't as if she were invading the privacy of someone who would object; and Mr. Snow would want to know what was inside. Upon reflection, it seemed she had an obligation to inspect the contents of the box.

Digging her fingers into the soft fill dirt surrounding the box, she found the edge of the lid and, quivering with curiosity, cautiously eased it open.

"Oh, my heavens!"

Her fingers flew to her lips. Incredibly, she stared down at rows and rows of stacked gold coins. A veritable fortune glowed in the cloudy light of the approaching storm.

"There must be . . ." Lifting one heavy stack in a shaking hand, she counted, then stared wide-eyed as she performed a swift calculation. There were four rows of ten stacks each, and fifteen coins in a stack. The box contained six hundred dollars.

She was rich.

Relief swamped her bones. Sitting down hard, her feet and skirts sprawled in front of her, she shook her head in disbelief and smothered a shout of sheer elation.

She was saved. Thank God, thank God!

No longer did she have to torment herself with thoughts of suicide, or make herself ill worrying about losing another ox, or begrudge each mouthful of food. If Mr. Clampet wasn't the town's wealthiest and most prominent citizen, she wouldn't have to marry him; she could purchase her freedom. She could buy eggs when next they became available. She could purchase fresh meat for the stew pot and a new tent, and sunbonnets and lip salve. She could send Cora home and hire a new girl if she chose. Finally, she would be able to sleep and stop wandering around the campsite in the middle of the night. She could pack away the headache powders.

Leaning forward over her knees, Augusta covered her face with both hands and swallowed back a surge of hysterical tears. This was a miracle.

But when she reached greedy hands into the box to gather the heavy coins, she suddenly halted and drew a sharp breath. What if the Eagglestons were traveling west to meet someone? What if someone knew about this money and was waiting to receive it? Rightfully, the money belonged to the Eaggleston heirs.

But she had found it. If she hadn't tripped over the lid, the money would have been lost forever.

Still . . . this money did not belong to her. Surely Cody Snow would know how to locate the Eagglestons' heirs.

But . . . if she gave the box to Snow, then the half-breed would learn about the money and steal it for himself. Everyone knew Indians were thieves. And what did she really know about Cody Snow? Maybe he would just keep the money. She stared at the coins and considered various outcomes.

Whether she welcomed the responsibility or not, she could see that it was her Christian duty to protect the poor Eagglestons' money. Clearly, the safest way to do that was to tell no one of her discovery. She would conduct her own search for heirs and when she found them, if they existed at all, she would be proud to inform them that she had saved their inheritance from plunder.

Yes, that was exactly the proper course.

Having settled the matter, and having determined the box was too heavy to carry, she eagerly dug her hands inside and pulled up the coins, pushing them into her gloves and down the front of her bodice. When her gloves were stuffed, she ran back to her wagon, climbed inside, and frantically looked for a safe place to hide the coins. For the moment her hatbox would have to do. After emptying the coins into the crown of her best Sunday hat, she dropped out of the wagon and hurried back to fetch another load.

On her second trip to the wagon, she experienced a bad scare. Glancing up, she spotted Cora standing in the opening of Winnie's wagon, observing her with a puzzled expression.

For one paralyzing instant, Augusta felt a stabbing jolt of guilt, as if Cora had caught her in the act of doing something shameful and wrong.

She stood frozen, a furtive look pinching her face, until she realized that her actions would not make sense to Cora. Cora could not see the buried box of coins. All she saw was Augusta clutching two lumpy gloves that might have been filled with pebbles, for all Cora knew.

The realization released her and she glared, then hurried to empty the second batch of coins into her hatbox before she rushed back to the cache for another load.

Who would have guessed that Cora would volunteer to sit with Winnie Larson while the others attended the service? Or that she would chance to look out the back of the wagon at the very moment when Augusta was rushing the coins to her hatbox? She worried, then decided it didn't matter. Even if Cora was smart enough to conclude that something momentous had occurred, she would never guess the staggering truth.

The hymn died on the breeze as Augusta dug into the buried box and stuffed coins into her gloves. She heard Cody Snow's deep voice rumbling a hasty prayer and understood she wouldn't have time to gather all the money.

For the first time in her ladylike life, Augusta Josepha Boyd swore. Hearing the sounds of voices returning from the grave sites, she slapped down the lid of the cache and jumped to her feet, kicking dirt over the lid. Hiding the stuffed gloves in the folds of her pelisse, she walked around the Eagglestons' wagon and fell in with the others as if she had been with them from the beginning. Perrin threw her a cold stare and Bootie lifted an eyebrow, but no one else seemed to realize she had been absent from the grave site.

There was enough time to empty the coins into the hatbox before Cora's head appeared in the oval of canvas.

"Oh! You startled me." She pressed a bare dirty hand to her throat and inhaled deeply. "How many time must I tell you not to creep up on people?"

"What on earth were you doing out there?"

"Can't a lady relieve herself without having to make an account of it?" she snapped. Cora's disbelieving silence plucked at her nerves. "Really, Cora. Shouldn't you be in the driver's seat? Mr. Snow will be wanting to get under way immediately."

Cora's sharp eyes slowly inspected the interior of the wagon bed. "Ain't you coming?"

"I have a fierce headache. I believe I'll put down some blankets and try to rest back here."

Cora's gaze settled on one of the gold coins that had fallen to the planks. She nodded slowly. "Whatever you say."

"Exactly," Augusta answered sharply. Bending, she curled her fingers around the coin. "How careless of me. Now, where did I put my purse?"

"It's in the canvas pocket above the sourdough jar. Where it always is."

Augusta stiffened. "How curious that you would know that."

Cora rolled her eyes. "Like I ain't turned this wagon out countless times, then repacked it on the other side of a gully or a stream or a deep draw."

Cora disappeared from view and in a moment Augusta heard her skirts flapping as she passed along the side of the wagon. Another minute elapsed, then she heard Cora shout, "Gee haw! Giddap, you lazy beasts!" The wagon lurched forward and turned into a long curve that would take them back to the trail. The first fat splats of rain struck the canvas above Augusta's head.

Cora peeked inside, then pulled the front drawstring to close out the rain. Augusta did the same at the back flap. The rain was a stroke of luck, she thought. Now she didn't have to worry about Cora spying on her.

Kneeling, she fumbled in the dim light for the hatbox and pulled it to the rocking floor. Wind buffeted the canvas, and the light was watery inside the closed wagon. But what light filtered inside glowed on the pile of gold coins filling the crown of her best Sunday hat.

For a long moment, she simply stared. Then, reaching a trembling hand, she counted the coins. There were two hundred and sixty-two gold pieces. Which, added to the money in her purse, elevated her fortune to two hundred and ninety-two dollars.

Stuffing a fist in her mouth, she smothered a shout of jubilation. Had there been more space, she would have leaped to her feet and danced with joy. She felt an insane urge to split open a sack of sugar and fling handfuls out of the back of the wagon simply because now she could buy more.

Sitting on the floor of the wagon, unaware of the rain pelting the canvas, oblivious to the sway and jolt of the wheels, she gazed down at the coins in her lap and burst into tears.

At that moment Augusta couldn't have said whether she

wept with gratitude for the coins filling her lap, or with regret for the coins she had been forced to leave behind.

On Thursday they camped near other trains at the base of Chimney Rock, one of the trail's most famous landmarks. Soaring Chimney Rock, and the formations at its base, had become the great guest book of the plains. Travelers carved their initials or names on the rocks, and left messages with a former trapper who charged a nickel to pin a note to his communication board.

After milking Hilda's cow and scouring out the breakfast skillet, Perrin washed at the rain barrel, then combed the dust out of her hair before pinning it in a knot above her collar. She chose her second-best bonnet, the one adorned with silk roses, and since the day was bright and warm, she wore a lightweight paisley fringed shawl.

"Are you ready to go?" she called to Hilda, excited by the prospect of an excursion and the novelty of new faces from the other trains. Also, Cody had told her people used this gathering spot to sell items they had discovered were too heavy to continue transporting or that they had decided they didn't want. There would be lemonade, and possibly pemmican, which everyone wanted to sample. Chimney Rock offered an atmosphere and turmoil as exciting as a country fair, and was as eagerly anticipated.

Hilda pushed their tent poles inside the wagon and dusted her hands across a gingham apron. She tucked a strand of blond hair beneath the braids crossing her head. "You go on ahead. I promised I'd wait for Winnie."

"Oh." Perrin leaned close to the mirror, hiding her disappointment. Hilda was friendly and cheerful, a good traveling companion, but she hadn't become a friend as Perrin had secretly hoped. The fact that Hilda was welcome anywhere in camp but Perrin was not, opened a subtle but wide rift between them.

Instinctively, she turned toward Mem's and Bootie's wagon, and considered asking Mem to accompany her to the

Chimney Rock. But Mem had been uncharacteristically distant and withdrawn for several days.

For a moment Perrin wavered. Maybe she should just forgo a closer look at the Chimney Rock rather than subject herself to the awkwardness of going alone. She could, after all, see the Chimney Rock's tall, craggy profile from here.

But she would miss reading the names carved in the rock and posted on the old trapper's message board. She would miss the lemonade and browsing the array of items for sale.

Giving herself a shake, she straightened her shoulders and her backbone. She had been alone all of her life; why should today be different? After giving Hilda a wave, she set out on her own, lingering well behind the other brides, lest it appear that she hoped to join them. She knew better than to court rejection.

In the end, the discomfort of being unaccompanied was offset by the pleasure of the outing. Sipping cool sugary lemonade, made with real lemons instead of citric acid and a few drops of essence of lemon, Perrin strolled along a row of impromptu stalls, dubbed Heartbreak Alley. Here she inspected various wares, bought a jar of blackberry jam, and exchanged stories of the trail with a tired-looking woman standing behind a display of china lovingly set out on a blanket.

When a family appeared who seemed interested in buying the china, Perrin moved on to examine a long plank that was pinned edge to edge with hundreds of messages. Some were amusing, some were sad, all were interesting, a small glimpse into someone else's life, someone else's problems.

A blacksmith named Hank Berringer declared himself a wronged man and sought information about his runaway wife. A man from Illinois had lost a mule named Ornery and would wait a couple of days in Fort Laramie in case anyone found her. There were dozens of messages of encouragement from people traveling ahead of following relatives. It was impossible to read all of the papers fluttering on the pins.

"Mrs. Waverly?" Cora called to her from the opposite end

of the board. "Can you read?" she asked when Perrin joined her. "Would you read this here message to me?"

Perrin leaned to the note Cora tapped, squinting to decipher crabbed misspelled handwriting. "'Urgent. Anyone with information concerning Mr. and Mrs. Edgar Eaggleston, post here. Will return in a week.'" The date at the bottom was Monday, two days previous. The message was unsigned.

Cora nodded sharply as if the message confirmed something she had been mulling in her mind, then she turned away from the board and scanned the crowds. Her thoughtful gaze settled on the folds of mauve silk banding Augusta's straw bonnet. "Interesting," she murmured.

"We should call this to Mr. Snow's attention so he can post a reply," Perrin commented. Then something occurred to her. "Cora, if you can't read, how did you chance to select a message about the Eagglestons from hundreds of others?"

"Someone else was reading this one and I wondered what was so upsetting about it," Cora replied absently, her gaze following Augusta's mauve ribbons along Heartbreak Alley.

Perrin watched too. Augusta moved from stall to stall, seemingly insensible to the stir her beauty caused. She didn't appear to be enjoying the day. A frown tugged her pale brow, and even from a distance she appeared distracted. When Ona touched her sleeve to catch her attention, she jumped and glared as if she'd been struck by a rattler.

Cora glanced over her shoulder at the message Perrin had read, then contemplated Augusta with a sulky expression. She seemed particularly interested in the net over Augusta's arm, filled with small items purchased from the desperate vendors along Heartbreak Alley. As if she'd forgotten Perrin, she moved into the crowd and in a minute was lost from sight.

Perrin lifted on tiptoe and scanned the throngs of people, searching for Mem's auburn hair or Bootie's fluttery little figure. She spotted one of the teamsters from the bride train, John Voss, she thought it was, who waved to her, and she noticed Sarah and Lucy waiting in line before the lemonade stand, but she didn't see Mem.

Mem would have been the perfect companion with whom to explore the rocks. Mem would have insisted they carve their names and would have made the event a great adventure.

But even after joining the multitude of people scrambling among the rocks at the base of the chimney formation, Perrin didn't spot Mem's tall figure. After a time, the names carved in stone absorbed her interest and imagination to the extent that she didn't mind viewing them alone. But she did wish the lemonade stand wasn't so far away. The rocks captured the sun's heat and every breath drew in hot dust kicked up by the crowd on the ground below.

Sitting on a rock that bore the inscription CALIFORNIA OR BUST, Perrin blotted her forehead and fanned her flushed face with the edge of her shawl.

"Shall I carve your initials?" a deep voice said above her.

Shading her eyes, she gazed up at Cody Snow. He lifted his hat to her, letting sunlight shine through waves of dark hair. It was such a bright warm day, and she'd had such a fine time so far, she couldn't stop the smile that curved her lips. "I'd like that very much. If you wouldn't mind."

His gaze dropped to her mouth and something flickered in his eyes, eyes so blue that she thought of summer skies and periwinkles. Perhaps it was his tanned skin that made the blue appear so intense. "You should smile more often," he said. His own smile was wide, engaging, and slightly lopsided.

The compliment caught Perrin by surprise. Feeling the heat of the sun on her cheeks, she looked toward the broad plains. "There's a message on the board inquiring about the Eagglestons."

"I left a reply." Bending down beside her, he removed a knife from the sheath on his belt. "Full name, or just initials?"

He turned his face toward her and she realized how closely

he knelt to her skirts. She could feel the exciting heat of him, could glimpse a nest of dark curls peeking from the bottom of his opened collar. The dizzying scent of strong soap and sunlight rose from his skin. Blushing, she shifted her gaze.

"Initials will do." She tried to concentrate, tried not to think about the solid maleness of him. It occurred to her that Cody Snow completely dominated the space he occupied. There was no room for anyone else.

"And thank you. It's nice to think there will be a record that I passed this way," she said, watching his hands on the knife and the rock. An odd certainty popped into her head. Those strong callused hands would be as skilled with a woman as they were with a knife or a gun. "Are you married, Mr. Snow?"

At once she was horrified by her blurted question. As gossip traveled swiftly in small groups, she had heard his story weeks ago. Learning his history had done nothing to quiet the strange restless longings that troubled her in his presence.

"My wife died in childbirth three years ago," he said tersely, leaning to blow dust out of the P appearing beneath his blade. "The infant died also."

"I'm sorry," Perrin commented softly, gazing down at her lap. His words were clipped and brief, but she sensed anger and pain behind them. After a pause, she inquired, "How long were you married?"

"Four years."

"I was married to Garin almost four years."

Here against the rocks, the sun fell on them heavily enough to draw a zigzag of sweat from Cody's temple. Fascinated, Perrin watched the tiny stream trickle toward his jawline. She experienced a sudden shocking urge to brush the perspiration away with her fingertips, then press her fingers to her lips and taste him. The intensity of this thought scandalized her and she quickly turned her head away, fearing her thoughts were writ large across her face.

"Cody?" she asked in a low voice. "Why do you always

seem so annoyed and angry? Do I do something that irritates you?"

He rocked back on his heels and his eyes darkened. "Ellen died giving birth to a baby that was not mine. I trusted her completely, and she betrayed me."

Slowly, Perrin nodded. "So now you dislike all women?"

"About as much as you dislike all men."

She wet her lips and tried to look away from him, but found she couldn't. They gazed into each other's eyes, measuring, making assumptions. "If you expect the worst, you're never disappointed."

"That's how I see it," he said.

Their locked eyes created a tension between them that drew her nerves taut, made her hands tremble to the extent that she tightened them around the jar of blackberry jam. The hard speculation in his gaze dried her mouth and she couldn't swallow.

Once she wouldn't have understood what was happening between them. But that was long ago, before Garin, before Joseph.

Now she understood what it meant to think about a man day and night, to hear his voice in dreams, to lose herself in thoughts of his hands or while remembering the glow of sunshine among the small dark hairs shading his jaw. She recognized the tension in her lower stomach, the aching in her breasts.

The odd thing was that she had seldom felt this level of arousal with Garin and never with Joseph. But she could not look at Cody Snow without yearning to touch his hard lean body, without wondering how his mouth would taste or how his hands would feel on her naked skin. She didn't know when this had happened, but it had.

Dropping her head, she watched her gloved fingers nervously smoothing her skirts across her thighs and she caught a deep breath. In Clampet Falls, Oregon, a farmer named Horace Able awaited her arrival. Perhaps he tried to imagine her, thought about her, was planning his life around her.

Shamefully, she had not entertained a single thought about Horace Able. She knew she would marry him regardless. But Cody Snow . . . with his strong tanned hands and jaw, with his dangerous cobalt eyes that probed and challenged, him she thought about all the time.

And he didn't want a woman in his life any more than she wanted a man in hers. Yet there was something electric that vibrated the air when they were together, as charged as the heat lightning that flashed across the vast prairie skies.

"It's finished," he said in a thick voice. When she turned to him, his shoulders had swelled against his shirt, as hard as the rocks surrounding them. Serge trousers pulled tight around his thighs and cut a deep V around his crotch.

"What?" she whispered, feeling faint. The sun beat down on her bonnet and perspiration dampened the sides of her waist. When she noticed droplets of moisture glistening in the crisp dark hair curling from his shirt collar, her head reeled and she couldn't think.

"Your initials," he said, staring at her mouth.

Blindly, she dropped her gaze to the raw cuts in the rock. "Yes," she said in a low voice, swaying toward him. "Yes, thank you."

"Perrin." He spoke so low that only she could have heard. But what she heard in his voice caused a shiver of apprehension to trace down her spine. This couldn't be happening. It couldn't.

"Mr. Snow?"

They both jerked at the shout, then turned toward Thea Reeves, who was climbing toward them, with Ona Norris immediately behind. Sunshine and pleasure flushed Thea's pretty face.

"Will you carve our initials in the rock?" Thea called cheerfully, adjusting the strap of the canvas bag that held her sketch pad and pencils. "I'll give you a sketch of the Chimney Rock in exchange for your labor."

It wasn't until Perrin noticed Ona's stern gaze that she remembered how close Cody knelt by her side and realized how his proximity might be interpreted.

Springing to her feet and blushing furiously, she thanked him again for carving her initials, then she murmured something to Thea and Ona before escaping and scrambling down the formation to the crowds below.

With a shock of truth, she recognized the excursion had ended for her. Today had not been about viewing the Chimney Rock or inspecting Heartbreak Alley. It hadn't been about reading the names carved in the rocks or leaving her own mark there.

She had come in hopes of seeing Cody, of spending a few minutes alone with him. And this was not the first time she had tried to maneuver time alone with him.

Admitting that her thoughts and actions had begun to revolve around Cody Snow made her feel heartsick. That she could be so deeply attracted to one man when she had promised to marry another shamed her. Her growing desire for Cody made her as sinful and as debased as the other brides believed she was.

But she couldn't help herself. Her woman's body didn't understand that Cody was forbidden to her.

The pleasure vanished from the bright day, and she felt like weeping. Perhaps Augusta was right to label her a harlot.

CHAPTER
* 11 *

My Journal, June, 1852: We've only traveled six hundred miles, but we can no longer pretend to ignore the hardships, the lack of privacy, the dirt, no fresh food, terrible weather, exhaustion, and the tedium of daily sameness. Sometimes I wish I hadn't come. Papa wanted this marriage. I'm no longer certain that I did.

Lucy Hastings

Mem blinked down at Lucy, horror dampening her eyes. In the ghastly shadows cast by a flickering lantern, Lucy's skin seemed to shrink over her bones, creating gaunt hollows and peaks. Tears rolled out of the girl's eyes as she pitched forward, gripped by another series of agonizing cramps. Her body writhed in convulsive spasms.

"So thirsty," she gasped when she could speak. Her eyes were wet and hot. With a shaking hand, Mem raised a cup of water to Lucy's cracked lips, then sponged the sweat off her forehead. Fever racked her tortured body even though she shivered uncontrollably. One minute Lucy clasped extra blankets close to chattering teeth; the next instant, she desperately tried to kick the coverings away from her, but her legs were too weak to move the blankets. Tears swam through her despair, and her whisper broke on a sob. "I'm dying."

"Shhh, don't waste energy trying to talk."

Sarah returned from emptying the vomit bucket and quietly climbed into the wagon. She replaced the pail on the floor near Lucy's head, inspected the bluish cast of Lucy's face and fingernails, then met Mem's eyes. Sadness pinched her expression. Pressing her lips together, she shook her head.

Mem smothered a sound and stared down at Lucy in disbelief. This morning Lucy's complexion had been pink and fresh, her eyes clear and bright. She had milked Sarah's cow and hung the buckets on the back of the wagon to slosh into buttermilk; she had packed the tent. For most of the morning, she drove the oxen while Sarah rolled out pies on the wagon seat beside her.

At the noon rest stop Lucy ate her midday meal despite an upset stomach and the onset of diarrhea. Several times during the early afternoon Mem had noticed Lucy climbing out on the tongue of the wagon, then jumping clear of the wheel, a feat they had all mastered so they could get off the wagon without stopping. Distressed, Lucy had dashed off to answer nature's urgent call.

When Lucy didn't return from her last flight, Sarah had become worried and pulled her wagon out of line, an event unusual enough that Cody Snow appeared at a gallop. When he learned that Lucy had not returned, he rode off with Miles Dawson. They found Lucy a mile behind, lying beside the trail in a pool of vomit, too weak to stand.

Now, eight hours later, Lucy Hastings was dying.

Sarah sat on a low stool beside the bed they had made for Lucy in the wagon. She touched Mem's hand and spoke in a whisper. "There's no sense both of us missing our rest. Get some sleep."

Mem blinked hard. "I just can't believe . . . it came on her so fast!"

"Cholera is like that." Raising the bottom of the blankets, Sarah trickled vinegar on the hot bricks that Perrin had delivered a few minutes ago. She tucked the blankets firmly into place, then watched beads of perspiration roll down Lucy's gray-blue face. The girl moaned and whispered a plea for water before she rolled to one side and vomited weakly into the bucket.

Lucy lay back exhausted. Her lips moved, but no sound emerged. "Pray for me."

Tears streaming from her eyes, Mem backed out of the wagon and dropped to the ground. Sagging against the tailgate, she inhaled deeply, drawing the cool night air into her lungs. The odors of vomit, diarrhea, sour sweat, and fear hung in her nostrils. She continued to see Lucy's shrunken bluish flesh.

Gradually she became aware that the camp was restless and few people were in their tents. Cody Snow and Heck Kelsey stood beside the arms wagon, talking quietly and smoking with the men on night watch. When she looked toward Smokey Joe's fire, she discovered Smokey Joe was awake, pouring coffee for Perrin, Hilda, Bootie, and Ona. The women sat on logs around Smokey Joe's fire, staring into the flames. Someone moved in the enclosure within the squared wagons, murmuring softly to the cows and oxen. Figures drifted between the wagons, speaking in subdued voices before reforming into other small groups. No one slept tonight.

Leaning on the tailgate of Lucy's and Sarah's wagon, Mem stroked the headache at her temples and listened to the soft sounds of Lucy's dying, to the murmur of Sarah's prayers. Anxious voices floated on the night breeze, reaching her like sighs.

After a while, she scrubbed her eyes with the heels of her hands, then stepped away. It was useless to think she would sleep tonight. Yet she didn't want to join the others who waited, as she did, for Lucy's suffering to end the only way it could.

Stumbling over her hem, she veered from the low fires burning beside most of the wagons, and walked into the darkness, wandering aimlessly toward a clump of cottonwoods that loomed dark and silvery in the light of a half moon.

"How can a person hope to sleep with so many people moving about?" Augusta complained, crawling out of her tent. Lifting a thick blond braid, she pulled her shawl up beneath it, then approached the fire to warm herself.

Cora peeked inside a Dutch oven nestled in the coals. "It's

confirmed. Lucy Hastings is dying of cholera," she said in a shaky voice.

"What on earth are you doing?"

"I'm baking cornbread. So is Winnie. Hilda will contribute some butter and Thea can spare a comb of honey." Cora replaced the lid of the Dutch oven and pushed a wave of dark hair out of her eyes. "It's going to be a long night. People get hungry."

Augusta folded her arms across her bosom and contemplated the Dutch oven. It occurred to her that Cora Thorp was mighty free with *her* provisions. If Augusta hadn't found the Eagglestons' gold, she would have been beside herself at the thought of feeding the camp. But she had found the Eagglestons' money. It was hers. To borrow from, she hastily amended, at least until she was certain that the Eagglestons had left no legitimate heirs.

Since discovering the message posted at the Chimney Rock, she had spent a lot of time thinking about the Eagglestons and possible heirs. The message had not sought information about "my parents" or "my aunt and uncle." The message had inquired about the Eagglestons as one would inquire about friends or a casual acquaintance. She was close to concluding that the Eagglestons probably had no heirs.

"You might have consulted me before you agreed to give away my supplies," she said sharply. Cora was getting too big for her britches, forgetting who employed whom.

In a week the train would arrive at Fort Laramie, and Augusta was considering leaving Cora at the fort. Long ago Cora had worn out her welcome.

Her final decision, of course, would depend on the availability of a replacement. Gazing at the firelight glimmering on Cora's sullen face, she decided instantly that she *would* hire another maid. Even if the new wench was as sulky and complaining as Cora, she wouldn't *be* Cora. The new maid wouldn't dare look at Augusta as if trying to read hints of shame or guilt in her employer's face. The very idea.

Adjusting her shawl around her shoulders, she sat on a

camp chair before the fire and extended her hands and feet toward the flames. The smell of hot cornbread made her mouth water.

"Have you heard whether the rest of us are in danger?" That was the fear that had kept her awake and worried. She thought the women who tended Lucy were mad to place themselves at such risk. If cholera decimated the train, it would be their fault. Which would be small comfort to those who sickened and died.

"I overheard Mr. Snow and Mr. Coate talking," Cora replied, gazing into the flames. "From what they said, it sounds like Lucy drank some bad water. That's how she got it. I think that's what they said. Anyway, Mr. Coate went around asking each of us if we'd scooped any water from that puddle near someone's old camp, you know, close to where we stopped last night. He thinks Lucy drank water from that puddle either last night or this morning."

Augusta stiffened and her eyebrows rose. "He didn't ask me!"

"I answered for you. I knew you didn't drink no water from a puddle. Not you."

"Well, you're right. But I might have." Irritation brought color to her cheeks. "He should have asked me directly."

"Maybe Mr. Coate don't like being insulted." Firelight shone as fiery pinpoints in Cora's dark eyes. A sly expression pursed her lips. "Course, I guess I know what that's all about. When are you going to admit you got a powerful hankering for that man?"

Augusta sprang to her feet, sputtering with outrage. The smirk on Cora's thin lips made her fingers twitch with fury. "How . . . how *dare* you! How . . ." She could hardly speak through the rage choking her throat. Shaking, she stood so close to the fire pit that it was a wonder her hem didn't burst into flame. "I will not tolerate any more insults from you! When we reach Fort Laramie, I'm putting you off this train. I was going to give you enough money to go home, but your filthy mouth has changed my mind. I don't care if you starve in the streets or have to sell yourself to the soldiers! You deserve whatever happens to you!"

She watched the smirk fade as Cora slowly rose to her feet, the lid of the Dutch oven forgotten in her hand. Augusta was so furious that she wanted to slap the wench and box her ears. Since she had vowed to control such un-Boyd-like feelings, and it was a promise she meant to keep, she spun on her heel and stalked away from the fire, moving into the darkness away from the camp and the temptation to slap Cora's face.

She didn't stop until she entered a copse of mature cottonwoods. After checking over her shoulder to make sure the distant fires of the camp were still within sight and she was in no danger of getting lost, she lifted her skirts and climbed a gentle incline toward a grassy rise at the top. At the highest point, she could see the broad expanse of the Platte flowing across starlit plains like a wide silver ribbon. Like so many things, the river's appeal was deceptive

Quicksand lurked beneath its shallow depths. It was too muddy to support bathing or drinking. Along this stretch, the water contained enough alkali to poison man and beast. Leaning against the trunk of a tree, Augusta glared at the sluggishly moving water and decided it was exactly like Cora. Deceptive, muddy-spirited, and poisonous.

"You shouldn't wander this far from camp, Miss Boyd. Especially alone, and never at night."

She jumped and her heart slammed in her chest. Whirling, she searched among the tree trunks, straining to see him among the shadows. "Where are you? Show yourself at once!" It was just like an Indian to creep up on a person and scare her half to death.

"Forgive me. I didn't intend to startle or frighten you." Webb stepped up beside her as the moon emerged from behind a slow-drifting cloud. Silvery light bronzed his skin and made his eyes appear lustrous and bottomless. A wandering night breeze toyed with the fringe on his jacket and leggings, ruffled the hair loose on his shoulders.

Augusta caught an involuntary breath and her fingers closed convulsively on the edges of her shawl. "Did you follow me?" she demanded in a whisper, gazing up at him. He stood too close, close enough that her skirts almost touched his leggings. A tremble of awareness began in her toes and jolted upward, shooting fingers of strange heat through her body.

Discovering herself alone with him, where no one could see or hear them, was her worst fear. And her constant fantasy. She feared he would rape and kill her. She fantasized that he would take her in his arms, crush her to his wide chest, and kiss her with such passion that both of them blazed like twin columns of fire. This fantasy held the power to bring perspiration to her brow and a violent blush to her cheek, though she hated such daydreams and was shamed by them.

"I saw you leave the camp." His strange accent emerged from the darkness like a caress, making everything he said seem exotic and disturbingly intimate. "I came to escort you back."

This was how her fantasy began, with these very words, spoken in the same dangerously intimate tone.

Weak with fear and anticipation, revulsion and yearning, Augusta sagged against the tree trunk, staring up at his mouth. Her breath quickened and her bosom rose and fell beneath her fingertips. Even as her lips dried, a shameless dampness flooded her secret woman parts.

She gazed at him helplessly. At this point in the fantasy, she stroked his hair. She wanted to know if it was coarse or soft. In the fantasy she did what she longed to do now, she ran her palms over his chest and shoulders, exploring the rocklike muscles she had seen bulging in the sunlight. And then he pulled her firmly against his body and she felt his hardness.

A dizzying feeling of faintness overcame her at the thought of his hard man's body pressed against hers.

Webb frowned at her, then she heard a sharp intake of

breath as he read and understood the yearning in her eyes. Slowly, giving her every opportunity to step away and stop him, he raised his hand to the braid trembling on her shoulder.

"I have never seen a more beautiful woman," he murmured in a low thick voice. Gently, he tugged her braid, drawing it through his palm. "You are gold in sunlight, silver in the moon."

This too he had done and said in her fantasy. She wet her lips and her mouth parted. Her breath emerged in tiny explosive gasps. When the back of his hand brushed her shoulder, she twitched as if lightning had scorched through her clothing and set her skin on fire.

For the first and only time in her life, Augusta burned for a man, wanted him, *needed* him to quench the fires he ignited within her body. She felt paralyzed, unable to move. Cataclysmic desire shook her frame, resonated through her body. Her bosom swelled with quickening breath, and she couldn't think, couldn't reason, didn't realize that her expression had gone slack and sensual, that her passion for him burned in her eyes.

"Oh, God," she whispered, her voice breaking on a half sob of despair and longing. She stared at the firm hard lines of his mouth, trembled violently in his shadow as he stepped forward.

Helplessly, she sagged against his chest as his arms came around her. Then she buried her hands in his hair and raised her trembling lips.

Mem didn't mean to spy on them.

She heard Augusta first, moving through the cottonwoods, and she froze in silence, listening hard, worried that it might be a stalking wolf. By the time she spotted Augusta standing atop the rise, glaring toward the river, it would have embarrassed them both for Mem to announce her presence. No one welcomed the knowledge that she was being observed unaware.

While Mem stood quietly, wondering if she could withdraw without calling attention to herself, Webb appeared out of the shadows, his arrival so silent that she had not heard his approach. Her first glad instinct was to call his name and press forward and join them. But before she spoke, she noticed the taut body postures and sensed an abrupt tension so heated that it almost crackled. The shout of greeting died on her tongue.

A minute passed and then it was too late. If she called out now or made a sudden noise, they would assume that she had been silently snooping. Damn. She was trapped into doing exactly what would have mortified her to contemplate. That she was in the appalling position of lurking in a dark patch of woods, spying on two people, shocked her nearly as deeply as the sickening realization that she could not look away.

Pressing a hand against her mouth, she stood as still as a stone and helplessly watched as Webb walked to the tree trunk Augusta leaned against. She couldn't overhear what they said to each other, but she didn't need to. The gist of their words reflected on Augusta's sensual expression.

Wistfully, Mem gazed at the moonlight shining luminous on Augusta's oval face and sudden tears swam in her eyes. Augusta Boyd in the moonlight was so beautiful that no mortal could hope to compete. Her face had softened and glowed with inner passion. Bathed in shimmering moonlight and trembling beneath Webb's intent gaze, she was a wood nymph, a fairy goddess, the quintessential male dream of beauty and sensuality.

And Webb . . . Mem saw him in profile, tall and strong, his shoulders swelling with desire. He stood wide-legged, his manhood rampant, his hair fluttering back from his face. He looked down at Augusta as if the world had vanished and only this woman remained, only this moment of tension and desire in the moonlight.

Mem bit her lip and lowered her head. She would have bargained the remainder of her life to have Webb Coate look at her as he looked at Augusta. And she would have flown into his arms as Augusta did. She would gladly have surrendered her virginity, her unknown bridegroom, her reputation, the rest of her life, to drink passionate kisses from Webb Coate's hard mouth, to sink to the ground in his arms and surrender to the rapturous mysteries only he could reveal.

But it was Augusta whom he kissed. Augusta's buttocks that he cupped and pulled roughly against his hips. Augusta who moaned and whimpered in his muscular arms.

And it hurt. The sight of their shared passion stabbed through Mem like a blade. Grinding her knuckles against her lips, she fought to smother a cry of pain, tried to focus her thoughts on her headache instead of the cause of it.

Two commands screamed inside her head. Forget Webb Coate. Run away before the pain of watching destroys you.

Whirling blindly, she ran crashing out of the cottonwoods and undergrowth, stumbling and tripping. Choking on tears, she fled toward the dying flicker of the campfires.

Webb held her against him so tightly that she could hardly breathe. Moving in a way that made her wild with urgency, he rubbed against her in an exciting, shocking grind of iron-hard manhood that she felt through her skirts and in the hot pit of her stomach. The volcanic thrill of what he was doing brought sweat to his brow and hers. Her pantaloons were wet with her readiness for him. So crazed with passion was she that she didn't notice her swollen lips or swelling breasts. All she thought about was the hard thrilling pressure of his manhood teasing her own need, driving her insane with wanting him.

Then she heard someone running through the underbrush.

Wrenching her lips from Webb's, she froze in horror. Her fingernails dug into his shoulders. "Someone's out there!"

"Whoever it is," he murmured in a husky voice, "he's moving away, not toward us."

Shock glazed her eyes. "Someone saw us!"

He smoothed a hand over her cheek; his thumb caressed her lips. "If he saw anything, it was only my back." His other hand rested high on her waist, just beneath her breast and her wildly beating heart. "He couldn't have seen you."

Augusta stared into black eyes smoldering with desire. She saw moonlight on darkly bronzed skin, saw his grandfather's nose and wide, contoured lips. She saw high broad cheekbones and fluttering black hair.

She saw an Indian.

Panic and revulsion exploded in her heart. An *Indian* had touched her, had kissed her. Shock sucked the strength out of her knees and she almost collapsed to the ground.

Oh, dear God. What had she done? Had she lost her mind?

Moonlight had destroyed her reason. She had allowed this dirty half-breed to place his hands on her body. He had dared to press his uncivilized, barbaric lips to the lips of a Boyd.

Drawing back, teeth bared, she slapped his face hard enough to snap his head to one side. Instantly, his hand dropped from her waist and he stepped backward. His expression shifted in the moonlight and shadows until only his burning eyes indicated the unexpectedness of her blow and his anger.

"You assaulted me!" she hissed, shaking with the horror of it. Frantically, she rubbed at her arms, trying to scrape off the touch of him, trying to scrub away the memory of his strong arms binding her close to his chest.

He said nothing. He stood silent and rigid, his stare piercing her. A cool breeze stirred his hair, teased along the fringes adorning his leggings and jacket. He stood so still that she could not see his chest move.

"You filthy savage!" She lashed the words at him, shaking so badly that she had to lean one hand on the tree trunk to remain standing. "How dare you touch a white woman? If I tell the others, they'll cut out your heathen heart! They'll hang you!"

His stare was so powerful that she almost faltered. Then she felt the moisture cooling on the pantaloons that rubbed her inner thighs and she could have wept for the hideous shame he had visited upon her.

"Barbarian! Rapist! I'll . . . if you ever come near me again, I'll . . ."

But he had faded into the darkness like a shadow. Frantically, she scanned the cottonwoods, searching for a trunk that appeared to move.

When she was certain that she was alone, she threw herself to the coarse grass and sobbed uncontrollably.

The hollowness of her threats devastated her. There was no circumstance under heaven that could force her to tell anyone what had happened here tonight. She would rather die than admit she had permitted an Indian to touch her.

And she could not claim that he had tried to rape her. Someone had seen Augusta Boyd step willingly into the arms of a filthy half-breed. Someone had seen her locked in his savage embrace, flushed with eagerness and desire.

Waves of shame and anguished regret rocked her body, and she wished the earth would open and swallow her. If only she knew who had spied on them, who had seen. If only she could explain somehow. If only she knew who it was, she would offer that person everything she owned to hold his or her tongue.

Fresh horror bit into her chest as she realized that someone in camp could destroy her with an innuendo, with a few words. A storm of weeping shook her frame.

She hated Webb Coate. This was his fault. She wished with all her suffering soul that he was dead.

Beating the ground with her fists, she wept and thought that she could not bear this latest tragedy. He was an *Indian*! A heathen who undoubtedly had never seen a tablecloth, who would have the table manners of an animal. Despite the cultured speech he mimicked, she just *knew* he couldn't read, couldn't even sign his name. What Indian could? Everything he owned, he carried on the back of his horse. He was nothing. A nobody!

And she had let this savage illiterate nobody, this worthless barbarian put his hands on her.

She wanted to die.

Cody glanced up from the arms wagon as Webb strode out of the darkness. The look in his burning black eyes caused the men around the fire to fall silent and exchange uneasy looks.

"Trouble?" Heck Kelsey asked, standing. He dropped a hand to the pistol at his waist.

Webb strode past them without speaking, moving toward the molasses wagons.

John Voss swallowed a last bite of cornbread, then also stood, his frown following Webb. "His gun's holstered," he observed. "Guess it ain't trouble that concerns us."

Cody flipped his cigar toward the fire pit. "Those who aren't on watch better turn in. It's a short night."

After the boys dispersed, he walked to the second molasses wagon and leaned against the back wheel, sensing Webb at the tail. He gazed at the stars, letting a minute pass. "You want to talk about it?"

"No."

Cody nodded and traced the Big Dipper, following to the North Star. He removed another cigar from his vest pocket, holding it between his fingers without searching for a light.

"Lucy Hastings died," he said finally.

Cody didn't know a single wagonmaster who had crossed the continent without burying a few passengers; an experienced master knew the grueling journey would exact a toll. But it never came easy. Death was always a shock. And the loss of a passenger felt like a personal failure.

He should have warned them not to drink ground water, just as he had warned them not to drink the alkali waters of the Platte. He should have chosen a different place to square the wagons. He should have found her earlier. He should have sent Miles Dawson to discover if there was a doctor on the train ahead or behind them. He should have been God.

Angrily, he glared at the cloudy sweep of the Milky Way. At the start of every journey he told himself that any passengers were merely high-paying freight. He told himself that he didn't care about their lives. His job was to get them where they had paid to go, not to nursemaid them, not to care about them.

But it didn't work. The trip was too long. They lived too closely together, too interdependently. Like it or not, want it or not, they came to know each other. And sometimes to care.

Damn it to hell, Lucy was only seventeen years old. In some societies, she would still have been regarded as a child. Scowling at the starlight, he saw her fresh smiling face. A preacher's daughter who sang hymns while she milked Sarah's cow, who read Bible verses when they stopped for the noon rest on Sundays. A pretty woman-child who gathered wildflowers while she walked, who laughed aloud at the antics of the prairie dogs.

She would never know a husband's embrace, would never hold her own child in her arms. Lucy Hastings's brief flame had flickered and died before her life had really begun.

The irony of Lucy Hastings's death was that without her, the bride train would never have formed. When her father, the Reverend Hastings, accepted young Reverend Quarry's request for Lucy's hand, he had worried about sending his daughter unaccompanied across the country. His concerns and Paul Quarry's response had resulted in Quarry organizing the bridegrooms' search for wives. Because her father and her fiancé had been concerned about Lucy's safety, Cody's train existed.

Without Lucy Hastings, none of the women on the train would have had bridegrooms waiting in Oregon. But Lucy's intended bridegroom was the only man among them who knew and loved his intended bride and would genuinely grieve her death.

Cody knew what Paul Quarry would feel. But at least Quarry's grief would not be scalded by the knowledge of betrayal.

His stomach tightened when he imagined Reverend Paul Quarry reading the letter Cody would post at Fort Laramie. Once, he had received a similar letter.

With a start he straightened and swore silently, then

walked around the end of the molasses wagon. Webb had gone.

For a long moment, he peered through the darkness toward the spot where Webb rolled out his blankets. It wasn't often that Webb allowed anything to penetrate his stoic serenity. Cody's gut instinct was to guess a woman. It had to be Augusta Boyd.

He shook his head. "To each his own preference." Hell, Webb would probably think Cody was mad if Webb knew how much time he wasted thinking about Perrin Waverly. Who was he to wonder at Webb's attraction to the selfish and imperious Miss Augusta Boyd?

Before turning in, he walked the perimeters of the camp, checking that all fires were extinguished, that the horses were securely tethered. When he reached Perrin Waverly's tent, he lingered beside the flap, picturing her inside asleep. This time he didn't indulge in any romanticized versions; he tried to picture her as she probably was. Dressed in her day gown, her braid unraveling, her lips slightly parted. It disturbed him to realize that reality was as arousing as the romanticized version.

What would he be feeling now if he were burying Perrin Waverly tomorrow morning instead of Lucy Hastings?

He stared down at the dusty tent flap. Never again did he intend to trust or give a woman the power to wound or destroy. It was a thousand times preferable to suffer an eternity of loneliness than to let some woman carve chunks out of his soul.

After a minute, he clenched his jaw and made himself stride away from her tent.

CHAPTER
* 12 *

My Journal, June, 1852. Lucy Hastings is dead. I looked at her for a long time, trying to understand why he was so upset. I never saw him alone with her.

I'm confused and more anxious every day. I'm afraid that he's sending me secret messages that I don't understand, so I think he's ignoring me. It must be that I fail to understand. Now I'm worried that he's disappointed in me, that I have failed him.

That would explain why he seems so eager to meet the whore every night. He's disappointed in me. He's punishing me. He wants me to see them together to test me.

Sometimes his silence makes me so furious that I want to punish him too. I imagine ways to do it. Then I get frightened by my thoughts and I have to punish myself. I resent that he does this to me, that he makes me think bad thoughts about him. Does he think I enjoy hurting myself?

My secret messages are plainer than his. I've left the cake and the ribbon. But his acknowledgment was so subtle that I didn't recognize it which made me wild inside.

I'm so angry, I'm furious at the oxen and the streams we have to cross. I hate the stinking sage and the prickly pear and the half cooked food and muddy water. I hate the noisy teamsters and Perrin Waverly and the haggard people we meet on the trail.

He's the only person who really knows me. Why is he doing this to me? His silence is cruel.

I'm so tired of waiting. Come to me, come to me, come to me.

"I wonder if we could walk a little," Perrin suggested, glancing back at Cora over her shoulder. Cora paced beside Augusta's wagon, wringing her hands in her apron and anxiously watching as Perrin joined Cody for their evening meeting.

Cody nodded curtly, then walked away from the squared wagons. Hurrying to catch up to his long strides, Perrin lifted her skirts away from the patches of prickly pear that plagued the entire Platte corridor. Every night she and Hilda spent an hour after supper picking thorns out of their hems and rubbing ointment on the scratches above their ankles. All the women hated the prickly pear. And the ubiquitous sage that ripped skirts and triggered sneezes. And the dust. And the lack of fresh water for bathing. And the afternoon heat, and . . .

Cody halted on a sandy rise, a dark silhouette against the blood-red sunset. He folded his arms across his vest.

"We're out of earshot," he said as she climbed toward him, then turned her face into the dying sun. As far as the eye could see, the western horizon burned scarlet, orange, and lavender. "What's so important that it couldn't be said back there?"

The vastness of sky and land overwhelmed Perrin, made her feel suddenly lost. The great prairie stretched endlessly before them, a featureless green and brown ocean tugged by dangerous and unseen currents. As this hour, crimson-dark shadows tiptoed across the immense expanse and she decided she had never seen anything so empty or so lonely as this terrible and beautiful country.

Dropping her head, she blinked down at the flap of leather tearing back from the side of her boots. This would be the second pair of soles she had worn out, walking behind the wagons. Sometimes it seemed frighteningly arrogant and desperately foolish to believe that a small group of humans and animals could cross this endlessly vast land one plodding step at a time.

"Perrin?"

Raising her head, she gazed into his eyes, into the blue of a thousand stormy skies. Cody's face was darkly tanned now. The creases splitting his cheeks seemed deeper tonight, still dusty from the day's travel. She studied him silently, wondering if he had been avoiding her, forcing their evening meetings to be as brief as possible, or if she only imagined it.

Drawing a breath, she gripped her hands together and forcefully told herself that she did not want to stroke his face and feel the softness of brown whiskery stubble beneath her palm. She didn't wonder about the texture of his skin or yearn to trace the contour of his lips with her fingertips.

"Cora Thorp wants to be a bride," she said.

Cody frowned at the sunset, his fists resting on his hips. "No."

"With Lucy gone . . ." She swallowed, finding it impossible to speak of Lucy's death. It was too terrible to think about. The memory of Lucy's lonely trailside grave would be painful for a long, long time. "There's an available bridegroom. . . ."

"The bridegrooms insisted on specific qualifications."

"No one works harder than Cora—you must have noticed that. We all felt sympathetic toward Jane Munger when Winnie couldn't help with the chores, but Cora has been doing everything herself all along. She's twenty-three. That's young enough to bear many children. She's the fourth of ten children, so she knows about families and babies. She's thin as a rail, but she's strong. Cora is exactly what those men in Oregon are looking for in a wife."

His steady gaze was unwavering. "First, Lucy's bridegroom knew and loved Lucy Hastings. Paul Quarry didn't want just a wife, he wanted Lucy. I doubt you can run in a substitution and expect him not to notice."

A rush of pink stained Perrin's throat. "That isn't—"

"Second, the Oregon men specified healthy, *educated* women. They're building for the future. They want women able to work hard, but equally important, they want educated women who will teach their children, who will bring culture to the community, who will polish the roughness off the edges of the territory. Cora Thorp is uneducated and about as polished as a granite chip. Bluntly speaking, Cora Thorp is a pair of hands and a strong back. The Oregon bridegrooms also want an educated mind."

Heat pulsed in Perrin's cheeks. "Is that how you and the bridegrooms see us? As callused hands and strong backs? A group of draft animals who can read and write?"

He stared at her. "That's stating it too callously. But if Cora had interviewed as a bride, I would have turned her away."

Perrin's hands curled into balls, and scarlet warmed her throat. "When the journey began, we had eleven brides. Were there only eleven bridegrooms?"

"No," he admitted after a reluctant pause. "There were twelve letters."

"So there's one hopeful bridegroom who isn't going to get a bride. Is that correct?"

He pushed back his hat, his strong features bathed in sunset red and orange. "Perrin, Cora isn't acceptable."

A spark of determination kindled in her eyes and her small chin set stubbornly. "Augusta intends to put Cora off the train at Fort Laramie and she refuses to give Cora any money to pay for her return passage to Chastity." Her eyes hardened as her voice sank to a throaty whisper. "Can you guess what will happen if Cora is abandoned at the fort with no money for food or shelter?"

Cody scowled into her flashing eyes. "This is between Cora and Augusta. The problem doesn't concern you or me."

"Yes, it does! I know what happens to a woman when she's left penniless. I know that brand of desperation all too well. I know what Cora will do just to stay alive, and I know how she'll feel about herself afterward. She will wear a taint for the rest of her life! We can't let that happen!"

"Damn it!" He slapped his hat against his thigh. "You don't recognize the word no. Why is it that other people's problems become something *we* must solve? That *we* can't allow to happen?"

Eyes locked to his, struggling not to let herself be distracted by the stomach flutter that always occurred when she gazed into his eyes, Perrin tried to frame an answer.

"I don't know why it's our problem, but it is," she said, frustrated by the question. She drew a breath. "If I can polish Cora a little, will that make a difference?"

"There's more to this than a clean skirt and how she holds a teacup. You know that."

They paced one direction, then the other, ending nose to nose, standing so close that Perrin inhaled the sweet tang of the venison he'd eaten for supper. She gazed at dying sunshine glowing in the soft fuzz on his chin and jaw, at the shining red highlights in his hair, and her heart rolled in her chest.

"Please, Cody," she whispered, yearning for him. Then she remembered what they were discussing and hoped he would mistake the sudden pink on her cheeks as an effect of the burning light. "All I ask is that you consider giving Cora a chance at a better life." She let her fingertips rest on his sleeve, unable to resist, then quickly withdrew them when she felt his muscled heat beneath the flannel. "Cora has been around Augusta for several years. She's undoubtedly picked up a lot of knowledge that she can use if she must. Please, I beg you to give her a chance. Don't abandon Cora in a military fort. Don't let that happen!"

His gaze dropped from her imploring eyes to her lips. "I didn't promise the bridegrooms a wife in the making, I agreed to furnish women ready-made to the qualifications they specified."

She noticed the pulse beating at the bronzed hollow of his throat and felt her breath involuntarily quicken. "Cora would be happy with so little. She'd work her fingers to the bone in return for a husband, a home of her own, and a brood of children. Just give her a chance. You gave Winnie a chance and look how well that turned out. Won't you please consider—"

She bit off the words, forgetting what she had intended to say. Cody stared into her eyes with a hard dangerous expression that mingled anger and desire. She smothered a gasp and felt her knees go weak.

"Damn it, Perrin. When you look at a man like that, it's hard to refuse you anything," he growled, his voice thick.

Her breath hitched in her throat and her heartbeat accelerated. Surely, she thought desperately, she hadn't heard him correctly. Uncertain, she wet her mouth and trembled at the sound that emerged from low in his throat as he watched her tongue dart over her lips. Unconsciously, she swayed toward him, drawn by the lean irresistible magnet that was Cody Snow.

"Then you'll let Cora be a bride? I've persuaded you?"

"Tell me something." His gaze traveled slowly over her flushed face, moving from brow to cheek to slightly parted lips. "Is this about Cora? Or about Augusta? I'm assuming if Cora changed status, she wouldn't remain in Augusta's wagon?"

Perrin's gaze steadied helplessly on his mouth. His lower lip was fuller than his upper lip. She hadn't noticed that before. "If Sarah agrees, Cora would like to take Lucy's place in Sarah's wagon," she whispered. Why couldn't she stop staring at his mouth?

"Augusta Boyd can no more drive a yoke of oxen than she can lasso a buffalo." He watched the pulse thudding at the opening of her collar. "If Augusta can't keep up with the train, it's she who'll have to remain in Fort Laramie."

Of course Perrin had realized that Augusta couldn't cope on her own. But she didn't let herself dwell on the possibility of Augusta leaving; the thought gave her too much shameful pleasure.

"I care what happens to Cora." She made a gesture of dismissal. "I don't care what happens to Augusta."

That wasn't entirely true. During the course of her twenty-six years, Perrin had learned that hatred could forge bonds as strong as love, could create a fascination as powerful as that which existed toward one held most dear. In that context, she did care what happened to Augusta Boyd. In her secret heart, she wanted Augusta to receive her comeuppance. And Perrin wanted to be there when it happened.

A sigh lifted her breast. "Will you at least think about allowing Cora to become one of the brides?"

Cody paced in front of the sunset panorama before he faced her and threw out his hands. "I'll think about it, damn it. But that's all, Perrin. I'll let you know my decision in three days, when we reach Fort Laramie. But don't promise Cora anything. I'm against this."

"Thank you!" If she hadn't known Cora and others might be watching, she would have flung herself against his chest and kissed him in gratitude.

Imagining it swept her breath away. She would kiss him and kiss him until she was drunk and dizzy with kisses, until she burned beneath his lips. She would press against his body until she felt his manhood steely between them, until they were both damp and gasping. She would . . . She caught herself with a sharp intake of breath.

Why did he obsess her like this? Why did the sight of him astride his horse make her feel weak inside? Why did her stomach flutter when she watched him pace along the wagon line shouting orders? What made her heart fly around inside her chest when she spotted him standing alone and hipshot against the evening sky?

Through word and action Cody had made it clear that he wanted no woman in his life. And Perrin was promised to a stranger in Oregon. Cody wasn't going to change and suddenly welcome a tarnished bride-to-be into his world. Plus, Perrin lacked extra funds to buy herself out of the marriage she had agreed to undergo. There was nothing between them but a chance meeting long ago, and now this journey.

That was all there could be.

Anything more would be fleeting and beyond the pale of decency. Perhaps a night of lust, an accident of loneliness and momentary need.

A shudder of apprehension rippled down Perrin's spine. A relationship with Cody Snow, no matter how exciting or how fulfilling, would become common knowledge within the small society of the train. She would irrevocably blacken herself with the others. She would unravel any progress she might have gained toward redeeming herself with the brides from Chastity, Missouri.

She couldn't risk that outcome. These women would be her neighbors for the remainder of her life. They might eventually forgive her for Joseph Boyd—possibly—but they would never forgive a second lapse, a lustful dalliance with Cody Snow.

Straightening her spine, regret and sorrow in her eyes, she stepped away from the heat and the scents of him and forced her thoughts to Cora. "I will proceed in the belief that you will not abandon a young woman to the soldiers' brothels, Mr. Snow."

"Perrin? Damn it, come back here!"

"I'm confident you'll reach the right decision," she called over her shoulder.

Cora ran forward as Perrin descended the rise, the blood-red sky behind her. "Lordy, lordy. There was all that to-ing and fro-ing, you walking after him, then him walking after you." Cora wrung her hands and peered anxiously into Perrin's face. "He said no, didn't he? He ain't going to let me be no bride! I just knew it! I ain't good enough for them swells in Oregon!"

Perrin caught Cora's fluttery hands in hers. "He said he'd think about it."

"He's just going to say no later!"

Biting her lip, Perrin gazed at the lone figure pacing angrily before a tableau of crimson and ink. "We have a lot to accomplish before we reach Fort Laramie. A lot to arrange." She turned to study Cora's pale anxious face. "First things first. We'll speak to Sarah."

Sarah eased her back against her hands. "You want to move from Augusta Boyd's wagon to mine. You'll ride with Hilda during the day if that works out, and Perrin will ride with me, but when we halt for the night, you'll return here and help with my chores? Is that the gist of it?"

"Yes, ma'am," Cora said, bobbing her head. "I'm a good worker, Mrs. Jennings. I can cook and bake. I can set up the tent in no time flat. I can . . ."

But it wasn't Cora whom Sarah Jennings examined with a coolly speculative expression. And this was more than Sarah's usual resistance to anything Perrin suggested. Perrin understood that she stood as the obstacle to Sarah's acquiescence.

When Cora's voice ran down, she said quietly to Sarah, "I'll walk behind the wagons when it's your turn to drive the oxen, and you can walk behind when it's my turn to drive. We needn't have more contact than is absolutely necessary."

Sarah had the breeding to blush. She waved a hand, then shrugged. "I miss Lucy, and it's hard on a person to drive all day with no relief." She still looked at Perrin. Then she sighed. "If the others agree to this project, then I'll do my part."

But she didn't appear happy about it. Still, Perrin thought, one of the necessary pieces had fallen into place. Concentrating on the positive, she thanked Sarah profusely, then went in search of Hilda with Cora trotting anxiously behind her.

They found Hilda on the banks of the Platte, scrubbing a stew pot beneath dusky shadows that deepened toward night.

Hilda's broad face widened into a cheerful smile as she listened to Perrin's request. "*Ja*, education is always good." She inspected Cora as if judging her capacity to learn. "You say you can read and write a bit already. I will teach you to do it well. This, I will enjoy. It will be more interesting than squinting through the dust at the back of another wagon."

Perrin smiled her gratitude. "What's required most urgently is to improve Cora's speech. She needs to sound more educated."

Determination hardened Hilda's brown eyes. She drew to her full height and became the formidable figure who had commanded the classrooms of Chastity, Missouri. "We begin at once."

Cora shrank like a small dark child standing in the shade of a sturdy blond Viking. Awed, and enormously intimidated, she swallowed twice, then nodded. "I'll do my best, Miss Clum."

"Yes, you will." Hilda pointed to a spot near the willows. "Sit. You can scrub the bread pan while we refresh your ABC's."

Perrin smiled, then lifted her skirts and went in search of Thea.

"Why should Thea teach a crude gravedigger's daughter the womanly graces?" Ona Norris demanded. "None of us would nod to Cora Thorp if we passed her in the street! We'd have no contact with such a creature if it weren't for this journey." Her expression added that the same dismissal applied to Perrin.

Perrin glanced at Thea's stricken expression, then returned to Ona. "Is that you speaking, Miss Norris, or is it Miss Boyd?"

The firelight leaping in their cook pit shadowed Ona's face and made her scowl appear deeper. "I shall overlook your rudeness and say only that I am capable of forming my own opinion!"

"And are you?" Perrin asked Thea softly. "Or do you agree with Ona that Cora Thorp is undeserving of our assistance?"

Thea's pretty face pinched into indecision. Ona was her wagon mate; agreeing to Perrin's proposal would create dissension between them.

"What would you have me do?" she inquired uneasily, aware that Ona had stiffened into a frieze of disapproval.

"You have a beautiful singing voice. I'd hoped you might teach Cora to sing. And perhaps to sketch a little. Embroidery is a refined skill she might find useful. Many of us admire your aptitude for the gentle arts."

Thea worried her lower lip between her teeth and considered the buffalo chips burning in the fire pit. The chips burned like peat and didn't smell as unpleasant as dried cow pies. At first everyone had expressed disgust at the necessity of gathering dried dung as they walked behind the wagons. Now they were grateful to find any fuel on this treeless plain.

Finally Thea raised apologetic eyes. "I can't teach anyone to sketch or paint who has no talent, Mrs. Waverly. And singing lessons are useless unless the student has a gift for singing. As for embroidery, well, it's Ona who . . . but she . . ." Thea's voice faded into red-cheeked discomfort.

"I understand," Perrin said quietly. Without another word, she left their fire.

"I couldn't possibly," Bootie protested, her hands fluttering through the deepening shadows.

Mem, who had scarcely spoken a word since Perrin's arrival, looked up sharply from the mending filling her lap. "Oh, for heaven's sake. You're refusing before you even know what the favor might be. Don't you have better manners than that?"

"Well, I swan, Mem Grant. It's so rude to chastise your own sister in front of . . . ah . . . in front of . . ."

Mem stood and moved to lean against the wagon's sideboard. She shoved at a wave of auburn hair falling across her forehead. "Don't pretend you can't guess why Perrin is here. Everyone's talking about what she's trying to do for Cora. Your precious Augusta, of course, is outraged." She returned Bootie's glare, then lifted her chin in Perrin's direction. "If there's anything I can do, you only have to ask."

Perrin glanced at her in surprise. When Mem had spoken of Augusta in previous conversations, she had done so with a tone of good-natured contempt. Tonight, there was something new in her voice, something angry and almost bitter.

"Actually, you both can help." She faced Bootie and arranged a smile on her lips. "If Cora becomes a bride, well, her clothes are wrong, and she doesn't own anything that would serve as a wedding dress. You have such wonderful style, Mrs. Glover, that I thought . . . well, I hoped you would take Cora's wardrobe in hand and see what you could do to make her presentable."

"Me?" Bootie blinked and a little starch came into her spine. She considered for a moment. "Well, I do have style, that's true." Her fingers preened the grimy lace collar at her throat. "I've always designed my own gowns. Mem's too." A look at Mem suggested that her efforts were largely wasted. "Oh, dear. Material! Where will we get the material we'll need?"

Perrin repressed a smile. "Perhaps Mem will accept the task of locating fabric. Surely most of us have a gown we can spare, something that might be refashioned for Cora. Or a length of cloth, some draperies, something that would serve."

Bootie tapped a finger against her chin, thinking, already flattered into compliance. "We'll need a good bonnet. Mr. Kelsey might be persuaded to make a frame, and we'll have to find trimmings. Then there's hair!" She rolled her gray eyes. "I swan, Cora's hair looks like a bird's nested inside. I'll have to do something with her hair. Then we have to think about . . ."

Before Perrin left their fire, she managed a word alone with Mem. Rocking back on her heels, she studied Mem's handsome face and the underlying bone structure. Mem would never be a beauty, but the years would be kind to her. When the beauty of her contemporaries had faded, Mem would still be striking.

"You seem rather listless lately. Are you well? Are the headaches severe?"

"No worse than usual," Mem said uncomfortably. Turning her head, she gazed toward the men gathered around Smokey Joe's cook wagon, then turned back to Perrin. "Do you ever wonder if it's morally right to marry a man whom you don't know and for whom you have no feelings?"

"Isn't it rather late to be asking that kind of question?" Perrin inquired in surprise.

Mem smoothed her hand along the edge of the sideboard. "When I read the advertisement for Oregon brides, all I thought about was the journey and what a wonderful adventure it would be. But lately, I've been thinking about Mr. Sails, my bridegroom. I'm wondering about . . . well, very unladylike things." She glanced up with a short embarrassed laugh. "I'm thinking there must be a large difference between offering oneself to a man one loves or surrendering to the affections of a man toward whom one feels ambivalent." Her cheeks flushed as coppery bright as her hair. "Is there?" she whispered, her eyes large and anguished.

"Oh, Mem," Perrin said softly. "Being Mrs. Sails is going to be the greatest adventure of all. There will be good times, exciting time, bad times, and discouraging times. But Mr. Sails will come to love you, I know he will. How could he not? You're intelligent and handsome, a skilled homemaker, capable, and wonderfully curious. There isn't a nonsense bone in your body. You're practical, and—"

"Perrin . . . that isn't what I asked."

"No, it isn't." She gazed into Mem's troubled brown eyes, and her voice sank. "The difference between lying with a man you love and one you don't is the difference between heaven and hell."

Mem trembled in the darkness. "That's what I feared," she whispered.

An hour before dawn the first gunshot exploded through Cody's dream. A fusillade of answering shots rang in his ears as he burst out of his tent and sprinted toward the arms and molasses wagons. Cutting through the middle of the squared wagons, he pushed through panicked animals and shoved bullets into his pistols as he ran.

The animals would have told him something was wrong even if the gunshots had not. Oxen, cattle, Smokey Joe's mules, and the teamsters' horses snorted, pawed, butted one another, then stampeded forward, sweeping Cody along. At once he understood a breech had opened in the square and the animals were flooding out onto the prairie.

Shouting and swearing, he fought through the surging mass and emerged behind the arms wagon. Dropping to the ground, he rolled beneath the wheels, his pistols in his hands.

"What the hell happened?" he shouted at Miles Dawson.

He couldn't see a goddamned thing through the dark and the dust kicked up by the animals spilling onto the plains. The noise of bawling animals, intermittent gunshots, and screams from the tents muffled Dawson's reply and he had to shout again.

Dawson crawled closer. "Bill Macy and Jeb Holden are both dead," he shouted in Cody's ear. Macy and Holden had been posted to the night watch. "One of the molasses wagons is gone. Stolen."

Instantly Cody understood he faced a crucial decision. He could pursue whoever had stolen the wagon, or he could order his men to round up the animals before they scattered to the four winds. He didn't have enough men to do both.

The need to chase the bastards who had invaded his camp and killed Bill Macy and Jeb Holden burned in his gut. But the last thing he needed was a bunch of women stranded out here with no oxen to pull their wagons.

"It was Indians!" Miles Dawson shouted in his ear, choking on the dust billowing beneath the wagon as the animals ran past them. "I saw them."

In this area, that meant Sioux. But Dawson's claim didn't hold water. There was unrest among the Sioux, but so far attacks on the wagon trains had been intermittent and directed at stealing animals, not wagons. And it was a safe bet that had the intruders been Indians bent on stealing something other than horses or cattle, they would have stolen the arms wagon, not a molasses wagon. The Sioux Cody knew would have scouted the train thoroughly before a shot was fired. That was another point. The Sioux had guns, but not enough to equip every warrior. He should have seen a few arrows if he was looking at an Indian raid.

Webb Coate hit the ground behind them and rolled under the wagon beside Cody.

"Six white men," he said between his teeth, squinting into the dust. "Painted and dressed like Dakota Sioux."

Cody's mind raced. With Macy and Holden dead, he had six men left, counting Smokey Joe, who couldn't shoot the side of a barn if he was standing in front of it. If he pursued the killers and thieves, he would be one man short of an even match.

He stared at the hooves thundering past his line of vision, churning up the darkness. "Jake Quinton," he said, spitting the name.

Webb nodded. "That's my guess."

CHAPTER
* 13 *

While Cody, Webb, Miles Dawson, and John Voss scoured the plains searching for lost animals, Smokey Joe and Heck buried the young teamsters, Bill Macy and Jeb Holden. Sarah delivered a eulogy, and Thea sang two hymns, her clear voice sweet and sad. After Heck Kelsey delivered a final prayer, Perrin cleared her throat and announced tersely, "We need to have a meeting."

Everyone, even Augusta, followed Perrin back to her wagon. Standing against the tailgate, she faced the brides, and this time she was too angry to be nervous.

"I spoke to Mr. Snow at first light." Anger was more comfortable than what she usually felt when she thought about Cody and she nursed it along. "First, we were not attacked by Indians, as you may have heard, but by men posing as Indians."

"One would expect Mr. Coate to protect his own by claiming the killers weren't savages," Augusta objected sharply.

Perrin ignored the remark. "Mr. Snow believes the outlaws' leader is a man named Jake Quinton. I'm not privy to the details, but apparently Mr. Snow and Mr. Quinton have a long and unpleasant history going back to Mr. Snow's army days."

"Jake Quinton? Good heavens! I met that man!"

The women turned as one to stare at Bootie Glover. Stammering and blushing bright pink, she related the incident at Addison's farm, her gaze darting apologetically from face to face. "So I just . . . well, Mr. Quinton said he knew Mr. Snow, he called him Captain Snow like many people do, so I . . ."

Sarah placed both hands on her hips and her mouth pursed in an incredulous expression. "Did you tell a stranger that we were transporting molasses and arms?" she demanded.

"I don't recall exactly what . . ." Bootie shot an imploring glance toward Mem, seeking help, but Mem appeared thunderstruck. She stared at Bootie as if she couldn't believe her ears.

Augusta tossed her head and narrowed her eyes. "I tried to warn her not to speak to that reprobate!" Accusation thinned her lips and she stared at Bootie. "Now look what you've done! If you had listened to me, those poor teamsters would still be alive!"

"Oh, my Lord!" Shock blanched the color from Bootie's lips and face and she would have collapsed if Hilda hadn't caught her by the elbows. "Oh, no! They're dead because of *me*?"

"We don't know that," Perrin interjected quickly. She threw Augusta a look of disgust. "What we do know is that two young men died trying to protect a wagonload of molasses barrels." She paused and frowned at the faces peering back at her. "Does this seem strange to anyone else?"

"Strange in what way?" Jane asked, still staring at Bootie.

Sarah nodded. "It's always seemed peculiar that our bridegrooms and Mr. Snow think there's profit in molasses. The profit must be so slim as to be negligible."

"I've wondered about that too," Perrin agreed. "Now I'm starting to doubt whether it's really molasses we're carrying."

"That is an offensive implication." Ona Norris crossed her arms over her bosom. "Captain Snow would not deceive us."

"Really?" Perrin snapped. "Men have made a virtue of deceiving women for centuries!" She had yet to meet a man she could rely on. Men lied and used as a matter of course.

Mem frowned. "Let's suppose you and Sarah are correct. If there's slim profit in molasses, then it follows that no one would want to steal it. So what are we hauling?"

"There's one way to find out." Perrin reached inside the back of her wagon and removed a hatchet. "Shall we?"

A chorus of suddenly angry voices urged her onward. In a body they converged on the remaining molasses wagon and Sarah and Perrin climbed onto the tailgate. Perrin drew back the canvas covering and everyone contemplated the stacked barrels stamped MOLASSES in red letters.

Perrin and Sarah looked at each other for a moment, then, heart beating loudly in her chest, Perrin drew a breath and swung the hatchet to knock the bung off one of the barrels.

She wanted Cody to have told them the truth; she wanted him to be the exception among the men she had known. It surprised her how much she longed to be wrong about her suspicions. But thin dark liquid trickled over the tailgate and spilled onto the ground. All she had to do was inhale to know it wasn't molasses.

"Whiskey!" Sarah said loud enough for all to hear. The fumes were unmistakable.

"This is not right! We should have been told!" Crimson flooded Hilda's cheeks and she threw out her hands. "Now that I know we've been carrying arms *and* whiskey, I am surprised we have not been waylaid before! I am furious!"

Heck Kelsey appeared at a run, skidding to a stop when he spotted the dripping barrel and the sea of accusing faces that turned to confront him.

"Did you know about this?" Hilda demanded, moving toward him like an enraged Valkyrie. "Did everyone know but us?"

"Ah," he said uncomfortably, reversing his course. He backed away from Hilda's advance. "Mr. Snow will be mighty displeased when he sees what you ladies have done here."

"Is that so!" Sarah shouted from the tailgate. "Well, you can just tell him that *we* are mighty displeased!"

"I, for one, am outraged!" Augusta snapped, pushing forward. "It's bad enough to place our lives at risk by transporting arms. But whiskey? Whiskey is a magnet to immoral men. Men who would not dream of stealing a gun would steal a barrel of whiskey in an eyeblink! We are going to be in danger all the way to Oregon!"

Murmurs of agreement buzzed like the sound of angry hornets. Heck Kelsey stepped backward and raised his hands. "This isn't my affair. You'll have to take it up with Mr. Snow," he said before he turned and fled rapidly toward the cook wagon.

Seething, her dark eyes snapping, Perrin faced the brides and waited for silence. "Mr. Snow believes Jake Quinton stole the wagon and killed the teamsters. Quinton must have figured it had to be something other than molasses too." She examined the angry faces glaring back at her. "We need to decide what we're going to say to Mr. Snow." They followed her scowl toward the plains, where three dark specks galloped after stray animals.

"I don't know what we say to Mr. Snow." Cora shook her head. "But watching that whiskey soak into the ground is like watching money drip away. A downright shame, if'n you ask me."

"I agree." Sarah dusted her hands briskly. "Fetch your cups, ladies. Last night and this morning have been a real trial; I'd say we all deserve a drink."

"Of whiskey?" Augusta gasped, appalled.

"Acquired a taste for it when I was in the army," Sarah said. She laughed. "Major Jennings, my late husband, always said whiskey tasted bad but felt good. Right now I could use a little feeling good. It was a bad night, and it's been one hell of a morning." Her gaze dismissed Augusta's gasp of disapproval. "Sometimes a swear word is the only word that will do."

"I've wondered what whiskey tastes like," Mem commented. "I've never had anything stronger than brandy." She joined Bootie, who leaned against the wagon yoke, weeping. "You could use a strong drink too."

"Oh, Mem," Bootie whispered, tears spilling down her cheeks. "When that man . . . I just didn't think! I didn't mean . . ."

"I know you didn't, and what happened isn't your fault. You couldn't possibly have guessed that Quinton was an outlaw and a killer." Mem placed an arm around her sister's shoulder and squeezed. Over Bootie's head she shot a venomous glare at Augusta. "Come on, we'll fetch our cups, sample a little whiskey, and we'll put this out of our minds."

When Perrin tasted the whiskey, it seared her throat and made her eyes water. Having never tasted anything stronger than sherry, she gasped, sputtered, then grinned weakly as the others applauded. Mem was next. She clasped her throat, coughed, blinked, then gamely swallowed another sip to shouts of laughter. Each had a turn at being the focus of tension-relieving laughter except Augusta and Ona, who looked on with steely-eyed censure.

When everyone had sampled the fiery whiskey, Perrin cleared her throat and spoke in a husky, liquor-choked voice. "You've had some time to think, so what shall I say to Mr. Snow?"

"You're our leader . . . what do you suggest?" Winnie asked.

For a moment Perrin couldn't respond. This was the first time anyone had referred to her as a leader, or had acknowledged that her opinion was worth hearing or considering. She gazed at their expectant faces and swallowed back sudden emotional tears.

"I know exactly what I'd like to say to Mr. Snow," she said when she could speak.

For the first time, they listened carefully. And to complete her small and very personal triumph, they all agreed with her. Even Augusta and Ona.

Leaving Webb and John to run the animals back into the square, Cody rode the camp perimeters to check on his passengers. His unease deepened as he passed one empty wagon after another.

By the time he trotted up to the cook wagon, his chest had tightened like sun-baked leather. "Where the hell are the women?" he demanded, halting in front of Heck and Smokey Joe.

Smokey Joe thumbed back his hat and grinned. "You got big trouble, Capt'n."

"Damn it, Smokey. Where the hell are they?"

Smokey Joe jerked a thumb over his shoulder. "Heck says they're over at the molasses wagon." His grin widened.

Leaning forward, Cody touched his bootheels to the buckskin's flanks and raced toward the molasses wagon. Smokey Joe's grin never portended anything pleasant. He reined hard when the whiskey fumes hit his face. Then he saw them.

Perrin Waverly, Bootie Glover, and Thea Reeves lay facedown on the prairie, sprawled out like they'd dropped where they'd been shot, which was his first chest-tightening fear. Only when he heard Bootie snore and saw one of Perrin's wool stockings twitch did he realize they were alive.

Relief collapsed his chest and made his thighs slacken. He had to tighten the reins to keep the buckskin from bolting away from the strong fumes wafting out of the wagon. Slowly, disbelieving, he swung from the women lying facedown on the dirt toward the raucous sound of singing.

Sarah perched on the edge of the tailgate, her stockinged feet swinging like a child's. She was singing loud, bawdy military songs to Mem and Cora, who held on to each other, weeping with hysterical laughter. Cody frowned. Sarah would be mortified when she recalled that she had sung such vulgar ditties, and Mem and even Cora would be appalled that they had laughed and shouted for more. *If* they remembered.

Hilda and Jane had collapsed spraddle-legged on the ground. They leaned against the back wheel of the molasses wagon, propped against each other, dead asleep. Hilda had vomited in her lap.

Finally he spotted Winnie. She sat Indian-fashion on the bare prairie, a tin cup cradled in her lap. She faced east, staring toward home while huge silent tears rolled down her cheeks. She was chanting Willie or Billie over and over in a singsong voice.

Closing his eyes, Cody rubbed a hand down his jaw. They were all stone-dead drunk.

After taking another look at Perrin's exposed legs, he

wheeled the buckskin and returned to Smokey's cook fire. Smokey handed him up a grin and a cup of coffee laced with whiskey.

"Figure you could use a little bone tightening, Capt'n."

Cody swallowed the coffee and whiskey in one gulp, ignoring the scald as it burned down his throat. "Heck, if there's any whiskey left in that barrel, replace the bung. Then you and Smokey put the women in their wagons to sleep it off."

He frowned in frustration and slapped a hand against his saddle. He had two dead men. They'd lost half a day rounding up the animals. They would lose the remainder because the brides were too damned drunk to drive. Due to fog, swollen streams, and Lucy's death, they were already running a week behind schedule.

When it occurred to him that a couple of the brides were unaccounted for, he rode around the square, eventually coming to Ona Norris's tent. He found Augusta and Ona sitting in camp chairs on the shady side of the wagon, sipping tea. They were sober, but they might have been sucking lemons for the looks on their faces. Neither of them greeted him.

There were a dozen things he might have said. But he couldn't think of any of them. He stared at them; they stared coldly back.

Finally he glanced at the sky. "The temperature's dropping. It's going to hail. Another day wasted."

Swearing under his breath, he rode to check on the animals, feeling the women staring icily at his back.

Smokey Joe's rise-and-shine gong ratcheted through Perrin's head like a series of clanging explosions. She awoke to find herself on the floor of the wagon, aching in every joint. Hilda's knee was in her face. Slowly, they sat up, clasping their heads and whimpering.

Squinting, Perrin peered at Hilda, who was in greater disarray than Perrin had ever seen her. One braid had come unraveled and tangled blond waves dropped to Hilda's waist.

Her skirt reeked and had stiffened with dried vomit. Bits of prairie grass clung to her gown and her loose hair.

"Ach! I am disgusting!" Hilda moaned, staring down at herself. She inhaled, then looked as if she might be ill again.

When she inventoried her own state, Perrin groaned. Dirt and grime caked her face; her stockings had twisted around her legs. A rip opened along her skirt seam, and she'd lost a shoe. Her eyes felt gritty and her mouth tasted so horrible that she gagged. She would have sold a portion of her soul for a hot bath.

Without speaking, their faces grim, she and Hilda changed clothing, then slowly emerged into a chilly overcast morning. Hilda sniffed the scent of frying bacon drifting from Smokey Joe's fire and her face turned green. She dashed for a clump of plum bushes, holding her stomach.

Leaning over the water barrel, Perrin scrubbed her cheeks until they burned, tried to comb the dirt and grass out of her hair, then kindled their fire and hung a pot of coffee over the flames. She didn't bother stirring up a batch of johnnycakes; Hilda wouldn't eat anything and neither could she.

Thirty minutes later, partially fortified by two cups of strong coffee, she tottered to her feet, drew a deep breath of courage, and went in search of Cody Snow. Two by two, the brides fell into step behind her. They were all shamefaced and bleary-eyed except Augusta and Ona, who refused to look at the others except with self-righteous disgust.

When Perrin spotted Cody, saddling the buckskin, she veered toward him, struggling to hold her head up. Each step on the uneven ground jarred her brain and made her wince. The only thing that offered the slightest pleasure was seeing Cody's soaring eyebrows when he noticed all the brides advancing on him. To give him credit, he recovered quickly and strode forward to meet them. Halting, he folded his arms over his chest.

"Well?" he asked coolly, studying Perrin's white face and shaking hands. Anger flickered in the depths of his eyes.

His attitude made it easy. How dare he use that tone of

voice, as if *they* needed to explain themselves. "You deceived us!" she snapped angrily. Murmurs of assent lifted from the women behind her.

The fury that trembled on her lips was personal. She had wanted Cody to be different. She had begun to believe that he was. But he was like the other men she had known. Deceivers, all of them. Instead of the truth, a man said what a woman wanted to hear. And when he was caught, he insisted that the woman was in the wrong, never him.

"You lied to us!" she accused, spitting the words at him.

"Would you ladies have slept better knowing you were carrying arms *and* whiskey?" His calm tone infuriated her.

"Don't try to blame us for your deceit! We should have been told!" She resonated with the heat of past deceptions.

She told herself this was not Garin Waverly exploiting a young girl's loneliness with honeyed words. This was not Joseph Boyd manipulating her sympathy and gratitude. This was Cody Snow, who had treated her fairly and straightforwardly. Until now. But nothing she said to herself lessened her anger at him for being revealed as a deceiver like the others.

"We refuse to risk our lives by traveling all the way to Oregon with arms and whiskey." Because she had allowed herself to begin to trust this man, his deception cut all the deeper.

"Is that right?" Cody's eyes narrowed dangerously and his hands dropped to lean hips and tightened into fists.

Perrin leaned forward from the waist. "That's right!"

"And what do you propose to do with your bridegroom's investment? Abandon the wagons beside the trail?"

"We demand that you sell the arms and whiskey in Fort Laramie." Another chorus of agreement sounded. Strong conviction asserted itself against the morning ravages of strong drink.

Cody swept them with a silencing glare. "That is not an option. If there are two things a military post has an abundance of, it's arms and whiskey. Our freight will fetch three times the price in Oregon, and that's where it's going."

Perrin thrust out her chin and sparks flashed in her eyes. "Then we aren't."

Cody's shoulders jerked and he stared at her. He hadn't expected this. After studying her unyielding scowl, he lifted his gaze to the other women. Their faces were equally determined.

"We don't have time to waste on foolishness. Put out your fires and get in your wagons. We'll depart in ten minutes." One or two of the brides started to turn away, but Perrin's voice stopped them.

"No," she said firmly, her refusal ringing in the crystal air. "We aren't going anywhere until we have your promise that you'll dispose of the whiskey and the arms in Fort Laramie. That's our condition for proceeding."

"You aren't going to get it," he snapped.

Spinning on the heel of a worn pair of shoes, she marched through the aisle opened for her by the brides. They glared at him, then closed ranks behind her, united in their decision and determination. Shoulders stiff, they returned to their wagons, presumably to search for headache elixirs.

Cody signaled Smokey Joe to announce it was time to mount the wagons. Smokey's dinner gong banged out the call, and Cody finished saddling his horse, giving them time to take their places. Then he waved his hat and shouted, "Waaaaagons, hoooo!"

The wagons didn't move. No one stirred. The oxen didn't turn out of the square and plod toward the trail.

Cody sat on his horse, scowling. He and feisty little Mrs. Waverly had come head to head. She had instigated a mutiny.

"Well, we'll see how things look after she's had a day to sit on that pretty little butt and think about it," he muttered as Webb rode up beside him.

He hadn't overlooked the significance of the brides' united support, but his anger focused on Perrin. Grinding his teeth, he rode toward his two remaining teamsters, shouting orders.

An hour later, Perrin noticed without much interest that Miles Dawson and John Voss were unyoking the oxen. As the day wore on, a few of the women summoned the energy to bake bread or roll out pies. Winnie and Cora wandered off in search of ripe plums. Everyone else nursed aching heads or dozed on the shady side of their wagons and swore never again to sample whiskey. Everyone wished they had access to clean water and a bath. But all they had was the dirty Platte, not fit for man nor beast.

From time to time throughout the day Perrin glimpsed Cody talking to the men, gesturing angrily. He rode out with Webb and a few hours later returned with enough antelope that Smokey Joe gave each of the wagons a chunk of fresh meat for the stew pots. Near suppertime, she spotted Cody standing with Webb, studying the remaining whiskey wagon.

The very best part of the day was when each of the brides found a reason to stop by Perrin's wagon and then praise her for standing up to Cody and reassure her that they were united in their position. When Augusta appeared, Perrin froze, dumbstruck.

Ostensibly, Augusta came to return a cup of sugar that neither Perrin nor Hilda could recall having lent her.

"I guess we showed *him* a thing or two," she said firmly, pouring her cup into the sugar sack that Hilda held open. "He'll not endanger *our* lives!" This was the closest Augusta would ever come to voicing approval of something Perrin had done.

Perrin nodded, and waited. Because, of course, Augusta, being Augusta, couldn't leave it at that.

She gave Perrin a cold stare. "I know what you're trying to do with Cora," she said sharply. "You want to keep her with the train as an annoyance to me."

Perrin leaned away from the bread dough she kneaded at the sideboard. With the back of one floury hand, she pushed at a strand of loose hair.

"I want to keep Cora on the train so she won't ruin herself in order to eat, find shelter, or buy her passage home," she said bluntly. "Cora will remain with you until Fort Laramie, then she'll move to Sarah's wagon. Since you can't care for yourself, I expect it will be you who leaves us once we reach the fort."

"Oh, you'd like that, wouldn't you?" Augusta growled, baring her teeth.

"It wouldn't break my heart," Perrin snapped.

"Well, it isn't going to happen. I intend to engage a new maid at the fort!"

Perrin forced her jaw to relax, made her fists open. "Somehow I doubt you'll find many maids in a military post."

"You forget . . . I'm a Boyd!" Holding her skirts close as if being near Perrin might contaminate her, Augusta swept away, red circles flaming high on her cheeks.

Perrin watched her go, then returned to the bread dough, cuffing it across the sideboard as if she were slapping the superior expression off of Augusta Boyd's smug face.

Throughout the day, she continued to catch glimpses of Cody and expected him to request a meeting. But he didn't.

On the morning of the third day, Cody walked toward the sunrise, then swore and flung his hat to the ground. Tilting his head back, he sucked in a long breath of cool morning air.

"Did you put out the word that every day lost on this foolishness is going to hurt us at the end of the journey?"

Heck Kelsey, Miles Dawson, and John Voss nodded solemnly. Webb stood to one side, hands in his back pockets, watching the sun push over the horizon.

"We told them about the snow and how we're trying to beat it," Heck murmured. He shook his head. The others did the same.

"Hellfire and damnation!" Fury and frustration exploded inside Cody's chest. Two trains had passed ahead of them while they were stuck here. With every minute, they fell further and further behind schedule.

"We're going to experience sanitary problems if we remain at this site another day," Webb commented, his gaze on the sunrise. "The animals have eaten every blade of grass. The water barrels are low. There isn't a buffalo chip within two miles; there won't be any fires tomorrow."

Cody stared at the crosses marking the graves of Bill Macy and Jeb Holden. The women had covered the mounds with stones and wildflowers. Heck had carved the teamsters' names on pieces of scrap lumber. The graves were a constant rebuke, reminding Cody that he should have done something differently. He should have hanged Jake Quinton when he'd had the opportunity.

"Them women got you beat, Capt'n," Smokey Joe said, flipping his long gray braid over his shoulder. His lips twitched.

"Half beat," Cody snarled. He started toward Perrin's wagon. "Prepare to move out!" He would do what he had to. It was time to end this stand-off.

She spotted him coming and walked out onto the prairie to meet him, stopping when they were ten feet apart. "Well?" she demanded suspiciously, lifting one silky eyebrow.

"Here it is, take it or leave it," he snapped. "I'll sell the whiskey in Fort Laramie. But the arms go with us to Oregon. If we sell the arms in Fort Laramie, your bridegrooms aren't going to realize enough profit to buy you . . . ladies . . . your houses. Is that what you want? To live in tents?"

"That isn't the whole story, now, is it? I believe you hold a financial interest in these transactions too, Mr. Snow!"

"That's correct. We've lost the profit from the stolen wagon, and I'm willing to take a reduced profit on the remaining whiskey. But I'm sure as hell not willing to part with the arms and ammunition at give-away prices! That wagon represents the bulk of our anticipated profits. So if you aren't willing to compromise, I'll—"

"You'll what, Mr. Snow?" Her damned chin thrust forward and sparks flashed in her eyes. He'd never met a woman he'd wanted to turn over his knee more than this one. She irritated him in the best of circumstances, enraged him in other situations.

Right now, he couldn't believe that he had ever questioned her leadership abilities. She was a born fighter.

"We'll take the arms and whiskey wagons and we'll leave your butts right here. That's what. We'll go on without you."

"Is that so?"

"You're damned straight! You've heard my offer and that's it. No negotiation. The boys and I are leaving in thirty minutes. So make up your mind if you're coming with us."

"Wait. We aren't finished."

He turned, expecting instant capitulation, but there was no sign of surrender in her expression.

"What about Cora? Does she get to be a bride?"

"Is that a condition?" He couldn't believe this.

"It could be."

She was pressing an advantage. She had to know he was in a frenzy to settle this problem and get moving again. Anger exploded behind his chest, and pride told him to dig in and show her who was running this outfit and who made the decisions.

Experience and common sense prevailed. If getting this expedition under way depended on Cora Thorp being designated a bride, then to hell with it. Mr. White just got himself a bride.

"Congratulate Miss Thorp. I'm sure she'll make a fine farmer's wife," he snarled between clenched teeth.

"Thank you, Cody," she said, her voice suddenly soft.

He glared, fuming. "The minute Cora can't pay her way, I'll put her off the train. And one more thing. I don't appreciate being blackmailed. I won't forget this. Now talk to the others and make your decision." He left her to go saddle his horse.

Twenty minutes later all the brides appeared, led by Perrin wearing that stubborn look he had learned to despise. The others scowled as if they would gladly have drawn and quartered him.

"What is it now?" he demanded, his voice harsh.

"We think you are the worst wagonmaster we have ever heard of and we rue the day you were assigned to take us across the continent!" That was her beginning. "You have shown and continue to show a reckless disregard for our lives and well-being."

Several of the brides murmured, "Hear, hear!"

Cody drew a deep breath and tried to control the burst of temper choking him. "Are you coming, damn it? Or are you going to stay here and sulk?"

Perrin glared at him. They all glared at him.

"We accept your terms," she snapped. "Since we don't appear to have a choice. But we want your guarantee that you'll sell the whiskey in Fort Laramie and that Cora joins us as a bride."

"Agreed. Now all of you get your behinds in those wagons. I mean right now!" They tossed their heads as if flinging invisible daggers at him. After fifteen minutes he cantered to the front of his train and shouted, "Waaaagons, hoooo."

To his relief, the oxen began turning out of the square.

God, he hated to deal with women. Most especially, he hated dealing with one small dark-haired, flashing-eyed beauty who was causing him more trouble than he had experienced on his last three journeys put together.

He wanted to fling her on a bed and show her who was the boss.

His scowl faded and he laughed out loud when he realized he wasn't sure who would win that particular struggle.

By the time they finished unloading the wagons and building barges to float the beds and wheels across the swollen, sparkling Laramie River, then reassembled and reloaded on the other side, dusk muted the sky and everyone reeled with exhaustion. The lights of Fort Laramie proved no enticement to people too fatigued to move aching muscles. Everyone tossed down a cold supper, set up tents, and fell into damp bedrolls.

As bone-weary as she was, Mem couldn't sleep. She tossed and turned, stared at the roof of the tent, tossed some more, listened to Bootie whimpering in her slumber, rolled this way, tried that way, then finally sighed and gave it up.

Although she suspected she could have fired a gun through Bootie's pillow without waking her, Mem crept from the tent as quietly as she could and stepped into the cool night air. The rise in altitude and a late afternoon hailstorm had left a chill that felt more like early winter than late June.

It surprised her how much of a hardship the weather continued to be. Hot sun blazed in their faces most of the day, but the temperature plummeted at night. The climate never felt just right, it was always too hot or too cold. Sudden storms had become the norm, billowing up out of the north to drench them or batter their bonnets with hail. And for several weeks, they'd been watching tornadoes rip across the prairie. Thus far, prayers had held the tornadoes at bay, but they'd suffered from hot winds and swirling dust.

Pulling her shawl close around her shoulders, Mem tossed back her long auburn braid and peered toward the glowing coals of the fire Smokey Joe had earlier coaxed into flames by standing over it with a borrowed parasol to shield his efforts from the hail and light rain. To Mem's relief, the night sky was clear and Smokey Joe's cook pit was deserted.

She seated herself on a damp log beside the embers, sighed, and gazed up in time to see a shooting star streak across the sky. It struck her as amusing that earlier today, suffering from the heat, she had wished for rain. But when the temperature sank, and marble-sized hail began to pelt them, she had wished for the return of the sun. Smiling, she touched her sunburned nose and forehead, feeling peeling skin. In the last day or so, all of the women had suffered sunburns.

It was daunting to realize that half of the journey still lay ahead. Mem's smile faded and her shoulders slumped. The joy had gone out of the trip.

The pleasure, the zest, the sense of adventure . . . she had left them behind in a dark copse of whispering cottonwoods.

Several minutes elapsed before she became aware that someone had joined her at the far end of the log. She jumped and clutched her shawl before she recognized his profile.

"Forgive me if I startled you," Webb quietly apologized. When Mem silently started to rise, he quickly inquired, "Are you having another of your headaches?"

She hesitated. She ought to go. If she possessed a grain of sense, she wouldn't do this to herself, wouldn't torture herself by remaining here with him. She commanded her legs to rise and walk away. Do it right now. Leave.

"I'm worried about Bootie," she heard herself say. She settled on the log and gazed into the embers. "She thinks she killed those two teamsters." She related Bootie's encounter with Jake Quinton at the Addison farm.

"I learned about the incident when it happened," Webb interrupted. "Miss Boyd told us."

They lapsed into an uncomfortable silence at the mention of Augusta's name.

Mem lowered her head and released a slow quiet sigh. They were clever about their desire for each other. She had observed them intently. Had she not witnessed their passion beneath the cottonwoods, she could actually have believed that Webb and Augusta disliked each other. Augusta couldn't keep her eyes off of Webb Coate, that was true; but she glared as if the very sight of him offended her. When Webb was forced to look at Augusta, his eyes flattened and went cold. Only one who had seen them wrapped in each other's arms as Mem had would guess the truth.

She touched the braid falling over her shoulder and remembered Webb pulling Augusta's braid through his hands. With all her aching heart, she wished she had never wandered into the cottonwoods that night.

"The teamsters' deaths had nothing to do with your sister. Tell her she isn't to blame."

"I've told her again and again. Telling her does no good."

"Cody and Jake Quinton have a history that goes way back." Speaking quietly, his mingled accents soft on her ear, Webb told her about Cody sentencing Quinton to six months of hard labor and Quinton's vow for revenge. "He'll dog us all the way to Oregon. It won't end until Quinton is dead."

Mem nodded. "I'll tell Bootie." She hesitated. "May I tell Perrin also?"

"If you like."

Suddenly Mem's spirits soared. Webb had confided in her. He trusted her judgment. Sliding a look from the corner of her eye, she studied his strong face, shadowed by the dim light.

He sat forward, elbows on knees, his head tilted back to gaze at something on the dark prairie. Black hair fell to his shoulders, tapered hands rested lightly at the top of his shins.

Mem's heart rolled in her chest. She loved the quiet powerful look of him. The strength and stillness that radiated from a spirit that could never be conquered. She loved the blend of cultures that reflected in his features, his fluid movements.

Helplessly, hopelessly, she conceded that she loved everything about him. The melodic sound of his voice, and the way he listened. The way his black eyes sparkled when he was amused, and the stories he told. She loved the gracefulness of his walk, as if he were one with the earth and sky, as if he inhabited a world invisible to others.

Mem's heart glistened in her eyes. With all her plain unvarnished soul, she wished she had been born Augusta Boyd.

But she was not Augusta. She would never be a beauty or turn men's heads. She would never stir Webb Coate's passion. He would never look at her as he had looked at Augusta in the moonlight.

Yet, she told herself, there was something between them, a

companionship that was intimate and comfortable. They had shared confidences with each other as only good friends did.

A sigh stirred her bosom. If friendship was all that Webb could offer, then she would accept his friendship, and gladly. Twenty-eight-year-old spinsters were accustomed to settling for crumbs; she didn't even mind anymore. Her blunder lay in forgetting for a while who she was, a tall ungainly creature who was too plain and too outspoken to arouse men's passions.

Rising, she studied the fringe on his jacket rather than meet his steady black gaze. "I believe I'll return to our tent and try to get some rest. My headache's gone." Surprisingly, it was true. It occurred to her that Webb Coate's company was more effective than any headache nostrum she had ever swallowed.

He nodded, then shifted toward the darkness. "You've been keeping your headache inside your tent. Perhaps you will come to Smokey Joe's fire again. . . ."

Her eyebrows lifted as swiftly as her heart. He had missed her company since she'd been avoiding him, was that what he was saying?

"Good night, Tanka Tunkan," she said softly, not trusting herself to say more.

She thought he smiled, but the shadows were too dense to be certain. "Good night . . . Mem."

He had called her Mem! Absurdly pleased, feeling as if she had won a stupendous victory, she floated back to her tent.

What on earth had made her think the joy had fled from the journey? Other than her father and Bootie's dear husband, Robert, no man had called her Mem. Her name, a silly one, she'd always thought, sounded almost like a caress when spoken by a man.

Crawling inside the tent, she rolled next to Bootie and clasped her thin pillow in her arms. It was a long time before she fell asleep, a smile on her lips.

CHAPTER
* 14 *

Augusta rode in the whiskey wagon, seated beside Heck Kelsey at the reins. Ahead, low barren hills sloped away from the whitewashed adobe bricks that surrounded Fort Laramie. After struggling to cross deep ravines and rushing streams to reach this unpromising place, she had expected more reward for the effort. But there was nothing appealing about Fort Laramie. It had been plunked down in the midst of scrubby junipers and sagebrush, without a single tree to offer shade from the harsh sun.

She began to understand why the other brides had chosen not to visit the fort, deciding instead to send money and requests for fresh provisions with Cody or Heck. Biting her lip, Augusta almost wished she had remained in camp. Right now she could be enjoying an all-over bath in the clean waters of the Laramie River. She hadn't had a real bath in three weeks.

But, she thought grimly, unlike the others she had business to conduct. She didn't intend to leave the fort until she hired a maid to replace Cora. Doing so would prove Perrin Waverly wrong, an event she anticipated with smug pleasure.

Also, she hastily reminded herself, if opportunity presented, she would discreetly inquire if anyone had been asking after the Eagglestons. It eased her conscience to promise that she would seize the chance should it happen along.

In the meantime, she would borrow just a teeny-tiny bit more of the Eagglestons' money and treat herself to fresh eggs and vegetables, perhaps some marmalade if she could find any in the post's stores. Also, she wanted some rice powder to lower the color in her sunburned cheeks.

A small sigh passed her lips. It was so nice to hear the clink of gold coins rubbing together in her little wrist bag when the wagon tilted over a stone or a rise. It sounded safe.

"So, lassie, are ye 'aving a gud journey?" Heck Kelsey asked, sliding a look at her.

The various accents he affected amused the others, but Augusta found them irksome. She supposed Heck Kelsey was in love with her, but it wasn't especially flattering. He was merely a blacksmith.

She touched his sleeve with the tips of her gloves, a gesture intended to soften a blatant rejection. After all, she occasionally needed him to repair a wheel or a bit of harness.

"I have a headache, Mr. Kelsey. I'd rather not talk."

"I am zo zorry, Mademoiselle." As she hadn't toured the Continent, she didn't know if he genuinely sounded French.

Another sigh fluttered between her lips. She had to endure the company of a frustrated actor, and there was no place to look during the drive to the fort except at Webb Coate's back.

As the wheels bumped closer to the gates, Webb and Cody dropped back to ride alongside the wagon. Her heart lurched and the beat accelerated as she realized that Webb would be on her side. Pressing her lips together, she fixed her gaze forward. She wouldn't permit herself to glance at his profile.

But she was conscious of him as she was every moment of every waking day. Whenever he passed nearby, her senses opened and she found herself acutely aware of every small thing he did or said. Gripping her hands in her lap, she desperately tried not to remember his long fingers stroking her hair or the hard thrilling pressure of his lips crushing hers. A light sheen of perspiration appeared on her brow, and she clenched her teeth to suppress the moan that built in her throat.

That she was capable of lust shocked her deeply. And it shamed her to the core that the object of her lust was a barely civilized heathen. Whenever she looked at Webb or tormented herself with thoughts of him, she shrank from the sound of a dozen generations of Boyds rolling in their graves.

Even so . . . even so. Lowering her head, she touched

gloved fingertips to a hot forehead and closed her eyes lest she surrender to temptation and look full at him.

It kept her in a constant state of agitation to think that whoever had snooped on them in the cottonwoods also watched them in camp, waiting to see her betray her dirty secret. To thwart this unknown sneak, she seized every opportunity to make a scathing remark about Webb Coate. When she absolutely had to look at him or address him, she made herself concentrate on what he was instead of how he made her feel. She displayed her superiority and revulsion to him and to whoever spied on them.

The whiskey wagon rattled through the gates of the fort and she looked around, first letting her gaze linger on Webb's stoic features. A stab of disappointment pierced her chest when she discovered he faced forward, not looking at her. Of course, she didn't want a dirty savage looking at her. She was glad that he had learned his lesson. Still, if he would just . . .

She shook her head so fiercely that her bonnet wobbled atop her blond curls. Business was her purpose here, nothing else.

Sharpening her concentration, she scanned the people inside the fort and crowding the balcony railings. She saw trappers, soldiers, travelers, traders, but the only women she noticed were sullen-faced Indian squaws. The Indian women moved in the shade near the walls, like shadows themselves. Most were wrapped in blankets, the edges raised to cover much of their faces. But some stood hipshot and brazen, touching their breasts and calling in low voices to the men who passed on the boardwalks.

Turning aside in shocked disgust, Augusta examined the other side of the fort. The only white woman she spotted was leaning far over a balcony railing, screaming obscenities at a departing man. Her hair swung loose over her shoulders, and she wore a wrapper that gaped to the waist.

Augusta blinked hard, looked around her, and her heart sank. There existed a very real possibility that she was the only woman in Fort Laramie clad in hat and gloves, or wearing a clean skirt and a waist decently closed to the throat. She had not seen a single female with whom she could bear to exchange a word. The thought of sharing her wagon with such creatures horrified her.

When she realized Cody Snow had called her name twice, she turned blank eyes in his direction.

"Heck will send Lucy Hastings's belongings back to Chastity, and the goods that belonged to Bill Macy and Jeb Holden. Also, he has some items to pick up for the brides. I'll auction the whiskey; Webb will hire more teamsters." He stood on the ground, gazing up at her with coolly expressionless eyes as if totally indifferent to the Boyd name and her own personal charms. Well. She didn't care much for him either. "Meet us by the flagpole at midday. That should allow you time to settle your business."

Nodding, Augusta swept a slow second look around the interior of the fort. Anxiety clogged her throat. She hadn't a notion where to begin. "I thought you would accompany me," she said in a high thin voice.

Tilting back the brim of his hat, Cody frowned in undisguised exasperation. "My duties don't include playing nursemaid, Miss Boyd. You have two choices. You hire yourself a maid or you arrange passage home. Whichever, you'll have to manage it on your own. I made that clear before we left camp."

The mere suggestion of returning to Chastity made her heart lurch. She gripped the edge of the wooden seat and didn't move until the whiskey wagon stopped. Then she halted her descent when she noticed the hard-eyed, bearded faces of the men loitering in the post square. They watched with hot eyes, rape in their stares. They nudged each other and shouted vulgar comments that frightened her half to death.

She could not imagine spending a day in this hideous crude sin-hole of a place, let alone waiting here for a train to carry her back to Chastity. And she would rather die where she stood than destroy her pride by returning to Chastity.

Without thinking, she looked for Webb, her gaze imploring protection and reassurance. But the cold flatness in his gaze informed her that he had observed her disgust at the sight of the Indians sitting on the boardwalks, their bare feet in the dirt.

A flush of embarrassment deepened the color in her sunburned cheeks. Webb was as far removed from the half-naked savages lolling about the post as butter from grass. Still, it occurred to her that one of the ugly squaws could easily be a relative of his. The filthy Indian reeling drunkenly past the wagon might be a half-brother or a cousin.

This reminder of who he was sickened her. He was not her kind. And when she saw his lip curl back from his teeth, she understood that he read her expression perfectly. She stared at him, then swung her eyes away and watched the drunken Indian scratch his crotch. Her backbone stiffened and her chin lifted. So be it. If Coate thought his kind repulsed her, he was right. He would think twice before he attempted to assault her again.

"Miss Boyd?" Heck Kelsey stood below her, his hand extended to assist her from the wagon.

Aware that dozens of male eyes stared, watching for a glimpse of ankle, her heart pounding in fright, she reluctantly stepped from the wagon, holding her skirts tightly to her body.

But she did not go in search of a new maid. She simply could not make herself leave the safety of the wagon. Moreover, hers was a fool's errand; she had understood that for several minutes.

Instead, she passed the morning in hopeless frustration, standing beneath the boiling sun beside the flagpole, quaking like an aspen, staying always within Cody Snow's sight. She waited, perspiring beneath her thin useless parasol while Cody auctioned off the whiskey barrels, waited while he posted letters to Lucy's Oregon fiancé, and to Lucy's family and the families of the dead teamsters. Then, after the whiskey barrels had been dispersed, she fidgeted while Cody approved two rough-looking teamsters that Webb had hired, then waited some more until Heck Kelsey finally returned and assisted her back into the wagon. It wouldn't occur to her until later that Heck was taking fresh provisions back to everyone but her. She had completely forgotten about eggs or vegetables or rice powder.

When her tailbone jarred against the hard wooden seat as Heck shouted the oxen back toward the sanctuary of their camp, tears of relief dampened her eyes. Fort Laramie, and the rough men who occupied it, had frightened her badly.

Shortly before they reached the familiar haven of squared wagons, Cody dropped back to ride beside her. He touched his fingers to the tip of his hat and nodded.

"Did you hire a maid or a driver?" he shouted over the rattle and creak of wheels and harness.

He knew perfectly well that she had not wandered more than four feet from the wagon all morning. "I am going to Oregon," she stated flatly. She could not return to Chastity destitute, could not live in some rented hovel within sight of the mansion she had once commanded. Her need to marry Mr. Clampet had not changed.

She could not go back.

But how could she go forward without someone to drive her stupid oxen and do for her?

"I'll spell this out for you, Miss Boyd, so there's no misunderstanding. I can't and won't spare a man to drive your wagon. And the other brides are under no obligation to do your work for you. If you cannot drive, cook your meals, or set up your tent . . . I have no place for you on this train."

She stared into his tanned face and felt her stomach cramp in sudden fear.

"We're leaving in the morning. If you're going to wait at the fort until you can arrange transportation back to Chastity, I'll try to find you a private room, try to discover when the next train heading east is expected. But you need to inform me of your plans immediately or I won't be able to assist you."

She didn't see him touch his heels to the buckskin's side and canter on ahead. Fear, powerful and debilitating, had paralyzed her.

"Excuse me," Augusta called, stopping beside Sarah Jennings's wagon. Sarah and Cora were busily rearranging the wagon, packing Cora's belongings into the space recently occupied by Lucy Hastings's goods. "Moving Cora's things isn't necessary," she added grandly.

"I beg your pardon?" Pausing over a trunk, Sarah wiped her hands on her apron and tucked a lock of dark hair into the bun on top of her head. "What are you talking about?"

"Why, dear Cora, of course." She made her lips curve in a smile that Cora didn't return. The cheeky creature scowled back with suspicion flaring in her ferret's eyes. "I've decided to forgive you," she said, resenting each honeyed word. "You can remain with me for the rest of the journey."

Cora's mouth dropped. Even Sarah blinked in surprise.

Augusta waved a hand in modest dismissal, misunderstanding their reaction. "I know it's difficult to believe that I could find it in my heart to forgive your rudeness and insolence, but forgiveness is a virtue that I've always—"

"No," Cora snapped, "what's hard to believe is that you think I'd rather be your lick-spittle than be a bride." She stared hard. "Well, you're wrong! I'm going to be a bride and get me a husband just like the rest of you. I ain't never going to be your slave again!" She bent to a box and lifted it up to Sarah.

Sarah stood on the wagon's tailgate looking down at Augusta as if watching someone who had taken leave of her senses. A flicker of pity darkened her eyes.

"All right," Augusta snapped at Cora, suddenly furious. How dare a mere Jennings look at her like that? "I'll pay you a weekly wage for your labors. Will that satisfy you?"

Cora's fingers tightened on the corners of the box she held

against her chest. Her gaze narrowed. "I don't want your ill-gotten gains. I want to be a bride."

Augusta's breath stopped and her stomach looped into a slow roll. "What do you mean, my 'ill-gotten gains'?" she demanded.

A hard knowing look came into Cora's eyes. "You know exactly what I mean. I ain't taking no dead man's money!"

The implied accusation was so unexpected, so paralyzing, that it left Augusta breathless and gasping. Cora knew. Somehow she had guessed. Throwing out a hand, Augusta steadied herself against the edge of the tailgate, and her mind raced. How would Sarah interpret this conversation? Be calm, she ordered herself frantically, be calm. Sarah would believe Cora referred to Augusta's deceased father. Of course.

But she understood at once that Cora had resurfaced as a threat. And Cora was not going to return to Augusta's wagon. A wave of dizziness shook through her body. When it passed, her lips curled back from her teeth.

"You don't know what you're talking about," she hissed. "You're only making wild guesses." The sudden doubt drawing Cora's cheeks told her this was true. "You're nothing but rubbish! Your father digs graves and your mother takes in wash! I wish I'd never brought you with me!"

Sarah jerked as if the desperate words had been addressed to her. Her face went hard and cold. "Excuse us, Miss Boyd. Miss Thorp and I have work to do. Perhaps you do too." Her dark eyes swept Augusta's dusty skirts and curls, drawing a pointed contrast to her own and Cora's freshly laundered clothing and shining clean hair. They had spent their morning at the river.

Turning away, they continued their work, speaking to each other as if Augusta were not standing three feet away.

When the panic eased enough that her knees unlocked, she tossed her head and strolled away as if she hadn't a care.

Ona Norris's eyes widened into an appalled expression.

She gaped as if Augusta had sprouted horns through her hair. "You want *me* to do *what*?" The teacup in her hand jerked and spilled tea down her skirt.

Augusta clucked her tongue and shook her head over the spilled tea, then repeated the offer. "We get along well, you must admit, so I decided it would be agreeable if you moved from Thea's wagon to mine. You're preforming half the chores now," she explained in a reasonable tone. "By expending a little more effort, you could earn a tidy nest egg between here and Clampet Falls. If you save the wages I'm offering, you can begin your married life with something put aside."

She congratulated herself for hitting upon the perfect solution. Beaming, she leaned back in her camp chair and waited for Ona to accept the opportunity to share her wagon. Ona impressed her as clever enough to grasp the beneficial aspects of observing a true lady at close quarters. There was much she could teach the girl.

The teacup slipped from Ona's fingers and fell to the ground. She stood, shaking with offense. Surprised, Augusta gazed at her in bewilderment. What on earth?

"I am *not* a servant, Miss Boyd!" Crimson pulsed in her cheeks. "I nursed my cousin in response to a signal from God, not because I was paid, and not because I was a servant!"

"Your cousin has nothing to do with . . . I didn't even know that you'd nursed any—" Ona's low snarl cut her off.

"How *dare* you offer this insult!" Fury set Ona's stare on fire. An incoherent sound sputtered from her throat, then she ground her boot on the teacup that had belonged to Augusta's mother before she caught her skirts around her and stormed away from Augusta's fire.

Anger and confusion pinched Augusta's lips. Truly, she didn't understand Ona's response. She had genuinely believed Ona would accept her offer, and happily. Instead the ungrateful chit had broken her mother's teacup. It was unforgivable.

"Well," she said, trying to bolster spirits that had begun to flag. She gave her head a brave little toss. "Ona Norris isn't the only pebble on the road."

Ignoring the nervous cramps in her stomach, she patted her hair and smoothed her skirts, irritated that she hadn't yet solved this matter so she too could bathe in the river.

Jane Munger was her next choice.

Jane raised a hand before Augusta could state her proposition. "Don't bother, Miss Boyd, I've already heard that you're trying to hire a slavey." Her chin lifted and a twinkle of insolent amusement sparkled in her eyes. "I'm not interested in being your lackey, not for any price."

Augusta raised her own chin. She didn't give a fig for Jane Munger's opinion. Who was Jane Munger, anyway? No one had ever heard of the Mungers.

"You flatter yourself if you think I intended to offer you a position," she said haughtily. "I doubt you could meet my qualifications. I have very exacting standards."

"Oh, Cora assured us that you do, Miss Boyd," Jane said with a wink at Winnie.

Furious, cheeks flaming, Augusta spun away.

Halting out of Jane's and Winnie's sight, she tried to think whom to approach next. Bootie? Out of the question; the silly fliberty gibbet burst into tears every time she saw Augusta, then launched into a weepy explanation of why she had spoken to Jake Quinton. Winnie was still too frail to be of any use, and Augusta didn't care for her anyway. Thea was hopeless, capable of burying her nose in her sketchbook and entirely forgetting her chores. Since Hilda had agreed to teach Cora how to speak properly—a waste of time, in Augusta's opinion—Hilda would probably take Cora's side. Sarah was too uppity and held too high an opinion of herself. Mem was too independent and outspoken. There wasn't one of them whom Augusta liked, and they were so consumed by envy and jealousy that none of them would help her. Such spiteful creatures were probably enjoying her predicament.

Swallowing in panic, she had just reached the frightening

conclusion that no one was going to save her when she spotted Perrin Waverly walking toward her. Lord in heaven, this was the last thing she needed right now. If her legs could have moved, she would have sped away.

Perrin stopped a few feet in front of her. "Mr. Snow instructed me to inquire if you wish to return to Fort Laramie this evening or before we depart in the morning?"

This should have been the satisfying moment when Augusta displayed her new maid, proving Perrin's prediction wrong. But everyone in camp knew there was no new maid.

She glared, hating Perrin with every fiber of her being.

"I'm not leaving!" she snapped, spitting the words in a low shaking voice. "You're not going to abandon me in that filthy fort!"

Perrin's hands closed into fists. "You would have left Cora there!"

"If I have to drive those damned oxen myself, I'm going to Oregon!" There was no choice. The realization made her sick.

They stared at each other, fingers twitching with the urge to rip and tear.

"I'll inform Mr. Snow of your decision," Perrin said abruptly. She spun in an angry swirl of faded calico.

Augusta stood rooted to the ground, unable to move. Someone nearby was cooking rice and dried apples for supper. The scent made her salivate. From behind came the fragrant smoke of a roasting hare. Augusta's stomach rumbled, and she recalled hopelessly that she hadn't eaten since dawn.

Bootie's voice drifted from the nearest wagon. "I swan, Mem, washing all that laundry plain wore me out. Would you mind setting up the tent tonight?"

Laundry. Food. The tent. Panic blotted Mem's reply.

Legs shaking with trepidation, Augusta listened to the evening sounds of supper being prepared, tents being erected. From the far side of the square, she heard Thea singing, heard Smokey Joe's mouth harp. Voices called from wagon to wagon and someone, maybe Hilda, was laughing.

One of the new teamsters stood beside a juniper bush, smoking and talking to Cody Snow.

When Augusta realized Cody was watching her, she made herself move, lurching forward on wooden legs. Toward the fire that had burned out in her fire pit, the fire she didn't know how to rekindle. Toward a stack of disgusting buffalo chips that she dreaded to touch. Toward a tent packed somewhere in the back of her wagon, a tent she had no idea how to erect.

Tears swam in her eyes and she felt herself slowly strangling.

Cody walked up behind the knot of women standing in the darkness watching Augusta. "It's time you ladies returned to your wagons," he said sharply, startling them. "We leave at dawn."

Thea, Ona, and Jane looked at each other, then smiled and walked toward their wagons, whispering in gossipy undertones.

When they'd gone, Cody lit a cigar and stood in the deeper shadows alongside the arms wagon. She'd managed to get a half-assed fire going, but it wasn't large enough or hot enough to boil a cup of water. Unless she'd found some dried fruit among her provisions, he guessed she would go to bed hungry tonight.

He waited to see what she would do with the tent. She'd pulled the poles and canvas to the tailgate of her wagon, and there it sat in a jumbled pile.

Dragging on his cigar and frowning, he watched her approach the scant light given off by burning twigs and buffalo chips. She extended shaking hands to the flames and stared down at them, then she covered her face and slowly sank to her knees, shoulders heaving.

"Damn it." His frown deepened. Those were not tears designed to manipulate, wound, or impress.

It crossed his mind that one person could never truly know another. He hadn't supposed Augusta Boyd possessed genuine tears. Nor had he anticipated that she would try to continue on her own.

This pampered, spoiled woman had never done a lick of real work in her entire life. He couldn't imagine that she would be successful driving a team of caring for herself. If he allowed her to try, she would slow his train and he'd lose time he could not afford to lose. Her health would suffer from inevitable exhaustion and malnutrition. He didn't intend to lose another passenger either.

He straightened, flicked his cigar toward a clump of sage, and started forward, but something stopped him.

She had jerked her head up and turned toward the tailgate. Wiping her eyes, she started to rise, then stopped. Pressing her hands to her cheeks, she closed her eyelids and whispered something, then tilted her head as if listening to a reply.

Curiosity piqued, Cody hesitated, then watched her push to her feet and stumble toward the tailgate. She spoke again, then placed her hands on the tent poles and waited. Looking at the poles as if she'd never seen them before, she finally lowered them to the ground, her expression helpless. She waited.

Straining to see and hear, Cody scanned the shadows moving in darkness behind her wagon. Her cow was there. He spotted the gray bulk of grazing oxen. That he saw no hint of another person first puzzled him, then suggested who stood on the far side of the wagon. Confirmation arrived in the next minutes.

Augusta dragged the tent poles to a spot not far from her puny fire. She waited, then glanced toward the tailgate. After sighing and swaying on her feet, she returned to the wagon and fumbled inside until she located a hammer. Weeping with frustration and self-pity, she went back to the tent poles and tried to hammer one into the baked earth. She missed the pole altogether, struck her thumb with a yelp, and dropped both the pole and the hammer.

A patient whisper encouraged her to try again. Shoulders

sagging, she bent toward the tongue of the wagon. Cody clearly heard her reply. "I can't! You do it!"

He didn't hear Webb's answer, but it wasn't hard to guess. Webb would instruct her, but he wouldn't perform the work for her. If she was to remain with the train, she had to become self-sufficient. She stamped her feet, pounded her fists against her thighs. A choking sound emerged from her throat, then she wiped tears from her eyes and bent to retrieve the fallen hammer.

Cody watched until she managed to drive the first pole into the ground far enough that it remained upright.

Considering, he contemplated the patch of darkness where Webb must be standing. There was something wrong here. If Webb wanted to help her, why didn't he step forward and show her how to set the tent instead of hiding in the shadows, half-whispering instructions that she was having a hell of a time following?

After reflecting, he decided Webb must have a reason for not wanting anyone to know he was helping Augusta remain with the train. Reluctantly, Cody decided to give her a week. He would do that for his friend's sake.

If Augusta wasn't holding her own by the time they reached Emigrant's Gap, Cody would send her back. Someone at the gap would be headed east. He wouldn't have a choice. His train was too far behind schedule already. He couldn't risk further delay while she learned what she should have learned two months ago.

He watched another minute, then moved away in the darkness. He didn't notice Mem Grant until he crashed into her and almost knocked her to the ground.

"I'm sorry, I didn't see you."

"I couldn't sleep," she said in a low agitated voice. She looked past him, watching Augusta's dimly lit form.

Both of them clearly heard Webb's voice. "Position the second pole on a direct line four feet behind the first."

Mem spun so abruptly that her skirts whipped around

Cody's legs. She walked rapidly, staying in front of him until they reached the corner of the square, then she turned.

"None of us will help her!" When Cody didn't say anything, she spoke again, her voice strained. "There isn't a person on this train whom Augusta hasn't offended!"

Her vehemence surprised him. "Miss Boyd was wrong to suggest your sister is responsible for Jake Quinton's attack." Perrin had related Augusta's painful remark. "I'll speak to Mrs. Glover if you think it would help." He was shooting in the dark, trying to guess why the usually levelheaded Miss Grant sounded so bitter.

"Augusta is . . . she's so . . . Oh, never mind!"

A long coil of auburn gleamed in the starlight, spinning out from her shoulder, then she was gone, swallowed by the deep shadows along the back side of the square. Cody could have sworn she was crying, but tears were so foreign to his impression of Mem Grant that he decided he must be mistaken.

He glanced back toward the sound of pounding. From what he could glimpse and guess, he doubted Augusta Boyd would have much of the night left by the time she assembled her tent. She wasn't going to be at her best tomorrow morning when she learned how to drive two yokes of stubborn oxen.

There was one bright glimmer lining this particular dark cloud. At least this time, Perrin Waverly wouldn't pace after him pleading the case of a bride about to be returned home.

He was almost disappointed. Their meetings had been brief and terse since the incident he privately thought of as the Great Whiskey Debacle. To his utter surprise and immense irritation, he missed the few minutes they spent together after finishing the business of the day.

Moving in the darkness, he strode toward his bedroll. This had been one hell of a day. First, he'd learned at the fort that Jake Quinton had sold a wagonload of whiskey two days previously. Second, he'd had to sell the remaining whiskey against his better judgment. Third, since Quinton had gotten there first, Cody's profits were soberingly lower than what he had expected, only a fraction of the gain he would have realized in Oregon. Fourth, there was the problem with Augusta Boyd. And finally, he couldn't stop thinking about Perrin Waverly's cinnamon eyes and strawberry mouth.

And now, what was this? Frowning, he knelt beside his bedroll and peered through the darkness.

Someone had used his knife to pin a handful of dried twigs to his blankets.

He couldn't really accept that someone had driven a knife through his blankets until he carried the bedroll to Smokey Joe's fire and examined it in the light.

Son of a bitch. Lifting his head, he listened to the silent camp. Who in the hell had done this? And why?

CHAPTER
* 15 *

My Journal, June, 1852, Augusta is suffering as she de-
serves to. Every night her wagon comes into camp an
hour after the rest of us have finished supper. Her face is
beet red from the sun and peeling like a lizard. Jane said
her hands bleed from driving all day without anyone to
relieve her at the reins. I'm glad.

I'm still furious that Cody didn't tell me about the mo-
lasses being whiskey. He can keep secrets from the oth-
ers, but he should not keep secrets from me! I defended
him in front of the others! He made a fool of me!

I was so angry that I used his own knife to pin the
dried flowers where he couldn't fail to find them. A week
has passed and still he hasn't apologized.

I get so furious that I shake all over. He looks at the
whore the way I want him to look at me. I can't bear to
see them together. It makes my stomach heave. Last night
I vomited behind the wagon.

What does he want from me? Why is he waiting and
tormenting me?

I've done everything I had to do to open the way for
our love, and it was not easy for me. I loved Ellen, he
should know that. I turned down two offers of marriage
while I waited for him. I traveled after him when he
didn't come for me. I joined this train. I have endured
great hardships for his sake. Since this terrible trip
began, I have been hungry, thirsty, exhausted, and fright-
ened. I've done all this for him. I've forgiven him again
and again and again.

When will it end? When will he stop testing me and
speak? What does he expect me to do?

I wanted to punish him so badly that I had to slash my

arm below the elbow. For a minute I hated him for making me do this. But I hate the whore more.

Does he want me to punish her? Is that the final test so he will know how much I love him?

CHAPTER
* 16 *

My Journal, July 1, 1852. When I review my sketches, I see that our features are thinner, our hands callused. Our sun-damaged faces and calicos are filthy, our hair flies untended from careless buns. Our losses and hardships reflect in weary eyes that also display growing confidence and a knowledge of new abilities. Oddly, many of us look stronger.

Thea Reeves

North out of Fort Laramie, Perrin eyed the mountain ranges flanking the trail. As the altitude climbed, afternoon sun burned through thinner air and broiled exposed flesh. Skin dried and lips blistered. Cracked hooves crippled limping oxen; subsequently, several were shot and abandoned beside the treeless trail. Gnats and mosquitoes swarmed thick during daylight hours; at dusk the insects became a torment.

Perrin sat coughing in a stream of smoke blowing off the buffalo chips smoldering in the fire pit. Smokey Joe insisted mosquitoes hated smoke and avoided it. Slapping at her neck and sighing, she decided that Smokey Joe was wrong.

After scratching the bumps and bites on the backs of her hands, she pulled apart a biscuit and inspected it with dismay. Enough mosquitoes had mixed into the dough that the biscuits were speckled inside. Mosquitoes floated in the gravy over her rice.

Hilda covered the bugs in her biscuit with the last of the plum jam, then waved furiously at a cloud of insects swarming around her hair. Her face was sunburned and swollen. "Smokey Joe claims if you rub spit on the bites they won't itch as much."

"Spit helps," Perrin agreed. She looked at Hilda and they burst out laughing. Three months ago neither could have foreseen a time when they would eat insect-infested food or rub spit on their skin. "How is Cora progressing with her lessons?" Perrin inquired, standing to change seats with Hilda.

Hilda took her turn in the smoke, coughed and rubbed her eyes, smearing soot across one cheek. "It's been less than two weeks, but Cora is an eager pupil. Did you ask the others to correct her speech when they hear her commit an error?"

"I did." Glancing up, Perrin watched Cody walking toward their fire, and set aside her supper plate. By some enigmatic process, she often sensed his presence before she saw him.

Purple shadows lengthened across a sky flashing with heat lightning; it was dark enough that she couldn't see Cody's face clearly, but she would have recognized the spread of his shoulders anywhere, knew the slight swagger in his walk and the sound of his footsteps. She would have known it was Cody merely by listening to her own accelerated heartbeat.

"I'm sorry I wasn't able to meet earlier," he apologized, stepping into the light of their fire. His eyes were tired and his voice irritable tonight. "An altercation erupted at the gap. One of the trains tried to go through out of turn."

"Was anyone hurt?" Hilda inquired anxiously.

The trains had bottlenecked at Emigrant's Gap. At this point wagons from both directions converged on the narrow passageway. Four trains camped on the west side, waiting for the eastbound traffic to come through before being allowed to proceed.

"A couple of hotheads from Murchason's train are nursing broken knuckles and jaws, but no one got shot." Cody pushed his fingers through the dark hair tumbling across his forehead. He looked at Perrin. "I'm in no mood to sit. Would you object to a stroll while we catch up on the day's business?"

Perrin's feet ached from walking behind Sarah's wagon most of the afternoon. The barren rocky soil absorbed the sun's heat, had burned through thin shoes and scorched her soles. She had been looking forward to soaking her feet in a bucket of water from the muddy creek not far from their campsite.

But a glance at Cody's tight jaw signaled his frustration. He'd pushed them hard this week, hoping to make up a few days, only to encounter this delay at the gap. Hiding a wince, Perrin stood on sore feet and fetched her shawl.

Maintaining a careful space between them, they followed the creek for several yards, then climbed a stony ridge that offered a view of the campsites chosen by the waiting trains. Perrin gazed over the plain at dozens of cook fires, small brave beacons that represented someone's dreams for a new and better life. The small points of hope twisted her heart.

Gathering her skirts, she sat on a granite rock, watching a cloud of fireflies dancing to the crickets' nightly serenade. She would have smiled but for the tension drawing Cody's body.

"I'm going to send Augusta back on the next eastbound train through the gap," he announced abruptly. "She can't keep up."

Perrin caught a sharp breath as a battle erupted in her mind. Personal grievance, armed and warlike, stood arrayed against a lone figure of justice.

"She's improving every day," she said finally, the words emerging with great reluctance. "When we made camp yesterday, Augusta was only thirty minutes behind us."

"She can't continue like this. Have you seen her?"

Of course she had, and he knew it. All the brides had gloated over Augusta's greatly altered appearance. Gone were the fancy blond curls Augusta had fussed over while Cora made breakfast, then cleaned up. Now her hair was matted and dulled by dust, skinned into a careless knot on her neck. Sun had scorched her pale skin, peeled away, then burned again. As no one had told her that spit eased the pain of insect bites, she had scratched her face and arms until they bled. Her clothing was torn and dirty, and she didn't look as if she had eaten or slept in days.

If she had been anyone other than Augusta, the women

would have hastened to her aid, appalled by what was happening.

"I've seen her," Perrin murmured, rubbing her temples.

"Every day I expect her to ask to be sent back." Cody turned, standing on the ridge with the starlight and the campfires glowing behind him. Perrin gazed at his wide-legged stance, and her chest tightened painfully.

"She hasn't said anything to me about returning."

She stared at Cody another minute, disturbed by deep inner stirrings that she had believed long conquered. Desperately, she tried to thrust his powerful presence out of her mind, tried to ignore the provocative way he stood, the way his strong, capable hands rested on his hips, the way his voice curled under her skin and whispered to her body.

Think about Augusta, she commanded herself despairingly, not this man whom she longed for.

She too had expected Augusta to give up and ask to go home. Augusta's hands were so blistered and swollen she could hardly grip the reins. Some nights she didn't attempt to kindle a fire, but crawled directly into her unstable tent. If she slept there or wept, no one knew. Perrin suspected a little of both.

"Damn," she swore softly, striking her thigh with a fist. Why was it so painful to observe what was happening to Augusta?

"Why would a woman like Augusta Boyd want to travel to Oregon and marry a stranger? It doesn't make sense."

Perrin battled to concentrate on the question instead of the man who posed it. "Initially I thought she was doing it because she was upset and confused by Joseph's death, making a mistake she would regret." Lifting her head, she found Cody in the darkness, startled to discover him staring at her with burning eyes. She wet her lips. "I thought the first time Augusta missed her regular bath, she'd demand to turn back."

"It doesn't matter," Cody said in a strained voice. "What matters is she can't keep up."

Perrin nodded. Tilting her head, she slapped at a swarm of mosquitoes and mopped her throat with the edge of her shawl. It was hot tonight, and the rocks retained the day's heat. When she lowered her head, she suddenly became aware that she sat at eye level with Cody's belt buckle. Her gaze dipped slightly, then she abruptly jumped to her feet, feeling wild inside.

"I know you're frustrated by the delay," she said, speaking the first words that fought through the shameful thoughts that made her breath quicken. "But we need a rest period. The recent pace has been very hard."

The words died when he stepped close enough that her skirt brushed his trousers. He stared intently at her mouth, hunger flickering deep in his eyes. Weakness sapped her resolve as Perrin realized this was the first time in weeks that they had been alone together beyond the sight of the others.

"I've missed you," he said in a low thick voice as if he too realized they had left the camp far behind them.

Perrin's throat dried; she wet her lips. She ordered herself to step away from him. But she couldn't. Oh, God, she could not move, could hardly breathe. A hot tingle of anticipation shot through her body as electric as the stars flashing in the steamy night. "I see you every morning and every evening," she whispered in a husky voice. Even her voice trembled.

"You don't speak a word that isn't necessary, then you run away." His eyes plundered her face, ravished her lips.

The night closed in to suffocate her, hot, humid, filled with the love songs of mating insects. Years of wanting . . . something . . . tightened her chest and vibrated through her limbs. Weeks of wanting *him* thinned her voice. A haze of yearning narrowed her vision on his strong face. His face, as tense with desire as her own, his face, which she dreamed of, waking and sleeping. A groan closed her throat. "Cody, please. No. . . ."

One powerful hand caught her waist and pulled her roughly against him. The sudden shock of his lean body hard against hers burned the breath out of Perrin's lungs and she gasped. Lifting her hands, she steadied herself against his chest. His muscles went rigid at her touch, and she felt herself dissolve in the heat of the night and the heat of his arousal.

The instant his arms closed around her and she felt the power of his need, his hips pressing hard against her skirts, her head spun and she knew she was lost. Vibrating with her own need, she gazed up into his blazing eyes, unable to speak, unable to breathe. A surge of pent-up desire flattened her resistance. She had waited a lifetime for this moment, this man.

"I've imagined holding you in my arms a thousand times," he whispered in a thick voice. "If you tell me to stop, I will. It will be the hardest thing I'll ever do."

A sound like a sob scraped her throat as she let herself fall into the pool of desire darkening his eyes almost to black. The movement of his hips drove her mind to frenzy.

"Cody," she whispered, his name husky on her lips. His breath in her hair, his hot hands on her waist made her mind reel and she couldn't remember why this was wrong. How could anything this exciting and wonderful be wrong? The slow grind of his hips ignited a flash fire deep within her stomach. A light dew of perspiration appeared on her brow as she felt a wildness building inside. The intensity of her response melted her knees to straw and she might have fallen if he hadn't caught her against him.

"I want to make you call my name," he said, tilting her head up to stare into her eyes. "I want to feel your legs wrapped around me and watch your eyes widen." A low groan rumbled from his chest as his fingertips stroked her throat, following the heat of her skin to the first button of her shirtwaist.

His touch burned through Perrin's blood and bone, as if her body had been only kindling awaiting the flame of his fingertips, as if she had needed merely a touch to ignite her. Gasping, she realized that no man had ever drawn this heat or this sense of wild urgency from her. If he didn't kiss her now, she would burn to cinders in his arms, consumed by her own need and frantic desire.

When his head lowered, her arms flew around his neck and her lips opened hungrily beneath his. Lightning shot through her body like damp flame. She had not expected that his kiss would be gentle, not after this long a wait, and it wasn't. His mouth was almost savage on hers, as fierce and demanding as the emotion that rocked her senses.

They had been rushing toward this moment from the beginning. Walking into his arms had been as inevitable as sunrise. They had fought their attraction for each other, had erected barriers to no avail. Neither of them wanted this complication, yet neither could have stopped it. Their passion was as hot and electric as the lightning that opened the black night along the horizon.

"Oh, my God," she whispered when his mouth released her, leaving her weak and trembling with desire. She pressed her forehead against his shoulder. Her fingers tightened into fists on his chest and she squeezed her eyes shut, concentrating on the hard heat of muscle and bone. Her body molded against his length, returned the hot insistent pressure of his hips. She could no more have turned back her hunger for him than she could have altered the spin of the earth.

"I can't get you out of my mind," Cody murmured, kissing her forehead, her eyelids, her mouth. "Damn it, you've possessed me."

Perrin moaned and arched her throat. "I start the day thinking about you; I go to bed thinking about you." The dizzying scents of smoke and soap and male perspiration filled her nostrils, mixing like an elixir that she drank into her own body, filling herself with the essence of him. Beneath her bodice, her breasts swelled and ached, a hot tension climbed her inner thighs, moving toward the flooding dampness of readiness.

When his hands moved up her waist to cover her breasts, she sucked in a sharp breath. Long before her mind would admit her desire for him, her body had recognized this man, wanted him, and now claimed him.

Leaning over her, Cody gazed into the starlight and desire reflecting in her large dark eyes, then he lowered his mouth to hers in a hard, possessive kiss that ignited mind and body. His kiss was almost cruel in its fierce need. His mouth claimed total ownership, insisted on total surrender. Anything less would have left Perrin reeling with disappointment. The powerful urgency between his legs hardened against her, seeking the hot wetness between her own.

His eyes were smoky with passion, his voice thick. "Say my name," he murmured against her lips, commanding her.

"Cody," she whispered in a throaty voice made full by the desire that rocked her body in waves. "Cody, Cody."

A groan issued from deep in his throat. His lips took hers with passionate force, demanding, possessive, conquering her mouth as he would conquer her body, with hard rough need.

His mouth, his tongue . . . his hand buried in her hair. His body, lean and hard and taut . . . his arms like iron cords crushing her body to his . . . the pressure of his manhood, powerful and thrusting. These images swirled and mixed with the starlight and the night and the passion that rocked her body and set fire to slumbering desires she had thought long dead.

Lips locked to each other's mouths, hands flying over faces and hair and shoulders, fingers exploring, stroking, caressing, they sank to their knees on the rocky starlit ridge. When his hands again covered her breasts, Perrin gasped against his lips at a caress that scorched through thin calico and chemise. Her nipples rose like pink stones, hard and aching with need.

He bent her to the ground, piling her shawl beneath her head, and she pulled him down on top of her. Passion fired each gasping breath. Her need for him blinded her to everything but his mouth, his burning eyes, his body. And his touch. His touch inflamed her; each fiery stroke was a skilled tease that whirled her deeper into blind need and wanting him.

Drunk with starlit kisses, they rolled on the rocky ground, striving to thrust and meld, closer, closer, until Perrin was almost sobbing. Only then did his hand drop between them to jerk at his belt and fumble with the buttons on his trousers. Only then, when she was shaking and dazed, did she lift her skirts and kick out of her pantaloons.

They came together with explosive, cataclysmic force. When his hot fullness penetrated her, Perrin cried out and a momentary weakness of intense pleasure pervaded her body. Then she lifted to meet each hard exciting thrust, her fingers flying over his face, tangling in his hair. She whispered his name over and over, mindlessly pleading, encouraging, needing him.

Pacing himself, Cody ravaged her lips, staring deeply into her wide eyes. Again and again he brought her to the brink of release, teased her until she thrashed beneath him in a drenched frenzy, clawing at his shoulders, sobbing his name. Never in a hundred tortured dreams had Perrin imagined lovemaking could be this rapturous, this fiery, this thrillingly exciting. Not once had she considered that a man might focus on her pleasure or elevate her satisfaction before his own.

"Cody! Oh, Cody!" Sweat dampened her temples, soaked her bodice. She was drowning in the hot liquids of passion, burning with fires that leaped higher until finally, finally he led her soaring to the rim of the precipice and then ... and then his body took her over the edge and spun her out among the stars that burned overhead.

A moment later Cody's shoulders convulsed and he clasped her so tightly that Perrin would have cried out had her joy been less intense. His head dropped to her breast, and they both struggled for breath.

Rolling onto his back, he pulled her close and cradled her head against his shoulder, stroking the hair that spilled out of her bun. Gulping for breath, they gazed up at the stars, listening to the hum of insects and the distant murmur of voices in the camp.

"Are you all right?" he murmured gruffly, his lips in her hair, his arms around her.

Sudden tears glistened in Perrin's eyes. He had ruined her for any other man. Never again would lovemaking be like this. Never again would her passion be so intense that she would surrender to a man because she felt as if she would die if she didn't. Never before and never again would her arousal be as intense, as selfishly focused, nor would she ever again know a man who cared for her pleasure as well as his own.

Closing her eyes, she inhaled the mingled scents of their cooling bodies and wondered how she could have been one man's wife and another man's mistress without ever knowing that she too could experience a release so rapturous that for an instant she had believed her body was flying apart.

She tilted her face up to him and Cody kissed her, gently now. "You taste like apples and raisins," he murmured, smiling. Laughing softly, she kissed him back. "This isn't how I imagined it," he murmured, stroking her cheek. "I imagined a featherbed, you with your hair spread across a pillow. . . ."

"I imagined—" But she bit off the words and stiffened in his arms. Someone climbed the ridge, sending small stones skittering in the darkness.

"Mr. Snow?" One of the new teamsters paused, then called again. "Mr. Snow!"

They lay perfectly still in each other's arms, hardly breathing. The teamster halted not ten yards in front of them, slapped his hat against his thigh, cursed, then headed back down the ridge, shouting Cody's name.

The teamster brought with him a chill wind of sobering reality. Heart pounding in her breast, Perrin sat up abruptly in the darkness and pushed down her skirts. If the teamster had arrived five minutes earlier, she and Cody would have been so engrossed in each other, so lost in passion that neither would have noticed if the teamster had sat down beside them. Wrapping her arms around her legs, she dropped her forehead to her knees, shaking at the knowledge of near-disaster.

"Perrin?" He touched her hair, the nape of her neck.

"This cannot happen again," she whispered. "It must not."

All the reasons against them flooded her mind. The bridegroom who awaited her in Oregon. The women who would be her neighbors. A reputation she struggled to overcome. Raising her head, she stared blindly toward the cook fires in the distance. But for the span of a few minutes, her future might have been destroyed.

She felt Cody watching her, felt the tension in his hand on her neck. "After tonight, do you really think you and I can stay away from each other?" he asked.

"I wanted this as much as you did," Perrin admitted in a low choking voice. She was thankful the night was moonless, that he couldn't see the scarlet firing her cheeks. "Wanting you makes me shameless," she whispered, dropping her head. "And letting myself get swept away . . . maybe I am the harlot Augusta says I am."

"Perrin, for Christ's sake!" He stood abruptly, tucking his flannel shirt inside his pants, reaching for the buttons.

"This was an accident, that's all it was." She watched her fingers pushing at the rocky soil. "I'm going to be married at the end of this journey. That hasn't changed." Her heart fluttered, then crashed when he didn't deny what she was saying. Silently she stood and found her pantaloons, rolled them into her shawl. She wanted him to hold her, to tell her that tonight had not been an accident, that it had meant something. But he didn't reach for her. He kept glancing toward the squared wagons, searching for the teamster who had come looking for him.

"This happened because—"

"You're wanted in camp," she interrupted abruptly. Holding her shawl and pantaloons tightly against her chest, she faced him across the granite boulder. "What happened was inevitable." She drew a breath and made herself sound indifferent, as if she didn't care what he thought, as if she didn't care that he didn't step forward to take her into his arms. "Now it's over. We can put this behind us and pretend it never happened."

She felt his stare and sudden coldness. "What the hell are you saying? Are you telling me to leave a gold piece when I go?" Sarcasm roughened his voice.

Perrin jerked as if he'd slapped her.

Striding around the stone, he grabbed her chin and lifted her face, his eyes burning down at her. "Was that all this was to you? Scratching a sudden itch?"

"What else?" she snapped, jerking away from him. Lifting a hand, she tested the bruises he'd left on her chin. "I can recall at least six times that I've heard you tell someone that you don't plan to remarry. I was meant to overhear, wasn't I?"

"You think that because we . . ." he waved toward the ground and the spot where they had lain together. "You expect me to propose marriage?"

His incredulity wounded her like a knife thrust in the breast. "What would follow if you'd taken a *decent* woman? A *respectable* woman?" The accusation lashed out of her, propelled by pain and sudden anger. "What would you do then?"

"Perrin, for God's sake. We're adults. You're an experienced woman."

Her eyes closed, and she reeled backward a step. If she lived to be a hundred, she would never outlive Joseph Boyd. She had been a fool to hope that she could polish a reputation tarnished beyond salvation. She would always be an "experienced woman." And it would always be said in that knowing voice.

"A whore, you mean," she whispered, swaying on her feet.

Trembling, tears glistening in the starlight, she started to say more, choked, then spun in a whirl of calico and ran blindly down the rise.

Mem rested on the heavy stick she was using to stir the

laundry boiling in a large pot hung over the fire pit. She shoved at a wave of hair falling forward on her forehead, then shaded her eyes against the harsh morning sun.

"Why in the name of heaven are you trying to help Augusta Boyd?" she asked quietly, curiosity deep in her brown eyes.

"Cody is going to send her home."

"No one is going to weep if Augusta leaves the train."

"If it were anyone else, we'd all help," Perrin said stubbornly, inspecting the gray water boiling around Mem's and Bootie's skirts. Since she had not slept much anyway, she'd risen before dawn to wash her own accumulated laundry.

"It isn't anyone else," Mem said flatly. "Of all people, why is it you proposing this nonsense?"

"Maybe I know how it feels to be alone, to feel helpless and outcast," Perrin said, her voice sharper than she had intended. "Maybe I want to prove to Mr. Snow and to all of you that I meant it when I said I'd be fair as the representative. Maybe I won't like myself very much if I'm willing to help Winnie and Cora, but not Augusta. Maybe I did something recently that I'm not proud of, and I'll feel like I've atoned somewhat if I do something right even if I don't want to do it." She hadn't wanted to say any of that. She covered her eyes with a hand. "Everyone else has refused to help. I hoped I could count on you."

"Augusta is petty and selfish and insufferable. She treated Cora like cow flop. She treats Bootie like a personal servant."

"She must be frightened and suffering, and she's alone."

Mem returned to the stirring stick and gripped it hard. "Send her home. I say good riddance to bad rubbish."

That's exactly what Perrin longed to say. But a mulish sense of justice wouldn't let her. Plus, she did know what it felt like to be outcast and alone.

Augusta carried two heavy buckets of water from the river and hung them over the fire to boil as Cody or Webb or someone had instructed eons ago. When the water had boiled, she would fill her water barrel, then wash the grime off her hands and face.

Tears of pain swam in her eyes as she gazed down at her hands. Blisters formed on top of blisters. Bloody fluid leaked from those that had burst. Her hands hurt so much that she couldn't make a fist without weeping.

Even her face hurt; the wagon had become so disorganized that she couldn't find her long-brimmed bonnet or the salve that might have offered some protection from the burning sun. For the first time in her life, she had a severe sunburn.

Dropping her head, she wiped her eyes, agonizing over raw hands and the skin peeling off her forehead and nose, disfiguring her. Thank heaven her mother had not lived to see this. Or to see the soiled clothing she wore, another first in her life. Her mother would have disowned her.

A tear leaked from beneath pale eyelashes. She was so tired, so bone-dead fatigued. She hadn't known a person could be this exhausted and still survive. Her stomach rumbled; she was sick with hunger. Beneath her dirty clothing, her dirty skin chafed; she itched all over, tormented by insect bites.

She couldn't go on. The panicked realization settled over her like a chunk of marble about to drop and crush her life.

"Here." A hand reached down, offering a bottle of milky liquid. "This will soothe your sunburn and ease the sting of the insect bites. From now on, rub spit on the bites first thing."

Shoving at stringy loops of hair, she rocked back on her heels and gazed up at Perrin. Old instincts died hard. Her first impulse was to summon her pride and slap Perrin's hand away.

But her face was blistered and burned; she had scratched the insect bites until they swelled and bled. She hurt. Wordlessly, she accepted the bottle, shook it once, then began to slather the nasty-smelling stuff on her face and the back of swollen hands. Immediately the fire diminished on her cheeks and her shoulders. She collapsed in a long sigh of gratitude.

"Are you boiling that water for laundry?"

Augusta stared at her lap and drew a deep breath. A dozen scathing replies died on the tip of her tongue.

"I don't know how to do laundry," she whispered, imagining that she heard her pride crashing in little pieces around her. "I'm trying to get more drinking water, and water to wash myself. I'm dirty." The amazement of it thinned her voice. Tears pooling at the back of her throat threatened to drown her.

"The teamsters set up a bathing area at the river."

"No one told me!" Tears glistened in the sunlight. She could have spared herself the handles of the heavy buckets cutting into her wounded palms.

"Go take a bath." Perrin scanned the disarray of Augusta's camp. "I'll tidy up here. When you return, I'll teach you how to put up a wash. You can eat with Hilda and me tonight. We'll show you how to bake bread and make a basic stew."

Shock widened her gaze. "Why would you do that?"

Perrin stared at her. "Mr. Snow asked the same thing when I wanted to help Cora. The answer is, I don't know. Maybe because it's the fair thing, the right thing to do. It kills me to say this, but you deserve a chance just like anyone else."

"He's going to send me home on the first train going east, he said so." She returned Perrin's stare, too miserable and too panicked to question her next words. "I can't go back. You're the representative—you have to speak to Mr. Snow in my behalf! After what you did to my father, you owe me!"

"I did nothing to Joseph; I don't owe you anything!"

"You—"

"You amaze me." Perrin's hands closed into fists at her sides. "Right now, I am all you have. No one else would help. Just me. Do you understand? You have offended a group of generous, kind-hearted women to the extent that they would rather see you suffer than endure a moment of inconvenience themselves."

"They're nobodies!" The strength of outrage energized a body that had been too weary to stand just minutes before. She came to her feet with a snarl on her lips, hating it that Perrin Waverly—Perrin Waverly!—had come to her assistance. "Why should I care what a group of nobodies thinks about me?"

Perrin's beautiful face settled into hard angry lines. "Will you for once stop congratulating yourself for being a Boyd? Will you just once stop riding the coattails of your ancestors and think about who *you* are? Haven't you ever wanted people to like you or admire you because you're you, not just because of an accident of birth?"

Augusta drew back as if she'd suffered a blow to the stomach. "Shut up!" she hissed, shaking.

"What do *you* plan to add to the illustrious Boyd line?" Perrin asked scornfully. She cast a disdainful glance around the mess surrounding Augusta's wagon. "Helplessness? Selfishness? An ability to offend everyone you meet coupled with a lack of kindness and an inability to care for yourself? Is that your contribution to the great exalted Boyd line?"

"Shut up, shut up! I won't listen to this!"

"Look at you! Why in the name of heaven didn't you *ask* for help? Is your stupid Boyd pride that overweening?"

Augusta clapped her palms over her ears, scowling at the anger crackling in Perrin's eyes and face. She felt flogged by Perrin's fury and didn't understand it. If they had traded places, Augusta would have gloated.

"None of you would have helped me anyway!"

"The day you bend enough to ask for help is the day you become a real person and not the useless thing you are!" Perrin stepped backward and raised a shaking hand to her face, fighting for control. "I'm sorry," she whispered. "I came to help you, not attack you."

Augusta gathered her pride and found the strength to toss her dirty hair. "Dirty water finds the lowest level," she snapped. "I expect no less from you."

Perrin spread her fingers and stared through them. "You and I will always despise each other."

"I have good cause to hate you!"

"And not enough sense to keep from showing it even when I'm the only person willing to help you." They glared at each other, then Perrin dropped her hand and almost shouted. "Go take your bath. Maybe if I don't have to look at you, I'll remember why I'm stupid enough to try to help. Maybe I won't change my mind."

Icy reality chilled Augusta's bones. She remembered the earlier scene with Cody Snow, her tears and his implacability. She must be a lunatic to insult Perrin, the one person who might change Snow's mind as she had changed his mind about sending Winnie home, about letting Cora become a bride.

What in the name of heaven was she doing? What kind of insanity pushed her toward destruction?

Swallowing hard, she wrung her hands and frantically tried to perceive a way to backpedal without sacrificing what remnants remained of her dignity.

"I can't return to Chastity," she blurted. Even the thought made her feel suicidal. "If you help me, if you'll make Snow change his mind, I'll pay you a generous sum!" Perrin's mouth fell open. "I have plenty of money. And you—"

"My services are not for sale," Perrin mumbled, her face pale. "If you don't leave right now, I swear I'll—"

Augusta took one look at Perrin's face, then turned and hurried toward the river. When she considered that her future, her life, depended on the fairness and fighting spirit of her worst enemy, she groaned in despair and began weeping again.

"Goddammit!" Cody pushed back his hat, then swung around to face her. "I wish just once you'd stop interfering!"

"I'll help her. Hilda will help a little too." She stared back at him from flat expressionless eyes. Standing in the sunlight, tendrils of dark hair fluttering from the edges of her bonnet, she was so stubbornly beautiful that she made his stomach cramp. She had felt so right beneath him.

"I'd think you'd stand by cheering when Augusta rode out heading in the other direction! Instead, you want to help her." He shook his head in amazement and disbelief.

"Believe me, I'd love to see Augusta leave. But when I was picked as the women's representative, I promised to be fair. Whether I like it or not, sending Augusta back to Chastity isn't fair! At least not without giving her a chance."

"I gave her a week."

"She's come a long distance in a week. Remember, this is a woman who had never even dressed her own hair before coming on this journey. Right now she's overwhelmed and she's too exhausted to think, let alone function. Give her another week, let us help her, then if she's still falling behind . . . then send her home and good riddance. But let us try. You let us try with Winnie."

Cody ground his teeth. He itched to shake her until her bones rattled, until he knocked the starch out of her spine. Wanted to kiss the pinched expression off her mouth. He glanced at Smokey Joe, who was sorting a bucket of wild strawberries not six feet away.

"I want to speak to you privately."

She glared at him. "There's nothing you have to say that can't be spoken right here." She too slid a look toward Smokey Joe, who made no secret that he eavesdropped on every word.

Fuming, Cody strode toward a field of sunflowers, hoping she would follow. When she didn't, he returned to where she waited, her face stony and turned away from him.

"All right, damn it. I'll give Augusta one more week. That's all. And I'm agreeing to this solely because you asked it, no other reason." To hell with Smokey Joe and whatever he made of this odd conversation.

Perrin nodded, then caught her skirts against a puff of dusty wind, starting to turn away.

"But Winnie leaves on the train coming through the gap now."

She spun back to him, her dark eyes narrowing. "You have to send someone back? Is that it?" she snapped, sarcasm whipping her voice. "Don't punish Winnie because of your contempt for me!"

"My contempt? Or your indifference?" He glared at her. "I just returned from finding Winnie and bringing her back. She spent the night in Murchason's camp," he said, disliking himself for enjoying the shock dawning on her expression as she suddenly noticed the bruises on his face, the cut on his chin. "In exchange for a bottle of laudanum, Winnie spent the night with a bastard named Clavell."

He'd beaten Clavell to within an inch of his life. He wished he had finished the job.

Perrin gasped. "Oh, my God." Her face paled beneath her sunburn and she swayed on her feet as if the marrow had leaked out of her bones. Throwing out a hand, she leaned on his arm.

Her touch made him suck in a quick breath. His eyes narrowed and his groin tightened sharply. Immediately she snatched her hand away and high color flooded her face. She pressed her palms against her stomach, then looked up at him, cheeks flaming.

"Cody . . ." Large imploring eyes searched his.

"No," he said firmly, not mistaking her meaning. "Winnie goes home. If I'd sent Winnie home when I wanted to, she would not have spent the night with Clavell. She'd have only half the distance to travel to get home to Chastity, only half the dangers to face. I hope to Christ that she isn't pregnant."

Perrin nodded once, then walked away from him without a word, her head down, a hand at her eyes.

He watched her skirt swaying from her hips, saw the pale nape of her neck.

Abruptly Ellen came into his mind. Ellen, whom he had trusted and loved. Ellen, who had become another man's mistress while he was on campaign in the Dakotas.

Stiffening, he watched Perrin for another minute, then he turned and strode in the opposite direction. The surest way to avoid that kind of pain was never to love again.

But he couldn't get her out of his mind. Even the wind whispering through the sunflowers seemed to murmur her name.

CHAPTER
* 17 *

"Mr. Snow agreed to give you one more week," Perrin said coldly. "Hilda and I will each spell you at the reins once a day so you can get some rest. We'll teach you a few basic recipes so you can feed yourself and maintain your strength. This afternoon, we'll show you how to put up a wash so you'll have clean clothing to wear." Her eyes narrowed. "I hope you have a good memory, because we'll only show you once."

Augusta lowered the tortoiseshell comb she pulled through wet hair and closed her eyes. She had bathed, then immediately reapplied the lotion Perrin had given her. Since she was standing in front of a mirror hanging on the side of the wagon, Perrin supposed Augusta knew how grotesque the dried milky lotion made her appear. But relief from sunburn and stinging insect bites had momentarily conquered the towering Boyd pride and vanity.

"Thank you," Augusta whispered.

Those two words shocked them both. They studied each other warily, then Perrin hurried toward Winnie's tent before Augusta added something that would spoil a moment that made her seem almost human.

Wringing her hands, Jane tried to say good-bye while the teamsters transferred Winnie's goods into one of the wagons heading east, but Winnie was sobbing too loudly to hear.

"You're going home," Perrin said, echoing Jane's words. She pinned Winnie's good hat on top of chestnut curls.

Winnie grabbed her hands. "Please, please, please! Give me another chance. Please, don't let him send me back! Please!"

"Oh, Winnie," Perrin whispered. Tears swam in her eyes.

"I'll never do it again, I swear! I just . . . I kept thinking about Billy Morris, and I knew the laudanum would help, so I . . . but, Perrin!" Her fingernails dug into Perrin's hands, tears flooded her cheeks. "If I go home, I won't be strong enough to resist! I'll die. Please, help me!"

Perrin turned aside, blinking hard at the teamsters transferring Winnie's belongings. She had wept and pleaded for Winnie again this morning, but Cody was intractable. Winnie had thrown away her second chance.

Perrin rubbed her forehead. Was there something more she could have done to help Winnie? Anything? In the end, all she had accomplished was to put Winnie through the hell of withdrawal and delay the inevitable. For the rest of her life, she would blame herself for Winnie's fall from grace.

"I'm sorry," she said helplessly, watching Winnie's expression fade from pleading to hopeless resignation.

In silence, she and the others followed as Cody escorted a weeping Winnie Larson to the eastbound train, then helped her up onto the wagon seat beside a grizzled old man whom Cody had hired to drive her. Winnie covered her face and sobbed into her gloves.

Jane dabbed her eyes with the hem of her apron. "She was so happy to be free of the opiates," she whispered. "She really believed she would never be tempted again."

"Winnie brought shame to herself and her family. She's killing herself," Sarah stated flatly. She dashed an angry hand across her lashes. "Now we've lost two. Lucy and Winnie."

They watched the eastbound train roll past oxen carcasses and piles of abandoned furnishings. Then Smokey Joe banged his gong, signaling it was time to mount their wagons. Murchason's train had entered the gap. Cody Snow's train was next in line.

The trail dropped south again. Now they could see the soaring craggy peaks of the Continental Divide. The sight stunned and awed them, taking the heart out of everyone.

Bootie lowered Cora's wedding dress to her lap, putting

down her needle, and swept a fearful frown toward the towering peaks. "I swan, I just don't know how we're going to get over them."

"We'll go through South Park," Jane explained. "It's a natural break. Easy as apple pie. You won't even know you're crossing a mountain range."

"Hold still," Thea cautioned, gazing at Jane, then down at her sketch pad. "How will I finish this if you keep fidgeting?"

Twin lines puckered Jane's brow. "I told you, I don't want my portrait shown in your display."

Mem set aside the lamp wicks she was plaiting, stretched her back, then leaned to inspect the lace Jane tatted for the collar on Cora's wedding dress. "What display is that?" she asked Thea.

Thea waved her charcoal stick. "You know how Cora is always looking for a way to earn money. . . ."

"She's doing the men's laundry," Bootie contributed.

"She wants to display my work when we meet up with other wagons at South Pass. She says she'll set up a display and do the selling if I'll pay her a twenty percent commission on sales."

"A commission?" Bootie inquired, blinking. "Fancy that. Where did Cora learn such a word, and what does it mean?"

"I'm serious, Thea," Jane said, frowning. "I don't want my portrait offered for sale."

Mem let the conversation swirl around her for another minute before she wandered away from the group, walking across some of the driest, most barren land she had seen. No wonder the oxen were going lame one after another. Cactus hugged the ground; the spines wreaked havoc on the poor oxen's feet. There was no water; dust choked everyone. It was a dismal stretch of country.

For thirty idle minutes she watched Miles Dawson and the teamsters wash the hooves of the limping oxen with strong soap, scrape away diseased flesh, then pour on tar or pitch. If the treatment was successful, perhaps tomorrow the train would make more than the six meager miles they'd traveled today.

Continuing around the squared wagons, she lingered a moment to observe Sarah, Hilda, and Cora sitting in the hot shade beside Sarah's wagon, their heads bent over a chalk slate. Mem called a word of encouragement, then walked toward Perrin's wagon.

"Feeling any better?" she inquired, finding Perrin resting on the shady side of her wagon, fanning her face and looking limp in the dusty heat.

"A little. Thank you for the ointment."

At the gap, where they had last done laundry, someone had moved Perrin's clothing from a thicket of willows and draped the garments over a stand of poison oak. Cody's clothing had ended up on the poison oak as well. Unaware, they had worn the clothes, then both had fallen ill for several days. Perrin had taken the worst of it. Her face and limbs were still swollen and lumpy, on fire with an itching that no treatment completely eased.

"It was an unfortunate accident," Mem said, sitting on the ground beside Perrin's camp chair where she could view the snowcapped mountain peaks. They were as inspiring as she had hoped mountains would be if she was ever lucky enough to see any.

"I wonder if it was an accident," Perrin commented, idly scratching her arms. When Mem lifted an eyebrow, she sighed. "Strange things have happened lately. Sand mixed with the coffee grounds, a hole in the sugar bag. We lost five pounds before Hilda noticed. Maybe I'm just . . . but it is odd."

"You push yourself too hard. You'd regain your strength faster if you'd stop wearing yourself out helping Augusta."

"Augusta will make it now." They gazed past the animals being doctored in the square, inhaling the pungent thick scent of hot tar. Despite the relentless heat, Augusta worked around her wagon, practicing new and still shaky skills. Perrin waved a fan in front of her swollen face. "She's determined. She isn't going home." A whiff of grudging admiration underlay her flat tone.

"Good for her," Mem answered tersely. "Too bad for us."

They lapsed into a comfortable silence, lulled by the heat, until Mem grew too restless to sit still any longer. She pulled her long legs up under her and stood. The unremitting heat made her sleepy unless she kept moving.

Rubbing her peeling sunburned forehead, she scanned the desolate hills surrounding them, then brightened. "Ah, here they come again. At least I think it's them, that Indian family." Three dots emerged from a distant ravine, moving slowly toward the train. "Last night I traded some bread loaves for a pair of quilled moccasins. Did you trade for anything?"

"I exchanged a jar of strawberry jelly for some beadwork." Perrin yawned, started to scratch the itchy welts on her chest, then made herself replace her hand in her lap.

Mem hesitated, then lowered her head and shook the dust from the folds of her dark skirt. "Perrin? There's something I've been wanting to . . . well, have you noticed . . . that is, do you think there's a special fondness between Augusta and Webb Coate?"

Perrin's eyes flew open and she laughed, cracking the white ointment that slathered her face. "Absolutely not! Last night I was showing her how to turn out her wagon when the Indians came. As far as Augusta is concerned, Indians—and that includes Webb—are uncivilized barbarians. Creatures to fear and despise. She can't say a civil word about Webb." She examined the patches of color blooming on Mem's cheeks. "Why do you ask?"

The scarlet deepened on Mem's cheekbones and she wished she had held her foolish tongue. Worse, the words kept coming. "Webb and I meet nearly every night by Smokey Joe's fire; we've done so almost from the start of the journey." When she observed Perrin's surprise, she clasped her hands tightly. "Webb is my friend, and I'm his. We've confided things about ourselves that no one else . . . well, that's neither here nor there." She frowned at the distant peaks, then lowered her head. It felt so good to talk about him, just to speak his name aloud. "It upsets me to think that I'll never see him again after we reach Oregon."

Perrin studied her flaming cheeks. "And you really think he cares for Augusta?"

"I know he does." She had come this far; there was no point turning coy now. "Webb helped her that first week. He's the one who told Augusta how to make her first fire and set up her tent. I overheard him whispering instructions to her."

"No, you didn't," Perrin disagreed, suddenly smiling.

"I beg your pardon?"

"You heard Heck Kelsey." When Mem gaped in disbelief, Perrin laughed. "When Heck finally told Cody what he'd done, Cody didn't believe it either. I did, because Webb was with Sarah and Cora and me when Heck was standing behind Augusta's wagon pretending to be Webb. Haven't you heard Heck imitate Cody and Webb before? Heck Kelsey can mimic any accent he has ever heard."

"But why . . ." Mem frowned. Was it possible? Her mind raced. She *had* heard Heck mimic Smokey Joe and others.

"It's Heck who's sweet on Augusta, Mem," Perrin said gently. "Smokey Joe teases him about it all the time. Webb wanted to send Augusta back to Chastity when Cody first suggested it."

Mem's heart leaped. She tried to speak, but couldn't, then hastily excused herself before Perrin could ask the questions rising in her large dark eyes.

She took a few steps, holding her hem away from the spiny cactus, then stopped. No, she would not allow herself to exalt that it was Heck who had assisted Augusta. It might not change anything. She *knew* there was something between Augusta and Webb because she had seen them together that awful night. And she had watched Augusta yearning after him with long glances.

But she was not going to torture herself with painful thoughts today. She'd done enough of that.

So what would she do? The rest of the morning and an idle afternoon stretched before her, promising nothing but monotony and boredom. When was the last time Mem Grant, great adventuress, intrepid explorer, had done something worthy of recording in her journal? Her descendants would read her journal and conclude that she was a dullard.

Her clear gaze settled on the dots walking out of the low hills and she considered, thinking about the Indian family, who apparently intended to pay a return visit to their camp.

After a moment's reflection, a slow smile appeared on her lips. Yes, this was the very thing. Whirling, she returned to her wagon and managed to locate an old hat and a pair of sturdy walking shoes without attracting the notice of the women working on Cora's wedding dress. After packing a flour sack with assorted trinkets for gifts, she set off across the barren ground at a brisk pace, walking toward the approaching dots.

Mem's impulsive adventure became the most glorious, most enlightening day of her life to date.

The Sioux village was small, only a dozen lodges, and the inhabitants were dumbfounded by the sight of her. The women recovered first, collecting around her to inspect her clothing, her sunbonnet, her sunburned face, and her astonishing auburn hair. She was equally fascinated by their soft doeskin tunics, and beadwork adorning their leggings, their shining braids.

Laughing, and struggling to recall the phrases Webb had taught her, she passed out the trinkets she had brought and indicated with gestures that she would like to examine a tepee, would enjoy seeing whatever they cared to show her.

She was aware that the village men engaged in a heated discussion concerning her arrival, questioning the man whose wife had agreed to bring Mem to the village. There appeared to be a lot of consternation, many comings and go-

ings from the largest tepee, and numerous male glares
thrown in her direction.

As she expected the men to banish her at any minute, she
pressed the women to take her inside a lodge at once, hoping
that out of sight meant out of mind. She wanted to glimpse a
way of life that charmed and surprised her.

The first surprise had been discovering pine and scrubby
cottonwood trees. The Indians had found shade in this empty
land, and a tiny creek that trickled past the lodges. The second surprise was discovering how cool it was inside the buffalo hides draping the lodge poles. Air flowed beneath the
gap between ground and hides. The flap turned back at the
peak allowed for circulation. It was quite comfortable inside.

Once her eyes adjusted to the airy dimness of the tepee's
interior, she could admire the efficiency of her hostess, a dignified older woman who invited her inside with the courtesy
one princess might extend another.

By the nature of the articles arrayed on each side of the
tepee, Mem could see that the lodge was arranged to accommodate women on one side, men on the other. She seated
herself on a pile of buffalo robes mounded invitingly on the
women's side. Her hostess beamed, then barked an order at a
younger woman, who hastened to fetch a bowl of food and a
container of cool water.

Mem drank the water gratefully, then sampled a bowl of
meat stewed with wild onions. To her taste, the dish needed
salt, and the meat was too gamy for her palate, but she
smacked her lips, smiled broadly, and politely swallowed
every bite. Immediately another bowl appeared before her.
Too late she remembered Webb absently turning his cup upside down when he finished drinking. Gamely, she finished
the second bowl of food, then patted her stomach, smiled and
smiled, and turned her bowl upside down before her. The
women beamed back at her.

During the next hours the Indian women showed her their
pouches of dyed quills and how they sewed the quills to
moccasins and jackets and doeskin gowns. She watched a

girl scraping an antelope hide, took a turn at it herself, admired a dozen children of various ages, observed their war-like games.

Pipe smoke wafted from the largest lodge, and occasionally a fierce-looking man emerged to stare at her, but none of the men spoke to her. Gradually the novelty of her visit dimmed and the women went about their chores and every-day life, laughing and calling to each other, leaving Mem to happily amuse herself by quietly observing.

Near four in the afternoon, a brief flurry erupted as two men trotted into the circle of tepees. Mem's eyebrows lifted in sheepish surprise when she recognized Webb's mustang.

For his entrance into the Sioux camp, he had stripped to the waist and loosened his black hair, letting it flutter free over bared shoulders. He'd twisted an eagle feather into his hair near the crown, and he rode bareback. Mem gazed at the hard muscles twitching on his naked chest and her mouth dried.

She wasn't the only woman affected by Webb Coate's powerful physique. The Indian girls cast him quick sparkling glances, then clapped hands over their mouths to smother giggles. The older women admonished them sharply, but they too ran speculative gazes over Webb's buttocks and thighs as he dismounted before the large tepee. They all giggled and glanced at Mem when Webb gave her a hard angry look before he ducked into the lodge.

At once Mem understood she was in trouble. But she decided it was worth it. For a few hours she had observed a different culture, a distinctive way of life, and had been captivated by all she had seen. She suspected this brief visit would be a highlight of her journey.

Accompanied by two of the many dogs in camp, dogs that never seemed to bark, she walked away from the voices shouting and murmuring in the large tepee, choosing to wait for Webb beside the willows bordering the trickle of water.

Here two naked chubby toddlers dug in the damp soil, playing beneath the watchful eye of an old grandmother as

wrinkled as a dried apple. The grandmother refused to acknowledge Mem's presence, but the toddlers babbled happily and waved their digging sticks before returning to their
play in the mud.

She smiled at the youngsters and imagined Webb's childhood in their dark eyes. She had seen him in the young boys
hunting mice with small bows and arrows, had visualized
him as one of the adolescents racing their ponies to win
small wagers.

Sighing, she seated herself on a flat rock and wondered
what it would be like to live a nomadic life, following game
and the seasons, living one's life in a cozy tepee, sleeping on
the softness of a buffalo robe.

The freedom and the closeness to nature appealed deeply.
Then she thought about relinquishing a bed and the sunny
smell of clean linen sheets. She considered giving up salty
food and a warm winter house, lamps to read by and a cook-
stove. She thought about never remaining in one place long
enough to plant a garden.

There were difficulties with this culture that placed it beyond her comfort level. Her hostess for lunch had been an
older wife; there was a younger wife as well. Both undoubtedly had watched their husband ride off to raid neighboring
villages, not knowing if he would return alive. And there was
something nasty hanging on a pole in front of the big lodge
that Mem suspected might be a scalp. One of the women
seemed quite proud of it.

No, despite some genuine attractions, Mem couldn't visu-
alize herself living as an Indian. A life without basic comforts was, alas, not for her. And the hint of savagery
disturbed her. Still . . . there was much here to envy.

"Enjoying yourself?" a voice inquired over her head. And
then, in Sioux that Mem couldn't interpret, "Perhaps someone would prefer a different site for the little ones."

The old grandmother did not look up at Webb, but she
nodded and pushed to her feet. Surprisingly lithe, she led the
children farther along the creek. Watching her go, Mem re-

called that adult men and women did not address one another directly or publicly look each other in the eyes.

Since she didn't know if the villagers watched, she did not turn and look at Webb's face. She waited until he stepped around the rock and halted in front of her, folding his arms across his naked chest. At this moment he resembled a young god, with sunlight creating a halo around his black hair, the blue sky and lavender mountains behind him.

Her heart rolled in her chest. Had there ever been a more beautiful man? Surely his rightful place was on Mount Olympus, seated at the hand of Zeus.

"Did Mr. Snow send you to fetch me?" she asked quietly.

He glared at a spot directly above her head. "Broken Paw sent a rider to the train. He feared the whites would believe he'd taken you hostage and would send a war party to rescue you."

Mem frowned, nervously arranging the folds of her skirt across the rock. "I didn't think of that."

"You disappeared. No one knew where you'd gone." His voice was flat with anger. "Cody pulled the teamsters off treating the oxen and sent them all over the countryside searching for you." The muscles swelled on his shoulders and forearms. "This was a foolish and dangerous stunt, Mem."

Foolish, yes. She could see that now. But it had never entered her mind that she might be in danger. She looked up at him defensively. "I've been treated with the utmost courtesy."

"I know that because I know Broken Paw. But not all villages welcome intruders. You could very well have placed yourself in grave danger. As it is, the teamsters and half the brides are convinced you were carried off by hostiles against your will. Miles Dawson wanted to ride into this village with guns blazing to avenge your capture. If a man less knowledgeable than Cody Snow was wagonmaster of the train, people might have gotten killed because of your impulsiveness."

Her mouth dropped and she stared at him directly. "I came here of my own free will and I have not been ill treated. I've had a delightful afternoon!"

Exasperation added to the anger in his black eyes. But as they stared at each other, Mem finally spied a tiny hint of amusement. "What in the hell were you thinking of?"

"I wanted to see an Indian village," she answered simply, spreading her hands. "It's been wonderful." Sadness darkened her eyes. "But this will all vanish one day, won't it?" When he said nothing, she continued speaking.

"The skins around their lodges are buffalo. They sleep on buffalo robes, use every part of the animal for something vital to their existence." She met his gaze. "But how many buffalo herds have we seen? Three? Four? And how many white buffalo hunters? Hundreds." She shook her head, idly tucking up an auburn strand. "Eventually there won't be a buffalo left on the plains. Then what will these people do? How will they live?"

She recalled the tall piles of buffalo hides covering the ground at the gap, awaiting transportation east. The mountainous piles had stunk and attracted clouds of flies. That's what Mem had noticed, the flies more than the hides. Now she saw the forest behind the trees. The plains buffalo were being systematically slaughtered. When the buffalo vanished, so would the village behind them.

Appalled by her vision of the future, she frowned up at Webb. "If I were an Indian, I would hate the white men who killed the animal I need to live." The conflict and pain drawing his cheeks confirmed her speculation. "It's all going to explode, isn't it? Our culture against theirs?"

He stared at her. "Yes. That's one of the reasons why this will be the last trip west for me and for Cody."

"You'll return to England and manage your father's affairs."

He nodded, his eyes so black she could not distinguish the pupils. "What kind of woman has thoughts such as these?" he asked curiously, studying her face.

Her head dropped back and she gazed up at him. "You know who I am better than anyone else. Even Bootie. I'm a woman who wants to know things. A woman too inquisitive for her own good."

He studied her with a clarity that caused Mem to suck in a quick, soft breath. "I see you, Woman Who Wants to Know Things."

"I see you, Tanka Tunkan," she whispered.

Not taking his eyes from hers, he clasped her shoulders and drew her to her feet. Mem's heart beat so loudly that she thought certain he must hear drums in his ears. For a full minute, he gripped her shoulders while he studied her face.

Then he leaned down, gazing into her eyes all the while, and she knew he would kiss her. A soft sigh parted her lips and she closed her lashes, trembling with anticipation.

It was not the passionate kiss he had bestowed on Augusta in the moonlight. Mem's afternoon kiss was gentle, exploratory, perhaps an experiment. He moved slowly, tentatively, as if he expected her to jerk away from him. In truth, she could not guess what kissing her meant to him.

But for her, Webb Coate's kiss was a bolt of raw lightning, a hot thrill that raced from her mouth to rock body and spirit. This was the kiss she had abandoned hope of ever experiencing, but had dreamed of a hundred times. She understood now that her dreams were weak and pallid things compared to the genuine event.

When his mouth released hers, he gazed down at her with surprise in his black eyes, then he clenched his jaw. His fingers tightened on her upper arms and she thought he would kiss her again. Instead, he lifted his magnificent head and gazed toward the village before he looked at her again. "You have a brave heart, Woman Who Wants to Know Things."

"I wish we didn't have to return to the train," Mem whispered, wetting her lips. What people said to each other after kissing was unknown to her. She wanted him to kiss her again, wanted him to kiss her as passionately as he had kissed Augusta. In this moment of happiness and yearning, she longed to furnish a tepee with his things on one side, her things on the other. "I wish we could run away and travel with the village."

His speculative stare traveled over her face, her eyes, her lips. It seemed to Mem that his dark gaze burned her skin, leaving a fiery stain in its wake. Beneath her hot fingertips, his naked chest felt like sculpted rock. If she could have moved, even breathed, she might have run her hands over his body as she longed to do.

"I see you," he said again, his voice wondering and slightly puzzled.

Mem laughed. "I have always seen you, my dear friend."

"Come," he said finally, releasing her arms. He looked at her again, then walked toward his mustang.

She followed, knowing they adopted roles for the sake of village custom. The women emerged to surround her and bid her farewell in a language she cursed herself for not understanding. Webb spoke to the men, then he tossed Mem up on the mustang and mounted behind her. Slowly, they rode out of the shady ravine.

Dazed and wondering where today would lead, Mem was totally unaware of the children running after them. All she could think about was Webb's naked chest pressed against her back. The touch of him scalded her senses. For the first time, it occurred to Mem Grant that she was a lustful creature, a woman of the flesh.

Good heavens. Her eyebrows soared and a broad smile curved lips that still tingled from his kiss. She, Mem Grant, prim and proper spinster, was a woman brimming with lust. My, my. The realization delighted her. She hoped she was wanton too. Maybe, with the right man, she could even be a bit brazen. Wicked little shivers rippled through her body. When Webb's thighs curved around her buttocks and his arms reached around her for the reins, she closed her eyes and swayed dangerously, enjoying the wonderful new sensations awakening within her body.

Oh, yes. If the thoughts reeling hotly through her mind

were any indication, she was exquisitely capable of being wanton and brazen. With the right man. This man.

Not trusting herself to speak, she relaxed in his arms, remembering every tiny detail of his tentative kiss, as they rode out onto the cactus-studded barren plain.

"What the . . ."

The murmur near her ear tightened with tension. Mem's eyes flew open and she stiffened against his chest.

Now she heard distant whoops, saw rising dust circling the wagon train. "The train is being attacked!"

Her words were lost to the wind whistling past her ears as Webb dug his heels into the mustang's flanks and the mustang leaped forward.

Both of them leaned, Webb to urge the mustang faster, Mem to grip the flying mane and hang on for dear life. Webb didn't shout instructions; she knew instinctively that when he drew the mustang up in a cloud of swirling dust, she was to throw herself off. When she pushed up from the parched ground, spitting dust, he was gone, lost in billowing coils.

Ignoring the cactus spines stinging her palms, Mem crouched and ran, diving underneath the wagon in front of her. Knowing Webb, it didn't surprise her to discover she was beneath her own wagon, and Bootie was staring at her with tear-stained eyes.

"Oh, Mem, you poor, poor dear! Did the savages . . . did they abuse you?" she whispered, her voice shaky with horror.

"Of course not!" Gunshots exploded from riders circling the wagons, answered by shots fired from the teamsters.

"What did they do to you?"

"Bootie!" She thrust up on her elbows, bumped her head on the bottom of the wagon, and gazed in exasperation at her disheveled sister. "We're in the middle of an attack!"

Bootie lay flat on her stomach, waving a hand at the dust flying in front of her face. "But what did they *do* to you? We were all so worried and terrified for your sake!"

"I went to the Indians of my own volition. They served me

lunch and cool water. They showed me their homes, their sewing, and their children. I had a lovely time and I didn't want to come back! Nothing unpleasant occurred."

Pity saddened Bootie's eyes. "Oh, Mem. How very like you to put a brave face on it. You poor, poor courageous dear. We'll just try to rise above your horrible experience."

Mem dropped her forehead against crossed arms and made a sound of frustration that blew a puff of dirt and dust into her face. "If the attackers don't shoot us first, I'm going to strangle you. Who are those men, anyway?"

Bootie shouted to be heard over the gunshots and pounding hooves that flashed past them in the dust. "Jane thinks it's the Quinton gang. They rode up with no warning at all." A single tear cut a muddy track down her cheek. "It's my fault."

"That's ridiculous!" But nothing Mem had said or could say would convince Bootie that she was not to blame for Quinton's pursuit. Silently, Mem again cursed Augusta Boyd for putting the idea in Bootie's head, then she stretched out an arm and drew her sister close in a protective gesture. They huddled together beneath the wagon, choking on dust, picking cactus spines out of their flesh, wishing they knew what was happening.

And floating above it all, like a soft cloud above an icy peak, was Webb's kiss still lingering on her lips.

Cody held fire and leaped out of the way when Webb's mustang loomed in the billowing dust. The mustang jumped the tongue of the arms wagon. Seconds later, Webb appeared beside him, guns blazing at the men who rode whooping around the train.

One figure flew off his horse, then another. A lull opened in the dust and noise. "They're leaving," Cody yelled. Spinning in tandem, he and Webb pushed aside the wagon tongue, opening it far enough to get their horses out. "Close it behind us," he shouted when he saw Perrin's ointment-smeared face peering at him through spirals of settling dust.

Miles Dawson galloped through the opening first, then Heck Kelsey. Webb was next, with Cody a heartbeat behind him. Before they raced off in pursuit, he saw Perrin rushing toward the wagon tongue, Hilda, Ona, and Thea behind her.

Damn Jake Quinton to hell. Cody burned with the urge to leave Heck Kelsey in charge of the train, take Webb, and track Quinton to the ends of the earth.

Quinton and his men faded into the rocky ravines like gray shadows. If night hadn't been hard upon them, Webb could have tracked the outlaws until they split up, but Cody's duty was to defend the train. Reluctantly, he ordered his men back to camp.

They arrived in time to see the women mounding dry dirt over two shallow graves. Grim-faced, Cody halted the buckskin beside Perrin and inspected her swollen face. She had received a worse dose of the poison oak than he had. "Who?" he demanded sharply.

"None of us," she answered quickly, understanding his deepest concern. "Two of the attackers. No identification."

He nodded shortly, relief spreading through his chest like thick hot liquid. Then his eyes found Mem Grant, leaning on the handle of a shovel. He rode up beside her and let her see the anger frosting his gaze. "Don't ever leave camp alone again. If you plan to go farther than a hundred yards, you tell someone. Understand? You get one serious mistake, and you just had it."

"I'm sorry." She nodded up at him. "I should have told Perrin where I was going. I apologize for the concern I caused."

Not sorry that she had gone, but sorry she hadn't told anyone. Cody suppressed a sigh. But he also glimpsed why Webb admired this unusual woman. He was beginning to understand that each of the brides was remarkable in her own way. But Mem Grant was the only one of them who would have marched off alone to inspect an Indian village. Just as Perrin Waverly was the only one who would help Augusta.

"While you're all present," he shouted, calling for silence. "The attackers were Jake Quinton and his men. I saw Quinton."

"He wants the arms wagon," Perrin stated flatly.

"The carbines and ammunition are your future and mine." His steely gaze matched hers, unyielding. "That wagon goes with us to Oregon; we've settled that question. Without it, your bridegrooms will lose the homes they are undoubtedly building for you now."

"Will Jake Quinton keep attacking us?" The question came from little Thea Reeves, who still shook from head to foot.

"Very likely," Cody snapped. He glanced at Webb above the women's heads, then again to the sea of eyes. "How many of you know how to use a pistol or a carbine?"

Sarah Jennings stepped forward, and Jane Munger, which surprised him.

"From now on we're going to have shooting lessons every day at the noon rest and again after supper. I'll teach half of you at midday; Webb will take the other half in the evening. We'll continue that schedule until everyone can handle a carbine. I want each of you able to defend yourselves."

For an instant he thought of asking which of them had slashed his bedroll for the second time, then thought better of it. The slashing hadn't begun until after the new teamsters joined up at Fort Laramie. In his gut, he didn't believe slashing a bedroll was something a man would do. But he wasn't certain enough to make accusations.

His eyes met Perrin's. "I'd like to speak to you after supper, Mrs. Waverly. I'll expect a report of any damage done to the wagons, any injuries, however minor."

Before she could invent an excuse to refuse, he wheeled the buckskin and rode out to capture the livestock that had escaped during the fracas.

He hadn't spoken to Perrin alone since the night before they came through the gap, the night he had taken her. He hated his reaction, but his thighs tensed in anticipation.

He wanted her again. Worse, he suspected this was a woman whom no amount of sex would get out of his system. They had forged a bond that went deeper than physical need. Exactly what that bond was, he didn't know. But he was beginning to recognize it existed and had taken root inside him.

What disturbed him most was the question she had posed. At first he had considered it ridiculous, but upon reflection, perhaps the question was fair. What would he have done, what would he be thinking now, if she hadn't been an experienced woman?

Was she thinking that he had only used her to ease his body? That she was merely a convenience during a long journey?

The answers danced away from his grasp because he didn't want to analyze, didn't want to admit how he felt about her.

CHAPTER
* 18 *

They completed the day's business swiftly. All the women had puncture wounds from cactus, Thea had sprained her left wrist, none of the wagons had escaped without a few bullet holes. Heck Kelsey worked by lantern light to repair a couple of shot-up water barrels. Miles Dawson patched one of Smokey Joe's mules after discovering its ear had been injured in the fracas.

"We understand that our futures depend on profits from the arms and ammunition and we have to take the wagon to Oregon," Perrin conceded, watching the first bright stars poke holes in the night. "But we're all frightened of Quinton and his gang."

She and Cody stood near a thick spread of rabbit brush. The smell of powder and smoke still drifted in the air from the earlier shooting lessons, which had begun immediately. Perrin inhaled the faint sulfur odor, the smoke from buffalo chip fires, the scents of bacon and beans, and the warm dusty night.

Cody lifted a coffee mug to his lips, his eyes scanning the squared wagons. "How do you think the women would react if I left Heck in charge and took Webb after Quinton and his men?"

Perrin examined the knots rising and falling along his clenched jaw. "Heck Kelsey is a good man," she said after a lengthy silence. "But he's not a trained wagonmaster. I doubt Heck could have stopped Miles Dawson from riding hell-bent for slaughter into that Indian village to rescue Mem."

Perrin had spoken sharply to Mem about going off on her own, but she wasn't sure if Mem had heard a word she'd said. Mem had smiled and nodded with a vagueness that reminded Perrin of Winnie. Mem's mind was elsewhere.

Cody tossed the remainder of his coffee onto the ground,

threw the cup toward Smokey Joe's wagon. "I was afraid that's what you'd say." He hooked his thumbs in his back pockets and spoke without looking at her. "I've missed you."

Perrin stiffened and her chest tightened. "If we've covered everything, I need to set up our tent." She told herself that she didn't want to hear anything he might have to say. And yet . . . knowing she would see him tonight, she had used some of their precious water to scrub the white ointment off her face.

He stepped in front of her, blocking her escape. "Do you want me to say I'm sorry for what happened between us? I'm not sorry. Do you want me to swear it won't happen again? I hope it does. I can't get you out of my mind."

"Please, Cody, let me pass." Warm color flooded her throat and cheeks. Her body remembered another hot night, remembered hard callused hands caressing her skin. She remembered every detail and the memories tormented her.

Lifting a hand, he smoothed a tendril of hair off her cheek. "What do you want from me, Perrin?"

Surprised by the question, she hesitated, gazing into eyes shadowed by stormy color. The lines carving his cheeks had deepened. Everything sensible told her to step away from his touch, but his fingertips on her cheek rooted her to the earth and she couldn't move, could hardly breathe. "I don't want anything from you," she whispered.

His fingertips slid to the corner of her lips. "I know what I want. I think—I hope—you want the same thing." His gaze lit the darkness, smoldering down at her. "Perrin, for God's sake. You and I are circling each other like wildcats. Nothing has changed except half the time we're spitting at each other, and the rest of the time—"

"Cody, please. Don't do this." Her eyes closed and a small moan issued from her throat.

Although darkness deepened around them, someone might have noticed two shadows merging into one. The thought frightened her and Perrin forced herself to step away from him. Lifting a shaking hand, she pressed it to the corner of her lips. When she felt Cody move up behind her, she stiffened her backbone and her resolve.

"We made a mistake," she said in a low voice, looking down at the ground. "Now we put it behind us and go on."

Warm hands closed around her waist and she inhaled sharply. Then he kissed the nape of her neck and the hot touch of his lips made her sway and shudder with pleasure.

"Can you forget?" he asked hoarsely, his breath on her skin.

She would never forget.

"I want . . . I want . . ." Her heart pounded with anger and frustration and wanting him. Suddenly she felt an urge to whirl and strike him with her fists. She wanted to beat on his chest and weep until no more tears flowed. She wanted him to hold her and comfort her and tell her they would always be together. Fury erupted inside when she realized that could never happen.

Her trembling body didn't recognize the difference between anger and passion. The same rushing blood sped through her veins, the same heated flush stained her cheeks. Her pulse thudded in her throat and her breath quickened. Turning to face him, she saw Cody through her anger and felt a helpless melting flood her limbs. Day and night she thought about his rough hands coaxing her body to heights never before experienced, remembered his deep voice whispering her name in passion. She remembered every joyful, exciting minute.

Clenching her fists at her sides, she stared at him with flashing determination that flew in the face of everything she felt in her heart. "I won't be your mistress, Cody. I won't be your plaything for the duration of this endless journey." The refusal hurt because she wanted him so much. "If I can't believe that I'm better than an itch for some man to scratch, then I'm lost. I'll never win anyone's respect if I can't respect myself."

He stared at her, his arousal so strong that she could feel his need across the space that separated them. "You won't start respecting yourself until you start holding your head up. Do you know that you walk with your eyes on the ground, your head lowered?" His stare darkened to a scowl. "And, damn it, Perrin, you weren't just an itch that needed to be scratched!"

"Then what am I to you?" Her husky whisper vibrated with a need to hear an answer—an answer he couldn't give.

"I don't know, all right? I don't the hell know!" He pushed a hand through the hair falling forward on his forehead.

"What are you looking for, Cody? What do you want?"

"It's time to settle down," he answered finally, clenching and releasing his jaw. "I want some land, a place that's permanent. Some cattle. Horses."

"Are there people in your dream?" she asked, trying to see his face in the darkness. "Who lives in your house with you?"

"Just me," he stated firmly.

Not a woman who had been another man's mistress.

Perrin's hand slid away from her face and she gazed up at him with a helpless expression. "We're both frauds, Cody Snow," she said quietly. "Neither of us has the courage to trust or love. We're both cowards."

She felt his eyes burning against her back as she returned to her wagon. With all her heart, she wished she were running toward him, not walking away. But she refused to let another man ruin the reputation she was fighting so hard to rebuild.

They painted their names in tar on Independence Rock, paid three dollars a wagon to cross the high, swift Sweetwater River, entered a stretch of deep sand and constant dust. When the women had enough energy to talk, they joked weakly that the mosquitoes were the size of hummingbirds.

Slowly, the barren, overgrazed road climbed the eight-thousand-foot summit of the Rocky Mountains toward South Pass.

To the north, Augusta saw the stunning Wind River Peaks arising above wide gray swales. To the south rose the flat top of Table Mountain.

She flapped the reins across the backs of her oxen, the motion automatic now. The ugly buckskin gloves she had borrowed from one of the teamsters concealed hands that had toughened over the last weeks. Her blisters had hardened into calluses.

That wasn't the only amazing change she had undergone. When she pulled her collar away from her throat and peered into the mirror, she could see a line of darkly tanned skin above the milky skin below. Only her nose continued to burn and peel.

Now she could set up her own tent, and she had learned to start a fire unless the wind was especially strong. The coffee she drank in the mornings had been made with her own hands. She cooked her own breakfast and supper. The menu never varied. She ate bacon and beans for breakfast, soggy biscuits and fried ham for the noon meal and supper. Having mastered these items—and no one could be more surprised by her success than she was—it occurred to her that she might ask Sarah how to fry an antelope steak. It was stupid to continue refusing the game the men occasionally brought into camp because she didn't know how to cook it. She desperately craved variety in her limited diet.

But, amazingly, she was taking care of herself. Even more astonishing, for the first time in her life she had accomplishments beyond her illustrious name and ancestors.

Every day she grew stronger in knowledge and experience. But weaker with growing fatigue. It was beginning to worry her that it got harder and harder to pull herself out of her bedroll and face another grueling day.

Every time one of the brides jumped off a wagon to walk behind and rest shoulders stiffened from hunching over the reins, Augusta wished she had a wagon partner. It would be easier if there were someone with whom to divide the work, with whom to share the small things that happened each day.

It would have been nice to have someone notice the enormous changes she had made and perhaps offer a word of praise.

Biting her lip, Augusta twitched her oxen into line, following the wagon ahead of her, passing it, then turning her animals inward before she hauled up on the reins.

She remained on the hard wooden seat until one of the teamsters appeared to unyoke the oxen. Tonight they would let the beasts graze on the open range. It meant more work collecting them in the morning, but grass was sparse here, grazed out by the trains that had preceded them.

Climbing down, she flexed her legs and arms, working the cramps out before she dug a trench for a fire. She needed to cook her supper, fetch some water, wash out a few things, clean up the supper pot and dishes, set up her tent, roll out her bedroll, prepare the utensils for a quick breakfast, mend the stockings she was wearing, beg a little lamp oil from someone. Fatigue pinched her features at the thought of all that she needed to do.

But there was also a swell of pride at the knowledge that she would do what she had to. She knew how.

She had coaxed the chips into thin flames and ground some coffee beans before she felt someone watching. Startled, she jerked up her head.

"Cora!" For an instant she was absurdly glad for someone to talk to, even if the someone was only Cora. Then she noticed Cora's tight smug smile.

"It's hard, isn't it? Driving with no relief. Do your hands and shoulders shake at night when you crawl into your tent? Mine used to shake after I'd slaved for you all day."

The light went out of Augusta's eyes, and she stood up from the fire, wearily shaking coffee flakes from her dusty skirt. "What do you want?"

"Want? As a matter of fact, I came to offer help."

Suspicion thinned Augusta's lips. "What kind of help?"

"When we reach South Pass tomorrow, I plan to sell Thea's sketches while we're waiting for our turn to go through." A knowing smirk curved her mouth. "I wondered if you'd like me to ask my customers if they know anything about the Eagglestons."

Augusta's heart lurched and for an instant she thought her knees would collapse. Her breath stopped and she couldn't speak.

"You remember the Eagglestons, don't you?" Cora asked in a hard voice. "You should. You've been spending their money since you stole it off their dead bodies!"

Augusta gasped and threw out a hand to steady herself against the wagon wheel. "That is a lie!"

"Is it? I been thinking about this for a long time. You squeezed a penny till it shined before we buried the two teamsters. After that, you spent money on foolish trinkets and suddenly didn't mind buying fresh eggs and vegetables when they were available. I think you stole the Eagglestons' money."

"You're only guessing!"

"Not anymore, I'm not," Cora said smugly, studying the guilty crimson burning Augusta's face.

Augusta hid her shaking hands in the folds of her skirt. "No one will believe such a ridiculous story!"

"Probably not. The others think you're rich. But you ain't . . . aren't, are you?"

"Are you asking me to pay you not to spread ludicrous rumors? Is that it?" She could hardly speak the words. There wasn't enough air in her lungs to push the words out.

"No," Cora said promptly. "It's bad luck to spend a dead man's money. But I figure to pay you back for all you done to me." She studied Augusta and smiled. "Someone left a note way back at the Chimney Rock, looking for information about the Eagglestons. If I find him, I'm going to tell him that you stole the Eagglestons' money. I'll tell him about those trips you took out behind the Eagglestons' wagon and how you came back with your gloves stuffed full of coins. That's what you did, isn't it?"

"I didn't steal anything! I just . . . that was . . ." She was dying. She could not pull enough air into her chest.

"Save your lies for the Eagglestons' friend or relative. It's *his* money you're spending."

Augusta stared. "It was you that night, wasn't it?" she whispered. "It was you watching us in the woods."

"What are you babbling about?"

Augusta bit her tongue. Maybe it hadn't been Cora. She was too tired to think. Crazily, she wondered if Cora had felt this exhausted, this low in her mind when Cora was riding with her and doing all the work. How had she borne it?

Suddenly she thought of the army of servants who had staffed the Boyd mansion in Chastity, most of whose names she couldn't recall. Had they gone to bed too tired to eat their supper? Had they ached deep in their bones? Had they resented and hated her?

She had never had such thoughts before, had never tried to imagine the lives of the people who had served her.

Cora threw Augusta a look of pure contempt, then tossed her head and returned to Sarah's wagon.

It was customary to camp a day at South Pass and celebrate reaching the highest altitude of the journey. High-spirited teamsters and passengers galloped along drifts of snow, firing their sidearms and whooping. The children from a Mormon train plucked wild alpine flowers near icy patches. Everyone marveled at snow in late July.

Mem and Bootie strolled down a row of wagon beds, twirling their parasols and examining various arrays of goods. It seemed everyone had something to sell. When they reached the plank Heck had set up for Cora, they paused to admire Thea's sketches.

"My, my," Bootie marveled, leaning to inspect the prices. "Is anyone actually paying a whole nickel for these?"

Cora displayed a tightly sealed jar and rattled the nickels inside. "Sold five sketches so far," she announced proudly. "And the questions they do ask!" She rolled her eyes and laughed. "I swear, the man who bought Jane's sketch . . . well, he asked so many questions, I swear he fell in love with her portrait."

Bootie's gloves fluttered before her bosom. "Oh, dear! Jane didn't want her portrait displayed!"

"Oh?" Cora frowned. "Well, nobody told me."

Mem couldn't take her eyes off a sketch of Webb. Thea had portrayed him astride the mustang, returning to camp after a day riding out ahead of the train. His head was high, his body relaxed. Thea had captured the pride of a warrior, the grace of an Englishman.

On impulse, Mem dug a nickel out of her little wrist bag and dropped it on the wooden plank. "I'll take that one," she said, blushing to the roots of her hair.

Cora scooped the nickel up before the sun hit it. Carefully, she rolled the sketch into a cylinder and tied it with a piece of yarn. "Here's another that is especially good," she said, grinning as she pushed forward a portrait of Mem and Bootie carrying laundry toward a stream. Their sleeves were rolled up and their skirts tied back. Bootie looked pretty and flustered. Mem thought her own depiction was highly romanticized; she too looked almost pretty.

"Now, why would we pay a nickel for Thea's sketches when she'll give us one for nothing?" Bootie said, lifting an eyebrow at Mem. "And why would you want a portrait of that . . ." she saw Mem's posture stiffen, "our scout?"

Because I love him, Mem thought hopelessly. "I want to remember everything about this trip," is what she said aloud.

Sometimes it was hard to protect another person's secrets. Right now she longed to reveal Webb's family identity and background just to watch her sister's expression. A sigh lifted her chest and she adjusted her bonnet against the sun's glare. She hadn't had a headache in several days and had dared hope they were gone forever. But now her head pounded.

"Mem?" Bootie asked as they began the walk back to their wagon. "Where do you go at night?"

A flush stained her cheeks. "I beg your pardon?"

"Occasionally I wake up and you're not in our tent." Bootie tightened her hold on the potatoes she had paid a fortune for at one of the displays. She kept her gaze on the ground. "I hope you're not doing anything foolish," she said in a voice more serous than Mem had heard from her in years.

"Foolish . . . like what?"

"We have husbands waiting for us in Oregon. We'll live next door to each other, I'll insist on that, and we'll have a good life." She lifted eyes that were soft and gray and pleading. "Please don't do anything to spoil our future. Don't do anything you'll regret. Mr. Coate seems strange and interesting to you—I know you're curious about him—but, Mem, he's only a half-breed scout. A man who lives on a saddle. He can't give you a home or any of the things that make life comfortable."

"Why do you . . . well, that's just . . ." Mem blustered into silence. Had Bootie spied on her? Did anyone else know about her and Webb meeting beside Smokey Joe's fire? They walked a little farther, then she said in a low tone, "What if I told you that I . . . that Webb Coate and I are friends? Good friends."

Bootie didn't fall to pieces as Mem had half expected.

"It would make me very anxious," Bootie said finally, lowering her nose to sniff the potatoes. "Mr. Coate is not a savage as I used to think he was," she said after a brief hesitation. "He's polite and clean and he does his job well," she continued, listing the qualities she admired in a man. "He seems decent enough and respectable."

"But he's an Indian. Is that what you're trying to say?"

"It's unseemly to chase after one man when you're pledged to marry another. That's what I'm trying to say."

Mem stared at her sister, appalled. "Do you think I'm chasing after Mr. Coate?" A guilty flush stained her throat.

"And, you're right. He *is* an Indian. Not our kind."

The slur came almost as a relief. For an instant, it had

seemed as if Mem were speaking to a stranger. "You know," she said, frowning, "I just realized something . . . you'r doing your share of the work!"

Bootie rolled her eyes. "Well, I swan! Of course I am."

"You weren't at the beginning." Why hadn't she notice this before? Bootie had made tremendous progress toward fi nally growing up. There was no other way to say it. A burs of pride and surprise lit Mem's face. Before they reache their wagon, she praised Bootie extravagantly, then touche her sister's arm.

"Don't worry about me," she said in a voice of quiet re gret. "Mr. Coate and I are only friends. I enjoy his compan and he appears to enjoy mine. That's all it is or will ever be."

Heart aching, she accepted this was true. She and Web continued to meet every night by Smokey Joe's fire, but he' made no attempt to repeat the kiss they had shared at th Sioux village. Mem's lust and wantonness were wasted.

But her intellect had discovered a banquet. She and Web discussed religion, politics, literature, art, everything unde the sun. They discovered areas of accord, and entertaine themselves by arguing their differences far into the night.

Occasionally, she caught him gazing at her with smolder ing speculation. Then her heart raced into a gallop and sh waited breathlessly, hoping he would reach for her. But he never did.

As she had told Bootie, they were good friends, that wa all. Except one of the friends deeply loved the other.

When they reached their wagon, Bootie halted in dismay. They spotted the teamsters left to guard the arms wagon and Jane passed by them, headed for the stream carrying a baske of laundry; otherwise the camp was deserted.

"Everyone is still at the pass! We left too soon," Bootie exclaimed. "I could have bought that little pot I wanted."

"Go back and buy it, but I think I'll stay here. I have a headache." Actually, she craved solitude to study the sketch that she'd purchased from Cora.

After she persuaded Bootie to return to the festivities a

the mouth of the pass, she exchanged her good shawl for an older, warmer one, tidied the area around the wagon, then wandered toward the willows concealing the stream, intending to sit on the banks, hidden from view, and daydream a little over Thea's portrayal of Webb.

"There you are, you slut!"

Mem froze in the midst of the clump of willows that reached almost to her ears. Lifting on tiptoe, she spied the top of a man's hat; it seemed to rush along the top foliage of the willows, heading for the stream. Alarmed, she pushed forward, fighting out of the branches and onto a narrow sandy bank.

Twenty yards upstream, Jane Munger stood in the shallows, a soapy and dripping petticoat in her hands. She straightened abruptly, her face white, as the man crashed out of the willows. He glanced at a sheet of paper, then tossed it aside.

"It is you! I thought so."

"Hank!"

Before the paper floated into the water and was swirled away, Mem identified it as one of Thea's sketches. When she looked upstream, the man had rushed into the water, had grabbed Jane by the shoulders, and was shaking her so roughly that her head snapped back and forth. Stumbling, Mem gasped, then halted in shock, unable to believe her eyes.

Swinging a beefy hand, the man slapped Jane across the face so hard that it was more a blow than a slap. Jane would have fallen into the stream if he hadn't gripped one forearm so tightly that his fingers disappeared into Jane's sleeve.

Spittle flew from his lips and his face was purple with rage when he leaned forward, snarling curses into Jane's frightened face. She cringed, but she didn't scream.

"Hank, wait. Let me explain." Blood dripped from a cracked lip. Her eyes were wide and black with terror. She shook violently and cried out when he jerked her hard against his body and cruelly twisted one arm up behind her.

"No one runs out on Hank Berringer! Did you think
could humiliate me and get away with it? You bitch!"
jerked up on Jane's arm and Mem heard a sickening crack

The sound broke her paralysis. Lifting her skirts
shouting, she ran toward them. "Let her go, you bru
You're breaking her arm!"

Twisting, he shot a warning over his shoulder. "I'll
whatever the hell I want. This is my wife! Leave us alone.

One moment of distraction was all Jane needed. Jerk
out of his grip, she shoved hard against his chest with her
hand. He lost his balance and slipped into the water, fall
to his knees, cursing and snarling. Jane shouted, "Mem!
out of here or he'll kill you too! Run!"

Before she rushed headlong into the shallows, Mem
ticed Jane's dangling right arm and understood it was ind
broken. Then she was in water up to her knees, look
wildly around for something to use as a weapon. A ro
Jane's washboard? There wasn't time to reach the wa
board; the man was pulling himself out of the water.

Clutching her broken arm against her body, Jane kicke
him, but he caught her ankle and twisted hard, toppling
into the stream. Then he rose up, water pouring out of
shirt, his brutish eyes fixed on Mem. With a snarl, he cau
a fistful of her skirt and pulled himself up. In horror, it
curred to her that a man was about to strike her for the f
time in her life. She tried to hit him, but her blows boun
off his shoulders as a child's fists might have done. He w
shorter than she, but stocky and solid; his arms were like i
rods.

His fist hammered her on the jaw. The blow flung her
her buttocks on the sandy bank. Dizzy and disbelievi
shocked, she tried to sit up, her head ringing. He was com
toward her again when something soft and black whipp
across her cheek.

Before her dazed mind registered that the soft black thi
was cloth, a skirt, she recognized a high thin scream. Boo
flew past her toward the edge of the water. Her arm came

swinging a small iron pot. When the pot hit the man on the forehead, Bootie reeled backward from the impact. She fell on the bank beside Mem, gasping.

Blood spurted from his head. He blinked hard, touched the blood streaming into his eyes, then crumpled to his hands and knees in the water. Jane was on him in a flash, lips pulling back from her teeth in a snarl. She dropped on his spine with her knees, flattening him beneath the surface. When he started to thrash and flail, Bootie and Mem rushed into the water, but Jane shouted them away. They stood in the shallows, water swirling around their knees, and watched in helpless shock as Jane held the man's head beneath the surface until he stopped moving.

White-faced and shaking violently, Jane climbed off of him. Slowly, his body floated to the surface, limp in the water, and she hastily backed away. They all did, fighting the weight of wet skirts and the weakness of straw knees. Standing on the bank, shivering and silent, they watched as the current slowly tugged him to the center of the water, then pulled his body downstream.

When he floated out of sight, they collapsed onto the sand and sat shaking and fighting to catch their breath.

"Oh, Mem!" Bootie tilted her head back, gasping for air. "I was coming to show you the pot I bought. . . ." Her hands fluttered in front of her and she glanced at the water, but the iron pot had sunk out of sight. "Then I saw that horrible beast strike you, and I just . . ." She dropped her head and covered her face with a shudder. "I hit him and I killed him!"

Gingerly, Mem touched her aching jaw. She was going to have an impressive black and blue bruise. She put her arm around Bootie, who shook as if she had severe chills.

Jane spoke sharply. "You didn't kill Hank, Bootie. I did. You stunned him, but I held him under the water until the son of a bitch died."

When Mem could speak, she swallowed and stared at Jane. "He broke your arm. Your lip is cracked and you're going to have a black eye. I still can't believe it!"

"Oh, he's done a lot worse," Jane said, staring at the water as if she feared he would rise out of it. She rested her broken arm on her lap. "His name was Hank Berringer. He's my husband." She drew a long breath, then closed her eyes. "My name is Alice Berringer, not Jane Munger. I made up that name after I ran away from him. I thought if I ran far enough . . . But I should have known he'd come after me. I guess I did know."

Bootie's eyes widened to the size of pie plates. "You're going to Oregon to get married? But you already have a husband?"

Jane's dulled gaze fixed on the pile of laundry scattered beside the stream. "He broke my ribs. He broke my collar bone. This is the third time he's broken one of my arms. He kicked me in the stomach so hard that I lost two babies. He threatened to push my face into his blacksmith's forge." She turned blazing eyes toward them. "I'm *glad* the son of a bitch is dead! I hope he burns in hell!" She spat on the ground. "I knew he'd kill me if he ever found me. He would have killed Mem too just because she was here and he was mad." She focused a blazing gaze on Bootie. "You saved our lives. If you hadn't come when you did . . ."

Mem wet her white lips, brushed the sand off sodden skirts. "We need to see to that arm. And we'll have to tell Mr. Snow about this." Lips twisting, she peered downstream half expecting to see Hank Berringer's body caught in the willows that overhung the bank on the far side.

Jane closed her eyes. "I've imagined killing him a thousand times. I know what to do." She drew a long shuddering breath, cradling her arm against her body. "Give me until supper tonight, then you can tell Mr. Snow. Will you do that for me? Please?"

Mem considered Jane's story, her arm tightening around Bootie's trembling shoulders. "Where will you go?"

Jane's laugh was short and harsh. "There's always a man looking for a woman. It doesn't matter if he's in Oregon or in one of those trains up ahead. I'll find one to help me."

"There's a train scheduled through the pass this afternoon," Mem offered, swallowing hard. "Going to California." She didn't know why she was agreeing to this, except they had shared so much together, so many hardships. Plus, she knew what would happen if Jane were caught for murdering her husband. If they didn't hang her on the spot, they would send her back to Missouri to stand trial. They would hang her there, because a woman couldn't kill her husband no matter what violence he wreaked on her.

Jane inspected her arm. "Can I have your shawl?"

Silently, Mem rose to find her old shawl and shake the sand out of fringe and folds. After helping Jane fashion a sling, she and Bootie assisted her up the bank and out of the willows. They paused, looking at the deserted, sun-bleached wagons.

"I thought it would work," Jane murmured, tears of pain in her eyes. "I thought I could escape and find a second chance."

"Maybe you still will," Mem said, looking at Jane as if she had never seen her before. Jane Munger was a runaway wife named Alice Berringer. Hank Berringer was dead. She couldn't make herself believe it. Everything that had happened in the last half hour shimmered with distortion, as if none of it were real.

"You'll give me until after supper before you tell anyone?" When Mem finally agreed, Jane embraced her. "Tell Perrin that I wanted to confide the truth. Tell her that . . ." She closed her eyes, swayed on her feet. "Thank you. You were both true heroines. You saved my life."

Silent tears ran down Bootie's cheeks, tears she didn't seem aware of. She gripped Mem's hand so hard that Mem thought the bones in her fingers would crack.

Together they hung back and watched Jane hurry toward her wagon. They waited beside the willows until Jane reemerged, carrying a carpetbag in her uninjured hand. She gazed at them as if memorizing their faces, then she turned and walked toward the trains camped close to the entrance to the pass.

"She'll be all right," Mem commented after a few minutes. They watched Jane veer toward a dozen men working near a row of wagons with CALIFORNIA OR BUST scrawled on the canvas.

Bootie shook the water out of her skirts and pulled back her shoulders. "Mem? Would you say saving your life and Jane's makes up for me running my mouth at Jake Quinton?"

Mem blinked. "I'd say so, yes. Definitely.

"Good." Satisfaction gleamed in her eyes. "I can't wait to tell Augusta that I did something heroic. Me!" She stepped forward, then halted and looked back at Mem. "Oh, dear. Can you help me find my warm shawl? It doesn't feel like July at all. Why can't we have a fire as big and cheery as everyone else has?"

Mem stared, then burst into semihysterical laughter. Bootie was still Bootie, a bit scattered, a bit fluttery. Yet Bootie was not the same woman she had been at the beginning of the journey. Never again would she be as helpless or as dependent as she had been for most of her life. This was a new Bootie Glover.

"Find us some wood or some cow chips and I'll build you the biggest fire in camp."

"As soon as I change clothing, I'll hunt for fuel." She grinned suddenly. "I'll take a pot with me. Just in case."

Shaking her head, Mem followed toward the wagon. "Bootie?" When Bootie paused, about to climb into their wagon, she said softly, tears in her eyes, "I'm so glad you came with me on this trip. I'm proud you're my sister, and I love you."

"Oh, Mem! You've never said that before." Bootie's face lit with joy. "I thought perhaps you didn't want me to come. I even thought . . ." She stopped and sunlight sparkled in the tears on her lashes. "I love you, too. I always wished I could be like you. But I never could be."

"You're wonderful just being yourself."

They hugged each other and it was a good moment, a fine moment, spoiled only by the thought that they had played a role in a man's death. And by Mem's sudden realization that she had lost Thea's sketch of Webb. She told herself that she didn't need a sketch to keep his memory alive. All of her life, she would remember this remarkable journey, and Bootie, and Webb Coate.

CHAPTER
* 19 *

My Journal, August, 1852. Jane ran away. I'm glad. Jane had sharp snoopy eyes. Sometimes I saw her looking at me and then at Cody and she knew. If she hadn't run off after murdering her husband, I would have had to punish her.

I want to punish someone for how badly I feel. I want to. It's all building inside. I can hardly stand up straight, my stomach hurts whenever I see him with his whore. I'm so afraid something that began as a test for me is turning into something else, so afraid that he's starting to care more for her than for me. I've warned her. She better take heed.

I came so close to flying at him and screaming. I'm tired of secrets. Weary to death of this game we're playing. He's scaring me with the whore, testing the depth of my love and trust. I don't know how much longer I can stand it. I'm so confused.

I've figured out that he won't admit our love until near the end of the journey. He doesn't want to cause jealousy among the others. But he doesn't mind showing favoritism to the whore. This makes my head hurt because I don't understand.

The only thing that calms me is to look into his eyes. He sat across from me at Smokey Joe's Friday night sing-along. I saw his love. I felt it. I understood the secret messages he sent. Why can't it be like that always? I was so happy. Then the next day, he looked through me as if I were invisible. And I wanted to rip and tear and bite and claw.

She said I was insane. I remember that sometimes. She was wrong. I'm not insane, I'm just so angry. So furiously angry.

The stretch southwest from South Pass to Fort Bridger was as desolate an area as Perrin had ever seen. Even the sage-brush dried and shriveled in temperatures that exceeded a hundred degrees by midday. Creek bottoms lay exposed like cracked pieces of a jigsaw puzzle. As water was too precious to waste on washing, thick dust coated faces, hands, and clothing.

Sarah inspected the dirt and grit beneath her fingernails then sighed and idly flapped the reins across the oxen's backs. No one had a full complement of oxen anymore. There were only two cows left from the dozen that had begun the journey.

"Did Mem say for sure that Jane—I just can't think of her as Alice—went to California?" Sarah inquired again.

For the third time, Perrin repeated the story Mem had told. The scandal of a runaway wife, a violent death, and Jane's abrupt departure had dominated conversations for a week. Mem's bravery and Bootie's heroism were toasted at every campfire.

Sarah shook her head. "I just can't believe it."

Bending, Perrin wrapped a length of rope around her boot to secure the flapping sole. She hoped to find boots for sale at Fort Bridger, which they would reach early tomorrow. After eyeing the position of the sun burning in the sky, she prepared to step out onto the tongue of the wagon and jump to the ground.

"I'll return in about two hours," she said, tying her bonnet strings beneath her chin.

"Wait." When Perrin looked at Sarah, she noticed a pink flush beneath Sarah's tanned cheeks. "You don't have to leave," Sarah said, keeping her gaze on the oxen's dusty backs. "Unless you want to."

Want to? Perrin almost laughed. The earth was so dry, the dust thrown up by the wheels so thick and dense, that she and Sarah were the only women who walked behind the wagons when it wasn't their turn to drive the oxen. So much dust and grime coated their hair that it looked gray in the sunlight.

"I agreed to help you drive so Cora could ride with Hilda and study. You made it clear that you didn't want my company. We agreed I'd walk behind while you drove, and you would walk behind while I drove."

Occasionally it struck Perrin how much she had changed in the last months. Once she would have lacked the courage to address painful subjects or to speak frankly.

"It's scorching hot out there. Look at the waves of heat shimmering off the ground." Sarah slid her a sidelong glance. "I don't want to walk. I don't imagine you do either."

"I don't. Thank you." Settling back on the seat, Perrin let her body relax into the tilt and sway of the wagon. The hard wooden seat still bruised her tailbone, still jarred the teeth in her head, but it was far, far preferable to stumbling behind the wagons, choking on clouds of hot dust.

They rode in silence for half an hour before Sarah cleared her throat with a self-conscious sound. "I'm going to say this straight out, Perrin. You and Joseph Boyd sinned against the values I hold most dear."

Perrin clasped her hands in her lap and gazed through a haze of dust at the back of the lead wagon.

"But I've come to respect you. I don't understand how I can condemn someone and also respect them, but that's how it is."

Turning her head aside, Perrin noticed the bleached bones of an ox, followed by a scattered pile of abandoned furniture. "You wanted to be the women's representative, didn't you?" she asked after a lengthy pause.

Sarah mopped sweat off her throat, then pushed her handkerchief back inside a rolled up sleeve. "I would have done a good job as our representative."

"Yes, you would have." Silence filled the next mile.

Sarah sighed heavily. "When you pleaded for Winnie, I asked myself if that's what I would have done. And the truth is, I would have asked Mr. Snow to send Winnie home the instant I discovered her problem with laudanum."

Perrin lowered her head and studied grimy fingernails. "That's what I should have done."

Turning, Sarah examined Perrin's face. "I was wrong. In

the end, Winnie threw away her second chance, but she *had* a second chance because of you." She considered. "After the major died, I thought my life had ended also. Since Chastity isn't exactly awash in eligible men, I dismissed any possibility of having another husband and eventual children. But what you said in your plea for Winnie applies to me too. This journey is my second chance. It's a second chance for all of us."

"Even me?" Perrin inquired softly.

Sarah hesitated. "I used to see you on the streets of Chastity. It always shocked me how modest and ordinary you looked, like a pleasant and decent person." She contemplated the pink rising in Perrin's cheeks. "I thought a sinner ought to look like a sinner. I resented that you seemed untouched by your sins."

Perrin pressed her lips together and lowered her head. Beside her, she heard Sarah release another long sigh.

"I've been watching you, and I've concluded that you must have had good reasons for taking Joseph Boyd into your bed." She waited, but Perrin offered no explanation. "It's not my place to judge; that's between you and your maker. But I've made enough mistakes in my life that I guess I can forgive you for making a few." Perrin kept her eyes fixed on her hands. She didn't know whether to be offended or say thank you.

"I have one more thing to say," Sarah added, scarlet tinting her face. "There are some who worry that you'll end like Winnie."

"I beg your pardon?" Perrin raised her head.

Sarah fixed her gaze on the back of the plodding oxen. Dots of color burned in her cheeks. "Winnie threw away her second chance. Some think you're on the brink of doing the same thing."

"I'm sorry. I don't know what you're talking about." But she could guess, and hot color seared her face too.

"We aren't blind. We've seen how you and Captain Snow look at each other," Sarah's hands tightened on the reins.

"We're going to be neighbors in Oregon, Perrin. Most of u‍
have decided to try to forget what happened with you an‍
Joseph Boyd. We'll try because we're grateful for your ef‍
forts and your help. We respect your fairness, especially wit‍
Augusta. That must have been hard. You've earned your sec‍
ond chance."

"But?" Perrin whispered.

Sarah met her eyes squarely. "But if you sin with Captai‍
Snow, and there are a few who think you might . . ." Sh‍
drew a long breath. "If you and Captain Snow . . . that is . . .'‍

"I understand your meaning," Perrin said in a low voice.

"We will select another representative if . . . you know‍
We will shun you. We will cut you on the streets of Clampe‍
Falls. We will not forgive or overlook a second lapse. Yo‍
will have thrown away your second chance exactly as Win‍
nie did."

Closing her eyes, Perrin leaned against the hard seat back‍
The isolation and imposed loneliness that Sarah threatene‍
settled over her now, providing a sample of what she coul‍
expect if she and Cody made another mistake.

"What if I told you that I love Cody Snow?" The hopeless‍
ness in her whisper shocked her as much as the admission it‍
self.

Silently, she repeated the words, testing their veracity. De‍
spair and truth pinched her features. She loved his strengt‍
and confidence, his assurance, and even his stubbornness‍
She loved the clear fairness of his thinking, his open mind‍
his genuine concern for others. She loved the roguish twinkl‍
in his blue eyes, the purposeful swagger of his stride. Sh‍
loved the way he made her feel when she was with him, as i‍
she were pretty and competent and capable and important, a‍
if she were the most desirable woman in the territories.

"Then I pity you," Sarah said finally, squinting against th‍
dust. "Your choice is love or honor." A silence followed‍
"Do you have the funds to repay your Oregon bridegroom‍
and spare yourself from marrying him?"

"No."

"Would Mr. Snow repay your bridegroom?"

Perrin mopped the sweat at her temples. "Mr. Snow has made it clear that he doesn't wish to remarry. He doesn't know how I feel."

"All I can say is there are people on this train who believe the worst of you. People who will never forgive if you deceive your bridegroom with another man, no matter who he is or how you feel about him." She stared at Perrin. "You'll pay a heavy price if you betray the man who's paying your passage to Oregon."

A space opened in the swirls of dust and Perrin could see the lead wagon turning off the trail toward the site where they would halt for the midday meal. In six hours she would meet with Cody to discuss the day's events. Her heart leaped ahead in anticipation, followed by a wave of desolation. Her future depended on controlling her confusing desire for him.

"Sarah? Since we're speaking frankly . . . who hates me enough to sneak into my wagon and slash one of my dresses into ribbons?" She had started the journey with three summer calicos; now she had only two, both of which were dusty and soiled.

"Good heavens!" Sarah's head whipped up with a shocked expression. "Someone cut up one of your dresses?"

Perrin nodded. "I . . . I had a valentine my father sent my mother. It was the only thing I had left from either of them. I kept it in a small locked chest. Whoever broke the lock and stole the valentine didn't steal my money. They took the thing I valued more than anything else."

She still couldn't talk about this without tears swimming in her eyes. The loss of the old valentine was a cruel punishment.

"Good heavens," Sarah said again, drawing up on the reins. "Perrin . . . I know there are those who don't like you, but . . . all I can say is be careful."

Fort Bridger was a trading post for trappers rather than a military garrison. Cody gave everyone two hours to visit the post and inspect the meager goods offered for sale. Unless they hankered for woven blankets and trinket items, he doubted his brides would discover much to interest them.

After the disappointed women returned to the wagons, Cody and Webb met James Conklin outside his log post house beside an outdoor display of hand mirrors and iron pots.

"The first cup of whiskey is on the house," Conklin announced, eyeing them.

"Not today," Cody said. Posts conducting heavy trade with Indians, as Fort Bridger did, were notorious for doctoring whiskey with tobacco and pepper. They thought the Indians liked their liquor hot. Any man who valued his innards wouldn't touch the stuff. "We're seeking information."

"Well, now, information is mighty expensive in these parts."

Removing a gold piece from his vest, Webb flipped it between his fingers, letting the sunlight flash beams of temptation. He gazed at the bald spot circling the top of Conklin's head. "Has Jake Quinton passed through here?"

Conklin snatched the coin when Webb let it spin in the air. "One of Quinton's boys was here." He walked away from them to straighten his display of hand mirrors. "Squaws love to admire themselves. They'll trade a fortune in pelts for a mirror."

Scowling, Cody stalked forward and tossed Conklin a gold eagle. "This buys the rest of your information." He let a hand drift to the butt of his sidearm.

Conklin grinned. "The man's name was Ryland. Said he and Quinton would be coming back this way before the snow flies. Said they might have a load of arms and ammunition, wanted to know what I'd give for cargo like that."

"What was your answer?" Webb asked sharply.

Greed glazed Conklin's little pig eyes. "Do you know what an Indian will pay for one carbine and a pouch of powder? He'll strip the hide off his family's lodge to buy a gun.

He'll steal his squaw's sleeping robes. A wagonload of guns and ammunition is worth a king's ransom."

Frustration exploded in Cody's chest. If he had harbored the slightest hope that Quinton would direct his attentions elsewhere, that hope died with Conklin's laugh.

Only Webb's fingers digging into his arm prevented him from raising a fist and showing Conklin just how much he appreciated having a bank-sized target painted on his train.

"We'll step up the schedule for the women's shooting lessons," he snarled as he and Webb mounted their horses.

The scrap of lace peeping out of his saddle blanket was so incongruous that he wondered how he had missed spotting it earlier. When he gave it a tug, four pieces of an old valentine fell into his hand. Curious, he tried to fit the ripped pieces together. The writing was so faded that he couldn't read the inscription or the name of the sender. Irritated by yet another small mystery, Cody threw the pieces over his shoulder and touched his bootheels to the buckskin's flanks.

Instinct suggested the mysteriously appearing items were intended to hold some meaning for him, but they didn't. The knife attacks on his bedroll were clearly a warning. Against what, he didn't have a notion. Stabbing his bedroll, cutting his water sack, and slashing the ties off his chaps suggested a man. But the cake, ribbon, and valentine argued for a woman.

He was certain now that neither of the new teamsters had tampered with his belongings. Perrin had been his first choice as the person leaving the articles, but his gut said it wasn't her.

So who was doing this? And what did it mean?

The best part of Augusta's day arrived when the train stopped for the evening and the brides lined up behind the arms wagon to receive their nightly issue of powder and shot. Then, while it was still light, they followed Cody to a target range that Miles Dawson had arranged away from the wagons.

After several weeks of practice, Augusta no longer shuddered as she shouldered her carbine and headed toward the improvised target area. Now she could shoot without the weapon's recoil throwing her to the ground; she could fire without closing her eyes, and she had learned to load on the run.

To her astonishment she was one of the most accurate shooters among the women. Once she understood that her surprising skill was not a fluke that would disappear at the next practice session, her confidence grew by leaps and bounds.

Her days passed in a series of impatient hours, waiting for the moment when she stepped up to the target. She liked the weight of the stock nestled against her shoulder, enjoyed the pungent tang that hung in the air after firing. It thrilled her each time she hit her target. She didn't even mind cleaning the gun afterward, as Cody insisted. Having the carbine in her wagon and knowing how to use it made her feel competent and powerful.

In Chastity, she had felt important and powerful enough to command deference. Now she understood how hollow her importance had been. There was nothing to do while driving the stupid oxen except think, and she had thought a lot about Perrin's comments. Her importance in Chastity had been based on social prominence, but that prominence resulted from her name and her father's accomplishments. Her standing in the community had nothing to do with her personally. She hadn't done a thing to deserve respect except be born as a Boyd. The insight shocked her deeply.

Now, with Webb Coate's continuing assistance, she was growing confident in genuine accomplishments that counted for something real. Never again would she be forced to wait for someone to dress her hair, cook her food, or wash her linens. She could drive a wagon, lay a fire, pitch a tent. And now she could defend herself. She would not have believed how exhilarating it felt to know she could do these things.

"I swan, Augusta. You could shoot the tip off a knitting

needle!" Bootie struggled to raise her heavy carbine to her shoulder. She closed one eye and squinted down the barrel. Slowly, it sank toward the ground in front of her.

"Sarah is the best shot," Augusta remarked. It was her goal to shoot as well as Sarah Jennings. "Mem isn't bad either. Course, no one's as skilled at wielding a pot as you are."

Everyone on the firing line turned to stare at her. Perrin was the first to burst into laughter, then they all did.

"I've never heard you jest before," Bootie said, smiling and blushing with pleasure.

Augusta blinked in surprise. Good heavens. She had indeed made a humorous remark. Everyone was smiling at her and Bootie. Flustered, she spun toward the target and squeezed off a shot.

Only a slight hesitation saved her from shooting Cody Snow, who dashed in front of her, running toward Ona Norris. Heart slamming in her chest, she fanned her face rapidly and tried to catch her breath. She had been an idiot to fire impulsively.

Cody glared a warning at her, then turned his attention to Ona. He snatched the barrel of Ona's carbine and jerked it toward the sky. Now Augusta noticed that Ona's gun had sagged, had pointed directly at Perrin's stomach before Cody ran forward.

"How many times must I tell all of you! Sky, ground, or target. Damn it, you don't point a gun at another person unless you are prepared to kill that person." He scowled at Ona. "A careless accident could cost one of you a husband. I've told you from the beginning. The Oregon men won't accept a crippled wife. They insist on brides who are healthy and whole."

Ona glared up at him, white-faced. "I'm tired of these secrets and games!"

"This isn't a game. And there are no secrets here. Quinton will be back, count on it!"

Augusta was surprised that prim, quiet Ona stood up to the

anger glittering in Snow's eyes. Ona's chin jutted, her cheeks flashed from white to red. She looked furious and her posture seemed oddly aggressive. Frowning, Augusta suddenly recalled Ona throwing down the teacup that belonged to Augusta's mother then deliberately crushing it in a fit of temper.

"I don't want to shoot a gun. I expect you to protect me!"

Cody examined her angry eyes and trembling mouth. "Fine," he said shortly. He took the carbine out of her hands, then walked to the front of the silently watching women. "When Quinton attacks again, and he will, ladies, here's what I want you to do. Sarah Jennings, Augusta Boyd, Mem Grant, and Perrin Waverly are our best shots. I want one of them on each side of the square, under a wagon. Hilda Clum, Bootie Glover, Cora Thorp, and Thea Reeves will run ammunition. Ona Norris will minister to any wounded. Are there any objections?" he demanded, staring at Ona.

No one spoke.

"Excellent." He ran an eye down the line of women, studying how they held their weapons. "That's enough for today. You're dismissed."

Ona whirled and ran past Augusta, heading toward her wagon. Augusta watched her go, thinking that not long ago she too had feared firearms, and she too had expected men to assume the responsibility for her protection. Perhaps she should speak to Ona and explain how it felt to contribute to her own defense.

She considered the idea while she cleaned her carbine, then dismissed it from her mind. Ona was a sullen little snip.

Before she returned to the wagon to prepare her evening meal, she scanned the faces of her shooting group, wondering if one of them was the person who had spied on her and Webb. Actually the incident had occurred so long ago that she believed Webb had been correct in assuming the snoop had not seen Augusta's face. If the spy had seen her, the story would have surfaced long before now.

She had begun to feel safe enough that occasionally her guard slipped. Twice now, she'd almost been caught gazing at Webb with longing in her eyes, first by Mem and then by that thorn in her side, Cora.

After coaxing her fire into a better showing, she hung a pot of soup over the flames, then poured a basin of water and washed her hands and face. She liked to delay lowering the tailgate as long as she could, liked to try to guess what Webb might have left her tonight. Sometimes he left food, a rabbit or a piece of venison, both of which she had learned to cook. Occasionally he left wood for her fire, a real treat. Twice, he had given her small wooden animals carved from the trunks of scrub oak. She treasured the carved deer and bear even though she suspected they were Indian things, and carried them in her pocket so she could touch them and think of him throughout the long lonely day.

Tonight, she found a bouquet of wild lupine. Gifts that made her life a little easier were better, but the bouquet was nice too, she decided, wondering what to do with it.

"Augusta?" Bootie's voice called from the deepening darkness. "Will you come with us to Smokey Joe's Friday Night?"

Every Friday, Smokey Joe offered his fire as a gathering place. Someone told stories or read aloud by the light of the flames. Sometimes the group sang the popular songs of the day. Sometimes they merely gossiped or exchanged personal histories.

"Perrin will be there," Mem casually announced, stepping up beside Bootie.

Learning that Perrin would be present made up her mind. "Thank you, but I believe I'll stay here and turn in early."

Undeniably, she owed Perrin a debt of gratitude. But Perrin Waverly was still the harlot who had seduced Augusta's father, and Augusta could not forgive that transgression. Hence, gratitude and hatred warred in constant conflict. The easiest course was to avoid those places where Perrin might be.

After scouring the soup pot and her bowl, she mended a torn hem beside her fire, then set out the breakfast utensils before she wrestled her tent out of the wagon and draped it over the poles she had set earlier. After laying out her bedroll, she returned to sit beside the low flames in her fire pit, listening to the sound of singing drifting from Smokey Joe's fire.

Sighing, she tilted her head back and gazed at a moon that reminded her of the moon that had hung in the sky like a lemon crescent the night Webb kissed her. Her eyes closed and her mouth softened. Every detail of that long-ago night was as fresh as the air she breathed. It might have happened yesterday.

A low sound of despair issued from her lips and she dropped her head. What was she going to do? Her nights were tormented by wanting a man she refused to speak to during the day. Their situation had not been clear-cut prior to Cody's ultimatum that she master camping skills in a week. Now she and Webb were caught in a set of complications that made her mind reel whenever she attempted to sort things out.

During the day, Webb appeared utterly indifferent to her. When he absolutely had to speak to her, his voice was cold, his eyes went flat and expressionless. But he left her a little gift almost every night. He hadn't spoken again since the first two nights when he'd taught her how to make a fire and set up her tent. But she sensed his presence, and there were the gifts.

She knew he ignored her during the day because he was respecting her wishes. But the more Augusta thought about him, the more she yearned to see him alone. Perhaps he would steal another kiss. Perhaps, she thought, indulging her newest fantasy, they could have a small clandestine romance during the remainder of the journey. Kissing only, nothing more, and they would be utterly and absolutely discreet, with no possibility whatsoever of discovery.

A harmless dalliance—which no one knew about—would add a little spice to the journey and break the monotony of her days. A few kisses would give Webb a memory to cherish all of his life, and a few kisses would satisfy her curiosity and get him out of her system. Allowing him to kiss her occasionally would be a way to thank him for helping her remain with the train.

She should thank him, she thought, she really should. Looking into the flames in her fire pit, she listened to the songs from Smokey Joe's fire. Webb seldom joined the group. Most likely he was with the men guarding the arms wagon.

She could stroll in that direction. She could inquire about the stream crossing scheduled for tomorrow and draw him away from the other men. They would walk into the dark hot night together. Perhaps their hands would brush. Perhaps he would take her into his arms and crush her to his magnificent body.

Oh, God, she was on fire for him. She burned for him.

He refused to be drawn from the men guarding the arms wagon. Twice, Augusta murmured a question and turned into the darkness, twitching the fringe of her shawl, enticing him to follow the moonlight gleaming in her hair. But Webb remained leaning against the wagon wheel, asking her to repeat her question.

Face flaming, furious that he was embarrassing her, Augusta fumed in the shadows where firelight faded into blackness, tempted to embarrass him in return. She would expose his little game and pay him back for making her feel foolish.

"I came to thank you for your assistance, Mr. Coate," she said crisply. "And for your gifts." Heck Kelsey and one of the new teamsters heard every word she said. They would tell everyone that the half-breed was leaving secret gifts for a white woman.

Leaving gifts truly was an outrageous presumption on his part, now that she thought about it. She stared at his strong cheekbones and powerful shoulders and felt her mouth tremble, felt a jolt of heat travel along her thighs. Suddenly she hated him for the way he made her feel, for what the sight of him did to her body. She hated it that he made her feel hot inside and restless with wanting. She utterly detested it that she felt dizzy with lust for an Indian savage.

"You don't need to hide behind my wagon like a sneak and a coward. You can offer assistance directly." A sick need to punish him for awakening her desire framed the sarcasm on her tongue. "Everyone knows I would never lower myself to become overly familiar with a half-breed. And I doubt you would assault me when a scream would bring half a dozen men running to kill you for daring to put your dirty hands on a white woman!"

Firelight honed his features as he stiffened against the wagon wheel. His black eyes raked her with such contempt that Augusta sucked in a hard breath and stepped backward.

Nausea clenched her stomach. This wasn't how it was supposed to go. She hadn't sought him out to make him hate her; she had come hoping to walk with him beneath the moon, longing to sigh in his arms. Instead, fear boiled up inside her and she lashed out at him. But fear of what? Fear of the very rejection that she read in his stare? But that was ridiculous.

His lip curled and his voice sliced the night like a blade. "You're mistaken, Miss Boyd," he said coldly. "I have not assisted you in any way. I have not given you gifts. I have not hidden in the shadows of your wagon."

Heck Kelsey and the new teamster slowly stood beside the fire, looking back and forth from Augusta to Webb. Heck became more agitated by the minute as he listened to the exchange between Augusta and Webb.

"You're lying," she accused flatly, enraged that he would try to make her look foolish by denying helping her and giving her presents. Suddenly she was glad events were unfolding as they were. She had needed this reminder that Indians were liars, and so stupid they would lie about something pleasant like gifts. "Do you think I didn't recognize your accent that first night?"

Webb's dark hair lifted from his shoulders as he whirled

to face Heck Kelsey. "There's only one person who could mimic my voice," he said, accusation heavy in his tone. "What the hell have you been doing, Kelsey?"

Heck cleared his throat and sent a weak smile toward Augusta. "I'm sorry, ma'am. I knew you needed help, and I just figured you'd listen to Mr. Coate where you might not listen to me. So I just . . . It was only those first two days that I pretended to be him. The gifts, well, those are from me."

"You?" Augusta's mouth dropped, and she stared at Heck in dawning horror. It was Heck Kelsey who had walked her through the survival tasks. Heck Kelsey who was leaving her the small gifts. Her mind raced, trying to recall if she had made any reference to that long-ago night in the cottonwoods and the kisses she had shared with Webb. She was too stunned and upset to remember.

Webb's deep exotic voice cut across Heck's mumblings. "You may rest assured that I'd never approach you or your wagon, Miss Boyd. I wouldn't risk spending one minute alone in your company."

He stared at her and his mouth twisted, then he turned on the heel of his moccasins. The darkness swallowed him.

Wringing her hands, Augusta tried not to look at Heck and the teamster who studied her with avid curiosity. She peered in the direction Webb had gone and willed him to return so they could begin again. Something had gone dreadfully wrong. How had her lovely fantasy taken such a terrible turn? Tears of frustration and confusion brimmed over her lashes.

"Miss Boyd?" Heck Kelsey swept off his hat and smiled like a moon-sick adolescent. "Can I escort you back to your wagon?"

She stumbled backward. "Leave me alone, you . . . you deceiver! You blacksmith! Don't ever speak to me again!"

Gathering her skirts, she bolted toward her tent and dived inside, her heart pounding so hard she thought it would burst from her chest. Placing both hands over her breast, and blinking at hot tears, she stared at the roof of her tent.

It had been Heck Kelsey, a smithy with a talent for accents, who had assisted her, who had left her tokens of affection. Not Webb, not the man she thought of day and night, not the man she longed for, dreamed of, desired with every breath she breathed.

Weeping, it occurred to her that she had captivated a blacksmith and been rejected by a half-breed. Tears of hysteria nearly strangled her. Generations of Boyds whispered scorn in her ears.

They camped at a rocky, cedar-shaded area surrounding the hot springs. Everyone trooped to observe a small geyser puffing away on the riverbank, and marveled at the novelties of nature.

"Such a luxury," Bootie sighed happily. "I didn't have to heat our tea water, I just scooped a pan of boiling water out of the pool over there." She toasted Mem with her cup.

Mem laughed and unpinned her hair, clean and shining from an earlier bath, and began to plait it in a loose braid for sleeping. "I'd be happy to stop right here," she said. "Think of it. Hot water all year around, a little geyser for a front-yard fountain, and the fragrance of cedars. Lovely."

After finishing her tea, Bootie rinsed her cup, then stretched and smothered a yawn. "There's something I've been meaning to say. You remember the day Jane ran off?"

Mem rolled her eyes, then bent to bank the embers in their fire pit. After laying out provisions for tomorrow's breakfast, she closed the wagon's tailgate. "How could I forget?"

"We talked about Mr. Coate that day, remember?"

Mem straightened warily. "I recall."

Bootie studied her expression. "Do you still meet Mr. Coate by Smokey Joe's fire every night?"

"Most nights," Mem replied defensively.

"Well, I've been thinking," Bootie said. After looking around to make sure no one could overhear, she stepped close to Mem and said in a low voice, "I know you came on this trip seeking adventure. Well, maybe Mr. Coate is your grand adventure. I just want to say that ... if ..." Crimson burned on her cheeks. "Well, there are things you can do so Mr. Sails will never know there was someone else. If you ever need to know those things, as a woman who was married once, I can advise you."

"Bootie Grant Glover! You do amaze me!" Mem stared at her sister. "Do I understand this? You're giving me permission to engage in a romantic tryst?"

"Certainly not!" Bootie pulled to her full diminished height. "I'm merely saying if disaster strikes, I won't abandon you." Flouncing her head, she dropped to her knees and crawled into their tent. The flap came down with an irritated snap.

Mem grinned. Then she sensed his presence and her smile altered to anticipation. Turning from the embers, she let her eyes grow accustomed to the darkness, then discovered him standing beside a cedar. She wondered how long he had been there, watching her with those black eyes that knew her so well. Sometimes she wondered how she had come to confide all her small secrets in this man, all but the secret she held close to her heart. But perhaps he knew that secret too, that she loved him. Perhaps he chose to pretend ignorance of the truth in her eyes.

Mem had not seen much of him in the last week. There had been several difficult stream crossings between Fort Bridger and the springs. Plus, he usually rode far in advance of the train, seeking comfortable campsites and searching for any trace of Quinton's gang. The one time they had met at Smokey's fire in the last week, she had known at once that something had changed.

For the first time their conversation had been strained. When he looked at her, she had not been able to guess his thoughts. And when she stood to leave, he stood also, staring at her as if she puzzled him. And then he had said the words she had never expected to hear from any man. "You are so beautiful." When she realized he was not jesting, she became so flustered that she hurried away.

But she had thought of nothing else since that night.

Drawing a breath, wondering what they would say to each other, she raised her skirt and walked away from the glow of the embers and into the darkness. The scent of cedar reached her before she saw him. She felt his hands on her shoulders before she heard him whisper her name. Her heart opened wide.

She didn't hesitate. It was the most natural thing in the world to finally step forward into his arms. Nothing had ever felt as right as when he drew her against his body and buried his face in her shining auburn hair. She closed her eyes and listened to his heart pounding against her own, inhaled the fresh clean scent of his hair and skin. She had imagined this moment for so long that she wondered if she were dreaming. Except no dream had ever made her knees go weak and her breath quicken.

"Mem," he said against her hair. "My beautiful Mem."

Her spinster's heart soared. And she trembled in his arms. For reasons she did not understand, tonight suddenly resonated with magic. But she did understand that for a while at least, the starlight and the cedars and this magnificent man were hers. Tomorrow she would wake to her ordinary plain self and perhaps discover that she had dreamed this moment. But right now, the night was enchanted, a dream that belonged to her.

Raising her hands, made bold by the magic of starlight, she framed his face between her palms, gazed deeply into his eyes, then lifted on tiptoe and brazenly pressed her lips to his. Instantly, she felt his hard arousal and the answering heat in her own loins. This was how it felt when two people discovered their desire for each other. It was like summer lightning, like electric currents racing along the skin, inflaming the senses. His kiss made her grow weak inside, yet strong. His hands tightening on her waist thrilled her and swept her breath away.

When his mouth released hers, he gazed long into her soft shining eyes. Smiling, she kissed him again, lightly, confidently. Without knowing when it had happened, she had made a momentous decision. "Yes," she whispered. "Yes, Tanka Tunkan."

"You are certain?" he asked hoarsely, speaking against her lips. "You have thought about this? About us?"

"I've never been more certain of anything." It didn't matter what her future held, what joys or what disasters. She only knew that if she did not follow her heart now, tonight, she would rue it all of her days. She did not want to look back one day and regret that her courage had failed. When she was old, she would warm herself by remembering this magic night and this man.

Taking her by the hand, pausing once to gaze at her and caress her cheek, Webb led her deeper into the cedar grove, led her to a starlit pool warmed by the hot springs. When Mem understood what he intended, she laughed softly. "Tonight is enchanted," she murmured, her fingers tugging clumsily at the hooks running down her bodice. "We may say anything we like, we can do whatever we desire. Tomorrow, all will be forgotten."

"No," he said gruffly, crushing her against his chest before he kissed her so deeply and thoroughly that she almost swooned like a schoolgirl. Gently, with a trembling hand, he opened her braid and spread her auburn hair over her shoulders. "Tonight is to be remembered always. Tonight is a promise, a pledge." His voice sank to a husky register. "Do you think I know you so little that I would ask only one night from you? Respect you so little? Love you so little?"

She swayed and thought certain she would faint. "Love me?" Her fingers dug into his shoulders. "Webb, please. Don't jest. I couldn't stand it if you were only—"

He covered her lips with his fingertips, then drew her close to his body. "In my mother's culture, a man pledges his spirit by washing his beloved's body in a stream. If the woman accepts him, he pledges his heart with his body." Gently, he covered her breasts with his hands, and it seemed to Mem that the faded calico melted away beneath his palms.

"Will you enter the pool with me, Woman Who Wants to Know Things?" He kissed her forehead. "If you do, you pledge yourself to me for now and all time."

Tears of great joy swam in her eyes. "But I thought you and Augusta—"

He silenced her with a deep, deliberate kiss that told her Augusta held no place in his heart or his thoughts. "I love you, Mem. Many a man has been blinded by fool's gold. Few are as fortunate as I to have found genuine treasure."

Mem threw her arms around his neck and returned his kiss with a passion that seared them both. Then, she who had never undressed before a woman, let alone a man, threw off her clothing and impatiently waited for Webb to do the same. When they both stood naked on the lip of the starlit pool, she drew a breath and satisfied her curiosity by looking directly at his bared body.

"Good heavens!" she marveled softly, her eyes widening. "I had no idea you . . . is that going to fit? Good heavens. I mean, will it . . . ah, will I . . ." Her concern ended in a violent blush from her and a shout of laughter from him.

"Flatterer," he said, grinning. He stepped into the pool, then turned and lifted his arms to her.

The warm water slid over her thighs up to her waist. Webb clasped her in his arms and she leaned into his strength. Slowly, methodically, tormenting them both, he washed her, his hands caressing her throat, her shoulders, her breasts. When his fingers touched her beneath the water, Mem gasped and felt her mind reel. No person could experience such arousal and remain conscious. Surely, the mind could not contain so much surprise and pleasure.

His kisses spun her senses into an enchanted realm. His touch stole her breath away. They made themselves complete the ritual bathing, then their hands flew urgently over faces and wet bodies. When she finally touched him . . . there . . . she grew dizzy and hot with desire.

Webb pulled his mouth from hers and, hoarse with passion, whispered in her wet ear. "Do you accept this man's heart, Woman Who Wants to Know Things?"

Smiling, knowing she was about to commit her life into his keeping, Mem kissed him. "Yes," she whispered. "Oh, yes, yes."

Lifting her in his arms, he carried her out of the warm pool and laid her on a bed of fragrant cedar boughs. He gathered her in his arms, his lips on her throat, and one hand slid between them. While he kissed her, tasting deep of her, his fingers manipulated her in ways Mem had never imagined, moved her to heights of desire and urgency that swept all rational thought from her mind. Nervousness and apprehension vanished and she squirmed and thrashed beneath him, surrendering wholly to the sensations he created. He murmured words of love, and she whispered his name and gave her heart and her love and her body.

When he entered her, she learned that everything fit perfectly. And she surprised and delighted them both by discovering she was as brazen as she had hoped she would be.

CHAPTER
* 20 *

My Journal, August, 1852. It is now clear that he has de-
ceived me from the first. Oh Lord, Lord, it hurts so much.
For three days I rode in the back of the wagon, sick in body
and spirit. When she came to ask how I was feeling, it re-
quired immense effort not to fly from my bed of despair and
slash the harlot as I slashed her dress. She has bewitched
him; she has stolen him from me.

Ellen accused me of imagining things. Ellen said I was
wrong in the head. But I don't imagine their lust for each
other. Thea notices too. So does everyone. They stand too
close; their hands brush; they gaze at one another with long-
ing in their eyes.

I ripped her valentine and let him find the pieces so he
would understand that I know about her. I know where his
misdirected lust lies. It changed nothing. He still goes to the
harlot with eagerness in his step and hunger on his mouth.
He ignores me as if he never promised to marry me, as if
there is not and never was an understanding between us.

Now, in front of everyone he tells me that we are not play-
ing a game, tells me there are no secrets. Liar, liar, liar! We
have always shared the secret of knowing we would be to-
gether one day. And what has this journey been if not a
game? I cannot bear knowing that he's used me so badly.
Now he has her and has abandoned me. The pain is like poi-
son in my veins.

What shall I do? The end of the journey is within sight.
Does he expect me to marry Mr. Riddley? That was never a
consideration. But I lack the funds to repay Mr. Riddley for
my passage. A horrible suspicion arises. Perhaps this is how
he intends to rid himself of me, by letting Riddley claim me.

He owes me better than this. Didn't I avenge his honor?
Didn't I place the pillow over Ellen's face and hold it there

until she stopped thrashing? I did this to my own cousin for him, because Ellen betrayed him. Yes, I also did it to clear the way for us. If the child had not been stillborn, I would have pressed the pillow over his face too. All that I did and would have done, I did out of love and because I believed he loved me too. And he would still love me if it wasn't for her!

He ignores my warnings. He embarrasses me before the others. He flaunts his harlot before me. Wait. Does he want me to prove my love by removing her *as I removed Ellen? I must think about this. I must try not to hate him as I hate* her.

CHAPTER
∗ 21 ∗

*My Journal, August, 1852. I finally got a futur It is coming
am hapy I made corn kakes to thank those who maked mad
me a weding dress I make my leters beter than I reed but
reed some to I am looking for the man whos money August
stold.*

Cora Thor

"Oh, Mem!" Perrin's knees gave out and she sat abruptl
on a lava boulder. Glad tears sparkled in the dying sunligh
and she blotted them, then pressed Mem's hands, too move
to speak. "I'm so happy for you both," she finally whispered

The joy blazing on Mem's face shone so brightly tha
looking at her was like gazing into the sun. "We told Booti
and Cody, and we want you to know, but we're not going t
make a general announcement until the journey is ended." A
charming blush tinted her cheeks. "We consider ourselves al
ready wed, but we'll have another ceremony in England fo
Webb's mother and friends."

"I knew Webb's father was English, but I had no idea tha
he was an earl. So Webb inherits the title and . . . Mem
You're a countess!"

Mem spun in a circle, her skirts flying out around her
When she came to a halt, her brown eyes sparkled like gems
"I know. Isn't it amazing?" She laughed out loud and her ex
pression turned mischievous. "Bootie is still dazed. I believe
she's having a bit of difficulty altering her perception from
'that Indian' to Lord Albany. But she's agreed to accep
Webb's invitation and come with us to England. I wish
you'd seen her face when we . . ."

Sinking to the ground, Mem drew up her knees, bubbling
with plans and the effervescence of her happiness. She told
Perrin that she and Webb had married in the Indian tradi-

tion, then they wrote to his mother announcing their news. She spoke of the Albany estate and the town house in London, the villa outside Rome. "I can't believe it," she finished, wonder bringing moisture to her lashes. "Oh, Perrin. I thought I'd married an Englishman's penniless son, but I married a wealthy earl. It's just so . . . so . . ."

"Wonderful," Perrin finished for her.

"And I haven't had any more headaches! I don't think I will ever again."

They gazed at each other, then burst into laughter. They laughed at the dust caking their faces and clothing, laughed at the tattered wagons squared around their campsite, laughed at Mem becoming Lady Albany, laughed at the delicious absurdity of fate.

Long after Mem had returned to her wagon, appearing to float rather than walk, Perrin remained seated on the lava boulder, watching the sun sink behind the ragged line of the Boise Mountains. She was genuinely glad for Mem, but Mem's shining joy underscored her own confusion and agitation.

Love or honor; the choice Sarah had given continued to haunt her thoughts. Regardless of her circumstance at the time, becoming Joseph Boyd's mistress had been an act of shame. Of all the reasons why Perrin had decided to make this journey, perhaps the strongest was an effort to escape a disreputable past and restore personal honor. How could she have guessed that fate would toss Cody Snow in her path? A long sigh lifted her breast.

Occasionally she forced herself to think about her intended bridegroom. She hoped Horace Able was personable, hoped he would be a good man. She prayed that she could learn to love him.

But her heart whispered a denial. Whatever else she might be, she was not fickle. She had not loved Garin Waverly, had not loved Joseph Boyd, she would never love Horace Able. She could give her heart but once, and it would be forever.

When she saw Cody walking toward her, his face lit by

the last of the sunset rays, she knew the choice was made. This was the man whose image lay carved on the surface of her heart. This was the man she would search for in every dark-haired stranger, in every twinkling pair of roguish eyes. She would imagine his laughter a thousand times before she breathed her last. Loving him would be the secret tragedy of her life.

Loving him would also be her greatest regret, because regardless of how much she loved him, the new person she had become during this journey would not compromise herself. Never again.

"Heck is fixing the axle on your wagon. This lava rock is raising cain with the oxen's feet, but Miles thinks—" He stopped talking when he saw her face. "When you look at me like that . . ."

Turning away from her, he swore and frowned back at the wagons. "Christ, Perrin! What in the hell are we doing?"

She gripped her hands in her lap. "We're trying to avoid each other so we won't make another mistake," she said in a low voice, thinking about Mem and Webb. She felt genuinely happy for Mem. But to her shame, a small rock of envy leaned against her heart.

Cody faced her, standing tall against the darkness. The first bright stars appeared to wreath his head. "I can't come near you without wanting you, without remembering how you felt in my arms, and how you tasted, and how . . ." A low groan issued from his throat. He closed his eyes for a long minute, then stared at her. "I didn't want this complication any more than you did. I fight caring about you every minute. I remind myself that you're stubborn and can be cantankerous. I tell myself you were another man's mistress. I tell myself you were indifferent to our lovemaking."

"You know I wasn't indifferent," she whispered. "I lashed out at you because I thought you saw me as a dalliance for this journey, that for you, I was a loose woman here for the taking."

"That statement insults us both," he snapped. "As for you

being a diversion for the trip . . ." He pushed a hand through his hair and shook his head. "I have nothing to offer beyond a temporary liaison." A storm tossed in his blue eyes. "Don't look at me like that. I told you Ellen took a lover. I don't like myself for saying this, but I can't get past the fact that you were another man's mistress."

She stared at him, then lowered her head. "I can't change the past. Not mine; not yours."

"I don't want to be made a fool of again."

Standing, Perrin faced him, her heart in her eyes. "Cody, surely you must know that not every woman betrays her husband. Do you think Mem would every betray Webb? Will Sarah betray the man she marries? Or Hilda?" Even the idea of these honorable women betraying their vows was unthinkable. Perrin could no more imagine any of them deceiving a husband than she could imagine herself doing such a thing.

Cody's hands opened and closed at his sides as if he wanted to pull her into his arms. But they stood in view of the wagons and they both knew that always someone was watching them.

"You once said that all men take. Is that how you see me, Perrin? Someone who takes and gives nothing back?"

He had taken her love and offered nothing in return, but she didn't tell him that. "You took nothing that was not freely given," she said in a low voice.

"You're wrong. Nothing is free," he said harshly, tracing her lips with his gaze. "I pay for that night by wanting you with every breath. I'm asking myself questions about Ellen, about myself, about things I thought were settled and decided long ago. I look at you and I don't know where the hell I'm going."

"I won't be your harlot, Cody Snow," she whispered, staring at him with stubbornness in her gaze. "If I surrender, I'll pay a heavy price for the rest of my life. And I would deserve whatever shame came my way because if we give in . . . it won't be impulsive, it will be deliberate. If we're

discovered, the others will punish me with a lifetime of loneliness. I couldn't bear that."

"Damn it, Perrin. You know I won't ask you to take that
risk." Thrusting his hands into his back pockets, he stood
frowning down at her in the last faint flare of light.

"Then we have nowhere to go," Perrin said softly, swallowing back tears. She wanted him with all her heart.

He stared at her. "I wish to hell that I'd never heard of
Joseph Boyd, damn his soul."

The Boise River, fed by mountain streams, thickly
wooded by handsome old cottonwoods, was a welcome sight
after nearly two weeks of dry eyes stung by alkali dust, of
the stink of hot sage and panting oxen. They had slogged
through steep-banked streams, banged across lava fields,
gone half mad from the attacks of mosquitoes, gnats, and
buffalo flies. They had pushed up rocky hills, paid an extor-
tionate fee to be ferried across the Snake River, and arrived
at Boise fatigued to the very marrow of their bones, and with
nerves drawn taut.

When Cody declared three days of rest, everyone was too
exhausted to cheer.

Augusta fell into her bedroll without supper and slept
twelve hours through. She awoke to discover the campsite
deserted except for the guards at the arms wagon. Apparently
everyone had walked into Fort Boise in search of fresh faces
and novelty.

Yawning, and looking forward to three whole days without driving, three wonderful days of rest and catching up on
her chores, Augusta cooked the last of the fresh turnips she
had purchased at Fort Hall, mashing them for breakfast along
with a pat of butter she had bought from Thea. Lucky Thea,
her cow was the only cow that had survived the journey to
this point.

While Augusta pinned up her hair in front of a mirror
hung on the side of the wagon, she considered buying another cow if one was available for sale at Fort Boise. Even if

the owner demanded us much as fifteen dollars, it would be nice to have fresh milk whenever she liked. And there was never enough butter.

"Oh!" She gasped, and jumped when a strange whiskered face loomed over her shoulder in the mirror. Spinning, she discovered a tall, big-boned man standing directly in front of her. His clothing was trail-tattered and filthy, bits of food had collected in an unkempt beard and mustache. Even this early in the day, he stank of cheap whiskey. "Who are you and what do you want?" she demanded in a voice higher than her normal tone.

She slid a glance toward the other wagons, saw no one. The arms wagon was on the far side of the square. At once, she realized the guards were near the noisy rushing river; they would not hear her if she screamed.

"You're Augusta Boyd, ain't you?" he said, inspecting her bright hair.

"Who are you?" He had the coldest eyes she had ever seen on a man, dead eyes, eyes that had never loved or shown pity. Even Jake Quinton had not frightened her as this man did. His steady dead stare made her stomach cramp in fear.

Her carbine was in the wagon where she could not get to it.

"My name is John Eaggleston," he snarled. His lips thinned when she choked and stumbled backward a step. A grunt snorted out of his nostrils. "You know the name. Damn me, she was right."

"She?" Augusta whispered. The edge of the sideboard pressed against her spine and she could retreat no farther.

"I been looking for this bride train ever since I read Snow's message at the Chimney Rock. Then some skirt up at the fort starts asking if anyone knows the name Eaggleston. Said Miss Augusta Boyd knew all about my brother and his woman, knew all about my money." He stepped closer and his face filled with menace. "I want my money."

"Your money?" She couldn't breathe. Panic lodged in her

throat, sent her heart crashing around inside her chest. Cora, she thought wildly, Cora had sent this man to find her.

His hand flashed forward and grabbed the front of her shirtwaist. He jerked her so close that she winced at the stink of rotted teeth and ancient sweat.

"Let me go!" The demand emerged as a frightened squeak.

"You've given me a merry chase, gal." He gripped her bodice so tightly that his knuckles bruised her breastbone. "After your wagonmaster's message, I rode back and found Ed's wagon. Found the graves. Found the hole where Ed must have buried the money box. But I sure as hell didn't find no gold. Been chasing this train since. Seems I was right, since that gal says you might just have my money." He gave her a violent shake that snapped her head back and forth. "Git it for me, girlie. Right now." Releasing her bodice, he flung her back against the sideboard hard enough to knock the air out of her lungs.

Panting, staring in disbelief, Augusta struggled to catch her breath, tried to think. Pushing against the shock of being violently seized was the panic of knowing she had only one hundred and fifty-eight dollars left of the two hundred and sixty-two gold dollars she had taken from Eaggleston's buried box.

She stared into John Eaggleston's dead eyes and knew he would not accept any explanation she might offer for the missing funds.

"How do I know it's your money?" she whispered, one hand pressed to the pulse thudding wildly in her throat. If she stalled for a minute, maybe her mind would begin to function again, maybe she would think of a way to escape.

The man's hand shot forward and gripped her by the throat, his fingers bruising into her skin. He leaned close enough that spittle flew in her face. "Listen to me, bitch. I killed two men to get that money. My mistake was leaving it in Ed's keeping. I ain't making no more mistakes." His cold eyes bored into her. "You got six hundred dollars of my money. You give it back, or I kill you. It's that simple."

Brides of Prairie Gold / 305

"Six hundred dollars!" His thick fingers cut her air, forcing her voice into a thin thread. Despairing, she realized that someone else had found the box and had taken the rest of the gold. But he believed she had it. "Please, let me speak."

He didn't release her, but he relaxed the pressure digging into her throat. His merciless gaze didn't slacken.

A torrent of babble poured from Augusta's lips. She told him about finding the box, told him—after a quick panicked review of her options—that she had taken only one hundred and fifty-eight of the gold pieces, which she was holding in safekeeping for him. She swore someone else had stolen most of his money.

His lip curled in fury. He didn't believe her. As casually as swatting a mosquito, he lifted his arm and backhanded her across the face. A snapping sound cracked in her ears, then pain exploded through her head. Blood gushed from her nostrils and dripped on her bodice. She heard a gurgling scream, then saw him raise his hand again. Terror and shock blanked her mind. He meant what he threatened. He was going to kill her.

Perrin woke slowly, stretching, yawning, indulging in the luxury of dozing for another few minutes. When she finally crawled out of her tent, the sun shone directly overhead and the campsite was deserted except for the oxen within the square and the lazy drone of insects. A rare day alone beckoned like a jewel.

Delighted by the prospect of solitude, she reheated the coffee Hilda had left for her, then nibbled a wedge of cornbread and listened with pleasure to the absence of voices.

Tomorrow she would turn out the wagon and give everything a good cleaning. There was laundry to catch up on, baking she could do ahead. But today was for herself. Maybe she would read awhile, a treat she had not indulged in in weeks. Or she could update her trip journal. Perhaps she would sit by the river and let herself daydream about Cody Snow. There was much to think about.

Something was changing with Cody, she read it in his eyes, felt it in the tension that drew his shoulders when they met to review the day's events. Sometimes she dared hope that he was falling in love with her. Other times she believed he was winning his fight against the attraction that drew them together.

Aching with pessimism, she paused with her coffee cup midway to her lips, her mind a hundred miles away. A full minute elapsed before she realized she was looking at Cora Thorp.

Cora walked toward the wagons, moving with a self-satisfied gait that could almost be mistaken for a swagger. She nibbled at a piece of fried bread wrapped in a strip of greasy paper.

As Perrin watched, coming to her feet with a frown, Cora halted abruptly. Her eyes widened and the fried bread fell to the ground. Both hands flew to her lips, then she spun, searching the line of wagons. Urgent frightened eyes fastened on Perrin.

"Quick!" she screamed. "He's beating her! It looks like he's going to kill her!"

Perrin didn't have a notion what Cora was talking about or what Cora could see from her angle. But the hysteria galvanized her. Grabbing the iron shovel leaning against the wagon wheel, she raced after Cora, who was running toward Augusta's wagon.

Augusta? Someone was beating *Augusta*?

When she skidded around the corner of the squared wagons, she saw what she had been unable to glimpse from her campsite, but what Cora had seen from a distance.

A brutish, bearded man was systematically battering Augusta Boyd, shaking her, hitting her, shouting something about money. Augusta flopped in his grip like a rag doll, beyond resistance. Her face and shirtwaist were covered in bright blood; Perrin couldn't be certain if she was fully conscious.

Shock stopped Cora and Perrin in their tracks. Perrin

couldn't believe what she was witnessing. She didn't know how long she stood as if rooted to the ground. It could only have been seconds, but it seemed as if an eternity elapsed. In that span of altered time, her gaze met Augusta's, and her history with this spoiled, self-centered woman rose like a specter between them.

Perrin recalled the icy snubs on the streets of Chastity, remembered all the insults and the shame that Augusta had thrown at her in Chastity and during this journey.

Finally she understood a truth she had not been able to acknowledge. As long as Augusta Boyd had breath in her body, there could be no second chance for Perrin Waverly. A week after the train arrived in Clampet Falls, every respectable woman would know that Perrin had been Joseph Boyd's mistress. Augusta would blacken her name, would see that she was ostracized and punished with a solitary and lonely life as an outcast.

In that frozen moment, Perrin gazed into Augusta's swelling eyes and knew Augusta did not expect her to intervene. Placing oneself in danger was not something Augusta would have done; she didn't expect it from another. She gazed at Perrin with dying eyes, filled with resentment and hatred even now.

It was only a blind instinct for survival that made her croak, "Help me!"

Perrin sucked in a deep trembling breath, then dashed forward and planted her feet behind the brute. He was so concentrated on beating Augusta that he didn't hear or notice Perrin's approach. Baring her teeth and gathering her strength, she raised the iron shovel and swung it as hard as she could. The impact of the shovel striking the side of the man's head shot up her arms and knocked her to the ground.

Caught in her skirts, swearing, gasping for breath, she struggled to rise, but was knocked flat again as Cora flew past her with a snarling scream.

The man had dropped to his knees, swaying, holding his bloody head with both hands. Rage contorted his features, as ugly as the obscenities spitting from his lips. One hand dropped to the sidearm strapped at his waist. "You're dead."

Then Cora was standing over him, bashing at his head with a chunk of granite. He elbowed her in the thigh and she fell backward with a howl of pain.

Lunging, Perrin clawed at the hand scrabbling for his gun. If his fingers hadn't been slippery with his blood and Augusta's, she couldn't have wrested the pistol from his grip. And it helped that Cora struck his shoulder with the rock. Finally, she had the gun and pulled to her feet. Then his fist caught her squarely in the stomach and she doubled over, tears of pain leaping into her eyes.

The pistol fired.

When the puff of smoke cleared, she was panting hard, staring in horror at a ragged scarlet hole in his chest. Flat expressionless eyes glared at her, his lips pulled back from his teeth, then he toppled slowly backward into the dirt. Cora jumped forward, gasping and sobbing. She struck him again and again with the rock until Perrin's voice penetrated her fear.

"In the name of God, stop!" She couldn't get enough air into her lungs. She was strangling. "He's dead." The gun weighed a hundred pounds. After letting it drop from boneless fingers, she staggered away from the wagon and vomited into the short, dry summer grass. She had shot a man. Had killed him. She didn't even know his name.

When she straightened, holding her stomach, her face the color of whey, Cora was poised beside the man, gasping and gripping her rock, ready to strike in case he suddenly sat up.

Augusta lay sprawled against the wagon wheel, drenched in blood. Her nose had been broken, her lips cracked. Both eyes were swelling shut, her throat was badly bruised. For an instant Perrin thought she was dead. Then Augusta's chest lifted beneath her blood-soaked bodice, and she made a whimpering sound.

"Jesus, God!" Miles Dawson and the teamster named Frank arrived at a dead run, kicking up dust as they skidded to a halt and stared wide-eyed at the scene. "What in the hell happened? How badly are all of you hurt?"

Now Perrin noticed that her hands were bloody from the struggle for the gun. Smears of crimson soiled her skirt and waist. Red speckles dotted Cora's face, hands, and waist. Augusta was awash in blood. Blood soaked her bodice, matted her hair, drenched her face and hands, splashed her skirt.

"It's my fault!" Cora said, breaking into sobs and covering her face. "I just wanted to embarrass and scare her, that's all. I didn't really think . . . I never dreamed that he would . . ."

Perrin fought to move past a numbing sense of unreality. She grasped Miles Dawson's arm and spoke in a low urgent voice. "Ride to the fort and get Cody." She glanced at Augusta. "Bring back a doctor if you can find one."

"We can't leave the arms wagon unguarded," Miles said. He looked at the dead man and swallowed, his eyes bugging.

Perrin dug her fingernails into his arm. "Do as I tell you, damn it." Leaning forward from the waist, she glared at him with icy authoritative eyes. "Get Cody!"

Miles peered at her face, then took off at a run toward the horses. Perrin pointed at Frank. "You can leave the arms wagon unguarded long enough to fetch some buckets of water. And I'll need help getting Augusta into her wagon. Don't just stand there, get us some water!"

Cora wiped her eyes and nose with the hem of her skirt. She hovered over Augusta, shuddering at all the blood. "Will she live? Oh, God, if I'm responsible for killing her . . ."

"Get a blanket and cover him. Please. I can't stand to look at him." Kneeling, she examined Augusta, who was breathing heavily through her mouth. The damage to her face was shocking. Perrin swallowed hard, then lowered her voice to a soothing tone.

"Augusta? Don't try to talk, just listen. As soon as Frank gets back with the water, we'll make a bed inside your wagon, then move you. Miles has gone to the fort to find a doctor." Gingerly, she stroked Augusta's shoulder, then stood as Cora returned with a blanket and flipped it over the dead man.

"Think, Cora. Does anyone on the train have any laudanum or opium? I don't know if she's hurting right now, but she will. And it's going to be bad." Panic swelled in her throat. "Oh, God. I killed a man. No, I can't think about that yet. We need clean rags to wash her. And we have to get her out of that bloody dress. If Miles can't find a doctor . . ." But she wouldn't think about that yet either.

The lumpish form beneath the blanket drew her gaze like a magnet. She had murdered a man. It didn't seem possible. She had shot him in the heart. Her empty stomach revolted and bile flooded her mouth. A silent scream rang in her head. Oh, Cody. Hurry. I need you.

The instant Cody saw Miles ride into the fort and leap off his horse, he knew something was bad wrong. Miles Dawson was a dependable hand; he wouldn't desert his post beside the arms wagon without a damned good reason. Cody left the men talking beneath the cottonwoods and strode rapidly forward, spotting Webb coming from the far side of the fort, a frown drawing his brow. They converged on Miles Dawson.

"Slow down, son. Start over at the beginning." Cody listened and his jaw dropped.

"All I know is there's a dead son of a bitch laying on the ground, and Miss Augusta, I think she's dead too. Miss Thorp and Mrs. Waverly have blood on them, but they don't seem hurt much. Mrs. Waverly sent me to fetch you and a doctor if I can find one. Frank stayed behind with the arms wagon."

Cody glanced at Webb. Webb nodded, then returned to the fort buildings, his expression seemingly unconcerned, his stride more rapid and purposeful than it would appear to a casual observer. If there was a doctor at the fort, Webb would find him. And Webb would know the dead man's identity before nightfall. He would accomplish this without alerting anyone that a problem existed.

"All right." Cody placed a hand on Miles's shoulder. "I'll get my horse, then you and I are going to ride out of here nice and slow, like nothing's wrong. Understand? We don't want anyone getting agitated until we learn what happened."

"I never seen a woman beat like that, Captain. Miss Augusta, she was the prettiest woman I ever—"

"Stow it. We'll talk later." Quickly, he scanned the people loitering in the shade beneath the porch roofs fronting a makeshift boardwalk. When he spotted Heck, he gestured him toward the horses. "Keep our people here for another three hours," he ordered curtly. "Are the wagons ready to roll?"

Heck's eyebrows lifted like rising half moons. "I thought we were going to rest here for another two days."

"We'll roll in three hours, as soon as you bring the women back to the train and we can get under way."

"What . . ."

"Not now." Wheeling the buckskin, he trotted toward Miles Dawson, grinding his teeth in frustration and wishing he had more information. Perrin. Was she injured? The possibility made him feel sick inside. He wanted to kick the buckskin into a canter, but knew it would be folly to raise questions until he discovered the answers himself. He and Miles rode toward the train at a leisurely pace until they dropped below a grassy rise. Then Cody galloped straight to Augusta's wagon.

He jumped from his horse and tossed the reins to Miles. "Go back to the arms wagon with Frank," he ordered. "I'll call you if I need you." If this had been a diversionary tactic, the arms wagon would have been gone by now. That he had spotted the wagon as they rode up provided enormous relief.

"Oh, Cody!"

Perrin flew into his arms and pressed her head to his chest as he ran his hands over her shaking arms, her throat, her face, checking for injuries. She was smeared with blood, but apparently it wasn't hers, thank God. He wrapped his arms around her and held her tightly while he whispered a prayer of gratitude.

She spoke against his chest and he only heard a fraction of what she said, but he understood that she had killed a man who was attacking Augusta. Holding her, stroking the hair that had fallen around her face, he looked over her head at the blanket-covered form on the ground.

Cora watched them, her mouth open in surprise, but he couldn't think about that now. "Who was he?"

Cora swallowed and tears sprang to her eyes. "He said his name was John Eaggleston." She wrung her hands. "I just wanted to scare Augusta, that's all. I just wanted to get back at her a little for being so mean. I swear I didn't know he would try to kill her!"

Perrin shivered against him, pressing close as if she wanted to melt into the heat of his body.

"Eaggleston, Eaggleston." Frowning, he tried to recall where he had heard that name.

The answer spilled out of Cora, reminding him of the man and woman he had buried. "I think Augusta found some money either in their wagon or near it, but I don't really know," she finished. "I just know that before we stopped to bury them she only had a few gold pieces that I ever saw, and afterward she had enough gold pieces to fill the brim of her Sunday hat. So I thought . . . but maybe it wasn't that way. I don't know. I just . . ."

"Where's Augusta now?"

"We put her inside the wagon." Cora lifted a bottle. "I went to look for something to help with the pain."

"Webb is searching for a doctor. Right now, I want you to stay with Augusta. I need to speak to Mrs. Waverly."

Mrs. Waverly was weeping on his chest and holding on to him as if they were very familiar with each other's bodies. Cody returned Cora's long stare. Whatever conclusions she might draw was a problem that would have to wait.

As soon as Cora climbed into Augusta's wagon, Cody

held Perrin a little away from his body and examined the
tears streaming down her cheeks. "First. Are you all right?"

"No," she whispered, looking up at him with those huge,
thick-lashed, cinnamon-colored eyes. "Cody . . . I killed a
man. I shot him with his own gun. Oh, God, I think I'm
going to be sick again."

He followed her toward a clump of chokecherries and held
her head, then helped her back to her own wagon and gave
her a ladle of water to rinse her mouth. Then he gently
pushed her into a camp chair and knelt beside her, taking her
hand.

"Tell me what happened. Take your time." When she finished talking, looking sick again, gaps remained in the story,
but he'd begun to grasp the outline of it.

"Perrin, listen to me. If you and Cora hadn't displayed extraordinary courage and attacked Eaggleston, he would have
killed Augusta. Once you were involved, he would have
killed you too. By shooting him, you saved Augusta's life,
and probably your own and Cora's."

She stared at him through tear stained eyes. "But I *killed* a
man!"

"And that's hard," he said, smoothing a tendril of dark
hair off her cheek. No one forgot the first time he shot and
killed a man, and no one emerged unchanged. "But you
saved three lives. Think about that, Perrin."

She pressed her fingertips to her forehead, and he watched
her trying to pull herself together. "What do we do now?"

"I'm going to get Miles and we'll bury Eaggleston. As
soon as a doctor has done what he can for Augusta, we'll
move out. What I want you to do is clean the blood off your
hands and skirt. Instruct Cora to do the same. Too many
people know what happened for this to remain a secret, but
maybe we can contain it until we've put Fort Boise well behind us. I don't want you detained for an inquiry into Eaggleston's death."

Slowly the shock faded from her beautiful eyes. He knew
the instant she was thinking clearly again. Her shoulders

slumped and her lips parted in a long breath. "Would they charge me with murder?"

Cody shrugged. "It's possible. We aren't going to let that happen."

"Cora saw me throw myself into your arms, didn't she?" Tilting her head back, she gazed at the sky. "I didn't think. All I knew was that I needed you."

"There's something I want to say, but now isn't the time." When she lowered her head and gazed at him, he cursed himself for imparting a wrong impression. "It's about money."

"Oh."

Why couldn't he tell her that he loved her? *Did* he love her? And if he did, was he ready to tear up his plans and his life? Was he prepared to take that kind of risk again? He pulled a hand down his face.

"Will you be all right if I leave you?"

She stared at him. "Yes." Standing, she swayed, then steadied on her feet. "I'll change and wash up, then I'll go to Augusta so Cora can . . ." She gave her head a shake. "I killed a man."

"Thank God he didn't kill you."

He made himself walk away from her.

Dr. Falkenburg filled a basin of water from the barrel, then washed his hands at the sideboard. "I've done what I can for her. And I've left two bottles of opiates with Mrs. Waverly." He dried his hands and squinted at Cody and Webb. "Miss Boyd endured a brutal beating, gentlemen. She'll need care for a least two weeks. But she'll recover."

"She was a beautiful woman," Cody stated in an expressionless voice. "Will she be disfigured?"

Dr. Falkenburg shrugged. "I did the best I could with her nose, but it's going to be crooked. She's lost two teeth. Other than that . . ."

Cody pressed a gold eagle into the doctor's hand, then he and Webb walked away from the wagon to watch Falkenburg ride back toward Fort Boise. "What did you find out?"

"He went by several names. John Eaggleston, John Ryland, John Sneed."

Cody glanced at Webb's frown. "Ryland? Like the Ryland who stopped at Fort Bridger and asked how much James Conklin would pay for a load of arms and ammunition?"

Webb nodded. "It's almost certain that Ryland or Eaggleston is part of Jake Quinton's gang. But I'm guessing what happened here is probably a personal issue. Eaggleston was asking about our train before we arrived. But he wasn't talking about weapons, he was talking about a box of gold pieces. When Eaggleston drank, his mouth ran. Consequently, it seems to be general knowledge that Eaggleston and his brother robbed a bank in central Missouri, then split up, intending to meet in Laramie. The brother was bringing the money from the bank robbery."

"We can piece together the rest," Cody said, swallowing the last of his coffee. "Eaggleston and his wife die along the trail. We stop to bury them. Maybe Augusta found Eaggleston's money or maybe she didn't, but Cora decides that she did. Cora's carrying a grudge, so she starts looking for anyone with an interest in the Eagglestons. She sends him to scare Augusta."

"The reason Cora didn't locate Eaggleston earlier is that he's been ahead of us until recently."

"Eaggleston must be a newcomer to Quinton's gang, or he would have found us when Quinton did."

"He's been looking for us. He probably figured whoever buried his brother also took the bank money. Something you need to know: Eaggleston was waiting at the fort for Quinton. Quinton can't be far behind."

Cody thought for a minute. "Once Quinton arrives at Fort Boise and begins inquiries, someone will recall that Eaggleston paid a visit to our train and hasn't been seen since. Quinton just found one more reason to come after us."

"Revenge and profit weren't enough?"

There was no humor in their quiet laughter.

CHAPTER
* 22 *

My Journal, 1852. I don't know what month it is or what day it is. I don't care anymore. I'm so tired, so exhausted and heartsick.

The whore has bewitched him; she has stolen Cody away from me.

Ellen accused me of imagining things. Ellen said I was insane. My own cousin said that. But I'm not imagining the way they stand too close, the way their hands brush and how they look at each other.

His flaw is that he is drawn to whores. So it was with Ellen, and now with Perrin.

I dreamed of Ellen last night and it was like I was standing over her again, pushing the pillow down on her face. When I woke, I remembered the baby and was glad it was stillborn, glad I didn't have to put the pillow over his face too. I couldn't have forgiven Cody if he'd made me put the pillow on the baby's face.

Cody sent the dream to me as a sign that we'll be together. But I'm so tired. How many whores do I have to kill? Is it fair to keep testing me like this?

Thea saw me cut my leg below the knee and she cried. She wanted to tell someone but I insisted it was an accident.

I've done so much for him, what does one more lie matter?

The journey is almost over, thank Heaven. Soon we'll be together. I wish I knew what he wants me to do about the whore. Does he expect me to rescue him from her like I did before?

I'm so terrible tired. Rage is the only thing that keeps me going. If he doesn't declare himself soon, I'll have to speak to him. I can't go much further trying to guess what he wants me to do. I just want to lie in his arms and rest.

Cody pushed them hard. Smokey Joe banged his gong before the sun rose, and they traveled into the long summer evening until the first pale stars appeared behind the sunset. Fatigue etched every face, hands cramped around the reins. Too exhausted to cook, the women gulped cold food and crawled into their tents, asleep before their heads hit their pillows. Even the glad news that the journey had reached its final stage did not penetrate weariness so deep it dulled thought.

Stumbling with fatigue, Perrin met Cody where he stood by the horses, checking the tether lines. She handed him a bowl of cold beans and bacon. "You need to eat something."

"Thank you." He pushed back his hat and lifted the spoon. "How's Augusta?"

Perrin ran a hand down the buckskin's dusty neck. "The swelling is starting to diminish around her eyes, and her lips have begun to heal. She's bruised everywhere, and every bump jostles her nose. The laudanum helps, but she's in pain."

Cora's claim that Augusta had stolen the Eagglestons' money was argued at every campsite during the midday rest stop. No one believed it. But Perrin had concluded that such a scandal was possible.

If the Boyd fortune had vanished, then Joseph's suicide finally made sense. Joseph would rather have died than confess to his daughter that her home would have to be sold, her life of pampered ease would end. If the noose had not killed Joseph Boyd, Perrin felt certain pride would have.

And, if the Boyd fortune was gone, then it explained why Augusta would endure an arduous journey to marry a stranger, why she hadn't turned back, and why she had delayed paying Cora.

If Augusta had begun this journey with insufficient funds, she might very well have stolen the Eagglestons' gold. Of course, her vanity would not have labeled it as theft.

Cody reached inside his vest and withdrew a leather bag. "I want you to have this."

"What is it?" Perrin asked. She turned the pouch between her fingers after he pushed it into her hands.

"It's two hundred and twenty dollars."

A hot flush climbed her throat. Her first instinct was to take offense and throw the pouch back at him. But a week ago she had killed a man; now she and the world were different.

Cody clasped her shoulders and the warm strength of his callused palms thrilled through her body. "I want you to use this money to repay Horace Able for your passage. I've thought about this, Perrin. You shouldn't marry Able unless you decide that's what you want. I want you to have a choice."

Just last week his gesture would have been an insult; only one kind of woman accepted money from a man who was neither husband nor kin. But today she was too tired to take offense.

"Can you really believe I ever wanted to marry and give myself to a stranger?" she asked wearily, looking at him.

Knots appeared along his jawline, then the air ran out of his chest. "No." Stepping away from her, he faced a gleam that flickered along the horizon. All day the oppressive smoke of forest fires had drifted in their direction. After watching the distant orange glow for a full minute, Cody turned back to her.

"All right. I don't want you to marry Able. Is that what you want to hear? And I don't want the others to turn against you if Cora tells them that she saw us embrace."

Such a possibility had certainly occurred to her. "Repaying my passage won't change whatever is going to happen." And something was brewing, she knew that. For days, most of the women had avoided meeting her eyes.

She squeezed the pouch. The bills crackled like the sound of liberty. And because she was not the person she had been before she killed a man, Perrin suddenly knew she would accept the money and the freedom it would buy her.

Lifting her head, she gazed into his sun-darkened face. "If

you're thinking that once I know I can purchase my freedom, I'll come to your bed . . . you're wrong."

All she had to do was take one step forward, one small step, and she would be in his arms, pressed against his strong hard body. That's what she yearned to do. "It isn't going to happen that way. Never again am I going to offer my bed or my body to a man who cannot or will not love me enough to offer me a future."

She met his gaze squarely. "Learning to respect myself again has been a hard fight over rocky terrain, and sometimes I've progressed only by inches. But I like this new person that I'm becoming, Cody. I never thought that could happen. Finally *I'm* willing to give myself a second chance. And I'm not going to throw away a good decent future for a man who desires me but who can't commit to me." Her chin rose and her eyes flashed.

Astonishment slackened his jaw. "Wait a minute. Did I say there were strings attached to that money? No, I didn't."

"I care about you. Too much. And if you weren't so stubborn, you'd admit that you care about me." Her gaze challenged him to concede the truth of what she was saying. But, of course, pride stayed his tongue. "But no, you have your plans and they don't include a woman. So . . . my plans don't include you."

"Perrin, you are the most irritating damned woman I ever met! And brazen too! You're all but demanding a marriage offer!"

"If I weren't so exhausted, I'd be embarrassed by this conversation." She glared up at him. "But the truth is, we *do* care about each other. You and me, we've seen each other in every kind of mood; we've seen the best and the worst. I know you want a ranch you can call your own. You know I want to carry my head high again. We understand each other. There's respect, and friendship, and passion between us. We'd be good together. But you're too damned pigheaded to even admit why you don't want me to marry Horace Able."

"Good God. There's no way you could have made a speech that blunt and immodest when I first met you!"

"You're right. I've changed. Killing Eaggleston taught me that life is short and uncertain. A person can't just wait and hope for what they want. A person has to speak up. Men have known this forever, but I'm just learning that I need to be direct, trust my instincts, and state what I want."

They glared at each other until the smoke from the forest fires stung their eyes and both had to blink. "Are you going to accept that money?" he demanded, choosing to address that issue and not the others she had raised.

"Yes," she decided after a minute's thought. "Because I don't want to marry Able if I don't have to. But I'll earn it. This is the fee I'll charge you for hiring on as an extra gun."

"*What?*"

"We all know Jake Quinton will try again to steal the arms and ammunition. When he comes, you expect me to be on the firing line. That's what the shooting lessons are all about."

He threw out his hands. "You're a good shot."

She couldn't help it. She was angry enough, fatigued enough to enjoy ruffling him. A tiny smile touched her lips. "Well, consider this." She tucked the money pouch inside her waistband. "If I don't marry one of the Oregon bridegrooms, then I'm not entitled to share in the profits when you sell the arms and ammunition. Therefore, I have no personal interest in risking my life to defend them. So, I'm charging you two hundred and twenty dollars for my services as a gunslinger."

Cody's mouth dropped and he stared at her in bewildered amazement. "That is the craziest damned logic I ever heard!"

"I'm so exhausted right now that my head feels like it's floating above my shoulders. Maybe that's why I can say these things." She lifted her chin and returned his stare. "But I happen to think it's illogical and damned insulting that you look at me like I'm the sole object of your desire, yet you can't admit that you care for me. Yes, I'll take this money, but I'm through thinking about you, Cody Snow! Through aching over you and daydreaming over you! I'm starting to believe you're just like Joseph Boyd and every other man I ever knew. You want to have your cake and eat it too. You want a woman who'll love you without asking anything in return, like a commitment for the future. Well, do you want to know what I say to that? I say you can go straight to hell!"

Turning smartly on her heel, she marched toward her wagon propelled by the steamy heat of anger. It wasn't until she settled into her bedroll that it occurred to her that she had come within an inch of asking him outright to marry her and then had told him to go to hell, all in the span of about ten minutes.

She hadn't a notion where she'd found the backbone to do either thing. But it sure felt good.

Mem told her that Sarah had called a meeting, but Perrin couldn't make herself believe it until the women passed her wagon carrying their camp chairs toward a flat spot relatively free of sage and sand burrs. No one looked at her.

Swallowing hard, she focused on the distant peaks of the Blue Mountains which rose like a forbidding wall across the western horizon.

She wasn't surprised. Mem had dropped uncomfortable hints, and Perrin had sensed a wave of silent condemnation. She didn't even blame Cora for telling what she had seen.

But she was surprised by how much it hurt. Thinking she was prepared for this was a mistake; she'd hoped for a miracle. Old instincts reared, powerful and compelling. She wanted to crawl into the back of her wagon, curl into a ball, and hide and weep.

Instead, she stiffened her shoulders and made herself follow behind the others. Feeling the heat pulsing in her cheeks, she stood behind the chairs arranged to face Sarah Jennings. Triumph gleamed in Sarah's dark eyes, or perhaps Perrin only imagined it. Perhaps what she saw was only an "I told you so."

"You all know why we're here," Sarah began. She looked tall and commanding, standing before an azure sky that enhanced her natural dignity. "Since both parties are present, we'll hear from each. Cora? You claim you saw Mrs. Waverly throw herself into Captain Snow's arms, that it was clear from what you saw that Mrs. Waverly and Captain Snow have more than a formal regard for one another. Is that correct?"

Standing, Cora wrung her hands and threw Perrin an imploring glance. "She was upset. We both were."

"Did *you* throw yourself into Mr. Snow's arms?" Ona inquired acidly. "Or was *she* more upset than you?"

"We were both . . . I'm sorry," Cora said to Perrin. "I just told what happened."

Sarah's voice sliced off further apology. "Is Cora's report true, Mrs. Waverly, or do you deny it?"

Perrin lifted flaming cheeks, speaking to the back of most heads. "I intend to repay Mr. Able for my passage. I no longer consider myself pledged to marry anyone."

"Did you consider yourself pledged to marry Mr. Able at the time when you and Captain Snow, ah, embraced?"

Sarah was offering her a chance to at least make an argument in her defense. A lie might avert what was about to happen.

But Perrin cared for these women. She loved Mem, and respected the rest. They had worked together, wept together, laughed together. She knew their strengths and their weaknesses. Unfortunately, they believed they knew hers. Regardless, she owed them better than a lie.

"Yes," she said quietly, her cheeks on fire. From the corner of her eye, she saw Mem drop her head and touch her fingertips to her lips. "I felt pledged to Mr. Able until yesterday."

Mem stood. "Thanks to my sister's inability to keep a secret—" she dropped an affectionate frown at Bootie— "everyone here knows that Mr. Coate and I have married in the Sioux tradition. Mr. Coate will repay the passage expenses for myself and for Bootie." She straightened her shoulders. "But at the time Mr. Coate and I performed our marriage ceremony, my situation was no different from Mrs. Waverly's. It could be said that I betrayed the man in Oregon whom I had agreed to wed. If you condemn Perrin, then you must condemn me also." She sat down.

"The situation is entirely different," Ona objected, jumping to her feet. Anger mottled her face. "You and Mr. Coate love each other and consider yourself married!" She whirled to face Perrin. "Do you and Captain Snow plan to marry?"

"No," Perrin whispered. The fury in Ona's eyes stunned her.

"Has he made you any promises? Has he told you that he loves you? Or has he merely succumbed to the lustful temptations of a proven whore? How many times have you given yourself to him?"

A faint hissing erupted as several of the woman drew in a sharp breath. They all stared at Ona in shock and disapproval.

Sarah stepped forward with a scowl. "Attacking Mrs. Waverly is as distasteful as the recent gossip. The issue before us is whether we wish Mrs. Waverly to continue as our representative. That is the only subject that concerns us today."

Trembling, scorched by the fire on her cheeks, Perrin pulled back her shoulders and prayed her voice would not break.

"I'll make this easy for you. I resign as your representative." Ona's ugly words continued to reverberate in her mind. What had she done to make the girl hate her so deeply? Drawing a deep breath, she concealed shaking hands behind her body. "I propose Sarah Jennings as the new liaison." She pulled another shallow breath into lungs that felt as if they were shrinking. "We've been taking turns driving Augusta's wagon. From this point forward I will drive Augusta's wagon alone."

Hilda was stuck with her at night, but she could spare

everyone her company during the day. Heaven forbid that she should contaminate any respectable women.

Angry, humiliated, and aching with embarrassment and pain, she turned suddenly, before they could see the tears brimming in her eyes, and she blindly walked away from them.

She had told Cody to go to hell. And now they had taken away a title and position that had made her feel good about herself. The loss of both created a painful hollow in her chest.

All she had left was herself. That's all she had ever had.

Smokey Joe, that font of information and gossip, told him what the women were up to. By the time Cody arrived at the meeting, Perrin was walking away, her face wooden, and Mem was running after her. Instantly he knew what had transpired merely by the sight of Perrin's rigid body and uncertain gait.

Tight-lipped and angry, he strode to the front of the group. "What you just did is small, petty, and wrong," he stated flatly, staring at them. He was breaking his rule of noninterference but didn't stop himself. "Perrin Waverly has represented you well. She's argued for you, worked for you, and worried about you. There isn't a person here who hasn't benefited from her kindness and concern. And no one could have been fairer than she has been." Anger smoldered in his icy gaze. "She turned to me for comfort, that's all. Any one of you would have done the same damned thing if you'd just shot and killed a man."

He saw Ona jab an elbow in Thea's ribs, then Thea stood and cleared her throat. "We understand that Miles Dawson was the first man to arrive on the scene. Did Mrs. Waverly also throw herself into his arms seeking comfort?"

The smug knowing look on her pretty face made him seethe. "I don't know."

Sarah coughed into her hand. "When he was queried on this point, Mr. Dawson said Mrs. Waverly did not seek comfort from him. He feels she was quite in command of herself."

Ona rose to her feet, flinging out an accusation. "Bootie claims she saw you give Mrs. Waverly a money pouch!"

Bootie shrugged. "Well, that's what I saw."

At once Cody understood they all grasped Ona's implication. Ona's tone made it glassy clear that she believed he'd been paying his whore. Dark color infused his face.

"I respect and admire Perrin Waverly. She's a beautiful and spirited woman and any man would be proud to have her share his bedroll. But she doesn't share mine. I began this journey with a private conviction that integrity and a sense of humor are solely male attributes. What I'm witnessing here does little to alter that opinion. But Perrin Waverly has proven that women do have integrity and personal honor. At least she does."

He stared into each face. Perrin's dismissal had not been unanimous; he was glad for her sake that she had supporters, albeit none with the courage to speak in her defense. It was also evident that nothing he said would change the opinions of those who condemned her. If anything, arguing in her favor may have injured her case. None of them viewed him as unbiased.

Later that evening his suspicion was confirmed when Smokey Joe made sure he overheard that Sarah Jennings was the new representative. Cody had not changed their minds.

Webb followed him out onto the edge of the high desert and they shared a smoke. When it was dark enough that his expression couldn't be seen, Cody made a sound of disgust.

"This is the first damned time that I've ever compromised a passenger!"

"You usually haul weapons and whiskey, not women," Webb commented placidly. He studied the fiery tip of his cigar.

"I think she wants me to marry her." Amazement roughened his tone. Every time he recalled how blunt she had been, he was freshly astonished. Women just didn't speak that frankly or that directly. And men raised the subject of commitment and marriage, not women. It was a man's decision.

"You could do worse. Perrin Waverly is a fine woman. What do you want, Cody?"

"Lately, I've been asking myself that question a dozen times a day." He drew on his cigar and frowned. He hadn't allowed himself to analyze how he felt about her until he heard himself lauding her integrity to the other brides. "I started this journey believing there would never be another woman in my life. I didn't think anything or anyone could change that. I didn't want another woman. Certainly not a woman who has been another man's mistress."

They watched a shooting star streak across the sky. "Are you going to spend the rest of your life punishing every woman for Ellen's sins?" Webb asked eventually. It was the kind of hard question only a very good friend would ask.

"Mrs. Waverly has sins of her own," he said sharply.

Webb peered at him through the darkness. "She can't change what she did before she met you." He let the words hang a minute. "Man wasn't meant to live alone, Cody. And Perrin isn't Ellen. She isn't a young, spoiled belle. Perrin is a woman of strength and character." He let those words hang too. "This solitary life you're planning . . . will it be better or worse without her?"

"She's stubborn, argumentative, doesn't know the meaning of the word no." He thought a minute, then released a long breath. "She never complains, works hard, is scrupulously fair, and sometimes there's a loneliness in her eyes that haunts me. They were goddamned wrong to reject her as their representative!"

Webb said nothing, but Cody sensed his smile and it infuriated him. "Even if there were no past history with Boyd, since the incident with Eaggleston she's started saying whatever pops into her mind. She's as blunt as a man!"

Webb clapped a hand on his shoulder and laughed out loud. "My friend, sometimes women have to hit us over the head with a blunt statement to get our attention."

"She told me to go to hell," he insisted indignantly. "She said she was through with me."

"Then you don't have a problem, since you claim you're finished with women anyway," Webb said, grinning.

Scowling, Cody flipped his cigar in a fiery arc. They stood in the darkness, silently observing the cook fires surrounding the squared wagons.

"Now that the California people have cut south and the traffic has thinned, I figure Quinton will make his move." Even at night the Blue Mountains loomed as a challenge. The mountains coupled to the problem of Quinton seemed daunting at this moment. "I wish you were two people," Cody said. "One to scout campsites and one to ride behind, checking for Quinton."

Webb studied the ebony wall of the Blues. "Better we settle it here than carry the fight into the mountains."

"He's out there," Cody said quietly, scanning the darkness. "I can feel him."

And he could feel Perrin as if her spirit reached out to him. When he turned to face the wagons, he saw her sitting alone beside her fire. She sat erect, her face expressionless, her body closed in on itself. Isolated in the solitude the others imposed on her.

Joseph Boyd had done this to her. Boyd had left her vulnerable to this kind of punishment. Or was it him? Was Cody the one responsible for her loneliness?

Again, Quinton and his gang struck shortly before dawn. Gunfire from the men guarding the arms wagon awoke everyone and sent them racing to rehearsed positions.

In the end, the skirmish lasted less than forty minutes. As Cody holstered his gun and rose to his feet in the chill swirling dust, he decided the hit-and-run attack had been more an information-gathering foray than a genuine attempt to steal the arms wagon. Cursing, he shoved back his hat and mopped dust and sweat from his brow. Now Quinton knew the train's defenses.

Webb walked out of the dusty darkness. "Perrin Waverly's been shot. It's a flesh wound, not serious." Webb's hand stopped him from striding forward. "Cody, she was shot from behind."

He understood at once and his stare deepened. "One of our people." His mind raced. She would have taken a position beneath her wagon. The animals were behind her in the enclosure formed by the wagons. "Damn it! How did this happen?" he demanded.

"Quinton's gang was riding off. She crawled out from under the wagon and stood up." Webb's eyes narrowed. "The last shot we heard must have been the shot fired at Perrin."

An absurd connection flashed through his mind. Although he saw no similarity whatsoever, he suddenly recalled his slashed bedroll. The incidents had ceased once they passed into the Oregon Territory. That puzzled him too.

By the time he arrived at Perrin's wagon, lanterns had been lit to aid the first glow of dawn. Sarah glanced up, then back to the bandage she was wrapping around Perrin's upper arm.

"It's not serious," she said briskly. "The bullet passed clean through, didn't hit bone. The wound will heal in a few days. Cora will drive Augusta's wagon."

Cody didn't give a damn who drove Augusta's wagon. He knelt beside Perrin, careful not to touch her as he wanted to. He gazed into her large pain-filled eyes. "Are you all right?"

"Yes."

He hesitated, aware that Sarah watched and listened, unsure how to ask what he suddenly needed to know or even if the question was reasonable. "Mrs. Waverly, have you experienced any strange incidents on this journey?"

Sarah cut the bandage with a small pair of scissors, then frowned at Perrin. "You didn't tell him?" she demanded.

He swore quietly. "If something has been going on, you should have told me immediately!"

She gazed at him with those cinnamon-colored eyes, huge in her pale face. "At first it didn't seem important."

In a halting voice, glancing occasionally at the blood seeping through the bandage on her arm, she related dozens of pranks that had escalated in seriousness to a slashed dress. As she spoke, Cody finally understood the old valentine that had appeared beneath his saddle blanket. Someone had been sending a message; someone had known of their attraction for a long time.

Pushing back his hat, he tugged at his hair. "Whoever stole your valentine stuck in under my saddle blanket. I didn't know what it was. I threw it away."

She nodded and moisture appeared in her eyes. She gazed down at her lap. "I've been ill for the last few days," she said when she could speak again. "Hilda hasn't felt well either. I think . . . I don't know . . . someone may have put something in our food. There was one night when we bought some fish from the Indians that visited camp. We prepared it immediately, but it tasted bitter. We didn't eat all of it."

"And now you've been shot." Cody studied her, wanting to take her into his arms.

"It had to be an accident," she said, searching his face.

He lifted an eyebrow at Sarah. "Having accompanied your late husband on campaigns, I imagine you've seen your share of wounds. Can you distinguish entry and exit?"

She nodded. Abruptly her frown altered to an expression of incredulity. She stared down at Perrin's arm. "Good heavens! But that means . . ."

Quickly, he told them about the cake, ribbon, slashed bedroll and blankets. The more serious incidents appeared to have happened in tandem with the escalating events targeting Perrin.

As the sun drifted above the horizon, Cody noticed how white her face was. When he considered that she might have been killed, his heart stopped. He wanted to pull her into his arms and hold her tightly and tell her how grateful he was that she was alive.

"Damn it," he said softly. There was no privacy on a wagon train. No place he could take her to cradle her in his

arms or tell her that he didn't like her coolness and didn'
like the indifference he suspected she only pretended.

Sarah's voice cut across confusing thoughts. "Who'
doing these things?"

Pulled from gazing at each other, Cody and Perrin looke
at her. Then Cody stood, opening and closing his hands at hi
sides.

"There are going to be questions," he said to Sarah, hi
eyes hard. "Answer truthfully. If Perrin's wound was not a
accident . . . then someone tried to kill her. Whoever did thi
needs to know we're aware of his intentions."

He met Perrin's large eyes before she lifted her chin an
looked away from him. Frustration tightened his jaw. Ha
Ellen ever irritated him this much? Had she confused hin
and stirred his guts the way this woman did when he looke
at her? He knew the answers. Ellen had never possessed a
great a potential to wound him as Perrin Waverly did.

The truth struck like a crippling blow to the belly. He wa
afraid of her. If he let it happen, he could love her as he ha
never loved another human being. And that love would giv
her the power to destroy him. What Ellen had done to hi
pride and his self-esteem would be as child's play compare
to what Perrin could do. If he let himself love her.

Leaving her, he strode into the pearly dawn. Someone ha
tried to kill her. And Quinton would attack again. His trai
was under siege from within and without.

Rocking back on his heels, he gazed at a chilly leaden sky
As if he didn't have enough trouble on his plate, he realize
winter would arrive early this year. Tales of passengers per
ishing in snowbound trains as early as mid-September dark
ened his thoughts.

From now on, every day counted.

Quinton's gang came at them every few days. Smokey Joe
took a bullet in the thigh and hobbled around on a crutch
Heck Kelsey made for him. They lost another two oxen to
gunfire, and one of Smokey's mules. Hilda smashed a finger

Thea crawled under her wagon and into a bed of stinging cactus. Nerves were pulled as tight as piano wire, and exhaustion tugged lips and eyelids.

Despite the hardship of traveling in the mountains, everyone expressed relief to enter the Blues and escape Quinton's persistent attacks. The heavy fir stands frustrated the outlaws' harassment and offered a respite from escalating attacks.

But their progress slowed to a crawl.

In short order, the brides discovered they were now embarked on the worst stretch of terrain so far experienced. Here everyone walked, stumbling over ragged stones the size of a tin mug. Shoes came apart, lacerations appeared on everyone's feet and ankles.

The wagons became cumbersome obstacles. They waited with pounding hearts as the vehicles were hoisted up steep slopes with ropes and pulleys. Courting injury and disaster, the women ran to block rear wheels with rocks as the wagons inched up perilous inclines. Occasionally they had to brace and push straining muscles against the tailgate of a wagon to keep it from rolling back and smashing to pieces should it break loose and crash down the side of a steep slope. Muscles quivered and twitched for hours afterward.

On the third day into the Blue Mountains, they all watched helplessly as an improvised winch snapped and the men's cook wagon hurtled end over end down the mountainside, spilling provisions and utensils.

Silently and trembling with exhaustion, everyone helped Smokey Joe salvage what he could. Then, shaking with anger and frustration, Cody agreed to two days' rest so Heck Kelsey could repair damaged wagons and rig a cart to haul the equipment Smokey Joe had been able to recover.

Since Cora had been driving Augusta's wagon while Perrin's arm healed, Cora decided to move back into Augusta's wagon. "It just makes sense in terms of convenience."

Surprisingly, Augusta had agreed to the suggestion, and seemed, in fact, to welcome Cora's return.

"Augusta's well enough to drive her own wagon," Perri
commented. Pausing to catch her breath, she set down th
box she was helping Cora move, then sat on a tree stump an
gently rubbed the arm where she'd been shot.

Instinctively, she scanned the firs, looking to see if anyon
watched her, perhaps with a carbine in his or her hands. Bu
she saw nothing except the distant icy cone of Mount Hoo
and another snowcapped peak she couldn't name. Seeing th
white glint of sunlight on snow called her attention to th
chill in the mountain air, and she pulled her shawl mor
closely around her body. These, the last days of August, fe
more like late autumn than the end of summer.

"Perrin?" Cora sat down beside her. "I been doing a lot c
thinking since we killed that Eaggleston. And I'm trying t
make amends where amends are needed. That's why I'r
going back to Augusta. To make up for sending Eaggleston
after her." A flush of regret tinted her cheeks. "I owe yo
amends too. I'm sorry I told about you and Captain Snow
My mouth just got going and I told everything without think
ing how some of them might take it. You been decent to me
and I'm just sick at heart that I've been the cause of so muc
trouble."

Perrin waved a hand, mildly astonished that she still pos
sessed the energy to lift it. The last few days had been ex
hausting. They had all lost weight. "No one can fault you fo
telling the truth," she said.

Cora used the edge of her shawl to mop sweat off he
brow. The altitude brought perspiration with every effort
"Well, it seems a shame," she said. "Now that you aren't th
representative and don't have to meet with the captain ever
day . . . well, I ain't the only one who's noticed there ain'
nothing between you two. And maybe I ain't the only on
who's starting to feel ashamed at how we been treating yo
too. What are you going to do when we get to Oregon?"

Perrin kept her eyes on the distant snowy caps. "I've bee
thinking about that. Hilda believes there will be many oppor
tunities for women and I agree with her. The territory need

teachers. Or I could cook or make a living taking in wash. Maybe I'll save what money I can and eventually try California."

Cora nodded. "Me, I'm glad to know there's a husband waiting. I never thought I'd have one." Bending, she picked up her box of belongings. "I guess it's hard for someone like me to understand why you'd choose to take in wash rather than a husband. My Ma took in wash. It's a hard job."

"So is marriage," Perrin said quietly.

Augusta saw them coming through the fir and alders. Turning, she frowned into the mirror hung on the side of the wagon. The distinctive perfect Boyd nose was crooked now. And when she smiled, which she seldom did, she exposed two gaps where small white teeth had been. A tiny but noticeable scar trailed from the corner of her lips across her chin.

Every day she practiced smiling without exposing her teeth. She was objective enough to know that her bridegroom would still find her attractive, but she would never again be considered stunning. She had paid for her theft with her beauty. And she would pay for her father's mistakes by surrendering the Boyd name to Owen Clampet.

Mrs. Owen Clampet. Augusta Clampet. The combinations offended her ear and her heart. *Clampet* sounded like a peasant's name. She stared at her missing teeth in the mirror.

At the end of this arduous, hideous journey, she would have lost everything on which she based her sense of self and importance.

"I've made space for your things in the wagon," she called to Cora, turning in disgust from the mirror. The sound of birds and the noise of Heck Kelsey's hammer seemed very loud as Perrin and Cora approached. Augusta drew a deep breath and pressed her hands together. She was convinced they stared critically at her nose and gloated over the ugly gaps between her teeth.

"I haven't had a chance to say this before," she began. She

had thought about what she would say, but the rehearsal didn't make it easier. She wasn't accustomed to being in someone's debt. "Thank you for saving my life."

Cora stopped near the battered front wheel of the wagon. "I have to know. Did you do it?" she asked bluntly, staring at Augusta's nose. "Did you steal that man's money?"

Augusta released a long low breath. Perrin shot a glance at Cora, but she too waited for Augusta's reply. "Yes," she said quietly.

It was the hardest one word she had ever spoken, and it released a flood of moisture beneath her arms. Shame pulsed in her face and dampened her eyes. But she owed them the truth. Without the foolhardy courage of these two women, she would be dead now.

She lowered her head. "My father invested badly and lost his fortune. Then he embezzled from his own bank. When he was about to be discovered, he hanged himself." She touched shaking fingertips to her forehead. Oddly, a hard knot unraveled inside and began to crumble away. To her astonishment, truth was easing the cramps she had suffered from the moment she learned of her father's death.

"I sold everything and paid his debts. I managed to keep his crime private." Raising her head, she faced Perrin and Cora, old enemies both, as she had never faced anyone else, stripped bare of pride. "I began this trip with forty dollars. It's all that was left of the Boyd fortune."

A long sigh collapsed Perrin's chest, and she sat on the wagon tongue. The defiance disappeared from Cora's eyes, and she leaned against the wheel.

"We weren't supposed to come unless we had at least two hundred dollars," Perrin stated in a level voice.

Augusta studied her face, but there was no sign of gloating. "It was either accept a husband in Oregon or become a beggar on the streets of Chastity. I had to come whether I had enough money or not."

Perrin nodded, understanding filling her large dark eyes.

And suddenly, truly for the first time, Augusta understood

how an unmarried woman could be desperate enough to invite a man to destroy her reputation. "Oh, God," she whispered. "If I'd stayed in Chastity, it might have happened to me!"

"But it didn't," Perrin said quietly, grasping where her thoughts had led.

"I blamed you." Shaking, she stared at Perrin's tired face. "I hated you. But . . . there was nothing else for you, was there?"

"Not then." Perrin stood. "And maybe there was nothing else for you but to take the Eagglestons' money when you found it. If it's any comfort, none of the others believe that you took the money." She glanced at Cora. "And they won't hear anything more from either of us."

Absurdly, astonishingly, she discovered that she didn't care what the others thought, but something inside her needed Perrin Waverly's understanding. Tears swam in her eyes.

"Why?" she whispered. "Why did you attack him and risk getting killed to help someone who hated you? Why did you do that for me?"

Augusta had asked herself this question over and over while she suffered the pain of healing. She had done nothing but revile Perrin from the first. She had done her best to incite the others against Perrin Waverly, had hated and despised her. She had blamed Perrin as the source of her misfortune and had wished her dead. Even as she thought Eaggleston was killing her, Augusta had hated this courageous woman. And Perrin had known it. Yet she rushed forward and placed herself in dire peril in an attempt to help someone who would have died hating her with the last breath.

Perrin gazed at her for a long time. "Mostly I did it for me," she said finally. "Because I couldn't live with myself if I stood by while a man beat a woman to death."

"Even if it meant that you might die too? Even if that woman was your sworn enemy?" Augusta whispered. There was nothing in her experience to help her understand Perrin's reasoning. "Even if that woman cursed you with her dying breath?"

"And I did it because you asked me to. For once in your life you asked for help."

Cora's smile broke the tension. "Seems like that bastard shoulda been afraid of us, if you ask me." She tossed her dark head and her eyes flashed triumph. "We're here and he ain't! Aren't. Isn't?"

Augusta drew herself up. She would never truly understand Perrin Waverly. And she needed time to reconsider her father's involvement in Perrin's ruin. But she owed this woman her life. Moreover, in an odd turn of fate, she was probably the only bride who could say the following words and mean them right now. "Welcome to my wagon and my campsite. I'm glad you're here."

Sudden tears appeared in Perrin's eyes.

"I made tea. I'd be happy if you both would join me."

"I—"

"A cup of tea is small payment for all that I owe you," Augusta interrupted. Her need was as great as Perrin's. She was so grateful to have company, even the company of women she had previously despised. "I haven't had the opportunity to thank you for driving my wagon while I recovered. And Cora . . . I'm glad you've come back. You do know it will be different than before, don't you? We'll share the work."

Cora studied her. "It was me that sicced Eaggleston on you. I ain't yet told you I'm sorry, but I am."

"I know. That's behind us now."

Later that night, after the supper dishes were scrubbed and the breakfast things laid out, Augusta and Cora sat by the embers, inhaling the scent of woodsmoke instead of burning chips and listening as the camp settled for the night.

"You're different now," Cora said, breaking the silence. "More like a real person, if you know what I mean. No offense."

A ghost of a smile touched Augusta's closed lips. "No offense taken." The temperature was dropping. They had pulled out the boxes of winter clothing and extracted heavier shawls. "You probably won't believe this, but I'm genuinely sorry they removed Perrin as the women's representative. She helped all of us at one time or another. Losing the position must have hurt her badly."

"I wish I hadn't been part of it. She loves Captain Snow," Cora added in a matter-of-fact voice.

"Oh." Augusta blinked. As old habits died hard, the word *harlot* leaped into her mind. She shoved it aside with difficulty. If she had learned one thing during this terrible trip, she had learned that she knew next to nothing about the human heart, not even her own. Perspiring slightly from the effort, she tried to assume a nonjudgmental tone. "Does he . . ."

"He does, but he don't know it. Or won't admit it."

"How do you know these things?" Augusta demanded irritably.

Cora chuckled. "I've always had a sense about men and women."

Instantly, Augusta blushed, recalling that Cora had guessed how she felt about Webb Coate even before she dared admit it to herself.

"I've been stupid and foolish," she heard herself confess. "I had a lot of time to think while I was recovering from Eaggleston's beating." She drew a long long breath, then said what previously would have been unthinkable. "You were right. I love Webb Coate." She heard Cora's gasp of surprise, but the skies didn't fall, and the earth did not disintegrate at the admission that a Boyd loved a half-breed. "I think he loves me too. I've been waiting for an opportunity to tell him if he still wants me . . . well, somehow we'll work everything out. It doesn't matter that he's penniless. I don't care. I just need to be with him."

"Oh, Lord," Cora muttered in a low voice. She released a long sigh. "Didn't anyone tell you? It's the worst-kept secret ever. I thought sure someone must have told you."

"Told me what?"

"About Webb and Mem Grant."

"Webb? And Mem?" Her face went white as Cora told her that Webb and Mem considered themselves married. She sat as still as a stone while Cora told the whole story in an expressionless voice. Then she stood on trembling legs. Without a word, tears streaming down her cheeks, she walked to her tent and crawled inside.

Webb was an English peer. He was wealthy. He'd been educated in Europe. He owned homes in Devonshire, in London, and in Rome. She had been wrong about everything. She had focused on the wrong things and had refused to see the man. But Mem had seen with clear eyes. Mem had taken everything that Augusta might have had.

She stared at the roof of her tent, tears of pain and regret trickling into her hair. She could have been a countess; instead she would marry a stranger with a peasant's name. She had spurned a fabulous life she had been born to live because a Boyd could not lower herself to love a savage. What a blind buffoon she had been. She had doubted he would recognize a tablecloth, this man who had dined with the nobility of Europe.

And now that she could admit her love for him, now that she didn't give a damn what anyone might think, it was too late. He despised her and loved Mem. Tears ran down her cheeks.

"Good-bye, my love, my savage Lord Albany. I will never forget you." His bronzed face and black eyes were permanently imprinted on her mind and heart, her first, her only love. She remembered him caressing her and kissing her in the moonlight, remembered sensations and yearnings she would never feel again.

"Oh, my dearest, I will long for you every time my husband touches me."

Sobbing, she buried her face in her pillow.

CHAPTER
* 23 *

My Journal, September, 1852. Augusta gave us her mother's tea set as a wedding gift and wished us a long and happy life together. Everyone has changed so much during this arduous journey. I wept today when I realized how much I will miss these courageous women when we part in three weeks. We have come so far. I pray to God that we complete this last leg of the trip without mishap.

Mem Coate, Lady Albany

Cody stood atop the cliff wall, gazing down at the dangerous, swiftly flowing currents of the wide Columbia River.

There were four possible choices to cover the remaining ninety miles to the Willamette Valley and Clampet Falls.

He could arrange ferries to carry them down the wild Columbia. But drowned passengers were a common result of ferry expeditions. Moreover, the ferries charged a fee comparable to extortion, and he suspected several of his brides had depleted the bulk of their funds.

They could abandon the wagons and hire Indians to float them downriver by canoe, also a soberingly dangerous undertaking, but not as expensive as the ferries. Or he could order Heck Kelsey to break up the wagons and build rafts from the wood. Rafts would eliminate expense, but might increase the danger.

Finally, he could opt to cross the rugged Cascade Mountains by taking the Barlow Toll Road around Mount Hood. *Road* was an egregious misnomer. The trail was no more than ruts passing over rough-hacked tree stumps, boulders, and daunting inclines. It wasn't a wise choice for travelers as exhausted and weakened as his brides had become.

None of the choices was attractive. Each possibility presented grave perils and mixed advantages.

"I must speak to you!"

Surprised by the tone of voice, he turned to discover Ona Norris standing directly behind him. He hadn't heard her approach. "Miss Norris, I've told you repeatedly that communications must go through the women's representative."

All of the women had changed throughout the journey. Perrin, despite being shunned by most, now carried her head high, and dignity and confidence distinguished her step. Augusta would never be a person Cody could warm to, but she had grown and matured into a capable woman. With the promise of a husband, Cora had bloomed. Hilda and Sarah shared expertise, provisions, and gave generously of themselves. Thea and Bootie were no longer the dreaming scatterbrains they had seemed at the beginning. And Mem had surprised everyone by blossoming into a beauty. All were stronger, tougher, more outspoken and self-sufficient than they had been at the initial interview where he first met them.

These were the courageous women who would tame Oregon and who would sacrifice their labor and their hearts to the territory's future. They would do it well and with distinction.

Except Ona Norris. Ona Norris had begun as a pretty, almost flirtatious girl, but would end the journey as an acid, furious harpy composed of jangled nerves and ugly moods. Cody gazed into her darting pale eyes and recalled a rabid dog he had shot in the Dakotas.

"We're almost there!" She spat the words as if accusing him of something. Bony fingers twitched in the folds of her skirt. Whatever poison she carried inside made her appear ten years older than Cody knew she was. Instead of making her stronger, the journey had robbed her of youth and inner resources.

"That's correct," he said, injecting a soothing note into his tone. Lifting his head, he cast a glance toward the wagons, looking for Sarah to take Ona off his hands. He spotted her momentarily, then she moved behind the wagons. "In less than three weeks, you'll have a husband and a home of your own."

She stared at him, then her shoulders dropped and she covered her face with her hands. "Thank God," she whispered. "I've waited so long—so long!—to hear you say that. Oh, Cody."

Only Sarah, Perrin, and Mem addressed him as Cody. His attention sharpened. Something was wrong here. "Mr. Riddley is waiting for you," he said carefully, unsure what he sensed. "I've met Riddley, and he's a good man."

Her hands dropped and she glared at him with slightly unfocused pale eyes. A hiss pulled thin lips back from her teeth.

"I'm warning you, no more games! No more! I've done everything you asked, succeeded at the tests you threw at me. I've punished the whore and driven her off. What more do you want from me? I've proven my love again and again!"

His mouth dropped and he stared in astonishment.

"Don't tease me with talk about Nathan Riddley. I need to know about *our* plans. I *need* to know, Cody. We're almost there and . . . I can't go on like this." Shaking, she covered her face again. "Sometimes I think I'm losing my sanity. That's what you've done to me. You have pushed me to the edge of darkness with your endless and cruel games! I should hate you for what you've done, but I still love you."

Speechless, he tried to frame words, failed, then tried again. "What in the name of God are you talking about?"

"About us!" she shouted, spittle flying from her lips. "You promised to marry me, don't pretend you didn't! I waited and waited. I tormented myself. I feared our secret love was hopeless. Then Ellen wrote and asked me to keep her company during her confinement. It was a sign from God, blessing our love."

"Ellen, my wife? Ellen wrote you?"

"After she died I waited for you to come for me. But you had to wait out the mourning period. I figured that out. And after the mourning period, I finally realized you were waiting for me to come to you, so I traveled to Chastity to my aunt and uncle. You should have come for me then, you should have, Cody. I wasn't going to say anything, but I'm angry now that you didn't!"

While she ranted about waiting, and her aunt and uncle, and all she had done to prove her love, he stared at her, stunned by what he was hearing. Finally he saw the faint resemblance to Ellen's family that had initially made him think Ona reminded him of someone. Mind racing, he shuffled backward through the years, trying to recall where and when he might have met her. He must have. If she knew Ellen, then she hadn't invented this tale.

Ellen. His wedding day. The home of Ellen's aunt, Eugenia Norris. With a small jolt, he realized Mrs. Norris must have been Ona's mother. The house overflowed with friends in dress uniform and friends of Ellen's family, dozens of people. He remembered entering the house, still a little drunk from all the toasts from the night before, and he had noticed a plain shy girl pressed into a corner gazing at him.

He stared hard at Ona. She was older now, but it could have been her, it must have been. Ellen's cousin. Imbued with the exuberance of the day, he had tried to draw the girl out of her corner. He remembered lifting her chin, smiling into her eyes, and flattering her outrageously. Perhaps he had inquired why the prettiest girl at the wedding was hiding in a corner. Perhaps he had begged for a dance later. She couldn't have been older than—what?—thirteen or fourteen years? No more than a child who momentarily blossomed in the light of an adult's attention.

To her, he must have seemed dashing and faintly exotic, the handsome young army officer about to marry her beautiful cousin. She had stared at him and blurted the comment, "I worship you." Cody remembered laughing, maybe he had said he loved her too rather than embarrass her. It was possible that, believing he bolstered the confidence of a painfully shy adolescent, he had made some stupid remark that perhaps he was marrying the wrong cousin. Dimly he recalled her saying something about waiting for him in case Ellen died, and concealing his distaste for such a remark by replying that she should wait for a love worthy of her. Apparently she had mistakenly believed he referred to himself.

The incident had been so fleeting, so slight and unimportant, that he had forgotten it, and her, entirely.

"It was you," he said abruptly, putting it together. "You placed the piece of cake in my vest—"

"Your own wedding cake!"

"And the ribbon—"

"From Ellen's bouquet. I even gave you part of the bouquet itself. Far better signs than you ever gave me!"

"Ona . . . you slashed my bedroll. Was that you?"

Crimson flooded her cheeks. "I thought you had abandoned me for the whore. That was before I understood you were testing me, before I realized what you wanted me to do. I didn't kill her, but I wounded her. If you still want me to kill her, I will."

"You're mad," he said softly. The journey west had driven others mad before her. He should have watched more carefully, shouldn't have made himself so inaccessible. Should have . . .

Her fingers curved and she dragged them across her breast like claws. "Don't say that!" She hissed at him, and her eyes darted. "Ellen said that, and I hate it!"

"Ona, listen to me." He didn't have a notion what he would say next and was almost relieved to be interrupted.

Two disastrous events occurred simultaneously. A snowflake tumbled lazily out of the sky and settled in Ona's dark hair, followed by another, then another. The sight appalled him. Before Cody could consider the consequences of early snow, Webb Coate broke out of the forest, running toward them. One glance at Webb's face, and Cody felt his gut

tighten. There was something worse than an early wet snow-
storm. And it was coming toward him.

They had awakened to frozen water buckets and a heavy,
chill fog floating among the firs and cedars, drifting as low
as the tansy and ragwort that grew thick against the forest
floor. The fog didn't burn off, but eventually rose to hover
near the tops of the trees, leaving dripping branches behind.
It was a cold unpleasant day.

Perrin unpacked her heaviest shawl and wrapped it around
her shoulders, then labored to coax damp wood into flames.
When she had the fire crackling, she sat beside the heat, grit-
ting her teeth as icy droplets spotted her skirt with moisture.
Warming her hands around a mug of coffee, she mentally
listed all the things she should do today. The chores seemed
overwhelming; the effort to build a fire had worn her out.

Everyone blamed the altitude for sapping their energy, but
in truth they were all weakened by malnourishment, minor
illnesses, and the rigors of the journey. Even Hilda, whom
Perrin considered indestructible, suffered a touch of dysentery. Thea continued to fight a runny nose and sore throat.
Bootie was slightly jaundiced. Everyone's flow cycles had
ceased two months ago. They had all lost weight.

Sighing deeply, Perrin sipped coffee which had cooled
rapidly in the cold air. Refusing to accommodate the indignities of dysentery or permit herself to rest, Hilda had gone off
to meet Cora for a reading lesson, and Perrin was alone. The
familiar sounds of the camp swirled around her, Heck's persistent hammering, Miles's murmur to the surviving animals,
the sound of women's weary voices calling out in inquiry or
annoyance.

The sounds opened a well of loneliness inside her chest.

Very soon the brides would marry and scatter to homes
along the Willamette Valley. Mem and Bootie would sail to
England. Perrin would seek employment in Clampet Falls,
her future an empty space waiting to be filled.

Perhaps she would occasionally glimpse Cody when he

rode into town to purchase supplies for his ranch. Perhaps they would nod to each other, or exchange polite howdy-dos. He might remark on the weather; she would agree. Then they would walk away as if this journey had never happened, as if they had not yearned for one another, as if they had not lain in each other's arms one warm night when the air itself sang of love and lovers.

No, she commanded herself, tilting her head to blink hard at a leaden sky. She would *not* think about him. She would not long for him or weep for him. She would not wish there had been no Ellen or no Joseph, would not mourn the past or the future.

If Cody wanted her, she was his. She had all but spelled it out for him. Since that humiliating conversation, she had felt him watching, had sensed his agitation and his black mood. She knew he thought about her and fought a private war as the journey approached an end. But he had said nothing, had offered no signal that anything had changed.

And how could it? Time would not erase the fact of Joseph Boyd. Or Ellen's betrayal. Or all the dark confusion those events unleashed in Cody Snow's heart.

And yet . . . something stubborn and dogged clung to the small hope that one day—soon, please soon—the sun would rise and Cody Snow would recognize and admit that he loved Perrin Waverly. He did love her. She read it in his eyes, felt it whenever he came near. He didn't want to love her, she knew that, but he did. And she knew that too. That was their tragedy.

A deep sigh lifted her breast and she clutched her shawl close to her throat. As soon as she could save enough money, she would go to California. Whatever she found in California would be easier to endure than the torment of waiting and hoping to glimpse Cody in Clampet Falls and the pain of loss that would wound like a blade when she did encounter him.

She blinked at tears in her eyes. She was wasting the morning torturing herself with thoughts of Cody Snow after she had promised she would not do this anymore. Standing abruptly, she shook icy droplets from her shawl, then looked around, seeking a diversion that would focus her thoughts on something, on anything, else.

Contemplating the forest, she decided a walk would clear her mind, and she could search the undergrowth for herbs to replenish her medical box. With luck, she might discover something to ease Hilda's discomfort or something to boost her own flagging energy.

After fetching a basket, she called across the wagons to Mem and gestured toward the forest, then she pushed through a thicket of wild blackberries, long since stripped of fruit, and entered the cool scented stillness of pine and alder.

An hour later, her basket brimming with interesting specimens, she returned through the tree trunks toward the sounds of the camp, pleased to note that she'd worked up an appetite for the salmon purchased from visiting Indians late yesterday.

She felt rather than heard a rush behind her. Before she could whirl or utter a sound, a dirty hand thrust across her shoulder and clamped over her mouth. The basket fell from her fingers, and she struggled silently with a man who dragged her backward.

Through the alders, she saw Bootie toasting her feet at Mem's fire, saw Ona Norris pacing in front of her wagon, pausing to frown toward Cody, who walked toward the cliff ledge overlooking the Columbia. She heard Heck Kelsey swear, then resume hammering. She was near enough to see them, hear them, smell the tang of woodsmoke curling from the fires.

A silent frustrated scream echoed in her head. *Cody! Look this way! Please. Help me, my love, help me!*

Desperately, she clawed at the man's thick hand and kicked backward. If she could only free herself long enough for one scream, please, just one scream.

He dragged her down an incline that blocked the view of camp, then twisted her roughly to face icy yellowish eyes. Perrin gulped breath to shout. Before she could scream he smashed her across the side of the head with his gun butt. Gasping, she dropped to her knees on the wet forest floor and her head erupted in excruciating pain. Slowly, she toppled backward. Then there was nothing.

Webb pushed Ona aside. Cody didn't think he noticed her. "Perrin's gone." He lifted a basket and a strip of torn dark material. "Mem saw her returning from a walk, but when she looked up a minute later, Perrin had vanished. Mem checked her wagon, asked everyone, then called me. I found these."

"Quinton," Cody said softly, his eyes raking the trees through snowflakes. There wasn't a doubt in his mind. "If he's harmed one hair on her head, I'll . . . We'll fan out the men. . . ."

Webb's steady gaze brought him to his senses. If he fanned his men through the forest, Quinton would pick them off as easily as plucking berries from a low branch. "Goddammit!" He slapped his hat against his leg. "There's no chance that she wandered off and got lost?" Hope stripped his voice naked.

"None. When Mem saw her, she was within shouting distance. From where I found this basket, she could see the wagons and the fires." Webb shook snow from his hair. "There was a scuffle. Her skirt caught and tore. The man's prints are deeper leading away than approaching. He carried her."

Cody didn't have to ask why Webb had not followed the tracks. The heavy early snow was falling thickly now, accumulating on the ground. Frustration and anxiety tightened the knots along his jaw. "If anything happens to her . . ."

"I hope Quinton rapes, then kills your whore!"

Cody blinked and both he and Webb looked at Ona, having forgotten her presence.

"She still has you bewitched!" Whirling, she ran into the snowflakes toward the wagons.

"What the hell was that about?" Webb asked.

Quickly, Cody sketched the story. "Apparently she believes I promised to marry her an hour before I married Ellen." He shook his head. "She thinks that she and I have been exchanging secret messages along the trail. She's the one who shot Perrin."

"She's mad," Webb stated flatly.

"I'll put a guard on her so nothing else happens." He shook snow from his hat and jammed it on his head. "But that problem will have to wait. Right now we need to decide—"

A voice shouted from the forest. "I've got one of your brides, Snow."

Both men dropped to a crouch and ducked into the undergrowth, guns in their hands. They scanned the trees, searching for a form, but snow and thick foliage distorted direction and distance.

"I'm offering a trade, which is more than you ever offered me. You get your bride back when I get them carbines and ammo."

Cody couldn't see a damned thing through the falling snow and thick tree trunks. "It's not my decision to make, Quinton. The arms belong to the brides and their bridegrooms. I only have part interest." He muttered to Webb, "See anything?"

"Nothing."

"Let the woman go, Quinton! You and I need to talk."

Quinton shouted an obscenity. "You got until tonight to pull the arms wagon out of line. Leave it at the first turnout on the Barlow Road. If you don't do as I say, I'll kill this bride and take me another one. I'll kill 'em all if I have to."

Sarah and Mem emerged in front of the wagons, holding their rifles and scanning the tree line. But now there was only silence. They turned anxious glances toward Cody and Webb.

"Damn women," Cody snapped. "They might as well paint a bull's-eye on their chests! Can you track him?"

"Not far," Webb answered shortly, staring through the falling snow at his wife. "She's got a mind of her own, that one." His expression blended equal measures of adoration and exasperation.

Slowly, Cody straightened, gripping his gun, half blinded by hatred for Jake Quinton. Quinton had Perrin. Christ. Of all the women, it had to be Perrin. Sweating, he battled a futile impulse to run into the trees, shouting her name.

Now an unthinkable possibility had been added to the choices he'd pondered earlier.

He strode toward Sarah and Mem, halting before them. "Call a meeting," he ordered Sarah. "I want everyone at Smokey Joe's fire in fifteen minutes. That will give me time to talk to the men first."

He met Webb's black eyes over Mem's head. There was sympathy in his friend's gaze. And also a reminder that Cody had to decide this dilemma from the perspective of the wagonmaster, not a man who had suddenly grasped the truth.

He loved her. If he'd needed a jolt to knock some sense in his head, he'd just received it. He would always love her. Perrin was his woman. Webb knew it. Even Ona Norris knew it.

Finally, Cody Snow knew it.

"By now you know that Quinton has Perrin." The snow was falling steadily. An inch had accumulated on the ground. He could hardly see the women standing at the back of the group.

The silence was so absolute that he could hear snow sliding off arching branches. He made himself speak the hardest words he had ever uttered. "I cannot trade Quinton the weapons and ammunition for Perrin, and I can't allow you to do it either. The profit from the arms will guarantee your future and the future of your bridegrooms." A low sighing sound reached his ears.

"Webb and Heck Kelsey will take the train on into the Willamette Valley over the Barlow Road. You'll move out as soon as the sky clears, no matter what time it is. You're going to travel fast and hard. This last leg will be worse than anything you've yet experienced, so get some rest."

"What will you do?" Sarah inquired.

"I'm going to kill Jake Quinton and rescue Perrin if Quinton doesn't kill her first."

Hilda licked lips that were dry and cracked by fever. "How many men does Quinton have with him?"

"We're guessing four or five. He couldn't have traveled as quickly or as quietly with more." Cody couldn't see Ona's face through the snow, but he could feel her stare. He hadn't had time yet to order her confined, but he would when the meeting ended.

Placing her fists on her hips, Mem glared at Webb standing at Cody's side. "Quinton said he would kill Perrin if he doesn't get the arms wagon tonight. If we move out and take the arms with us, we've as good as pointed a gun at her head. How could you agree to this plan?"

"I don't agree," Webb said quietly, folding his arms over his chest. He could guess what was coming and he smiled at her.

"I don't either," Mem snapped. "Give Quinton the wagon."

"That's easy for you to say," Cora objected. "But for the rest of us, that wagon decides whether we git houses or we don't. Whether we're warm this winter or we ain't."

Ona's voice called out of the snowflakes. "I say leave her!"

"Quinton has only four or five men, but we've got six if we don't count Smokey, who's on crutches." Sarah counted off names. "The two teamsters, Miles Dawson, Heck Kelsey, Webb Coate, and you. Why don't all the men go after Quinton and save Perrin?"

There was nothing Cody would have liked better. "We could ride off that direction," he said, pointing, "and they could be over there. With the men gone, Quinton's gang could ride in here and take the weapons and kill all of you. Moreover, finding Quinton's camp could take several days. And we don't have several days, ladies." He glared at the falling snow. "Time is running out. All the signs point to an early winter. This could be the first of several big storms. If we get trapped, we could be here all winter. I'll tell you flat out . . . not many of you will survive a winter in these mountains."

He ended by telling them that he would have ordered the train to roll minutes after he spotted the first snowflake. He would have done that in any case. The only difference now was that Webb and Heck would take them the last ninety miles. And Perrin was gone.

Augusta Boyd pushed through the women and walked up beside him. She met his eyes, then turned to face the group.

"I say to hell with the men's plan." Her blue eyes flashed. "Everyone here owes Perrin Waverly something better than abandonment. If it wasn't for Perrin, I wouldn't be here now. Neither would you, Cora. Who's been doing the chores so you can rest, Hilda? And Ona? Who walked three miles to the Mormon train to trade for oil to treat your cactus infection, then walked three miles back? Who comforted you, Bootie, after the incident with Jane's husband? Thea? Do you remember who caught you when you were almost swept away at the bathing hole outside Boise?" Her hard gaze found Sarah. "You wanted Perrin's position badly enough to incite the others to take it away from her. Maybe by now you've learned how hard she worked for all of us. I say we don't leave here without her."

Face flaming, Sarah hesitated, then stepped forward. "Augusta is right. I . . . Perrin confided in me, and I . . ." She looked at Cody. "I knew she was not acting promiscuously when she ran into Captain's Snow's arms. I'm ashamed that I didn't defend her and that I wanted to be the representative badly enough that I . . ." She bit her lips and dropped her head. "Since I've been doing Perrin's job, I've gone to bed without supper more nights than I can count because I've been busy solving problems for each one of you. Just as Perrin used to do. You know what you've asked me to do, but

352 / Maggie Osborne

you don't know how many others also need a problem solved. It's a tremendous amount of work. We didn't know because Perrin never complained."

"This is merely wasting time. All of you are leaving the minute the sky clears," Cody snapped.

"Quinton will just follow us," Mem said, turning toward the group. "I agree with Augusta. This train goes nowhere without Perrin. And we don't give that bastard the arms wagon either! I was wrong to suggest giving it to him."

Ona elbowed to the front, her eyes blazing. "Perrin Waverly is a whore! Have all of you forgotten that?" Her chin jutted at Cody. "That's why Sarah is our representative. That's why most of you stopped speaking to her! Well, that hasn't changed! And I, for one, am not willing to risk getting shot for the sake of a whore! I say we go without her!"

Cody's eyes were as hard as blue flint. "Maybe you'd also like to tell them you're the person who shot Perrin in the arm."

She looked up and gasped. Surprise and betrayal filled her eyes. "You wanted me to kill her!"

Thea's voice cut through a shocked silence. "Oh, Ona." She spread her hands and looked helplessly at the others. "She . . . she has this idea that she and Mr. Snow . . . but Perrin . . ."

"You are deranged," Sarah stated flatly, staring at Ona. "I should have figured out it was you who slashed Perrin's dress and did those things. As for Perrin . . . I regret what we did, and I'm embarrassed by my role in it."

"I hate all of you."

Cody nodded to Heck and Miles and they stepped forward to escort a hissing, spitting Ona Norris out of the circle and back to her wagon. "Tell Smokey Joe to make sure she stays there."

When Ona was gone, he returned to the others. "Whatever you ladies think you're suggesting, it isn't going to happen," he said curtly. "Webb predicts this storm will pass through rapidly. We should have some sun in about two hours, then this train is going to roll out."

"Well, I won't be on it," Augusta stated quietly. "I've been practicing twice a day for two months to shoot Jake Quinton. I'm going with you to find Perrin Waverly. I used to think Perrin was . . . but that doesn't matter anymore. I know she's treated me fairly and I owe her my life. I owe her better than leaving her to Jake Quinton's men."

Mem shot Cody a defiant glance. "I agree." She stepped up beside Augusta and stared at him. "Perrin is my friend, and I'm not going to Clampet Falls without her."

Bootie sighed, fluttered her hands, then joined Mem. "Well, I guess I'm staying too."

"I won't leave her behind," Sarah and Hilda said in the same breath. "She *is* a friend. One we've treated badly. That ends right here and now," Sarah added. Cora nodded firmly and stepped forward behind them.

Thea came forward too. "I'm with the rest of you. Perrin's been a friend to all of us. It's long past time that we showed her we're sorry for what we did to her. We were wrong. We began the journey together and we should end it together."

"None of you are staying!" Cody roared. "Get this camp packed up and ready to roll!" He was losing precious minutes dealing with nonsense, minutes he could have used to begin searching for Quinton and Perrin. His gut was in knots.

"When we go out to search for her, we'll have to move with stealth," Sarah advised, beckoning the women around her. "Walk as if you're stepping on a wet floor, lightly and quietly. We'll position one of our best shots in front, one in the middle, and one at the end."

"How many pounds of ammunition do you think we can each carry?" Augusta asked, flexing her fingers. "I need to test if I can shoot with my gloves. The cold is a problem."

"We might need bandages, so wear extra, clean petticoats."

"It's cold enough to see our breath. We don't want to signal our position," Mem pointed out. "Webb told me his people suck on ice in this kind of situation. We should too. It will cool our breath and we won't give ourselves away with puffs of vapor."

"I've been sketching the woods," Thea volunteered. "You know ... there's a cave not far from here. . . . If I were Quinton, that's where I'd hide."

They all stared at her, including Cody. "Can you draw a map showing us where this cave is located?"

"Give me five minutes," she said, then hurried off to fetch her sketchbook and pencils.

Bootie pursed her lips. "There aren't enough horses. We'll have to walk. So wear thick socks and your sturdiest boots."

Hilda blushed. "I am having this small health problem. We will need to stop frequently so I can run into the bushes and—"

"This has gone far enough!" Cody strode into their midst. "I swear I'll give Quinton the arms wagon before I'll let all of you get killed trying to implement some damned fool plan!"

Mem drew to her considerable height. "If you won't assist us, Captain Snow, at least be quiet and stay out of our way!" She sent Webb a loving look, then joined the circle of women that stepped around Cody and reformed.

Cody spun. "Do you support this?" he demanded.

Webb leaned against a tree trunk, his arms folded across his chest. He grinned and tilted his head toward Mem. "Looks like I don't have a choice." The grin faded. "You know I don't agree with leaving you behind to face Quinton's gang alone. And Mem's right. If Quinton gets away from you, he'll follow the train."

Cody ground his teeth together. He knew he wasn't thinking as clearly as he usually did. All he could think about was Perrin. What were they doing to her? What was she thinking?

Webb observed the women, then looked back at Cody. "You better listen in, Captain, or you're going to confront

Quinton wearing the wrong battle color." A faint grin returned.

"Son of a bitch!" They were discussing what to wear. And he realized their choice had sound logic behind it. They had decided to hide in the snowflakes by wearing white.

He waded into their center to take charge, although he had to concede they weren't doing badly on their own.

"If you damn fools are determined to do this, then here's how we're going to do it." He glared at the men watching and grinning. He gestured to them. "Get over here. Or do you plan to let these women face Quinton alone?"

Thea returned then, breathlessly waving the map she had drawn. Cody studied it for a full three minutes, with Webb looking over his shoulder.

Instantly they both knew this was where they would find Quinton and his gang. It was exactly the site Cody would have chosen in Jake Quinton's place. "How far?" he asked Webb.

"About thirty minutes from camp."

Lifting his gaze, Cody looked into Thea's eyes. "Thank you." His gaze narrowed. "And don't you ever wander thirty minutes away from the wagons again. Damn it!"

Smiling, she joined the others, then so did Cody. He talked for thirty minutes, rehearsed them for an hour. By the time he sent them to their wagons to don warm white apparel, it was almost two o'clock.

He and Webb checked their powder and balls. "We'll leave Smokey to guard the wagons and Ona." For a moment his thoughts wandered. No, he couldn't think about Ona now. "Hilda and Thea will be the slowest; both are in poor health. We'll let them set the pace."

If something happened to Perrin before he had the chance to tell her that he loved her, he would never forgive himself. What the hell difference did it make that she had been Joseph Boyd's mistress? And she was nothing like Ellen. Perrin was his now, and that's all that mattered. Not the past, just the future.

That he hadn't permitted himself to accept this truth proved that a man could be a fool in a hundred ways. And he'd run through just about all of them with Perrin. He had a lot of explaining to do. He prayed that she would forgive him and that she still wanted him.

"I just hope our brides don't shoot each other," he muttered, slamming balls into his pockets.

"The chances for avoiding an accident will improve if you assign Bootie to ammunition instead of giving her a gun," Webb commented. "I'm amazed my sister-in-law hasn't shot her toes off before today." He checked his gear. "We're ready."

Now, when he wanted the snow to conceal them, it began to thin. In an hour the sky would clear. Cody swore. And he threw up his hands when he spotted the women coming toward him in their wedding dresses and frilly white shawls.

"God help us."

They filed straight past him and entered the forest, not waiting to be led. Their attitude, he swiftly realized, was a lot less frilly than their attire. They were grimly prepared to confront the same outlaw who miles ago had killed Bill Macy and Jeb Holden. They were committed to protect the arms wagon and their future and to rescue one of their own.

Cody watched them and gradually his shoulders relaxed. God alone knew how this would turn out. But he'd led less motivated troops than this one, and three of the brides were as good with a carbine as any man who had served under his command.

"If we're going to lead this troop," he said between his teeth, looking at Webb, "we'd better move or they're going to leave our butts behind."

CHAPTER
* 24 *

Cold and miserable, Perrin huddled in her shawl near the mouth of the cave, away from the fire and the men who sat around it. Pale white woodsmoke curled along the roof of the cave and drifted past her, making her headache worse.

Dried blood matted her hair to her temple. Her ankle ached where the rope around it had chafed through her stockings and rubbed her skin raw. Cold penetrated her shawl and gloves and occasionally she shivered uncontrollably. But she didn't ask to move closer to the fire. She sat as far from the five men as the rope around her ankle permitted.

One was drunk and the others were moving in that direction. Already they celebrated the fortune they would gain from selling the carbines and ammunition. Without wanting to hear, Perrin listened to their plans, staring out of the cave at the snow gently accumulating on leaves and tree limbs.

Cody would never voluntarily surrender the arms wagon. He might want to, but his obligations as wagonmaster would not allow it. And the women would never agree. Their futures depended on the sale of the arms and ammunition. They would not squander their bridegrooms' investment or leave themselves without homes for the winter. She didn't blame them, didn't hold it against them. They had no real choice.

Perrin watched the falling snow and considered her situation.

Her heart insisted that Cody would not abandon her. He'd send the others on to the Willamette Valley, and he would stay behind to search for her. But he'd never find this secluded cave. If he did chance to eventually stumble on it, he would be too late. Quinton would make good on his threat. When Quinton didn't get the arms wagon, he would kill her, after his men took their pleasure. Every time one of them shifted, she started, thinking the rapes were about to begin. But so far the men only talked about it. She suspected they waited for the snow to stop so they could drag her outside the small cave.

Understanding that she was likely to die prompted Perrin to reflect over her life. Frowning, she recalled a lonely childhood and an isolated adulthood. Continuing, she reviewed her brief unhappy marriage to Garin Waverly, the period following his death, and the months with Joseph Boyd.

She couldn't genuinely regret either man. Each in his own way had filled a desperate need, and each in his own way had cared for her. They had stolen her self-esteem and her good name, but she had been a different woman then; she had let them do it.

A plume of vapor sighed from her lips. A woman's life was one long search for a good man. The mistakes were devastating.

Her one regret was that she had finally found her good man, but fate and Cody's own pigheadedness had decided she would never have him for her own.

She could have loved him so much. She could have erased Ellen's memory, could have shown him the security and trust and joy that a woman in love could bring to a man. She could have made him as happy as he would have made her.

Something moved beside a fir tree not far from the cave's entrance. Perrin's frown deepened and she peered through thinning snow. She saw nothing. She must have imagined . . .

Blinking hard, concentrating, she slowly scanned the forest. No puffs of vapor signaled the presence of a person or animal.

But the longer and harder she looked, the more she began to hallucinate snow-covered bushes draped in white ruffles. There was another one. And she spotted a strange short sheet of snow hemmed midway with dangling, yarnlike icicles.

One of the outlaws rose behind her, crouching so his head wouldn't scrape the roof of the cave. He threw a whiskey bottle past Perrin's head and she heard it shatter against the rocks a foot below the cave mouth. "Got to water the tiger," he said, reaching for his fly.

The others laughed as he paused beside Perrin, dug his fingers into her hair, and jerked her head back. He planted a wet whiskey kiss hard on her lips. "That's just a sample of what you're going to get," he said, bringing fresh laughter from the others before he stumbled out of the cave, straightened, then staggered into the trees and snowflakes.

Perrin spit and wiped a hand across her lips. Ordinarily she wouldn't have watched a man relieve himself, but she strained to see his dark coat moving among the firs.

Something white slipped across her line of sight. White wrapped hat, white scarf pulled over a nose. A white and brown poncho. And a flash of intense blue eyes that her heart recognized before her mind did. She sucked in a sharp breath and her pulse leaped. Cody! He was here!

Stiffening, she narrowed her gaze and focused intently. The ruffled bushes appeared to advance. Something stirred— an arm?—and she glimpsed a flash of auburn that vanished in an eyeblink. Mem!

Oh, God. They were all here. They had come to rescue her.

She heard a peculiar gurgling sound, and could no longer see the outlaw. Frantically, she wondered what Cody's plan was and how she might help.

She cleared her throat, mind racing. "Excuse me . . ."

"Hear that, boys?" Quinton's yellow eyes plundered her breast. "She's getting eager."

"I think something may have happened to the man who went outside. I thought I heard a call for help."

"Ole Everett can't pee without help?" They laughed. Several long minutes elapsed, then Quinton frowned at the mouth of the cave. "Frank, go see what in the hell is taking Everett so damned long. Maybe the stupid fool is too drunk to find his way back."

Do it, Perrin silently urged. She already knew she couldn't

untie the rope around her ankle, but she tested it a little by
drawing her knees up. Quinton glared and gave the rope a
sharp yank that cut into her skin. "You ain't going nowhere."

"I'm just moving so—Frank?—can get past."

Frank moved forward, crouching until he stepped past Perrin and could straighten just outside the cave.

All hell broke loose.

A shot exploded from one of the ruffled bushes. Bits of
rock flew from the top of the cave just above Frank's shoulder. He froze in surprise long enough for another shot to hit
him in the thigh and spin him around. Perrin jerked back her
feet as he struggled for balance, then he dived forward,
pulling his pistol as he fell.

Gunfire erupted around her as the men at the fire rushed to
the mouth of the cave, pistols blazing. Perrin seized the moment to grab the rope and, finding it slack, she rolled out of
the cave mouth and fell behind some prickly laurel. Flattening out, she covered her head with her arms and prayed she
wouldn't be struck by the blizzard of bullets.

The gun battle lasted several endless minutes, then suddenly the forest fell silent. When Perrin dared to open her
eyes, she saw two forms, Cody and Webb, crawling toward
the bodies strewn about the cave mouth. Holding her breath,
she watched as they split off in two directions.

"All right, everyone." Five minutes later, Cody stood at
the front of the cave. His voice carried easily in the clear
frosty air. The snow had almost stopped. "You can come out
now. We've got three dead outlaws and two wounded."

Cautiously, Perrin sat up. The wounded outlaws sat in the
cave looking down the barrels of Webb's pistols. The ruffled
bushes ran forward, faces exposed now.

"We did it!" Cora shouted, waving a smoking carbine.

Cody roared at them. "Who the hell fired that first shot?
We agreed I would fire first when the time was right!"

"It was me," Sarah shouted. "Thea was about to sneeze
and Hilda had to answer nature's call. We had to begin. It

would have been a good shot, but I fluffed it. Where's Perrin? Perrin?"

"Over here," she called, rising to her feet.

They converged on her in a rush, seven women wearing snowy white dresses and fancy shawls, waving carbines and hankies twisted around extra ammunition. Flushed with triumph and everyone talking at once, they made Perrin prove that she was not injured, then told her about the plan and how they had crept through the snowy woods, how they feared Thea would sneeze and give them away, how they just knew they had outshot the men and the victory belonged to them.

"Thank you," Perrin whispered, tears filling her eyes. "Thank you for not leaving me behind."

"Tell her," Cora said, giving Sarah a shove.

Sarah touched Perrin's hand and cleared her throat. "We talked and . . . well, we're ashamed of ourselves and sorry for how we treated someone who's become a friend. We were wrong."

Mem pushed forward, her shawl dropping back to expose shining auburn hair. "We hope you'll forgive us."

Perrin embraced her tightly. "There's nothing to forgive," she said, strangling on tears. "You were never part of it."

"But I was, and I'm ashamed of myself," Bootie said, coming forward. "I'm sorry."

"You been a better friend to us than we been to you, but that's going to change. And there's something else," Cora said, looking at Sarah. "Tell her the rest of it."

"We, ah, like I said, we talked, and . . . well, neither you nor Captain Snow are pledged to anyone else, so . . ."

"Oh, for heaven's sake." Hilda rolled her eyes. "A person could grow old waiting for you to get to the point. If you and Mr. Snow want to court, no one here has any objection."

"It's no one's business but yours," Mem snapped, glaring at the others.

When Perrin raised her eyes, Cody was standing at the mouth of the cave, hands on hips, staring down at her with

smoldering eyes. In all her life Perrin had never seen eyes
that rogue-blue, or a smile that promised so much.

"Since we seem to have everyone's permission," he said
dryly, a twinkle sparkling in his gaze, "I'd like to call on you
after supper tonight, Mrs. Waverly. I have some crow to eat,
some forgiveness to beg, and a future to discuss. Will you
welcome me at your fire, or do I have to plead for the next
ninety miles? I'll do it, but we'll be wasting time that could
be spent making plans and doing . . . other things."

She gazed up at him with shining eyes. She didn't intend
to make it easy for him, she wanted to hear three certain
words, but her heart sang in the knowledge that the time of
anxiety had ended. Everything was going to work out and
she and Cody Snow would be together. The future spread before her like a bright package waiting to be opened.

"You may call on me, Mr. Snow," she said primly, aware
that her hair was hanging, her gown was torn and soiled, a
rope hung off her ankle, and she was probably the most
bedraggled object of a man's courtship to pass through these
parts.

A cheer went up, and laughter and a few whispers of con-
gratulations, then Bootie's plaintive voice rose above the
others. "Now can we go back? I swan, I'm plumb freezing to
death!"

Cody called to them in a voice Perrin would never tire of
hearing. "Pack up, ladies. As soon as the men finish here,
we'll roll. We can get a few miles under the wheels before
supper." He stared at Perrin. And his eyes told her everything he would say later.

Dazed with happiness, she floated back to camp.

Cody placed the last stone on Quinton's grave, then stood
and wiped mud and snow off his hands. "Odd, isn't it?" he
murmured to Webb. "This man has been a thorn in my side
for years, and maybe I've been that to him . . . then, in
twenty minutes of gunfire, it ends." He fell silent. "I don't

think it was even me who shot him. I think Sarah Jennings killed him."

"What do you want to do with those two?" Webb jerked his head toward the cave where Heck held his gun on the two wounded outlaws.

"Tie them up. We'll take them to Clampet Falls and let the authorities there deal with them."

On the walk back to camp, Webb studied the clearing sky. "It doesn't matter who killed Jake Quinton."

"I wanted it to be me," Cody said between his teeth. "Quinton took my woman."

When Webb grinned, Cody glared at him. Then they both laughed, the sound ringing through the forest.

"You were right," Cody said when he could speak. "Is that what you're waiting to hear? At least I hope to hell that you're right. You're going to be dealing with one sorry sad son of a bitch if she doesn't forgive me and agree to marry me."

He bolstered a sudden flag of confidence by remembering the shine in her huge cinnamon eyes when she had gazed up at him.

The women lingered at Perrin's wagon, talking about the skirmish and their victory, and asking what had happened during the time Quinton's gang held her prisoner. Eventually Mem pointed out that the snow had stopped and weak sunlight poked through the clouds. Sarah hustled everyone away to break camp.

Perrin watched them go in their ruined wedding dresses, her heart filled to overflowing. Words seemed inadequate. How did one thank people for saving one's life? Or for being true friends? Mere words couldn't express the depth of emotion involved.

While she put water on to heat for washing the blood out of her hair, she thought about how far they had traveled from Chastity, Missouri. Alliances had formed along the way, broken, and reformed in new groupings. Old animosities had mellowed, love had blossomed. People had died. Bonds had been forged that would endure for a lifetime.

Hilda touched her arm, then embraced her. "I am so glad you are back and not badly injured," she said, lightly brushing the bruise on Perrin's temple with her fingertips. "You are a good woman, Perrin Waverly. I am ashamed that I let others influence me for a while." A blush lit her cheeks. "I will not let someone else decide my opinion again. If you will forgive me, you and I will be neighbors and friends for the rest of our lives." She smiled. "I will teach your children in my school."

Tears reflected the light in Perrin's eyes. "I'll tell them how fortunate they are to have you for their teacher."

"But now"—Hilda gave her a look of apology—"this damned dysentery . . . lucky for me we aren't still on the desert. Lots of bushes here." Leaving Perrin with a weak smile, she dashed toward the forest.

"I think we have laudanum in the wagon. I'll look," Perrin called. Conventional wisdom advised laudanum to treat dysentery although it wasn't noticeably effective. Walking to the back of the wagon, she lowered the tailgate and prepared to climb inside.

A dark form flew out of the wagon bed and knocked Perrin to the ground. Instinctively, she fought to protect herself. She managed to grip Ona Norris's wrist in time to halt the descent of a paring knife that would have plunged into her throat.

But Perrin was weak from the day's ordeal. And Ona was imbued with the strength of the insane. Slowly, but certainly, Ona overpowered her.

It was Sarah who reached him first, with Hilda running right behind her. "One at a time," Cody ordered them. "I can't understand what either of you is saying."

"Thea found Smokey Joe trussed up behind her wagon," Sarah said, gasping to catch her breath. "Smokey's been stabbed. He's lost so much blood, at first we thought he was dead, but he isn't. He'll live."

"And Ona was gone," Hilda added, wringing her hands.

"We found Ona at Perrin's wagon," Sarah gripped his sleeve. "Cody, she's got Perrin on the ground, a knife at her throat. Oh, God! Ona says she wants you to watch her slice Perrin's throat so you'll know that she loves you."

He didn't wait to hear more. He and Webb raced through the forest. When they arrived at Perrin's wagon, he skidded to a halt, then pushed through the white-faced women, absorbing the scene at a glance.

Ona sat braced against a tree trunk, holding Perrin against her chest. One arm looped around Perrin's body, pressing a paring knife against her throat. As Cody watched, a tiny red droplet welled at the tip of the knife, caught the frail sunlight for an instant, then trickled down into Perrin's collar. Perrin fastened huge dark eyes on him, but she didn't attempt to speak.

"I finally understood," Ona said eagerly. She smiled at him. "You're angry because I only wounded her. I didn't kill her like you wanted me to."

Lifting his hands, Cody advanced a step. He spoke in a calm expressionless voice. "You're wrong, Ona. I don't want you to harm Perrin Waverly or anyone else."

She nodded at the group watching in horrified disbelief. The movement caused another red drop to swell at the tip of the knife and Perrin winced. "You have to say that because they're listening, I understand. But I know you want her punished for coming between us. I want to punish her too."

Cody saw the muscles tighten along her thin arm. "Wait!" Sweat broke over his brow. "Perrin has learned her lesson. You don't have to punish her now. There's nothing standing between you and me."

"I warn you. Don't come any closer until it's done. I don't want you saying later that I couldn't kill her or that you had to do it for me."

Perrin's eyes flickered, then steadied. She gazed at him

with absolute trust, gazed at him with eyes that confirmed she loved him, eyes that said good-bye.

He wiped sweat from his brow and advanced another step. "Ona, you must listen to me. You can't do this."

"Oh, yes, I can!" She seemed to think he doubted her ability and fortitude to draw the knife across Perrin's throat. "I've done it before. I killed Ellen because she betrayed you. When I learned Ellen's baby couldn't be yours, I knew that was God's signal that I should kill the whore so we could be together." She nodded and another red drop appeared. Perrin pressed her lips together and closed her eyes.

"It was easy. I held the pillow over Ellen's face. I punished her for whoring like I knew you'd want me to." A frown puckered her brow and she gave him a puzzled, sad look. "I will be very angry if you continue to let whores distract you. I hope I never have to punish you for bringing another whore into our lives. That would break my heart."

Her arms remained tight, poised and ready to rip the blade across Perrin's throat. Suddenly Cody knew there was nothing he could say to stop her. He couldn't reach his pistol faster than she could jerk back the knife. And he didn't have a shot anyway, as she held Perrin against her body as a shield. Rage shook his body and frustration blacked his mind.

"Let her go," he snarled.

Instead Ona smiled and tightened her grip on the knife, digging the point into Perrin's throat. In horror, he realized she wanted to do it slowly.

A shot exploded from Cody's right. Ona's head jerked to the left and the knife dropped from her fingers, falling into Perrin's lap. In an instant Perrin was on her feet and running toward him, then she was in his arms. Screams rang in his ears. Someone jumped forward to press a handkerchief against the wound dripping blood on Perrin's collar and bodice.

Until Augusta walked around the wagon and lowered her carbine, Cody believed it was Webb who had killed Ona. But

Webb emerged from the forest in the opposite direction. He shook his head when Cody stared at him. "The angle was wrong."

Tightening his arms around Perrin's shaking body, Cody swung his gaze to Augusta. "That was one hell of a shot. But you might have hit Perrin!"

She dismissed the suggestion with an airily superior smile that exposed her missing teeth, but which would have made dozens of Boyds proud. There was almost a swagger in her step as she walked toward Perrin. "This makes us even. I don't owe you and you don't owe me. We start over from here."

Perrin flew out of his arms and embraced Augusta, both of them trembling. Cora took the carbine from Augusta's suddenly boneless fingers and Perrin and Augusta held each other tightly, weeping and speaking in voices Cody could not hear.

Shaking his head over the mysteries of women, he walked away from them, removing his coat, then gazing down at Ona Norris before he covered her. She had murdered Ellen. And she would have murdered Perrin. For an instant guilt slammed across his chest. It required several minutes to convince himself that the seeds of madness had been planted long before he met Ona Norris. He told himself that he was not responsible for Ellen's death. Perhaps he had not been responsible for Ellen's life or how she chose to live it either.

Kneeling, he placed his coat over Ona's body.

And finally he let Ellen go. Whatever crimes she had committed against him and their marriage, she had paid a terrible price for them. Ellen's image slowly receded into the past.

Standing, he turned toward the woman who would be his future. She met his eyes over Augusta's shoulder, then gently disengaged herself. Almost running, she came to him.

Whatever she sought in his gaze, she must have found it, because she smiled, then slipped her arm around his waist and leaned into his body when he dropped an arm around her shoulder.

His chest lifted in a deep breath. He was never going to let this woman go. After signaling Miles and Heck to begin digging Ona's grave, he waved his hat in the air.

"We've got ninety hard miles left to travel, and we can cover at least three of them yet today. Waaaagon's hoooo!"

"We should get some sleep. It's going to be a long, hard day tomorrow," Cody murmured. They sat on a log, Perrin's back nestled against his chest, his arms around her waist. The flames had long since died to embers.

"Hmmm," she said drowsily, burrowing deeper in his arms.

For the last hour, they had been trying to say good night to each other, but couldn't bear to part. Farther down the line of wagons he heard the soft murmur of the night watch, playing cards and talking quietly near the arms wagon. The rest of the camp had been asleep for hours.

Neither of them stirred, though the sun would rise soon. They had talked the night away, opening their hearts. Never again would they mention Ellen or Joseph Boyd. From now on, they would look forward, toward the future and each other.

"Cody?" She kissed his jaw, then looked back at the faint orange glow in the fire pit. "I'm eager for us to begin our life together, but . . . part of me will be sorry when we roll into Clampet Falls. Can you understand that?"

"Perhaps."

"While I was in Quinton's cave, I thought about all of it. How it began . . . Lucy Hastings, Winnie Larson, Jane Munger, and those boys we buried. I thought about Mem and Augusta, and . . . all of us. I thought about the Great Whiskey Debacle and the poison oak and . . . everything we've all endured together."

"Are you crying?"

"I love you, Cody Snow. Someday, I'm going to tell our grandchildren how I crossed a continent and found you."

Gently turning her in his arms, he kissed her, deeply, tenderly, trying to tell her with lips and body that which words were not powerful enough to convey. "You're trembling," he said softly against her mouth.

Perrin gazed into the blue eyes she loved so much. "I'm cold."

He kissed her forehead, then her eyelids. "It's probably warmer in my tent. But of course I wouldn't suggest anything improper, Mrs. Waverly."

"It's probably even warmer in your bedroll, Mr. Snow," she whispered, smiling.

Pulling back, he blinked at her. "Perrin, I was jesting. I don't want to do anything that would embarrass you before the others or lead them to—"

She placed a finger across his lips. "I have friends now," she said softly, her huge dark eyes glowing with love for him and with affection for the women with whom she had forged lifelong bonds. "And I think my friends would understand." The truth of what she said made her smile through a shine of happy tears.

"If they catch us, that is," he said in a thick teasing voice before he stood and swept her up in his arms. "Which I'll make sure they don't."

It was only a few steps to his tent.

As one journey drew to an end, another began.

The Brides

Perrin Waverly married Cody Snow in Clampet Falls, Oregon, on September 23, 1852. The Snows settled on a one-hundred-and-twenty-acre horse farm in the Willamette Valley and eventually had five children, one of whom was elected governor of Oregon. Perrin Snow was respected and much loved for her generosity and work in the community. Cody Snow died in 1881 while assisting in the rescue of travelers stranded in the Cascade Mountains. Mrs. Snow did not remarry. She died of natural causes in 1894.

Mem Grant and Webb Coate, Lord Albany, repeated their marriage vows on June 12, 1853, in Devonshire, England. Lord and Lady Albany and their four children traveled extensively during the 1800s. Between jaunts to Africa, Brazil, and the Orient, Lady Albany founded the Devonshire School for Curious Young Ladies. Lord Albany was shot and killed by an outlaw during a return trip to the American West in 1880. Lady Albany lived to celebrate the turn of the century.

Augusta Boyd married Owen Clampet, mill owner, in Clampet Falls, Oregon, on September 23, 1852. No children resulted from the marriage. Until the end of her life, Mrs. Clampet maintained a close friendship with Perrin Snow (née Waverly), Cora White (née Thorp), and Hilda Hacket (née Clum). Mrs. Clampet died of a self-inflicted gunshot in 1868 after her husband's mill burned to the ground, leaving the Clampets in financial ruin.

Hilda Clum married Orry Hacket, a farmer, in Clampet Falls, Oregon, on September 23, 1852. Mrs. Hacket was the second schoolteacher in the Willamette Valley and taught for twenty-nine years, her students including her own six children. One of her daughters published an account of Mrs. Hacket's journey from Chastity, Missouri, to Clampet Falls, Oregon. Mrs. Hacket died of natural causes in 1882, following the death of her husband shortly before.

Bootie Glover accompanied her sister, Lady Albany, to England, where she married Sir Eugene Wickett in December 1855. Lady Eugene was lauded for her soirees and her whist tournaments. The Wicketts had one daughter. Lady Wickett died in 1871 as a result of a carriage accident.

Sarah Jennings married Frederick Pim, a baker, in Clampet Falls, Oregon, on September 23, 1852. The Pims moved to San Francisco, California, in 1854, where they established a boardinghouse and later a prosperous hotel. The hotel, under the ownership of the Pims' eldest son, was destroyed in the 1906 earthquake. Mrs. Pim died of pneumonia in 1892.

Cora Thorp married Willard White, a farmer, in Clampet Falls, Oregon, on September 23, 1852. The Whites had three children. After Mr. White's death in 1860, Mrs. White married Albert Sparrow, with whom she had four children, one of whom served in the United States Senate. Mrs. Sparrow was a lifelong advocate for women's education. She died of tuberculosis in 1879.

Thea Reeves married Luther Frost, a furniture maker, in Clampet Falls, Oregon, on September 23, 1852. In 1853, the Frosts returned to St. Joseph, Missouri, where Mrs. Frost became a local celebrity after publishing a book of drawings depicting scenes along the Oregon Trail. Mrs. Frost died in childbirth in 1858.

Jane Munger, a.k.a. Alice Berringer, never remarried. Mrs. Berringer drifted through the West, never settling into a permanent home. Legend suggests she had a daughter with Kid Johnny, an outlaw living in Fort Worth, Texas, but this information cannot be confirmed. Mrs. Berringer died from a gunshot wound in 1862 after a brawl erupted in the saloon where she was working.

Winnie Larson died of an opiate overdose following a miscarriage that occurred ten days out of Chastity, Missouri, on her return trip.

The remarkable women of the Oregon Trail are not forgotten. Their names can be found carved on the Chimney Rock and Independence Rock, on old grave markers along fading wheel ruts. Their courage, their spirit, and their stories survive to inspire and lift the hearts of all women toward valor, determination, and pride. That is their legacy to those who continue to follow them west.

THROUGHOUT THE NEXT YEAR, LOOK FOR OTHER
FABULOUS BOOKS FROM YOUR FAVORITE WRITERS
IN THE WARNER ROMANCE GUARANTEED PROGRAM

FEBRUARY
HOT TEXAS NIGHTS   MARY LYNN BAXTER

MARCH
SWEET LAUREL   MILLIE CRISWELL

APRIL
PASSION   MARILYN PAPPANO
THE LISTENING SKY   DOROTHY GARLOCK

MAY
BEHOLDEN   PAT WARREN
LOVERS FOREVER   SHIRLEE BUSBEE

JUNE
GOLD DUST   EMILY CARMICHAEL

JULY
THIS LOVING LAND   DOROTHY GARLOCK

AUGUST
BRIDES OF PRAIRIE GOLD   MAGGIE OSBORNE

SEPTEMBER
SUNSETS   CONSTANCE O'DAY-
                                      FLANNERY

OCTOBER
SOUTHERN FIRES   MARY LYNN BAXTER
BELOVED   STELLA CAMERON

NOVEMBER
THE DECEPTION   JOAN WOLF
LEGACIES   JANET DAILEY